WORTH POCKET COMPANIONS

CRIME

Short Stories by Great Writers

WORTH POCKET COMPANIONS

Other titles in the series

ROMANCE

MYSTERY & SUSPENSE

TRAVEL & ADVENTURE

Crime

Short Stories by Great Writers

Selected by

ROSEMARY GRAY

WORTH POCKET COMPANIONS

First published in 2012 by
Worth Press Limited, Cambridge, UK
www.worthpress.co.uk

A catalogue record for this book is available
from the British Library

ISBN 978 1 84931 069 7

Cover design Bradbury & Williams
Typeset in Great Britain by Antony Gray
Printed and bound in China by Imago

Contents

VIRGINIA WOOLF

Virginia Woolf was born in 1882, the youngest daughter of the Victorian writer Leslie Stephen. After her father's death, Virginia moved with her sister Vanessa (later Vanessa Bell) and her brothers Thoby and Adrian to 46 Gordon Square, which was to be the first meeting place of the Bloomsbury Group. Virginia married Leonard Woolf in 1912, and together they established the Hogarth Press. Virginia published her first novel, *The Voyage Out*, in 1912, and she subsequently wrote eight more, several of which are considered classics, as well as two books of seminal feminist thought. Woolf suffered from mental illness throughout her life and committed suicide in 1941.

The Duchess and the Jeweller

Oliver Bacon lived at the top of a house overlooking the Green Park. He had a flat; chairs jutted out at the right angles – chairs covered in hide. Sofas filled the bays of the windows – sofas covered in tapestry. The windows, the three long windows, had the proper allowance of discreet net and figured satin. The mahogany sideboard bulged discreetly with the right brandies, whiskies and liqueurs. And from the middle window he looked down upon the glossy roofs of fashionable cars packed in the narrow straits of Piccadilly. A more central position could not be imagined. And at eight in the morning he would have his breakfast brought in on a tray by a manservant: the manservant would unfold his crimson dressing-gown; he would rip his letters open with his long pointed nails and would extract thick white cards of invitation upon which the engraving stood up roughly from duchesses, countesses, viscountesses and honourable ladies. Then he would wash; then he would eat his toast; then he would read his paper by the bright burning fire of electric coals.

'Behold Oliver,' he would say, addressing himself. 'You who began life in a filthy little alley, you who . . .' and he would look down at his legs, so shapely in their perfect trousers; at his boots; at his spats. They were all shapely, shining; cut from the best cloth by the best scissors in Savile Row. But he dismantled himself often and became again a little boy in a dark alley – selling stolen dogs to fashionable women in Whitechapel. He had once thought that the height of his ambition. And once he had been done. 'Oh, Oliver,' his mother had wailed. 'Oh, Oliver! When will you have sense, my son?' . . . Then he had gone behind a counter; had sold cheap watches; then he had taken a wallet to Amsterdam. . . . At that memory he would chuckle – the old Oliver remembering the young. Yes, he had done well with the three diamonds; also there was the commission on the emerald. After that he went into the private room behind the shop in Hatton Garden; the room with the scales, the safe, the thick magnifying glasses. And then . . . and then . . . He chuckled. When he passed through the knots of jewellers in the hot evening who were discussing prices, gold mines, diamonds, reports from South Africa, one of them would lay a finger to the side of his nose and murmur, 'Hum–m–m,' as he passed. It was no more than a murmur; no more than a nudge on the shoulder, a finger on the nose, a buzz that ran through the cluster of jewellers in Hatton Garden on a hot afternoon – oh, many years ago now! But still Oliver felt it purring down his spine, the nudge, the murmur that meant, 'Look at him – young Oliver, the young jeweller – there he goes.' Young he was then. And he dressed better and better; and had first a hansom cab, then a car; and first he went up to the dress circle, then down into the stalls. And he had a villa at Richmond, overlooking the river, with trellises of red roses; and Mademoiselle used to pick one every morning and stick it in his buttonhole.

'So,' said Oliver Bacon, rising and stretching his legs. '*So*. . .'

And he stood beneath the picture of an old lady on the mantelpiece and raised his hands. 'I have kept my word,' he said, laying his hands together, palm to palm, as if he were doing homage to her. 'I have won my bet.' That was so; he was the richest jeweller in England; but his nose, which was long and flexible, like an elephant's trunk, seemed to say by its curious quiver at the nostrils (but it seemed as if the whole nose quivered, not only the nostrils) that he was not satisfied yet; still smelt something under the ground a little farther off. Imagine a giant hog in a pasture rich with truffles; after unearthing this truffle and that, still it smells a bigger, a blacker truffle under the ground farther off. So Oliver snuffed always in the rich earth of Mayfair another truffle, a blacker, a bigger farther off.

Now then he straightened the pearl in his tie; cased himself in his smart blue overcoat; took his yellow gloves and his cane; and swayed as he descended the stairs and half snuffed, half sighed through his long sharp nose as he passed out into Piccadilly. For was he not still a sad man, a dissatisfied man, a man who seeks something that is hidden, though he had won his bet?

He swayed slightly as he walked, as the camel at the zoo sways from side to side when it walks along the asphalt paths laden with grocers and their wives eating from paper bags and throwing little bits of silver paper crumpled up on to the path. The camel despises the grocers; the camel is dissatisfied with its lot; the camel sees the blue lake and the fringe of palm trees in front of it. So the great jeweller, the greatest jeweller in the whole world, swung down Piccadilly, perfectly dressed, with his gloves, with his cane; but dissatisfied still, till he reached the dark little shop, that was famous in France, in Germany, in Austria, in Italy, and all over America – the dark little shop in the street off Bond Street.

As usual, he strode through the shop without speaking, though the four men, the two old men, Marshall and Spencer, and the two young men, Hammond and Wicks, stood straight and looked at him, envying him. It was only with one finger of the amber-coloured glove, waggling, that he acknowledged their presence. And he went in and shut the door of his private room behind him.

Then he unlocked the grating that barred the window. The cries of Bond Street came in; the purr of the distant traffic. The light from reflectors at the back of the shop struck upwards. One tree waved six green leaves, for it was June. But Mademoiselle had married Mr Pedder of the local brewery – no one stuck roses in his buttonhole now.

'So,' he half sighed, half snorted, 'so –'

Then he touched a spring in the wall and slowly the panelling slid open, and behind it were the steel safes, five, no, six of them, all of burnished steel. He twisted a key: unlocked one; then another. Each was lined with a pad of deep crimson velvet; in each lay jewels – bracelets, necklaces, rings, tiaras, ducal coronets; loose stones in glass shells; rubies, emeralds, pearls, diamonds. All safe, shining, cool, yet burning, eternally, with their own compressed light.

'Tears!' said Oliver, looking at the pearls.

'Heart's blood!' he said, looking at the rubies.

'Gunpowder!' he continued, rattling the diamonds so that they flashed and blazed.

'Gunpowder enough to blow Mayfair – sky high, high, high!' He threw his head back and made a sound like a horse neighing as he said it.

The telephone buzzed obsequiously in a low muted voice on his table. He shut the safe.

'In ten minutes,' he said. 'Not before.' And he sat down at his desk and looked at the heads of the Roman emperors that were graved on his sleeve links. And again he dismantled himself and became once more the little boy playing marbles in the alley where they sell stolen dogs on Sunday. He became that wily astute little boy, with lips like wet cherries. He dabbled his fingers in ropes of tripe; he dipped them in pans of frying fish; he dodged in and out among the crowds. He was slim, lissome, with eyes like licked stones. And now – now – the hands of the clock ticked on, one two, three, four . . . The Duchess of Lambourne waited his pleasure; the Duchess of Lambourne, daughter of a hundred Earls. She would wait for ten minutes on a chair at the counter. She would wait his pleasure. She would wait till he was ready to see her. He watched the clock in its shagreen case. The hand moved on. With each tick the clock handed him – so it seemed – *pâté de foie gras*, a glass of champagne, another of fine brandy, a cigar costing one guinea. The clock laid them on the table beside him as the ten minutes passed. Then he heard soft slow footsteps approaching; a rustle in the corridor. The door opened. Mr Hammond flattened himself against the wall.

'Her Grace!' he announced.

And he waited there, flattened against the wall.

And Oliver, rising, could hear the rustle of the dress of the Duchess as she came down the passage. Then she loomed up, filling the door, filling the room with the aroma, the prestige, the arrogance, the pomp, the pride of all the Dukes and Duchesses swollen in one wave. And as a wave breaks, she broke, as she sat down, spreading and splashing and falling over Oliver Bacon, the great jeweller, covering him with sparkling bright colours, green, rose, violet; and odours; and iridescences; and rays shooting from fingers, nodding from plumes, flashing from silk; for she was very large, very fat, tightly girt in pink taffeta, and past her prime. As a parasol with many flounces, as a peacock with many feathers, shuts its flounces, folds its feathers, so she subsided and shut herself as she sank down in the leather armchair.

'Good-morning, Mr Bacon,' said the Duchess. And she held

out her hand which came through the slit of her white glove. And Oliver bent low as he shook it. And as their hands touched the link was forged between them once more. They were friends, yet enemies; he was master, she was mistress; each cheated the other, each needed the other, each feared the other, each felt this and knew this every time they touched hands thus in the little back room with the white light outside, and the tree with its six leaves, and the sound of the street in the distance and behind them the safes.

'And today, Duchess – what can I do for you today?' said Oliver, very softly.

The Duchess opened her heart, her private heart, gaped wide. And with a sigh but no words she took from her bag a long wash-leather pouch – it looked like a lean yellow ferret. And from a slit in the ferret's belly she dropped pearls – ten pearls. They rolled from the slit in the ferret's belly – one, two, three, four – like the eggs of some heavenly bird.

'All's that's left me, dear Mr Bacon,' she moaned. Five, six, seven – down they rolled, down the slopes of the vast mountain sides that fell between her knees into one narrow valley – the eighth, the ninth, and the tenth. There they lay in the glow of the peach-blossom taffeta. Ten pearls.

'From the Appleby cincture,' she mourned. 'The last . . . the last of them all.'

Oliver stretched out and took one of the pearls between finger and thumb. It was round, it was lustrous. But real was it, or false? Was she lying again? Did she dare?

She laid her plump padded finger across her lips. 'If the Duke knew . . .' she whispered. 'Dear Mr Bacon, a bit of bad luck. . .'

Been gambling again, had she?

'That villain! That sharper!' she hissed.

The man with the chipped cheekbone? A bad 'un. And the Duke was straight as a poker; with side whiskers; would cut her off, shut her up down there if he knew – what I know, thought Oliver, and glanced at the safe.

'Araminta, Daphne, Diana,' she moaned. 'It's for *them*.'

The Ladies Araminta, Daphne, Diana – her daughters. He knew them; adored them. But it was Diana he loved.

'You have all my secrets,' she leered. Tears slid; tears fell; tears, like diamonds, collecting powder in the ruts of her cherry-blossom cheeks.

'Old friend,' she murmured, 'old friend.'

'Old friend,' he repeated, 'old friend,' as if he licked the words.

'How much?' he queried.

She covered the pearls with her hand.

'Twenty thousand,' she whispered.

But was it real or false, the one he held in his hand? The Appleby cincture – hadn't she sold it already? He would ring for Spencer or Hammond. 'Take it and test it,' he would say. He stretched to the bell.

'You will come down tomorrow?' she urged, she interrupted. 'The Prime Minister – His Royal Highness . . .' She stopped. 'And Diana . . .' she added.

Oliver took his hand off the bell.

He looked past her, at the backs of the houses in Bond Street. But he saw, not the houses in Bond Street, but a dimpling river; and trout rising and salmon; and the Prime Minister; and himself too, in white waistcoat; and then, Diana. He looked down at the pearl in his hand. But how could he test it, in the light of the river, in the light of the eyes of Diana? But the eyes of the Duchess were on him.

'Twenty thousand,' she moaned. 'My honour!'

The honour of the mother of Diana! He drew his cheque book towards him; he took out his pen.

'Twenty – ' he wrote. Then he stopped writing. The eyes of the old woman in the picture were on him – of the old woman his mother.

'Oliver!' she warned him. 'Have sense! Don't be a fool!'

'Oliver!' the Duchess entreated – it was 'Oliver' now, not 'Mr Bacon'. 'You'll come for a long weekend?'

Alone in the woods with Diana! Riding alone in the woods with Diana!

'Thousand,' he wrote, and signed it.

'Here you are,' he said.

And there opened all the flounces of the parasol, all the plumes of the peacock, the radiance of the wave, the swords and spears of Agincourt, as she rose from her chair. And the two old men and the two young men, Spencer and Marshall, Wicks and Hammond, flattened themselves behind the counter envying him as he led her through the shop to the door. And he waggled his yellow glove in their faces, and she held her honour – a cheque for twenty thousand pounds with his signature – quite firmly in her hands.

'Are they false or are they real?' asked Oliver, shutting his private door. There they were, ten pearls on the blotting-paper on the table. He took them to the window. He held them under his lens to the light. . . . This, then, was the truffle he had routed out of the earth! Rotten at the centre – rotten at the core!

'Forgive me, oh, my mother!' he sighed, raising his hand as if he asked pardon of the old woman in the picture. And again he was a little boy in the alley where they sold dogs on Sunday.

'For,' he murmured, laying the palms of his hands together, 'it is to be a long weekend.'

E. W. HORNUNG

Ernest William Hornung (1866–1921) was born in Middlesbrough, Yorkshire, and educated at Uppingham. From 1884 to 1886 he lived in Australia for his health and afterwards he wrote two novels with an Australian background, *A Bride from the Bush* (1890) and *The Boss of Taroomba* (1894). Returning to England, he married Constance Doyle, sister of Conan Doyle, in 1893. In 1899 his well-known book *The Amateur Cracksman* appeared, with its hero Raffles, the gentleman-burglar, conceived as a sort of foil to his brother-in-law's detective Sherlock Holmes. Raffles's Dr Watson is his admiring assistant and ex-fag Bunny. Three further collections of these adventures appeared, *Raffles* (1901), *A Thief in the Night* (1905) and *Mr Justice Raffles* (1909). During the First World War Hornung travelled in France with a mobile library for the use of the troops. *Notes of a Camp Follower on the Western Front* (1919) tells of his experiences and *The Young Guard* is a book of war poems.

Wilful Murder

Of the various robberies in which we were both concerned, it is but the few, I find, that will bear telling at any length. Not that the others contained details which even I would hesitate to recount; it is, rather, the very absence of untoward incident which renders them useless for my present purpose. In point of fact our plans were so craftily laid (by Raffles) that the chances of a hitch were invariably reduced to a minimum before we went to work. We might be disappointed in the market value of our haul; but it was quite the exception for us to find ourselves confronted by unforeseen impediments, or involved in a really dramatic dilemma. There was a sameness even in our spoil; for, of course, only the most precious stones are worth the trouble we took and the risks we ran. In short, our most successful escapades would prove the greatest weariness of all in narrative form; and none more so than the dull affair of the Ardagh emeralds, some eight or nine weeks after the Milchester cricket week. The former, however, had a sequel that I would rather forget than all our burglaries put together.

It was the evening after our return from Ireland, and I was waiting at my rooms for Raffles, who had gone off as usual to dispose of the plunder. Raffles had his own method of conducting this very vital branch of our business, which I was well content to leave entirely in his hands. He drove the bargains, I believe, in a thin but subtle disguise of the flashy-seedy order, and always in the Cockney dialect, of which he had made himself a master. Moreover, he invariably employed the same 'fence', who was ostensibly a money-lender in a small (but yet notorious) way, and in reality a rascal as remarkable as Raffles himself. Only lately I also had been to the man, but in my proper person. We had needed capital for the getting of these very emeralds, and I had raised a hundred pounds, on the terms you would expect, from a soft-spoken greybeard with an ingratiating smile, an incessant bow, and the shiftiest old eyes that ever flew from rim to rim of a pair of spectacles. So the original sinews and the final spoils of war came in this case from the selfsame source – a circumstance which appealed to us both.

But these same final spoils I was still to see, and I waited and waited with an impatience that grew upon me with the growing dusk. At my open window I had played Sister Ann until the faces in the street below were no longer distinguishable. And now I was tearing to and fro in the grip of horrible hypotheses – a grip that tightened when at last the lift-gates opened with a clatter outside – that held me breathless until a well-known tattoo followed on my door.

'In the dark!' said Raffles, as I dragged him in. 'Why, Bunny, what's wrong?'

'Nothing – now you've come,' said I, shutting the door behind him in a fever of relief and anxiety. 'Well? Well? What did they fetch?'

'Five hundred.'

'Down?'

'Got it in my pocket.'

'Good man!' I cried. 'You don't know what a stew I've been in. I'll switch on the light. I've been thinking of you and nothing else for the last hour. I – I was ass enough to think something had gone wrong!'

Raffles was smiling when the white light filled the room, but for the moment I did not perceive the peculiarity of his smile. I was fatuously full of my own late tremors and present relief; and my first idiotic act was to spill some whisky and squirt the soda-water all over in my anxiety to do instant justice to the occasion.

'So you thought something had happened?' said Raffles, leaning back in my chair as he lit a cigarette, and looking much amused. 'What would you say if something had? Sit tight, my dear chap! It was nothing of the slightest consequence, and it's all over now. A stern chase and a long one, Bunny, but I think I'm well to windward this time.'

And suddenly I saw that his collar was limp, his hair matted, his boots thick with dust.

'The police?' I whispered aghast.

'Oh, dear, no; only old Baird.'

'Baird! But wasn't it Baird who took the emeralds?'

'It was.'

'Then how came he to chase you?'

'My dear fellow, I'll tell you if you give me a chance; it's really nothing to get in the least excited about. Old Baird has at last spotted that I'm not quite the common cracksman I would have him think me. So he's been doing his best to run me to my burrow.'

'And you call that nothing!'

'It would be something if he had succeeded; but he has still to do that. I admit, however, that he made me sit up for the time being. It all comes of going on the job so far from home. There was the old brute with the whole thing in his morning paper. He *knew* it must have been done by some fellow who could pass himself off for a gentleman, and I saw his eyebrows go up the moment I told him I was the man, with the same old twang that you could cut with a paperknife. I did my best to get out of it – swore I had a pal who was a real swell – but I saw very plainly that I had given myself away. He gave up haggling. He paid my price as though he enjoyed doing it. But I *felt* him following me when I made tracks; though, of course, I didn't turn round to see.'

'Why not?'

'My dear Bunny, it's the very worst thing you can do. As long as you look unsuspecting they'll keep their distance, and so long as they keep their distance you stand a chance. Once show that you know you're being followed, and it's flight or fight for all you're worth. I never even looked round; and mind you never do in the same hole. I just hurried up to Blackfriars and booked for High Street, Kensington, at the top of my voice; and as the train was leaving Sloane Square out I hopped, and up all those stairs like a lamp-lighter, and round to the studio by the back streets. Well, to be on the safe side, I lay low there all the afternoon, hearing nothing in the least suspicious, and only wishing I had a window to look through instead of that beastly skylight. However, the coast seemed clear enough, and thus far it was my mere idea that he would follow me; there was nothing to show he had. So at last I marched out in my proper rig – almost straight into old Baird's arms!'

'What on earth did you do?'

'Walked past him as though I had never set eyes on him in

my life, and didn't then; took a hansom in the King's Road, and drove like the deuce to Clapham Junction; rushed on to the nearest platform, without a ticket, jumped into the first train I saw, got out at Twickenham, walked full tilt back to Richmond, took the District to Charing Cross, and here I am! Ready for a tub and a change, and the best dinner the club can give us. I came to you first, because I thought you might be getting anxious. Come round with me, and I won't keep you long.'

'You're certain you've given him the slip?' I said, as we put on our hats.

'Certain enough; but we can make assurance doubly sure,' said Raffles, and went to my window, where he stood for a moment or two looking down into the street.

'All right?' I asked him.

'All right,' said he; and we went downstairs forthwith, and so to the Albany arm in arm.

But we were both rather silent on our way. I, for my part, was wondering what Raffles would do about the studio in Chelsea, whither, at all events, he had been successfully dogged. To me the point seemed one of immediate importance, but when I mentioned it he said there was time enough to think about that. His one other remark was made after we had nodded (in Bond Street) to a young blood of our acquaintance who happened to be getting himself a bad name.

'Poor Jack Rutter!' said Raffles, with a sigh. 'Nothing's sadder than to see a fellow going to the bad like that. He's about mad with drink and debt, poor devil! Did you see his eye? Odd that we should have met him tonight, by the way; it's old Baird who's said to have skinned him. By God, but I'd like to skin old Baird!'

And his tone took a sudden low fury, made the more noticeable by another long silence, which lasted, indeed, throughout an admirable dinner at the club, and for some time after we had settled down in a quiet corner of the smoking-room with our coffee and cigars. Then at last I saw Raffles looking at me with his lazy smile, and I knew that the morose fit was at an end.

'I dare say you wonder what I've been thinking about all this time?' said he. 'I've been thinking what rot it is to go doing things by halves!'

'Well,' said I, returning his smile, 'that's not a charge that you can bring against yourself, is it?'

'I'm not so sure,' said Raffles, blowing a meditative puff; 'as a matter of fact, I was thinking less of myself than of that poor devil of a Jack Rutter. There's a fellow who does things by halves; he's only half gone to the bad; and look at the difference between him and us! He's under the thumb of a villainous money-lender; we are solvent citizens. He's taken to drink; we're as sober as we are solvent. His pals are beginning to cut him; our difficulty is to keep the pal from the door. Enfin, he begs or borrows, which is stealing by halves; and we steal outright and are done with it. Obviously ours is the more honest course. Yet I'm not sure, Bunny, but we're doing the thing by halves ourselves!'

'Why? What more could we do?' I exclaimed in soft derision, looking round, however, to make sure that we were not overheard.

'What more,' said Raffles. 'Well, murder – for one thing.'

'Rot!'

'A matter of opinion, my dear Bunny; I don't mean it for rot. I've told you before that the biggest man alive is the man who's committed a murder, and not yet been found out; at least he ought to be, but he so very seldom has the soul to appreciate himself. Just think of it! Think of coming in here and talking to the men, very likely about the murder itself; and knowing you've done it; and wondering how they'd look if they knew! Oh, it would be great, simply great! But, besides all that, when you were caught there'd be a merciful and dramatic end of you. You'd fill the bill for a few weeks, and then snuff out with a flourish of extra-specials; you wouldn't rust with a vile repose for seven or fourteen years.'

'Good old Raffles!' I chuckled. 'I begin to forgive you for being in bad form at dinner.'

'But I was never more earnest in my life.'

'Go on!'

'I mean it.'

'You know very well that you wouldn't commit a murder, whatever else you might do.'

'I know very well I'm going to commit one tonight!'

He had been leaning back in the saddle-bag chair, watching me with keen eyes sheathed by languid lids; now he started forward, and his eyes leapt to mine like cold steel from the scabbard. They struck home to my slow wits; their meaning was no longer in doubt. I, who knew the man, read murder in his clenched hands, and murder in his locked lips, but a hundred murders in those hard blue eyes.

'Baird?' I faltered, moistening my lips with my tongue.

'Of course.'

'But you said it didn't matter about the room in Chelsea?'

'I told a lie.'

'Anyway you gave him the slip afterwards!'

'That was another. I didn't. I thought I had when I came up to you this evening; but when I looked out of your window – you remember? to make assurance doubly sure – there he was on the opposite pavement down below.'

'And you never said a word about it!'

'I wasn't going to spoil your dinner, Bunny, and I wasn't going to let you spoil mine. But there he was as large as life, and, of course, he followed us to the Albany. A fine game for him to play, a game after his mean old heart: blackmail from me, bribes from the police, the one bidding against the other; but he shan't play it with me, he shan't live to, and the world will have an extortioner the less. Waiter! Two Scotch whiskies and sodas. I'm off at eleven, Bunny; it's the only thing to be done.'

'You know where he lives, then?'

'Yes, out Willesden way, and alone; the fellow's a miser among other things. I long ago found out all about him.'

Again I looked round the room; it was a young man's club, and young men were laughing, chatting, smoking, drinking, on every hand. One nodded to me through the smoke. Like a machine I nodded to him, and turned back to Raffles with a groan.

'Surely you will give him a chance!' I urged. 'The very sight of your pistol should bring him to terms.'

'It wouldn't make him keep them.'

'But you might try the effect?'

'I probably shall. Here's a drink for you, Bunny. Wish me luck.'

'I'm coming too.'

'I don't want you.'

'But I must come!'

An ugly gleam shot from the steel blue eyes.

'To interfere?' said Raffles.

'Not I.'

'You give me your word?'

'I do.'

'Bunny, if you break it – '

'You may shoot me, too!'

'I most certainly should,' said Raffles, solemnly. 'So you come at your own peril, my dear man; but, if you are coming – well, the sooner the better, for I must stop at my rooms on the way.'

Five minutes later I was waiting for him at the Piccadilly entrance to the Albany. I had a reason for remaining outside. It was the feeling – half hope, half fear – that Angus Baird might still be on our trail – that some more immediate and less cold-blooded way of dealing with him might result from a sudden encounter between the money-lender and myself. I would not warn him of his danger; but I would avert tragedy at all costs. And when no such encounter had taken place, and Raffles and I were fairly on our way to Willesden, that, I think, was still my honest resolve. I would not break my word if I could help it, but it was a comfort to feel that I could break it if I liked, on an understood penalty. Alas! I fear my good intentions were tainted with a devouring curiosity, and overlaid by the fascination which goes hand in hand with horror.

I have a poignant recollection of the hour it took us to reach the house. We walked across St James's Park (I can see the lights now, bright on the bridge and blurred in the water), and we had some minutes to wait for the last train to Willesden. It left at 11.21, I remember, and Raffles was put out to find it did not go on to Kensal Rise. We had to get out at Willesden Junction and walk on through the streets into fairly open country that happened to be quite new to me. I could never find the house again. I remember, however, that we were on a dark footpath between woods and fields when the clocks began striking twelve.

'Surely,' said I, 'we shall find him in bed and asleep?'

'I hope we do,' said Raffles grimly.

'Then you mean to break in?'

'What else did you think?'

I had not thought about it at all; the ultimate crime had monopolised my mind. Beside it burglary was a bagatelle, but one to deprecate none the less. I saw obvious objections: the man was *au fait* with cracksmen and their ways: he would certainly have firearms, and might be the first to use them.

'I could wish nothing better,' said Raffles. 'Then it will be man to man, and devil take the worst shot. You don't suppose I prefer foul play to fair, do you? But die he must, by one or the other, or it's a long stretch for you and me.'

'Better that than this!'

'Then stay where you are, my good fellow. I told you I didn't want you; and this is the house. So good-night.'

I could see no house at all, only the angle of a high wall rising solitary in the night, with the starlight glittering on battlements of broken glass; and in the wall a tall green gate, bristling with spikes, and showing a front for battering-rams in the feeble rays an outlying lamp-post cast across the new-made road. It seemed to me a road of building-sites, with but this one house built, all by itself, at one end; but the night was too dark for more than a mere impression.

Raffles, however, had seen the place by daylight, and had come prepared for the special obstacles; already he was reaching up and putting champagne corks on the spikes, and in another moment he had his folded covert-coat across the corks. I stepped back as he raised himself, and saw a little pyramid of slates snip the sky above the gate; as he squirmed over I ran forward, and had my own weight on the spikes and corks and covert-coat when he gave the latter a tug.

'Coming after all?'

'Rather!'

'Take care, then; the place is all bell-wires and springs. It's no soft thing, this! There – stand still while I take off the corks.'

The garden was very small and new, with a grass-plot still in separate sods, but a quantity of full-grown laurels stuck into the raw clay beds. 'Bells in themselves,' as Raffles whispered; 'there's nothing else rustles so – cunning old beast!' And we gave them a wide berth as we crept across the grass.

'He's gone to bed!'

'I don't think so, Bunny. I believe he's seen us.'

'Why?'

'I saw a light.'

'Where?'

'Downstairs, for an instant, when I –'

His whisper died away; he had seen the light again; and so had I.

It lay like a golden rod under the front-door – and vanished.

It reappeared like a gold thread under the lintel – and vanished for good. We heard the stairs creak, creak, and cease, also for good. We neither saw nor heard any more, though we stood waiting on the grass till our feet were soaked with the dew.

'I'm going in,' said Raffles at last. 'I don't believe he saw us at all. I wish he had. This way.'

We trod gingerly on the path, but the gravel stuck to our wet soles, and grated horribly on a little tiled veranda with a glass door leading within. It was through this glass that Raffles had first seen the light; and he now proceeded to take out a pane, with the diamond, the pot of treacle, and the sheet of brown paper which were seldom omitted from his impedimenta. Nor did he dispense with my own assistance, though he may have accepted it as instinctively as it was proffered. In any case it was these fingers that helped to spread the treacle on the brown paper, and pressed the latter to the glass until the diamond had completed its circuit and the pane fell gently back into our hands.

Raffles now inserted his hand, turned the key in the lock, and, by making a long arm, succeeded in drawing the bolt at the bottom of the door; it proved to be the only one, and the door opened, though not very wide.

'What's that?' said Raffles, as something crunched beneath his feet on the very threshold.

'A pair of spectacles,' I whispered, picking them up. I was still fingering the broken lenses and the bent rims when Raffles tripped and almost fell, with a gasping cry that he made no effort to restrain.

'Hush, man, hush!' I entreated under my breath. 'He'll hear you!'

For answer his teeth chattered – even his – and I heard him fumbling with his matches. 'No, Bunny; he won't hear us,' whispered Raffles, presently; and he rose from his knees and lit a gas as the match burnt down.

Angus Baird was lying on his own floor, dead, with his grey

hairs glued together by his blood; near him a poker with the black end glistening; in a corner his desk, ransacked, littered. A clock ticked noisily on the chimney-piece; for perhaps a hundred seconds there was no other sound.

Raffles stood very still, staring down at the dead, as a man might stare into an abyss after striding blindly to its brink. His breath came audibly through wide nostrils; he made no other sign, and his lips seemed sealed.

'That light!' said I, hoarsely; 'the light we saw under the door!'

With a start he turned to me.

'It's true! I had forgotten it. It was in here I saw it first!'

'He must be upstairs still!'

'If he is we'll soon rout him out. Come on!'

Instead I laid a hand upon his arm, imploring him to reflect – that his enemy was dead now – that we should certainly be involved – that now or never was our own time to escape. He shook me off in a sudden fury of impatience, a reckless contempt in his eyes, and, bidding me save my own skin if I liked, he once more turned his back upon me, and this time left me half resolved to take him at his word. Had he forgotten on what errand he himself was here? Was he determined that this night should end in black disaster? As I asked myself these questions his match flared in the hall; in another moment the stairs were creaking under his feet, even as they had creaked under those of the murderer; and the humane instinct that inspired him in defiance of his risk was borne in also upon my slower sensibilities. Could we let the murderer go? My answer was to bound up the creaking stairs and to overhaul Raffles on the landing.

But three doors presented themselves: the first opened into a bedroom with the bed turned down but undisturbed; the second room was empty in every sense; the third door was locked.

Raffles lit the landing gas.

'He's in there,' said he, cocking his revolver. 'Do you remember how we used to break into the studies at school? Here goes!'

His flat foot crashed over the keyhole, the lock gave, the door flew open, and in the sudden draught the landing gas heeled over like a cobble in a squall; as the flame righted itself I saw a fixed bath, two bath-towels knotted together – an open window – a cowering figure – and Raffles struck aghast on the threshold.

'*Jack – Rutter*?'

The words came thick and slow with horror, and in horror I heard myself repeating them, while the cowering figure by the bathroom window rose gradually erect.

'It's you!' he whispered, in amazement no less than our own; 'it's you two! What's it mean, Raffles? I saw you get over the gate; a bell rang, the place is full of them. Then you broke in. What's it all mean?'

'We may tell you that, when you tell us what in God's name you've done, Rutter!'

'Done? What have I done?' The unhappy wretch came out into the light with bloodshot, blinking eyes, and a bloody shirt-front. 'You know – you've seen – but I'll tell you if you like. I've killed a robber; that's all. I've killed a robber, a usurer, a jackal, a blackmailer, the cleverest and the cruellest villain unhung. I'm ready to hang for him. I'd kill him again!'

And he looked us fiercely in the face, a fine defiance in his dissipated eyes; his breast heaving, his jaw like a rock.

'Shall I tell you how it happened?' he went passionately on. 'He's made my life a hell these weeks and months past. You may know that. A perfect hell! Well, tonight I met him in Bond Street. Do you remember when I met you fellows? He wasn't twenty yards behind you; he was on your tracks, Raffles; he saw me nod to you, and stopped me and asked me who you were. He seemed as keen as knives to know, I couldn't think why, and didn't care either, for I saw my chance. I said I'd tell him all about you if he'd give me a private interview. He said he wouldn't. I said he should, and held him by the coat; by the time I let him go you were out of sight, and I waited where I was till he came back in despair. I had the whip-hand of him then. I could dictate where the interview should be, and I made him take me home with him, still swearing to tell him all about you when we'd had our talk. Well, when we got here I made him give me something to eat, putting him off and off; and about ten o'clock I heard the gate shut. I waited a bit, and then asked him if he lived alone.

' "Not at all," says he; "did you not see the servant?"

'I said I'd seen her, but I thought I'd heard her go; if I was mistaken no doubt she would come when she was called; and I yelled three times at the top of my voice. Of course there was no servant to come. I knew that, because I came to see him one night last week, and he interviewed me himself through the gate, but wouldn't open it. Well, when I had done yelling, and not a soul had come near us, he was as white as that ceiling. Then I told him we could have our chat at last; and I picked the poker out of the fender, and told him how he'd robbed me, but, by God, he shouldn't rob me any more. I gave him three minutes to write and sign a settlement of all his iniquitous claims against me, or have his brains beaten out over his own carpet. He thought a minute, and then went to his desk for pen and paper. In two seconds he was round like lightning with a revolver, and I went for him bald-headed. He fired two or three times and missed; you can find the holes if you like; but I hit him every time – my God! I was like a savage till the thing was done. And then I didn't care. I went through his desk looking for my own bills, and was coming away when you turned up. I said I didn't care, nor do I; but I was going to give myself up tonight, and shall still; so you see I shan't give you fellows much trouble!'

He was done; and there we stood on the landing of the lonely house, the low, thick, eager voice still racing and ringing through our ears; the dead man below, and in front of us his impenitent slayer. I knew to whom the impenitence would appeal when he had heard the story, and I was not mistaken.

'That's all rot,' said Raffles, speaking after a pause; 'we shan't let you give yourself up.'

'You shan't stop me! What would be the good? The woman saw me; it would only be a question of time; and I can't face waiting to be taken. Think of it: waiting for them to touch you on the shoulder! No, no, no; I'll give myself up and get it over.'

His speech was changed; he faltered, floundered. It was as though a clearer perception of his position had come with the bare idea of escape from it.

'But listen to me,' urged Raffles; 'We're here at our peril ourselves. We broke in like thieves to enforce redress for a grievance very like your own. But don't you see? We took out a pane – did the thing like regular burglars. Regular burglars will get the credit of all the rest!'

'You mean that I shan't be suspected?'

'I do.'

'But I don't want to get off scot-free,' cried Rutter hysterically. 'I've killed him. I know that. But it was in self-defence; it wasn't murder. I must own up and take the consequences. I shall go mad if I don't!'

His hands twitched; his lips quivered; the tears were in his eyes. Raffles took him roughly by the shoulder.

'Look here, you fool! If the three of us were caught here now, do you know what those consequences would be? We should swing in a row at Newgate in six weeks' time! You talk as though we were sitting in a club; don't you know it's one o'clock in the morning, and the lights on, and a dead man down below? For God's sake pull yourself together, and do what I tell you, or you're a dead man yourself.'

'I wish I was one!' Rutter sobbed. 'I wish I had his revolver to blow my brains out. It's lying under him. Oh my God, my God!'

His knees knocked together: the frenzy of reaction was at its height. We had to take him downstairs between us, and so through the front door out into the open air.

All was still outside – all but the smothered weeping of the unstrung wretch upon our hands. Raffles returned for a moment to the house; then all was dark as well. The gate opened from within; we closed it carefully behind us; and so left the starlight shining on broken glass and polished spikes, one and all as we had found them.

We escaped; no need to dwell on our escape. Our murderer seemed set upon the scaffold – drunk with his deed, he was more trouble than six men drunk with wine. Again and again we threatened to leave him to his fate, to wash our hands of him. But incredible and unmerited luck was with the three of us. Not a soul did we meet between that and Willesden; and of those who saw us later, did one think of the two young men with crooked white ties, supporting a third in a seemingly unmistakable condition, when the evening papers apprised the town of a terrible tragedy at Kensal Rise?

We walked to Maida Vale, and thence drove openly to my rooms. But I alone went upstairs; the other two proceeded to the Albany, and I saw no more of Raffles for forty-eight hours. He was not at his rooms when I called in the morning; he had left no word. When he reappeared the papers were full of the murder; and the man who had committed it was on the wide Atlantic, a steerage passenger from Liverpool to New York.

'There was no arguing with him,' so Raffles told me; 'either he must make a clean breast of it or flee the country. So I rigged him up at the studio, and we took the first train to Liverpool. Nothing would induce him to sit tight and enjoy the situation as I should have endeavoured to do in his place; and it's just as well! I went to his diggings to destroy some papers, and what do you think I found. The police in possession; there's a warrant out against him already! The idiots think that window wasn't genuine, and the warrant's out. It won't be my fault if it's ever served!'

Nor, after all these years, can I think it will be mine.

AMBROSE BIERCE

Born in 1842, Ambrose Bierce was the author of disquieting stories that have secured his place in both the weird tradition and in the wider world of American letters. He is also noted for his tales of the Civil War, which drew on his own experience as a Union cartographer and officer. His first job in journalism was as editor for the *San Francisco News-Letter* and *California Advertiser* (1868–72). In time, Bierce established himself as a kind of literary dictator of the West Coast and was so respected and feared as a critic that his judgement could 'make or break' an aspiring author's reputation. Well known by his mere initials, A. G. B., he was called by his enemies and detractors 'Almighty God Bierce'. He was also nicknamed 'Bitter Bierce' and his nihilistic motto was, 'Nothing matters.' Bierce is best remembered for his cynical but humorous *Devil's Dictionary*. In 1913, at the age of seventy-one, Bierce disappeared into revolution-torn Mexico to fight alongside the bandit Pancho Villa. Although a popular theory is that Bierce argued with Villa over military strategy and was subsequently shot, he probably perished in the battle of Ojinaga on 11 January 1914.

My Favourite Murder

Having murdered my mother under circumstances of singular atrocity, I was arrested and put upon trial, which lasted seven years. In summing up, the judge of the Court of Acquittal remarked that it was one of the most ghastly crimes that he had ever been called upon to explain away.

At this my counsel rose and said: 'May it please your honour, crimes are ghastly or agreeable only by comparison. If you were familiar with the details of my client's previous murder of his uncle, you would discern in his later offence something in the nature of tender forbearance and filial consideration for the feelings of the victim. The appalling ferocity of the former assassination was indeed inconsistent with any hypothesis but that of guilt; and had it not been for the fact that the honourable judge before whom he was tried was the president of a life-insurance company which took risks on hanging, and in which my client held a policy, it is impossible to see how he could have been decently acquitted. If your honour would like to hear about it for the instruction and guidance of your honour's mind, this unfortunate man, my client, will consent to give himself the pain of relating it under oath.'

The district attorney said: 'Your honour, I object. Such a statement would be in the nature of evidence, and the testimony in this case is closed. The prisoner's statement should have been introduced three years ago, in the spring of 1881.'

'In a statutory sense,' said the judge, 'you are right, and in the Court of Objections and Technicalities you would get a ruling in your favour. But not in a Court of Acquittal. The objection is overruled.'

'I except,' said the district attorney.

'You cannot do that,' the judge said. 'I must remind you that in order to take an exception you must first get this case transferred for a time to the Court of Exceptions upon a formal motion duly supported by affidavits. A motion to that effect by your predecessor in office was denied by me during the first year of this trial.

'Mr Clerk, swear the prisoner.'

The customary oath having been administered, I made the following statement, which impressed the judge with so strong a sense of the comparative triviality of the offence for which I was on trial that he made no further search for mitigating circumstances, but simply instructed the jury to acquit, and I left the court without a stain upon my reputation.

'I was born in 1856 in Kalamakee, Michigan, of honest and reputable parents, one of whom heaven has mercifully spared to comfort me in my later years. In 1867 the family came to California and settled near Nigger Head, where my father opened a road agency and prospered beyond the dreams of avarice. He was a silent, saturnine man then, though his increasing years have now somewhat relaxed the austerity of his disposition, and I believe that nothing but his memory of the sad event for which I am now on trial prevents him from manifesting a genuine hilarity.

'Four years after we had set up the road agency an itinerant preacher came along, and having no other way to pay for the night's lodging which we gave him, favoured us with an exhortation of such power that, praise God, we were all converted to religion. My father at once sent for his brother, the Honourable William Ridley of Stockton, and on his arrival turned over the agency to him, charging him nothing for the franchise or plant – the latter consisting of a Winchester rifle, a sawn-off shotgun and an assortment of masks made out of flour sacks. The family then moved to Ghost Rock and opened a dance house. It was called the Saints' Rest Hurdy-Gurdy, and the proceedings each night began with a prayer. It was there that my now sainted mother, by her grace in the dance, acquired the sobriquet of the Bucking Walrus.

'In the fall of '75 I had occasion to visit Coyote, on the road to Mahala, and took the stage at Ghost Rock. There were four other passengers. About three miles beyond Nigger Head, persons whom I identified as my Uncle William and his two sons held up the stage. Finding nothing in the express box, they went through the passengers. I acted a most honourable part in the affair, placing myself in line with the others, holding up my hands and permitting myself to be deprived of forty dollars and a gold watch. From my behaviour no one could have suspected that I knew the gentlemen who gave the entertainment. A few days later, when I went to Nigger Head and asked for the return of my money and watch, my uncle and cousins swore they knew nothing of the matter, and they affected a belief that my father and I had done the job ourselves in dishonest violation of commercial good faith. Uncle William even threatened to retaliate by starting an opposition dance house at Ghost Rock. As the Saints' Rest had become rather unpopular, I saw that this would assuredly ruin it and prove a paying enterprise, so I told my uncle that I was willing to overlook the past if he would take me into the scheme and keep the partnership a secret from my father. This fair offer he rejected, and I then perceived that it would be better and more satisfactory if he were dead.

'My plans to that end were soon perfected, and communicating them to my dear parents, I had the gratification of receiving their approval. My father said he was proud of me, and my mother promised that, although her religion forbade her to assist in taking human life, I should have the advantage of her prayers for my success. As a preliminary measure, looking to my security in case of detection, I made an application for membership in that powerful order the Knights of Murder, and in due course was received as a member of the Ghost Rock Commandery. On the day that my probation ended I was for the first time permitted to inspect the records of the order and learn who belonged to it – all the rites of initiation having been conducted in masks. Fancy my delight, when, in looking over the roll of membership, I found the third name to be that of my uncle, who indeed was junior vice-chancellor of the order! Here was an opportunity exceeding my wildest dreams – to murder I could add insubordination and treachery. It was what my good mother would have called "a special Providence".

'At about this time something occurred which caused my cup of joy, already full, to overflow on all sides, a circular cataract of bliss. Three men, strangers in that locality, were arrested for the stage robbery in which I had lost my money and watch.

They were brought to trial and, despite my efforts to clear them and fasten the guilt upon three of the most respectable and worthy citizens of Ghost Rock, convicted on the clearest proof. The murder would now be as wanton and reasonless as I could wish.

'One morning I shouldered my Winchester rifle and going over to my uncle's house, near Nigger Head, asked my Aunt Mary, his wife, if he were at home, adding that I had come to kill him. My aunt replied with a peculiar smile that so many gentlemen called on the same errand and were afterwards carried away without having performed it that I must excuse her for doubting my good faith in the matter. She said it did not look as if I would kill anybody, so, as a guarantee of good faith, I levelled my rifle and wounded a Chinaman who happened to be passing the house. She said she knew whole families who could do a thing of that kind, but Bill Ridley was a horse of another colour. She said, however, that I would find him over on the other side of the creek in the sheep lot; and she added that she hoped the best man would win.

'My Aunt Mary was one of the most fair-minded women whom I have ever met.

'I found my uncle down on his knees engaged in skinning a sheep. Seeing that he had neither gun nor pistol handy, I had not the heart to shoot him, so I approached him, greeted him pleasantly, and struck him a powerful blow on the head with the butt of my rifle. I have a very good delivery, and Uncle William lay down on his side, then rolled over on his back, spread out his fingers, and shivered. Before he could recover the use of his limbs I seized the knife that he had been using and cut his ham strings. You know, doubtless, that when you sever the *tendo Achillis* the patient has no further use of his leg; it is just the same as if he had no leg. Well, I parted them both, and when he revived he was at my service. As soon as he comprehended the situation, he said: "Samuel, you have got the drop on me, and can afford to be liberal. I have only one thing to ask of you, and that is that you carry me to the house and finish me in the bosom of my family."

'I told him I thought that a pretty reasonable request, and I would do so if he would let me put him in a wheat sack; he would be easier to carry that way, and if we were seen by the neighbours *en route* it would cause less remark. He agreed to that, and going to the barn, I got a sack. This, however, did not fit him; it was too short and much wider than he was; so I bent his legs, forced his knees up against his breast, and got him into it that way, tying the sack above his head. He was a heavy man, and I had all I could do to get him on my back, but I staggered along for some distance until I came to a swing which some of the children had suspended from the branch of an oak. Here I laid him down and sat upon him to rest, and the sight of the rope gave me a happy inspiration. In twenty minutes my uncle, still in the sack, swung free to the sport of the wind. I had taken down the rope, tied one end tightly about the mouth of the bag, thrown the other across the limb, and hauled him up about five feet from the ground. Fastening the other end of the rope also to the mouth of the sack, I had the satisfaction to see my uncle converted into a huge pendulum. I must add that he was not himself entirely aware of the nature of the change which he had undergone in his relation to the exterior world, though in justice to a brave man's memory I ought to say that I do not think he would in any case have wasted much of my time in vain remonstrance.

'Uncle William had a ram which was famous in all that region as a fighter. It was in a state of chronic constitutional indignation. Some deep disappointment in early life had soured its disposition, and it had declared war upon the whole world. To say that it would butt anything accessible is but faintly to express the nature and scope of its military activity; the universe was its antagonist; its method was that of a projectile. It fought, like the angels and devils, in mid-air, cleaving the atmosphere like a bird, describing a parabolic curve and descending upon its victim at just the exact angle of incidence to make the most of its velocity and weight. Its momentum, calculated in foot-tons, was something incredible. It had been seen to destroy a four-year-old bull by a single impact upon that animal's gnarly forehead. No stone wall had ever been known to resist its downward swoop; there were no trees tough enough to stay it; it would splinter them into matchwood and defile their leafy honours in the dust. This irascible and implacable brute – this incarnate thunderbolt – this monster of the upper deep, I had seen reposing in the shade of an adjacent tree, dreaming dreams of conquest and glory. It was with a view of summoning it forth to the field of honour that I suspended its master in the manner described.

'Having completed my preparations, I imparted to the avuncular pendulum a gentle oscillation, and retiring to cover behind a contiguous rock, lifted up my voice in a long, rasping cry, whose diminishing final note was drowned in a noise like that of a swearing cat, which emanated from the sack. Instantly that formidable sheep was upon its feet and had taken in the military situation at a glance. In a few moments it had approached, stamping, to within fifty yards of the swinging foeman who, now retreating and anon advancing, seemed to invite the fray. Suddenly I saw the beast's head drop earthward as if depressed by the weight of its enormous horns; then a dim, white, wavy streak of sheep prolonged itself from that spot in a generally horizontal direction to within about four yards of a point immediately beneath the enemy. There it struck sharply upward, and before it had faded from my gaze at the place whence it had set out I heard a horrible thump and a piercing scream, and my poor uncle shot forward with a slack rope, higher than the limb to which he was attached. Here the rope tautened with a jerk, arresting his flight, and back he swung in a breathless curve to the other end of his arc. The ram had fallen, a heap of indistinguishable legs, wool and horns, but, pulling itself together and dodging as its antagonist swept downward, it retired at random, alternately shaking its head and stamping its forefeet. When it had backed about the same distance as that from which it had delivered the assault, it paused again, bowed its head as if in prayer for victory, and again shot forward, dimly visible as before – a prolonging white streak with monstrous undulations, ending with a sharp ascension. Its course this time was at a right angle to its former one, and its impatience so great that it struck the enemy before he had nearly reached the lowest point of his arc. In consequence he went flying around and around in a horizontal circle, whose radius was about equal to half the length of the rope, which I forgot to say was nearly twenty feet long. His shrieks, crescendo in approach and diminuendo in recession, made the rapidity of his revolution more obvious to the ear than to the eye. He had evidently not yet been struck in a vital spot. His posture in the sack and the distance from the ground at which he hung compelled the ram to operate upon his lower extremities and the end of his back. Like a plant that has struck its root into some poisonous mineral, my poor uncle was dying slowly upward.

'After delivering its second blow the ram had not again retired. The fever of battle burned hot in its heart; its brain was intoxicated with the wine of strife. Like a pugilist who in his rage forgets his skill and fights ineffectively at half-arm's length, the angry beast endeavoured to reach its fleeting foe by awkward vertical leaps as he passed overhead, sometimes, indeed, succeeding in striking him feebly, but more frequently overthrown by its own misguided eagerness. But as the impetus was exhausted and the man's circles narrowed in scope and diminished in speed, bringing him nearer to the ground, these tactics produced better results and elicited a superior quality of screams, which I greatly enjoyed.

'Suddenly, as if the bugles had sung truce, the ram suspended hostilities and walked away, thoughtfully wrinkling and smoothing its great aquiline nose, and occasionally cropping a bunch of grass and slowly munching it. It seemed to have tired of war's alarms and resolved to beat the sword into a ploughshare and cultivate the arts of peace. Steadily it held its course away from the field of fame until it had gained a distance of nearly a quarter of a mile. There it stopped and stood with its rear to the foe, chewing its cud and apparently half asleep. I observed, however, an occasional slight turn of its head, as if its apathy were more affected than real.

'Meanwhile, Uncle William's shrieks had abated with his motion, and nothing was heard from him but long, low moans, and at long intervals my name, uttered in pleading tones exceedingly gratifying to my ear. Evidently the man had not the faintest notion of what was being done to him, and was inexpressibly terrified. When Death comes cloaked in mystery he is terrible indeed. Little by little my uncle's oscillations diminished, and finally he hung motionless. I went to him and was about to give him the *coup de grâce*, when I heard and felt a succession of smart shocks which shook the ground like a series of light earthquakes, and turning in the direction of the ram, saw a cloud of dust approaching me with inconceivable rapidity and alarming effect. At a distance of some thirty yards away it stopped short, and from the near end of it rose into the air what I at first thought a great white bird. Its ascent was so smooth and easy and regular that I could not realise its extraordinary celerity, and was lost in admiration of its grace. To this day the impression remains that it was a slow, deliberate movement, the ram – for it was that animal – being upborne by some power other than its own impetus, and supported through the successive stages of its flight with infinite tenderness and care. My eyes followed its progress through the air with unspeakable pleasure, all the greater by contrast with my former terror of its approach by land. Onward and upward the noble animal sailed, its head bent down almost between its knees, its forefeet thrown back, its hinder legs trailing to rear like the legs of a soaring heron. At a height of forty or fifty feet, as near as I could judge, it attained its zenith and appeared to remain an instant stationary; then, tilting suddenly forward without altering the relative position of its parts, it shot downward on a steeper and steeper course with augmenting velocity, passed immediately above me with a noise like the rush of a cannon shot, and struck my poor uncle almost squarely on top of the head! So frightful was the impact that not only was the neck broken, but the rope, too; and the body of the deceased, forced against the earth, was crushed to pulp beneath the awful front of that meteoric sheep. The concussion stopped all the clocks between Lone Hand and Dutch Dan's, and Professor Davidson, who happened to be in the vicinity, promptly explained that the vibrations were from the north to south.

'Altogether, I cannot help thinking that in point of atrocity my murder of Uncle William has seldom been excelled.'

MAURICE LEBLANC

Maurice Leblanc (1864–1941) was the French playwright, short-story writer and novelist celebrated for creating the popular rogue Arsène Lupin, the 'Prince of Thieves'. Lupin swaggered through a thirty-five-year career that made him internationally famous. Leblanc often had his tongue in his cheek, his plots being parodies of crime fiction, and on occasion he even had his hero lock horns with Britain's brightest detective Holmlock Shears (also sometimes referred to as Herlock Sholmes). Lupin was portrayed on the screen, both in silent and talking pictures; John Barrymore played the likeable scoundrel in MGM's *Arsène Lupin* (1932). His colourful character brought Leblanc wealth and fame and eventually the Legion of Honour.

Arsène Lupin in Prison

There is no tourist worthy of the name who does not know the banks of the Seine, and has not noticed, in passing, the little feudal castle of the Malaquis, built upon a rock in the centre of the river. An arched bridge connects it with the shore. All around it, the calm waters of the great river play peacefully among the reeds, and the wagtails flutter over the moist crests of the stones.

The history of the Malaquis castle is stormy like its name, harsh like its outlines. It has passed through a long series of combats, sieges, assaults, rapines and massacres. A recital of the crimes that have been committed there would cause the stoutest heart to tremble. There are many mysterious legends connected with the castle, and they tell us of a famous subterranean tunnel that formerly led to the abbey of Jumièges and to the manor of Agnès Sorel, mistress of Charles VII.

In that ancient habitation of heroes and brigands, the Baron Nathan Cahorn now lived; or Baron Satan as he was formerly called on the Bourse, where he had acquired a fortune with incredible rapidity. The Lords of Malaquis, absolutely ruined, had been obliged to sell the ancient castle at a great sacrifice. It contained an admirable collection of furniture, pictures, wood carvings and faience. The baron lived there alone, attended by three old servants. No one ever entered the place. No one had ever beheld the three Rubens that he possessed, his two Watteaus, his Jean Goujon pulpit, and the many other treasures that he had acquired by a vast expenditure of money at public sales.

Baron Satan lived in constant fear, not for himself, but for the treasures that he had accumulated with such an earnest devotion and with so much perspicacity that the shrewdest merchant could not say that the Baron had ever erred in his taste or judgement. He loved them – his bibelots. He loved them intensely, like a miser; jealously, like a lover. Every day, at sunset, the iron gates at either end of the bridge and at the entrance to the court of honour were closed and barred. At the least touch on these gates, electric bells would ring throughout the castle.

One Thursday in September, a letter-carrier presented himself at the gate at the head of the bridge, and, as usual, it was the baron himself who partially opened the heavy portal. He scrutinised the man as minutely as if he were a stranger, although the honest face and twinkling eyes of the postman had been familiar to the baron for many years. The man laughed, as he said: 'It is only I, Monsieur le Baron. It is not another man wearing my cap and blouse.'

'One can never tell,' muttered the baron.

The man handed him a number of newspapers, and then said: 'And now, Monsieur le Baron, here is something new.'

'Something new?'

'Yes, a letter. A registered letter.'

Living as a recluse, without friends or business relations, the baron never received any letters, and the one now presented to him immediately aroused within him a feeling of suspicion and distrust. It was like an evil omen. Who was this mysterious correspondent that dared to disturb the tranquillity of his retreat?

'You must sign for it, Monsieur le Baron.'

He signed; then took the letter, waited until the postman had disappeared beyond the bend in the road, and after walking nervously to and fro for a few minutes, he leaned against the parapet of the bridge and opened the envelope. It contained a sheet of paper, bearing this heading: Prison de la Santé, Paris. He looked at the signature: Arsène Lupin. Then he read:

Monsieur le Baron – There is, in the gallery in your castle, a picture of Philippe de Champaigne, of exquisite finish, which pleases me beyond measure. Your Rubens are also to my taste, as well as your smaller Watteau. In the salon to the right, I have noticed the Louis XIII cadence-table, the tapestries of Beauvais, the Empire *gueridon* signed 'Jacob', and the Renaissance chest. In the salon to the left, I have remarked the cabinet full of jewels and miniatures.

For the present, I will content myself with those articles that can be conveniently removed. I will therefore ask you to pack them carefully and ship them to me, charges prepaid, to the station at Batignolles, within eight days, otherwise I shall be obliged to remove them myself during the night of 27 September; but, under those circumstances, I shall not content myself with the articles above mentioned.

Accept my apologies for any inconvenience I may cause

ARSÈNE LUPIN

PS – Please do not send the larger Watteau. Although you paid thirty thousand francs for it, it is only a copy, the original having been burned, under the Directoire by Barras, during a night of debauchery. Consult the memoirs of Garat.

I do not care for the Louis XV chatelaine, as I doubt its authenticity.

That letter completely upset the baron. Had it borne any other signature, he would have been greatly concerned – but signed by Arsène Lupin!

As an habitual reader of the newspapers, he was versed in the history of recent crimes, and was therefore well acquainted with the exploits of the mysterious burglar. Of course, he knew that Lupin had been arrested in America by his enemy Ganimard and was at present incarcerated in the Prison de la Santé. But he knew also that any miracle might be expected from Arsène Lupin. Moreover, that exact knowledge of the castle, the location of the pictures and furniture, gave the affair an alarming aspect. How could he have acquired that information concerning things that no one had ever seen?

The baron raised his eyes and contemplated the stern outlines of the castle, its steep rocky pedestal, the depth of the surrounding water, and shrugged his shoulders. Certainly, there was no danger. No one in the world could force an entrance to the sanctuary that contained his priceless treasures.

No one, perhaps, but Arsène Lupin! For him, gates, walls and drawbridges did not exist. What use were the most formidable obstacles or the most careful precautions, if Arsène Lupin had decided to effect an entrance?

That evening, he wrote to the *Procureur* of the Republique at Rouen. He enclosed the threatening letter and solicited aid and protection.

The reply came at once to the effect that Arsène Lupin was in custody in the Prison de la Santé, under close surveillance, with no opportunity to write such a letter; it was, no doubt, the work of some imposter. But, as an act of precaution, the

Procureur had submitted the letter to an expert in handwriting, who declared that, in spite of certain resemblances, the writing was not that of the prisoner.

But the words 'in spite of certain resemblances' caught the attention of the baron; in them, he read the possibility of a doubt which appeared to him quite sufficient to warrant the intervention of the law. His fears increased. He read Lupin's letter over and over again. 'I shall be obliged to remove them myself.' And then there was the fixed date: the night of 27 September.

To confide in his servants was a proceeding repugnant to his nature; but now, for the first time in many years, he experienced the necessity of seeking counsel with someone. Abandoned by the legal official of his own district, and feeling unable to defend himself with his own resources, he was on the point of going to Paris to engage the services of a detective.

Two days passed; on the third day, he was filled with hope and joy as he read the following item in the *Reveil de Caudebec*, a newspaper published in a neighbouring town: 'We have the pleasure of entertaining in our city, at the present time, the veteran detective M. Ganimard who acquired a worldwide reputation by his clever capture of Arsène Lupin. He has come here for rest and recreation, and, being an enthusiastic fisherman, he threatens to capture all the fish in our river.'

Ganimard! Ah, here was the assistance desired by Baron Cahorn! Who could baffle the schemes of Arsène Lupin better than Ganimard, the patient and astute detective? He was the man for the place.

The baron did not hesitate. The town of Caudebec was only six kilometres from the castle, a short distance to a man whose step was accelerated by the hope of safety.

After several fruitless attempts to ascertain the detective's address, the baron visited the office of the *Reveil*, situated on the quai. There he found the writer of the article who, approaching the window, exclaimed: 'Ganimard? Why, you are sure to see him somewhere on the *quai* with his fishing-pole. I met him there and chanced to read his name engraved on his rod. Ah, there he is now, under the trees.'

'That little man, wearing a straw hat?'

'Exactly. He is a gruff fellow, with little to say.'

Five minutes later, the baron approached the celebrated Ganimard, introduced himself, and sought to commence a conversation, but that was a failure. Then he broached the real object of his interview, and briefly stated his case. The other listened, motionless, with his attention riveted on his fishing-rod. When the baron had finished his story, the fisherman turned, with an air of profound pity, and said: 'Monsieur, it is not customary for thieves to warn people they are about to rob. Arsène Lupin, especially, would not commit such a folly.'

'But – '

'Monsieur, if I had the least doubt, believe me, the pleasure of again capturing Arsène Lupin would place me at your disposal. But, unfortunately, that young man is already under lock and key.'

'He may have escaped.'

'No one ever escaped from the Santé.'

'But, he – '

'He, no more than any other.'

'Yet – '

'Well, if he escapes, so much the better. I will catch him again. Meanwhile, you go home and sleep soundly. That will do for the present. You frighten the fish.'

The conversation was ended. The baron returned to the castle, reassured to some extent by Ganimard's indifference. He examined the bolts, watched the servants, and, during the next forty-eight hours, he became almost persuaded that his fears were groundless. Certainly, as Ganimard had said, thieves do not warn people they are about to rob.

The fateful day was close at hand. It was now 26 September and nothing had happened. But at three o'clock the bell rang. A boy brought this telegram: 'No goods at Batignolles station. Prepare everything for tomorrow night. Arsène.'

This telegram threw the baron into such a state of excitement that he even considered the advisability of yielding to Lupin's demands.

However, he hastened to Caudebec. Ganimard was fishing at the same place, seated on a camp-stool. Without a word, he handed him the telegram.

'Well, what of it?' said the detective.

'What of it? But it is tomorrow.'

'What is tomorrow?'

'The robbery! The pillage of my collections!'

Ganimard laid down his fishing-rod, turned to the baron, and exclaimed, in a tone of impatience: 'Ah! Do you think I am going to bother myself about such a silly story as that!'

'How much do you ask to pass tomorrow night in the castle?'

'Not a sou. Now, leave me alone.'

'Name your own price. I am rich and can pay it.'

This offer disconcerted Ganimard, who replied, calmly: 'I am here on a vacation. I have no right to undertake such work.'

'No one will know. I promise to keep it secret.'

'Oh! nothing will happen.'

'Come! three thousand francs. Will that be enough?'

The detective, after a moment's reflection, said: 'Very well. But I must warn you that you are throwing your money out of the window.'

'I do not care.'

'In that case . . . but, after all, what do we know about this devil Lupin! He may have quite a numerous band of robbers with him. Are you sure of your servants?'

'My faith – '

'Better not count on them. I will telegraph for two of my

men to help me. And now, go! It is better for us not to be seen together. Tomorrow evening about nine o'clock.'

The following day – the date fixed by Arsène Lupin – Baron Cahorn arranged all his panoply of war, furbished his weapons, and, like a sentinel, paced to and fro in front of the castle. He saw nothing, heard nothing. At half-past eight o'clock in the evening, he dismissed his servants. They occupied rooms in a wing of the building, in a retired spot, well removed from the main portion of the castle. Shortly thereafter, the baron heard the sound of approaching footsteps. It was Ganimard and his two assistants – great, powerful fellows with immense hands and necks like bulls. After asking a few questions relating to the location of the various entrances and rooms, Ganimard carefully closed and barricaded all the doors and windows through which one could gain access to the threatened rooms. He inspected the walls, raised the tapestries, and finally installed his assistants in the central gallery which was located between the two salons.

'No nonsense! We are not here to sleep. At the slightest sound, open the windows of the court and call me. Pay attention also to the waterside. Ten metres of perpendicular rock is no obstacle to those devils.'

Ganimard locked his assistants in the gallery, carried away the keys, and said to the baron: 'And now, to our post.'

He had chosen for himself a small room located in the thick outer wall, between the two principal doors, one which, in former years, had been the watchman's quarters. A peep-hole opened upon the bridge; another on the court. In one corner, there was an opening to a tunnel.

'I believe you told me, Monsieur le Baron, that this tunnel is the only subterranean entrance to the castle and that it has been closed up from time immemorial?'

'Yes.'

'Then, unless there is some other entrance, known only to Arsène Lupin, we are quite safe.'

He placed three chairs together, stretched himself upon them, lighted his pipe and sighed: 'Really, Monsieur le Baron, I feel ashamed to accept your money for such a sinecure as this. I will tell the story to my friend Lupin. He will enjoy it immensely.'

The baron did not laugh. He was anxiously listening, but heard nothing save the beating of his own heart. From time to time, he leaned over the tunnel and cast a fearful eye into its depths. He heard the clock strike eleven, twelve, one.

Suddenly, he seized Ganimard's arm. The latter leaped up, awakened from his sleep.

'Do you hear?' asked the baron, in a whisper.

'Yes.'

'What is it?'

'I was snoring, I suppose.'

'No, no, listen.'

'Ah! yes, it is the horn of an automobile.'

'Well?'

'Well! it is very improbable that Lupin would use an automobile like a battering-ram to demolish your castle. Come, Monsieur le Baron, return to your post. I am going to sleep. Good-night.'

That was the only alarm. Ganimard resumed his interrupted slumbers, and the baron heard nothing except the regular snoring of his companion. At break of day, they left the room. The castle was enveloped in a profound calm; it was a peaceful dawn on the bosom of a tranquil river. They mounted the stairs, Cahorn radiant with joy, Ganimard calm as usual. They heard no sound; they saw nothing to arouse suspicion.

'What did I tell you, Monsieur le Baron? Really, I should not have accepted your offer. I am ashamed.'

He unlocked the door and entered the gallery. Upon two

chairs, with drooping heads and pendent arms, the detective's two assistants were asleep.

'Tonnerre de nom d'un chien!' exclaimed Ganimard. At the same moment, the baron cried out: 'The pictures! The *crédance*!'

He stammered, choked, with arms outstretched towards the empty places, towards the denuded walls where naught remained but the useless nails and cords. The Watteau, disappeared! The Rubens, carried away! The tapestries taken down! The cabinets, despoiled of their jewels!

'And my Louis XVI candelabra! – And the Regent chandelier! – And my twelfth-century Virgin!'

He ran from one spot to another in wildest despair. He recalled the purchase price of each article, added up the figures, counted his losses, pell-mell, in confused words and unfinished phrases. He stamped with rage; he groaned with grief. He acted like a ruined man whose only hope is suicide.

If anything could have consoled him, it would have been the stupefaction displayed by Ganimard. The famous detective did not move. He appeared to be petrified; he examined the room in a listless manner. The windows? . . . closed. The locks on the doors? . . . intact. Not a break in the ceiling; not a hole in the floor. Everything was in perfect order. The theft had been carried out methodically, according to a logical and inexorable plan.

'Arsène Lupin . . . Arsène Lupin,' he muttered.

Suddenly, as if moved by anger, he rushed upon his two assistants and shook them violently. They did not awaken.

'The devil!' he cried. 'Can it be possible?'

He leaned over them and, in turn, examined them closely. They were asleep; but their response was unnatural.

'They have been drugged,' he said to the baron.

'By whom?'

'By him, of course, or men under his direction. That work bears his stamp.'

'In that case, I am lost – nothing can be done.'

'Nothing,' assented Ganimard.

'It is dreadful; it is monstrous.'

'Lodge a complaint.'

'What good will that do?'

'Oh; it is well to try it. The law has some resources.'

'The law! Bah! it is useless. You represent the law, and, at this moment, when you should be looking for a clue and trying to discover something, you do not even stir.'

'Discover something of Arsène Lupin! Why, my dear monsieur, Arsène Lupin never leaves any clue behind him. He leaves nothing to chance. Sometimes I think he put himself in my way and simply allowed me to arrest him in America.'

'Then, I must renounce my pictures! He has taken the gems of my collection. I would give a fortune to recover them. If there is no other way, let him name his own price.'

Ganimard regarded the baron attentively, as he said: 'Now, that is sensible. Will you stick to it?'

'Yes, yes. But why?'

'An idea that I have.'

'What is it?'

'We will discuss it later – if the official examination does not succeed. But, not one word about me, if you wish my assistance.' He added, between his teeth: 'It is true I have nothing to boast of in this affair.'

The assistants were gradually regaining consciousness with the bewildered air of people who come out of an hypnotic sleep. They opened their eyes and looked about them in astonishment. Ganimard questioned them; they remembered nothing.

'But you must have seen someone?'

'No.'

'Can't you remember?'

'No, no.'

'Did you drink anything?'

They considered a moment, and then one of them replied: 'Yes, I drank a little water.'

'Out of that carafe?'

'Yes.'

'So did I,' declared the other.

Ganimard smelled and tasted it. It had no particular taste and no odour.

'Come,' he said, 'we are wasting our time here. One can't decide an Arsène Lupin problem in five minutes. But, *morbleau*! I swear I will catch him again.'

The same day, a charge of burglary was duly performed by Baron Cahorn against Arsène Lupin, a prisoner in the Prison de la Santé.

The baron afterwards regretted making the charge against Lupin when he saw his castle delivered over to the gendarmes, the *Procureur*, the *Juge d'instruction*, the newspaper reporters and photographers, and a throng of idle curiosity-seekers.

The affair soon became a topic of general discussion, and the name of Arsène Lupin excited the public imagination to such an extent that the newspapers filled their columns with the most fantastic stories of his exploits which found ready credence among their readers.

But the letter of Arsène Lupin that was published in the *Echo de France* (no one ever knew how the newspaper obtained it), that letter in which Baron Cahorn was impudently warned of the coming theft, caused considerable excitement. The most fabulous theories were advanced. Some recalled the existence of the famous subterranean tunnels, and that was the line of research pursued by the officers of the law, who searched the house from top to bottom, questioned every stone, studied the wainscoting and the chimneys, the window-frames and the girders in the ceilings. By the light of torches, they examined the immense cellars where the Lords of Malaquis were wont to store their munitions and provisions. They sounded the rocky foundation to its very centre. But it was all in vain. They discovered no trace of a subterranean tunnel. No secret passage existed.

But the eager public declared that the pictures and furniture could not vanish like so many ghosts. They are substantial, material things and require doors and windows for their exits and their entrances, and so do the people that remove them. Who were those people? How did they gain access to the castle? And how did they leave it?

The police officers of Rouen, convinced of their own impotence, solicited the assistance of the Parisian detective force. M. Dudouis, Chief of the Sûreté, sent the best sleuths of the iron brigade. He himself spent forty-eight hours at the castle, but met with no success. Then he sent for Ganimard, whose past services had proved so useful when all else failed.

Ganimard listened, in silence, to the instructions of his superior; then, shaking his head, he said: 'In my opinion, it is useless to ransack the castle. The solution of the problem lies elsewhere.'

'Where, then?'

'With Arsène Lupin.'

'With Arsène Lupin! To support that theory, we must admit his intervention.'

'I do admit it. In fact, I consider it quite certain.'

'Come, Ganimard, that is absurd. Arsène Lupin is in prison.'

'I grant you that Arsène Lupin is in prison, closely guarded; but he must have fetters on his feet, manacles on his wrists and a gag in his mouth before I change my opinion.'

'Why so obstinate, Ganimard?'

'Because Arsène Lupin is the only man in France of sufficient calibre to invent and carry out a scheme of that magnitude.'

'Mere words, Ganimard.'

'But true ones. Look! What are they doing? Searching for

subterranean passages, stones swinging on pivots, and other nonsense of that kind. But Lupin doesn't employ such old-fashioned methods. He is a modern cracksman, right up to date.'

'And how would you proceed?'

'I should ask your permission to spend an hour with him.'

'In his cell?'

'Yes. During the return trip from America we became very friendly, and I venture to say that if he can give me any information without compromising himself he will not hesitate to save me from incurring useless trouble.'

It was shortly after noon when Ganimard entered the cell of Arsène Lupin. The latter, who was lying on his bed, raised his head and uttered a cry of apparent joy.

'Ah! This is a real surprise. My dear Ganimard, here!'

'Ganimard himself.'

'In my chosen retreat! I have felt a desire for many things, but my fondest wish was to receive you here.'

'Very kind of you, I am sure.'

'Not at all. You know I hold you in the highest regard.'

'I am proud of it.'

'I have always said: Ganimard is our best detective. He is almost – you see how candid I am! – he is almost as clever as Sherlock Holmes. But I am sorry that I cannot offer you anything better than this hard stool. And no refreshments! Not even a glass of beer! Of course, you will excuse me, as I am here only temporarily.'

Ganimard smiled, and accepted the proffered seat. Then the prisoner continued: 'Mon Dieu, how pleased I am to see the face of an honest man. I am so tired of those devils of spies who come here ten times a day to ransack my pockets and my cell to satisfy themselves that I am not preparing to escape. The government is very solicitous on my account.'

'It is quite right.'

'Why so? I should be quite contented if they would allow me to live in my own quiet way.'

'On other people's money.'

'Quite so. That would be so simple. But here, I am joking, and you are, no doubt, in a hurry. So let us come to business, Ganimard. To what do I owe the honour of this visit?

'The Cahorn affair,' declared Ganimard, frankly.

'Ah! Wait, one moment. You see I have had so many affairs! First, let me fix in my mind the circumstances of this particular case . . . Ah! yes, now I have it. The Cahorn affair, Malaquis Castle, Seine-Inférieure . . . Two Rubens, a Watteau, and a few trifling articles.'

'Trifling!'

'Oh! *ma foi*, all that is of slight importance. But it suffices to know that the affair interests you. How can I serve you, Ganimard?'

'Must I explain to you what steps the authorities have taken in the matter?'

'Not at all. I have read the newspapers and I will frankly state that you have made very little progress.'

'And that is the reason I have come to see you.'

'I am entirely at your service.'

'In the first place, the Cahorn affair was managed by you?'

'From A to Z.'

'The letter of warning? the telegram?'

'All mine. I ought to have the receipts somewhere.'

Arsène opened the drawer of a small table of plain white wood which, with the bed and stool, constituted all the furniture in his cell, and took therefrom two scraps of paper which he handed to Ganimard.

'Ah!' exclaimed the detective, in surprise, 'I thought you were closely guarded and searched, and I find that you read the newspapers and collect postal receipts.'

'Bah! these people are so stupid! They open the lining of my vest, they examine the soles of my shoes, they sound the walls of my cell, but they never imagine that Arsène Lupin would be foolish enough to choose such a simple hiding place.'

Ganimard laughed, as he said: 'What a droll fellow you are! Really, you bewilder me. But, come now, tell me about the Cahorn affair.'

'Oh! oh! not quite so fast! You would rob me of all my secrets; expose all my little tricks. That is a very serious matter.'

'Was I wrong to count on your complaisance?'

'No, Ganimard, and since you insist – '

Arsène Lupin paced his cell two or three times, then, stopping before Ganimard, he asked: 'What do you think of my letter to the baron?'

'I think you were amusing yourself by playing to the gallery.'

'Ah! playing to the gallery! Come, Ganimard, I thought you knew me better. Do I, Arsène Lupin, ever waste my time on such puerilities? Would I have written that letter if I could have robbed the baron without writing to him? I want you to understand that the letter was indispensable; it was the motor that set the whole machine in motion. Now, let us discuss together a scheme for the robbery of Malaquis Castle. Are you willing?'

'Yes, proceed.'

'Well, let us suppose a castle carefully closed and barricaded like that of the Baron Cahorn. Am I to abandon my scheme and renounce the treasures that I covet upon the pretext that the castle which holds them is inaccessible?'

'Evidently not.'

'Should I make an assault upon the castle at the head of a band of adventurers as they did in ancient times?'

'That would be foolish.'

'Can I gain admittance by stealth or cunning?'

'Impossible.'

'Then there is only one way open to me. I must have the owner of the castle invite me to it.'

'That is surely an original method.'

'And how easy! Let us suppose that one day the owner receives a letter warning him that a notorious burglar known as Arsène Lupin is plotting to rob him. What will he do?'

'Send a letter to the *Procureur*.'

'Who will laugh at him, because the said Arsène Lupin is actually in prison. Then, in his anxiety and fear, the simple man will ask the assistance of the first-comer, will he not?'

'Very likely.'

'And if he happens to read in a country newspaper that a celebrated detective is spending his vacation in a neighbouring town – '

'He will seek that detective.'

'Of course. In anticipation of this scenario, therefore, let us presume that the said Arsène Lupin has requested one of his friends to visit Caudebec, make the acquaintance of the editor of the *Réveil*, a newspaper to which the baron is a subscriber, and introduce himself as said celebrated detective – then, what will happen?'

'The editor will announce in the *Réveil* the presence in Caudebec of said detective.'

'Exactly; and one of two things will happen: either the fish – I mean Cahorn – will not bite, and nothing will happen; or, what is more likely, he will run and greedily swallow the bait. Thus, behold my Baron Cahorn imploring the assistance of one of my friends against me.'

'Original, indeed!'

'Of course, the pseudo-detective at first refuses to give any assistance. On top of that comes the telegram from Arsène Lupin. The frightened baron rushes once more to my friend and offers him a definite sum of money for his services. My friend accepts and summons two members of our band, who, during the night, while Cahorn is under the watchful eye of his protector, removes certain articles by way of the window and lowers them with ropes into a nice little launch chartered for the occasion. Simple, isn't it?'

'Marvellous! Marvellous!' exclaimed Ganimard. 'The boldness of the scheme and the ingenuity of all its details are beyond criticism. But who is the detective whose name and fame served as a magnet to attract the baron and draw him into your net?'

'There is only one name could do it – only one.'

'And that is?'

'Arsène Lupin's personal enemy – the most illustrious Ganimard.'

'I?'

'Yourself, Ganimard. And, really, it is very funny. If you go there, and the baron decides to talk, you will find that it will be your duty to arrest yourself, just as you arrested me in America. Hein! the revenge is really amusing: I cause Ganimard to arrest Ganimard.'

Arsène Lupin laughed heartily. The detective, greatly vexed, bit his lips; to him the joke was quite devoid of humour. The arrival of a prison guard gave Ganimard an opportunity to recover himself. The man brought Arsène Lupin's luncheon, furnished by a neighbouring restaurant. After depositing the tray upon the table, the guard retired. Lupin broke his bread, ate a few morsels, and continued: 'But, rest easy, my dear Ganimard, you will not go to Malaquis. I can tell you something that will astonish you: the Cahorn affair is on the point of being settled.'

'Excuse me; I have just seen the Chief of the Sureté.'

'What of that? Does M. Dudouis know my business better than I do myself? You will learn that Ganimard – excuse me – that the pseudo-Ganimard still remains on very good terms with the baron. The latter has authorised him to negotiate a very delicate transaction with me, and, at the present moment, in consideration of a certain sum, it is probable that the baron has recovered possession of his pictures and other treasures. And on their return, he will withdraw his complaint. Thus, there is no longer any theft, and the law must abandon the case.'

Ganimard regarded the prisoner with a bewildered air.

'And how do you know all that?'

'I have just received the telegram I was expecting.'

'You have just received a telegram?'

'This very moment, my dear friend. Out of politeness, I did not wish to read it in your presence. But if you will permit me –'

'You are joking, Lupin.'

'My dear friend, if you will be so kind as to break that egg, you will learn for yourself that I am not joking.'

Mechanically, Ganimard obeyed, and cracked the eggshell with the blade of a knife. He uttered a cry of surprise. The shell contained nothing but a small piece of blue paper. At the request of Arsène he unfolded it. It was a telegram, or rather a portion of a telegram from which the post-marks had been removed. It read as follows: 'Contract closed. Hundred thousand balls delivered. All well.'

'One hundred thousand balls?' said Ganimard.

'Yes, one hundred thousand francs. Very little, but then, you know, these are hard times . . . And I have some heavy bills to meet. If you only knew my budget . . . living in the city comes very high.'

Ganimard arose. His ill humour had disappeared. He reflected for a moment, glancing over the whole affair in an effort to discover a weak point; then, in a tone and manner that betrayed his admiration of the prisoner, he said: 'Fortunately, we do not have a dozen such as you to deal with; if we did, we would have to close up shop.'

Arsène Lupin assumed a modest air, as he replied: 'Bah! a person must have some diversion to occupy his leisure hours, especially when he is in prison.'

'What!' exclaimed Ganimard, 'your trial, your defence, the examination – isn't that sufficient to occupy your mind?'

'No, because I have decided not to be present at my trial.'

'Oh! oh!'

Arsène Lupin repeated, positively: 'I shall not be present at my trial.'

'Really!'

'Ah! my dear monsieur, do you suppose I am going to rot upon the wet straw? You insult me. Arsène Lupin remains in prison just as long as it pleases him, and not one minute more.'

'Perhaps it would have been more prudent if you had avoided getting there,' said the detective, ironically.

'Ah! monsieur jests? Monsieur must remember that he had the honour to effect my arrest. Know then, my worthy friend, that no one, not even you, could have placed a hand upon me if a much more important event had not occupied my attention at that critical moment.'

'You astonish me.'

'A woman was looking at me, Ganimard, and I loved her. Do you fully understand what that means: to be under the eyes of a woman that one loves? I cared for nothing in the world but that. And that is why I am here.'

'Permit me to say: you have been here a long time.'

'In the first place, I wished to forget. Do not laugh; it was a delightful adventure and it is still a tender memory. Besides, I have been suffering from neurasthenia. Life is so feverish these days that it is necessary to take the 'rest cure' occasionally, and I find this spot a sovereign remedy for my tired nerves.'

'Arsène Lupin, you are not a bad fellow, after all.'

'Thank you,' said Lupin. 'Ganimard, this is Friday. On Wednesday next, at four o'clock in the afternoon, I will smoke my cigar at your house in the rue Pergolese.'

'Arsène Lupin, I will expect you.'

They shook hands like two old friends who valued each other at their true worth; then the detective stepped to the door.

'Ganimard!'

'What is it?' asked Ganimard, as he turned back.

'You have forgotten your watch.'

'My watch?'

'Yes, it strayed into my pocket.'

He returned the watch, excusing himself.

'Pardon me . . . a bad habit. Because they have taken mine is no reason why I should take yours. Besides, I have a chronometer here that satisfies me fairly well.'

He took from the drawer a large gold watch and heavy chain.

'From whose pocket did that come?' asked Ganimard.

Arsène Lupin gave a hasty glance at the initials engraved on the watch.

'J.B. – Who the devil can that be? – Ah! yes, I remember. Jules Bouvier, the judge who conducted my examination. A charming fellow!'

HESKETH PRICHARD

Major Hesketh Vernon-Pritchard (1876–1922) was a distinguished soldier, explorer, newspaper correspondent, travel writer, cricketer and campaigner for animal welfare who included many of his own exploits in his stories, especially those featuring November Joe, 'the Detective of the Woods'. Possibly the most unusual detective in this collection, November Joe uses his native skills for detective purposes in the wilds of Canada.

The Hundred-Thousand-Dollar Robbery

'I want the whole affair kept unofficial and secret,' said Harris, the bank manager.

November Joe nodded. He was seated on the extreme edge of a chair in the manager's private office, looking curiously out of place in that prim, richly furnished room.

'The truth is,' continued Harris, 'we bankers cannot afford to have our customers' minds unsettled. There are, as you know, Joe, numbers of small depositors, especially in the rural districts, who would be scared out of their seven senses if they knew that this infernal Cecil James Atterson had made off with a hundred thousand dollars. They'd never trust us again.'

'A hundred thousand dollars is a wonderful lot of money,' agreed Joe.

'Our reserve is over twenty millions, two hundred times a hundred thousand,' replied Harris grandiloquently.

Joe smiled in his pensive manner. 'That so? Then I guess the bank won't be hurt if Atterson escapes,' said he.

'I shall be bitterly disappointed if you permit him to do so,' returned Harris. 'But here, let's get down to business.'

On the previous night, Harris, the manager of the Quebec branch of the Grand Banks of Canada, had rung me up to borrow November Joe, who was at the time building a log camp for me on one of my properties. I sent Joe a telegram, with the result that within five hours of its receipt he had walked the twenty miles into Quebec, and was now with me at the bank ready to hear Harris's account of the robbery.

The manager cleared his throat and began with a question: 'Have you ever seen Atterson?'

'No.'

'I thought you might have. He always spends his vacations in the woods – fishing, usually. The last two years he has fished Red River. This is what happened. On Saturday I told him to go down to the strong-room to fetch up a fresh batch of dollar and five-dollar bills, as we were short. It happened that in the same safe there were a number of bearer securities. Atterson soon brought me the notes I had sent him for, with the keys. That was about noon on Saturday. We closed at one o'clock. Yesterday, Monday, Atterson did not turn up. At first I thought nothing of it, but when it came to afternoon, and he had neither come nor sent any reason for his absence, I began to smell a rat. I went down to the strong-room and found that over one hundred thousand dollars in notes and bearer securities were missing.

'I communicated at once with the police and they started in to make enquiries. I must tell you that Atterson lived in a boarding-house behind the Frontenac. No one had seen him on Sunday, but on Saturday night a fellow boarder, called Collings, reports Atterson as going to his room about 10.30. He was the last person who saw him. Atterson spoke to him and said he was off to spend Sunday on the south shore. From that moment Atterson has vanished.'

'Didn't the police find out anything further?' enquired Joe.

'Well, we couldn't trace him at any of the railway stations.'

'I s'pose they wired to every other police-station within a hundred miles?'

'They did, and that is what brought you into it.'

'Why?'

'The constable at Roberville replied that a man answering to the description of Atterson was seen by a farmer walking along the Stoneham road, and heading north, on Sunday morning, early.'

'No more facts?'

'No.'

'Then let's get back to the robbery. Why are you so plum sure Atterson done it?'

'The notes and securities were there on Saturday morning.'

'How do you know?'

'It's my business to know. I saw them myself.'

'Huh! . . . And no one else went down to the strong-room?'

'Only Atterson. The second clerk – it is a rule that no employee may visit the strong-room alone – remained at the head of the stairs while Atterson descended.'

'Who keeps the key?'

'I do.'

'And it was never out of your possession?'

'Never.'

November was silent for a few moments.

'How long has Atterson been with the bank?'

'Two years odd.'

'Anything against him before?'

'Nothing.'

At this point a clerk knocked at the door and, entering, brought in some letters. Harris stiffened as he noticed the writing on one of them. He cut it open and, when the clerk was gone out, he read aloud:

'DEAR HARRIS – I hereby resign my splendid and lucrative position in the Grand Banks of Canada. It is a dog's dirty life – anyway it is so for a man of spirit. You can give the week's screw that's owing to me to buy milk and bath buns for the next meeting of directors.

Yours truly,

C. J. ATTERSON.'

'What's the postmark?' asked Joe.

'Rimouski. Sunday, 9.30 a.m.'

'It looks like Atterson's the thief,' remarked Joe.

'I've always been sure of it!' cried Harris.

'I wasn't,' said Joe.

'Are you sure of it now?'

'I'm inclined that way because Atterson had that letter posted by a con–con– what's the word?'

'Confederate?'

'You've got it. He was seen here in town on Saturday at 1.30, and he couldn't have posted no letter in Rimouski in time for the 9.30 a.m. on Sunday unless he'd gone there on the 7 o'clock express on Saturday evening. Yes, Atterson's the thief, all right. And if that really was him they saw Stoneham ways, he's had time to get thirty mile of bush between us and him, and he can go right on till he's in Labrador. I doubt you'll see your hundred thousand dollars again. Mr Harris.'

'Bah! You can trail him easily enough?'

Joe shook his head. 'If you was to put me on his tracks I could,' said he, 'but up there in the Laurentides he'll sure pinch a canoe and make along a waterway.'

'H'm!' coughed Harris. 'My directors won't want to pay you two dollars a day for nothing.'

'Two dollars a day?' said Joe in his gentle voice, 'I shouldn't a' thought the two hundred times a hundred thousand dollars could stand a *strain* like that!'

I laughed. 'Look here, November, I think I'd like to make this bargain for you.'

'Yes, sure,' said the young woodsman.

'Then I'll sell your services to Mr Harris here for five dollars a day if you fail, and twenty per cent of the sum you recover if you succeed.'

Joe looked at me with wide eyes, but he said nothing.

'Well, Harris, is it on or off?' I asked.

'Oh, on, I suppose, confound you!' said Harris.

November looked at both of us with a broad smile.

* * *

Twenty hours later, Joe, a police trooper named Hobson and I were deep in the woods. We had briefly paused to interview the farmer at Roberville, and then had passed on down the old deserted roads until at last we entered the forest, or as it is locally called, the 'bush'.

'Where are you heading for?' Hobson had asked Joe.

'Red River, because if it was really Atterson the farmer saw, I guess he'll have gone up there.'

'Why do you think that?'

'Red River's the overflow of Snow Lake, and there is several trappers has canoes on Snow Lake. There's none of them trappers there now in July month, so he can steal a canoe easy. Besides, a man who fears pursuit always likes to get into a country he knows, and you heard Mr Harris say how Atterson had fished Red River two vacations. Besides . . .' here Joe stopped and pointed to the ground, 'them's Atterson's tracks,' he said. 'Leastways, it's a black fox to a lynx pelt they are his.'

'But you've never seen him. What reason have you . . . ?' demanded Hobson.

'When first we come on them about four hours back, while you was lightin' your pipe,' replied Joe, 'they come out of the bush, and when we come near Cartier's place they went back into the bush again. Then a mile beyond Cartier's out of the bush they come on to the road. What can that circumventin' mean? Feller who made the tracks don't want to be seen. No. 8 boots, city-made, nails in 'em, rubber heels. Come on.'

I will not attempt to describe our journey hour by hour, nor tell how November held to the trail, following it over areas of hard ground and rock, noticing a scratch here and a broken twig there. The trooper, Hobson, proved to be a good track-reader, but he thought himself a better and, it seemed to me, was a little jealous of Joe's obvious superiority.

We slept that night beside the trail. According to November, the thief was now not many hours ahead of us. Everything depended upon whether he could reach Red River and a canoe before we caught up with him. Still it was not possible to follow a trail in the darkness, so perforce we camped. The next morning November wakened us at daylight and we hastened forward.

For some time we followed Atterson's footsteps and then found that they left the road. The police officer went crashing along till Joe stopped him with a gesture.

'Listen!' he whispered.

We moved on quietly and saw that, not fifty yards ahead of us, a man was walking excitedly up and down. His face was quite clear in the slanting sunlight, a resolute face with a small, dark moustache and a two-days' growth of beard. His head was sunk upon his chest in an attitude of the utmost despair, he waved his hands, and on the still air there came to us the sound of his monotonous muttering.

We crept upon him. As we did so Hobson leapt forward and, snapping his handcuffs on the man's wrists, cried: 'Cecil Atterson, I've got you!'

Atterson sprang like a man on a wire, his face went dead white. He stood quite still for a moment as if dazed, then he said in a queer voice: 'Got me, have you? Much good may it do you!'

'Hand over that packet you're carrying,' answered Hobson.

There was another pause.

'First of all, I'd like to hear exactly what I'm charged with,' said Atterson.

'Like to hear!' said Hobson. 'You know! Theft of one hundred thousand dollars from the Grand Banks. May as well hand them over and put me to no more trouble!'

'You can take all the trouble you like,' said the prisoner.

Hobson plunged his hand into Atterson's pockets, and searched him thoroughly, but found nothing.

'They are not on him,' he cried. 'Try his pack.'

From the pack November produced a square bottle of whisky, some bread, salt, a slab of mutton – that was all.

'Where have you hidden the stuff,' demanded Hobson.

Suddenly Atterson laughed.

'So you think I robbed the bank?' he said. 'I've my own down on them, and I'm glad they've been hit by someone, though I'm not the man. Anyway, I'll have you and them for wrongful arrest with violence.' Then he turned to us. 'You two are witnesses.'

'Do you deny you're Cecil Atterson?' said Hobson.

'No, I am Atterson right enough.'

'Then look here, Atterson, your best chance is to show us where you've hid the stuff. Your counsel can put that in your favour at your trail.'

'I'm not taking any advice just now, thank you. I have said I know nothing of the robbery.'

Hobson looked him up and down. 'You'll sing another song by and by,' he said ironically. 'We may as well start in now, Joe, and find where he's cached that packet.'

November was fingering over the pack which lay open on the ground, examining it and its contents with concentrated attention. Atterson had sunk down under a tree like a man wearied out.

Hobson and Joe made a rapid examination of the vicinity. A

few yards brought them to the end of Atterson's tracks.

'Here's where he slept,' said Hobson. 'It's all pretty clear. He was dog-tired and just collapsed. I guess that was last night. It's an old camping place this.' The policeman pointed to weathered beds of balsam and the scars of several camp-fires. 'Yes,' he continued, 'that's what it is. But the trouble is where has he cached the bank's property?'

For upwards of an hour Hobson searched every conceivable spot, but not so November Joe, who, after a couple of quick casts down to the river, made a fire, put on the kettle, and lit his pipe. Atterson, from under his tree, watched the proceedings with a drowsy lack of interest that struck me as being particularly well simulated.

At length Hobson ceased his exertions, and accepted a cup of the tea Joe had brewed.

'There's nothing hid round here,' he said in a voice low enough to escape the prisoner's ear, 'and his' – he indicated Atterson's recumbent form with his hand – 'trail stops right where he slept. He never moved a foot beyond that nor went down to the river fifty yards away. I guess what he's done is clear enough.'

'Huh!' said Joe. 'Think so?'

'Yep! The chap's either cached them or handed them to an accomplice on the back trail.'

'That so? And what are you going to do next?'

'I'm thinking he'll confess all right when I get him alone.' He stood up as November moved to take a cup of tea over to Atterson.

'No, you don't,' he cried. 'Prisoner Atterson neither eats not drinks between here and Quebec unless he confesses where he has got the stuff hid.'

'We'd best be going now,' he continued as November, shrugging, came back to the fireside. 'You two walk on and let me get a word quiet with the prisoner.'

'I'm staying here,' said Joe.

'What for?' cried Hobson.

'I'm employed by bank manager Harris to recover stolen property,' replied Joe.

'But,' expostulated Hobson, 'Atterson's trail stops right here where he slept. There are no other tracks, so no one could have visited him. Do you think he's got the bills and papers hid about here after all?'

'No,' said Joe.

Hobson stared at the answer, then turned to go. 'Well,' said he, 'you take your way and I'll take mine. I reckon I'll get a confession out of him before we reach Quebec. He's a pretty tired man, and he don't rest nor sleep, no, nor sit down, till he's put me wise as to where he's hid the stuff he stole.'

'He won't ever put you wise,' said Joe definitely.

'Why do you say that?'

' 'Cause he can't. He don't know himself.'

'Bah!' was all Hobson's answer as he turned on his heel.

* * *

November Joe did not move as Hobson, his wrist strapped to Atterson's, disappeared down the trail by which we had come.

'Well,' I said, 'what next?'

'I'll take another look around.' Joe leapt to his feet and went quickly over the ground. I accompanied him.

'What do you make of it?' he said at last.

'Nothing,' I answered. 'There are no tracks nor other signs at all, except these two or three places where old logs have been lying – I expect Atterson picked them up for his fire. I don't understand what you are getting at any more than Hobson does.'

'Huh!' said Joe, and led the way down to the river, which, though not more than fifty yards away, was hidden from us by the thick trees.

It was a slow-flowing river, and in the soft mud of the margin I saw, to my surprise, the quite recent traces of a canoe having been beached. Beside the canoe, there was also on the mud the faint mark of a paddle having lain at full length.

Joe pointed to it. The paddle had evidently, I thought, fallen from the canoe, for the impression it had left on the soft surface was very slight.

'How long ago was the canoe here?'

'At first light – maybe between three and four o'clock,' replied Joe.

'Then I don't see how it helps you at all. Its coming can't have anything to do with the Atterson robbery, for the distance from here to the camp is too far to throw a packet, and the absence of tracks makes it clear that Atterson cannot have handed the loot over to a confederate in the canoe. Isn't that right?'

'Looks that way,' admitted Joe.

'Then the canoe can be only a coincidence.'

November shook his head. 'I wouldn't go so far as to say that, Mr Quaritch.'

Once again he rapidly went over the ground near the river, then returned to the spot where Atterson had slept, following a slightly different track to that by which we had come. Then taking the hatchet from his belt, he split a dead log or two for a fire and hung up the kettle once more. I guessed from this that he had seen at least some daylight in a matter that was still obscure and inexplicable to me.

'I wonder if Atterson has confessed to Hobson yet,' I said, meaning to draw Joe.

'He may confess about the robbery, but he can't tell anyone where the bank property is.'

'You said that before, Joe. You seem very sure of it.'

'I am sure. Atterson doesn't know, because *he's* been robbed in his turn.'

'Robbed!' I exclaimed.

Joe nodded.

'And the robber?'

' 'Bout five foot eight, lightweight, very handsome, has black hair, is, I think, under twenty-five years old, and lives in Lendeville, or near it.'

'Joe, you've nothing to go on!' I cried. 'Are you sure of this? How can you know?'

'I'll tell you when I've got those bank bills back. One thing's sure – Atterson'll be better off doing five years' hard than if he'd – But here, Mr Quaritch, I'm going too fast. Drink your tea, and then let us make Lendeville. It's all of eight miles upstream.'

It was still early afternoon when we arrived in Lendeville, which could hardly be called a village, except in the Canadian acceptance of that term. It was composed of a few scattered farms and a single general store. Outside one of the farmhouses Joe paused.

'I know the chap that lives in here,' he said. 'He's a pretty mean kind of a man, Mr Quaritch. I may find a way to make him talk – though if he thought I wanted information he'd not part with it.'

We found the farmer at home, a dour fellow, whose father had emigrated from the north of Scotland half a century earlier.

'Say, McAndrew,' began Joe, 'there's a chance I'll be bringing a party up on to Red River month after next for the moose-calling. What's your price for hiring two strong horses and a good buck-board to take us and our outfit on from here to the Burnt Lands by Sandy Pond?'

'Twenty dollars.'

'Huh!' said Joe, 'we don't want to buy the old horses!'

The Scotchman's shaven lips (he wore a chin-beard and whiskers) opened. 'It wouldna' pay to do it for less.'

'Then there's others as will.'

'And what might their names be?' enquired McAndrew ironically.

'Them as took up bank-clerk Atterson when he was here six weeks back.'

'Weel, you're wrang!' cried McAndrew, 'for bank-clerk Atterson juist walked in with young Simon Pointarré and lived with the family at their new mill. So the price is twenty, or I'll nae harness a horse for ye!'

'Then I'll have to go on to Simon Pointarré. I've heard him well spoken of.'

'Have ye now? That's queer for he . . .'

'Maybe then it was his brother,' said Joe, quickly.

'Which?'

'The other one that was with Atterson at Red River.'

'There was nae one, only the old man, Simon and the two girls.'

'Well, anyway I've got my sportsmen's interests to mind,' said November, 'and I'll ask the Pointarrés' price before I close with yours.'

'I'll make a reduce to seventeen dollars if ye agree here and now.'

November said something further of Atterson's high regard for Simon Pointarré, which goaded old McAndrew to fury.

'And I'll suppose it was love of Simon that made him employ that family,' he snarled. 'Oh yes, that's comic. 'Twas Simon and no that grinning lassie they call Phèdre! . . . Atterson? Tush! I tell ye if ever a man made a fule o' himself . . .'

But here, despite McAndrew's protests, Joe left the farm.

At the store, which was next visited, we learned the position of the Pointarré steading and the fact that old Pointarré, the daughters, Phèdre and Claire, and one son, Simon, were at home while the other sons were on duty at the mill.

Joe and I walked together along various trails until from a hillside we were able to look down upon the farm, and in a few minutes we were knocking at the door.

It was opened by a girl of about twenty years of age; her

bright brown eyes and hair made her very good-looking. Joe gave her a quick glance.

'I came to see your sister,' said he.

'Simon,' called the girl, 'here's a man to see Phèdre.'

'What's his business?' growled a man's voice from the inner room.

'I've a message for Miss Pointarré,' said Joe.

'Let him leave it with you, Claire,' again growled the voice.

'I was to give it to her and no one else,' persisted Joe.

This brought Simon to the door. He was a powerful young French-Canadian with up-brushed hair and a dark moustache. He stared at us.

'I've never seen you before,' he said at last.

'No, I'm going south and I promised I'd leave a message passing through,' replied Joe.

'Who sent you?'

'Can't tell that, but I guess Miss Pointarré will know when I give her the message.'

'Well, I suppose you'd best see her. She's down bringing in the cows. You'll find her below there in the meadow,' he waved his arm to where we could see a small stream that ran under wooded hills at a distance of about half a mile. 'Yes, you'll find her there below.'

Joe thanked him and we set off.

It did not take us long to locate the cows, but there was no sign of the girl. Then, taking up a well-marked trail which led away into the bush, we advanced upon it in silence till, round a clump of pines, it debouched upon a large open shed or byre. Two or three cows stood at the farther end of it, and near them with her back to us was a girl with the sun shining on the burnished coils of her black hair.

A twig broke under my foot and she swung round at the noise.

'What do you want?' she asked.

She was tall and really gloriously handsome.

'I've come from Atterson. I've just seen him,' said November.

I fancied her breath caught for the fraction of a second, but only a haughty surprise showed in her face.

'There are many people who see him every day. What of that?' she retorted.

'Not many have seen him today, or even yesterday.'

Her dark blue eyes were fixed on November. 'Is he ill? What do you mean?'

'Huh! Don't they read the newspaper in Lendeville? There's something about him going round. I came thinking you'd sure want to hear,' said November.

The colour rose in Phèdre's beautiful face.

'They're saying,' went on Joe, 'that he robbed the bank where he was employed of a hundred thousand dollars, and instead of trying to get away on the train or by one of the steamers, he made for the woods. That was all right if a Roberville farmer hadn't seen him. So they put the police on his track and I went with the police.'

Phèdre turned away as if bored. 'What interest have I in this? It *ennuies* me to listen.'

'Wait!' replied November. 'With the police I went, and soon struck Atterson's trail on the old Colonial Post Road, and in time come up with Atterson himself, nigh Red River. The police takes Atterson prisoner and searches him.'

'And got the money back!' she said scornfully. 'Well, it sounds silly enough. I don't want to hear more.'

'The best is coming, Miss Pointarré. They found nothing. Though they searched him and all round about the camp, they found nothing.'

'He had hidden it I suppose.'

'So the police thought. And I thought so too, till . . . ' (November's gaze never left her face) 'till I see his eyes. The pupils was like pinpoints in his head.' He paused and added, 'I got the bottle of whisky that was in his pack. It'll go in as evidence.'

'Of what?' she cried impatiently.

'That Atterson was drugged and the bank property stole from him. You see,' continued Joe, 'this robbery wasn't altogether Atterson's own idea.'

'Ah!'

'No, I guess he had the first notion of it when he was on his vacation six weeks back. He was in love with a wonderful handsome girl. Blue eyes she had and black hair, and her teeth was as good as yours. She pretended to be in love with him, but all along she was in love with – well, I can't say who she was in love with – herself likely. Anyway, I expect she used all her influence to make Atterson rob the bank and then light out for the woods with the stuff. He does all she wants. On his way to the woods she meets him with a pack of food and necessaries. In that pack was a bottle of drugged whisky. She asks him where he's going to camp that night, he suspects nothing and tells her, and later off she goes in a canoe up Red River till she comes to opposite where he's lying drugged. She lands and robs him, but she don't want him to know who's done it, so she plays an old game to conceal her tracks. She's a rare active young woman, so she carries out her plan, gets back to her canoe and home to Lendeville . . . Need I tell any more about her?'

During Joe's story Phèdre's colour had slowly died away.

'You are very clever!' she said bitterly. 'But why should you tell *me* all this?'

'Because I'm going to advise you to hand over the hundred thousand dollars you took from Atterson. I'm in this case for the bank.'

'I?' she exclaimed violently. 'Do you dare to say that I had anything whatever to do with this robbery, that I have the hundred thousand dollars . . . Bah! I know nothing about it. How should I?'

Joe shrugged his shoulders. 'Then I beg your pardon, Miss Pointarré, and I say goodbye. I must go and make my report to the police and let them act their own way.' He turned, but before he had gone more than a step or two, she called to him.

'There is one point you have missed for all your cleverness,' she said. 'Suppose what you have said is true, may it not be that the girl who robbed Atterson took the money just to return it to the bank?'

'Don't seem to be that way, for she has just denied all knowledge of the property, and denied she had it before two witnesses. Besides, when Atterson comes to know that he's been made a cat's-paw of, he'll be liable to turn king's evidence. No, miss, your only chance is to hand over the stuff – here and now.'

'To you!' she scoffed. 'And who are you? What right have you . . .'

'I'm in this case for the bank. Old McAndrew knows me well and can tell you my name.'

'What is it?'

'People mostly call me November Joe.'

She threw back her head – every attitude, every movement of hers was wonderful.

'Now supposing that the money could be found . . . what would you do?'

'I'd go to the bank and tell them I'd make shift to get every cent back safe for them if they'd agree not to prosecute . . . anybody.'

'So you're man enough not to wish to see me in trouble?'

November looked at her. 'I was sure not thinking of you at all,' he said simply, 'but of bank-clerk Atterson, who's lost the girl he robbed for and ruined himself for. I'd hate to see that chap over-punished with a dose of gaol too . . . But the bank people only wants their money, and I guess if they get that they'll be apt to think the less said about the robbery the better.

So if you take my advice – why, now's the time to see old McAndrew. You see, Miss Pointarré, I've got the cinch on you.'

She stood still for a while. 'I'll see old man McAndrew,' she cried suddenly. 'I'll lead. It's near enough this way.'

Joe turned after her, and I followed. Without arousing McAndrew's suspicions, Joe satisfied the girl as to his identity.

Before dark she met us again. 'There!' she said, thrusting a packet into Joe's hand, 'But look out for yourself! Atterson isn't the only man who'd break the law for love of me. Think of that at night in the lonely bush!'

'My!' ejaculated November as he looked after her receding figure, 'she's a bad loser, ain't she, Mr Quaritch?'

* * *

We went back into Quebec, and Joe made over to the bank the amount of their loss as soon as Harris the manager (rather against his will) agreed that no questions should be asked nor action taken.

The same evening I, not being under the same embargo regarding questions, enquired from Joe how in the world the fair Phèdre covered her tracks from the canoe to where Atterson was lying.

'That was simple for an active girl. She walked ashore along the paddle, and after her return to the canoe threw water upon the mark it made in the mud. Didn't you notice how faint it was?'

'But when she got on shore – how did she hide her trail then?'

'It's not a new trick. She took a couple of short logs with her in the canoe. First she put one down and stepped on to it, then she'd put the other one farther and step on to that. Next she'd lift the one behind, and so on. Why did she do that? Well, I reckon she thought the trick good enough to blind Atterson. If he'd found a woman's tracks after being robbed he'd have suspected.'

'But you said before we left Atterson's camp that whoever robbed him was middle height, a lightweight and had black hair.'

'Well, hadn't she? Lightweight because the logs wasn't much drove into the ground, not tall since the marks of them was so close together.'

'But the black hair?'

Joe laughed. 'That was the surest thing of the lot, and put me wise to it and Phèdre at the start. Twisted up in the buckle of the pack she gave Atterson I found several strands of splendid black hair. She must 'a' caught her hair in the buckles while carrying it.'

'But, Joe, you also said at Red River that the person who robbed Atterson was not more than twenty-five years old?'

'Well, the hair proved it was a woman, and what but being in love with her face would make a slap-up bank-clerk like Atterson have any truck with a settler's girl? And them kind are early ripe and go off their looks at twenty-five. I guess, Mr Quaritch, her age was a pretty safe shot.'

GRANT ALLEN

Charles Grant Blairfindie Allen (1848–99) was a British author, philosopher and scientist whose two most notable works were literary breakthroughs. The first, *The Woman Who Did* (1895), created a sensation on its publication because of its frank discussion of sexual matters. The second, *An African Millionaire* (1897), contained a series of tales featuring Colonel Clay, the first important rogue in short crime fiction who is the hero, and not a subsidiary character or villain or anti-hero. He preceded Raffles, the gentleman crook, by two years. Allen's friend Arthur Conan Doyle completed his last novel (featuring an early female detective) *Hilda Wade*, using the author's notes, when Allen fell ill and died before he was able to finish it.

The Episode of the Diamond Links

'Let us take a trip to Switzerland,' said Lady Vandrift. And anyone who knows Amelia will not be surprised to learn that we *did* take a trip to Switzerland accordingly. Nobody can drive Sir Charles, except his wife. And nobody at all can drive Amelia.

There were difficulties at the outset, because we had not ordered rooms at the hotels beforehand, and it was well on in the season; but they were overcome at last by the usual application of a golden key; and we found ourselves in due time pleasantly quartered in Lucerne, at that most comfortable of European hostelries, the Schweitzerhof.

We were a square party of four – Sir Charles and Amelia, myself and Isabel. We had nice big rooms, on the first floor, overlooking the lake; and as none of us was possessed with the faintest symptom of that incipient mania which shows itself in the form of an insane desire to climb mountain heights of disagreeable steepness and unnecessary snowiness, I will venture to assert we all enjoyed ourselves. We spent most of our time sensibly in lounging about the lake on the jolly little steamers; and when we did a mountain climb, it was on the Rigi or Pilatus – where an engine undertook all the muscular work for us.

As usual, at the hotel, a great many miscellaneous people showed a burning desire to be specially nice to us. If you wish to see how friendly and charming humanity is, just try being a well-known millionaire for a week, and you'll learn a thing or two. Wherever Sir Charles goes he is surrounded by charming and disinterested people, all eager to make his distinguished acquaintance, and all familiar with several excellent investments, or several deserving objects of Christian charity. It is my business in life, as his brother-in-law and secretary, to decline with thanks the excellent investments, and to throw judicious cold water on the objects of charity. Even I myself, as the great man's almoner, am very much sought after. People casually allude before me to artless stories of 'poor curates in Cumberland, you know, Mr Wentworth', or widows in Cornwall, penniless poets with epics in their desks, and young painters who need but the breath of a patron to open to them the doors of an admiring Academy. I smile and look wise, while I administer cold water in minute doses; but I never report one of these cases to Sir Charles, except in the rare or almost unheard-of event where I think there is really something in them.

Ever since our little adventure with the seer at Nice, Sir Charles, who is constitutionally cautious, had been even more careful than usual about possible sharpers. And, as chance would have it, there sat just opposite us at the *table d'hôte* at the Schweitzerhof – 'tis a fad of Amelia's to dine at the *table d'hôte*; she says she can't bear to be boxed up all day in private rooms with 'too much family' – a sinister-looking man with dark hair and eyes, conspicuous by his bushy overhanging eyebrows. My attention was first called to the eyebrows in question by a nice little parson who sat at our side, and who observed that they were made up of certain large and bristly hairs, which (he told us) had been traced by Darwin to our monkey ancestors. Very pleasant little fellow, this fresh-faced young parson, on his honeymoon tour with a nice wee wife, a bonnie Scotch lassie with a charming accent.

I looked at the eyebrows close. Then a sudden thought struck me. 'Do you believe they're his own?' I asked of the curate; 'or are they only stuck on – a make-up disguise? They really almost look like it.'

'You don't suppose – ' Charles began, and checked himself suddenly.

'Yes, I do,' I answered; 'the seer!' Then I recollected my blunder, and looked down sheepishly. For, to say the truth, Vandrift had straightly enjoined on me long before to say nothing of our painful little episode at Nice to Amelia; he was afraid if she once heard of it, *he* would hear of it for ever after.

'What seer?' the little parson enquired, with parsonical curiosity.

I noticed the man with the overhanging eyebrows give a queer sort of start. Charles's glance was fixed upon me. I hardly knew what to answer.

'Oh, a man who was at Nice with us last year,' I stammered out, trying hard to look unconcerned. 'A fellow they talked about, that's all.' And I turned the subject.

But the curate, like a donkey, wouldn't let me turn it.

'Had he eyebrows like that?' he enquired, in an undertone. I was really angry. If this was Colonel Clay, the curate was obviously giving him the cue, and making it much more difficult for us to catch him, now we might possibly have lighted on the chance to do so.

'No, he hadn't,' I answered testily; 'it was a passing expression.

But this is not the man. I was mistaken, no doubt.' And I nudged him gently.

The little curate was too innocent for anything. 'Oh, I see,' he replied, nodding hard and looking wise. Then he turned to his wife and made an obvious face, which the man with the eyebrows couldn't fail to notice.

Fortunately, a political discussion going on a few places farther down the table spread up to us and diverted attention for a moment. The magical name of Gladstone saved us. Sir Charles flared up. I was truly pleased, for I could see Amelia was boiling over with curiosity by this time.

After dinner, in the billiard-room, however, the man with the big eyebrows sidled up and began to talk to me. If he *was* Colonel Clay, it was evident he bore us no grudge at all for the five thousand pounds he had done us out of. On the contrary, he seemed quite prepared to do us out of five thousand more when opportunity offered; for he introduced himself at once as Dr Hector Macpherson, the exclusive grantee of extensive concessions from the Brazilian government on the Upper Amazon. He dived into conversation with me at once as to the splendid mineral resources of his Brazilian estate – the silver, the platinum, the actual rubies, the possible diamonds. I listened and smiled; I knew what was coming. All he needed to develop this magnificent concession was a little more capital. It was sad to see thousands of pounds' worth of platinum and carloads of rubies just crumbling in the soil or carried away by the river for want of a few hundreds to work them with properly. If he knew of anybody, now, with money to invest, he could recommend him – nay, offer him – a unique opportunity of earning, say, forty per cent on his capital, on unimpeachable security.

'I wouldn't do it for every man,' Dr Hector Macpherson remarked, drawing himself up; 'but if I took a fancy to a fellow who had command of ready cash, I might choose to put him in the way of feathering his nest with unexampled rapidity.'

'Exceedingly disinterested of you,' I answered drily, fixing my eyes on his eyebrows.

The little curate, meanwhile, was playing billiards with Sir Charles. His glance followed mine as it rested for a moment on the monkey-like hairs.

'False, obviously false,' he remarked with his lips; and I'm bound to confess I never saw any man speak so well by movement alone; you could follow every word though not a sound escaped him.

During the rest of that evening Dr Hector Macpherson stuck to me as close as a mustard-plaster. And he was almost as irritating. I got heartily sick of the Upper Amazon. I have positively waded in my time through ruby mines (in prospectuses, I mean) till the mere sight of a ruby absolutely sickens me. When Charles, in an unwonted fit of generosity, once gave his sister Isabel (whom I had the honour to marry) a ruby necklet (inferior stones), I made Isabel change it for sapphires and amethysts, on the judicious plea that they suited her complexion better. (I scored one, incidentally, for having considered Isabel's complexion.) By the time I went to bed I was prepared to sink the Upper Amazon in the sea, and to stab, shoot, poison or otherwise seriously damage the man with the concession and the false eyebrows.

For the next three days, at intervals, he returned to the charge. He bored me to death with his platinum and his rubies. He didn't want a capitalist who would personally exploit the thing; he would prefer to do it all on his own account, giving the capitalist preference debentures of his bogus company, and a lien on the concession. I listened and smiled; I listened and yawned; I listened and was rude; I ceased to listen at all; but still he droned on with it. I fell asleep on the steamer one day, and woke up in ten minutes to hear him droning yet – '. . . and the yield of platinum per ton was certified to be –' I forget how many pounds, or ounces, or pennyweights. These details of assays have ceased to interest me: like the man who 'didn't believe in ghosts', I have seen too many of them.

The fresh-faced little curate and his wife, however, were quite different people. He was a cricketing Oxford man; she was a breezy Scotch lass, with a wholesome breath of the Highlands about her. I called her 'White Heather'. Their name was Brabazon. Millionaires are so accustomed to being beset by harpies of every description that when they come across a young couple who are simple and natural they delight in the purely human relation. We picnicked and went on excursions a great deal with the honeymooners. They were frank in their young love, and so proof against chaff, that we all really liked them. But whenever I called the pretty girl 'White Heather', she looked quite shocked, and cried: 'Oh, Mr Wentworth!' Still, we were the best of friends. The curate offered to row us in a boat on the lake one day, while the Scotch lassie assured us she could take an oar almost as well as he did. However, we did not accept their offer, as row-boats exert an unfavourable influence upon Amelia's digestive organs.

'Nice young fellow, that man Brabazon,' Sir Charles said to me one day, as we lounged together along the quay; 'never talks about advowsons or next presentations. Doesn't seem to me to care two pins about promotion. Says he's quite content in his country curacy; enough to live upon, and needs no more; and his wife has a little, a very little, money. I asked him about his poor today, on purpose to test him: these parsons are always trying to screw something out of one for their poor; men in my position know the truth of the saying that we have that class of the population always with us. Would you believe it, he says he hasn't any poor at all in his parish! They're all well-to-do farmers or else able-bodied labourers, and his one terror is that somebody will come and try to pauperise them. "If a philanthropist were to give me fifty pounds today for use at Empingham," he said, "I assure you, Sir Charles, I shouldn't know what to do with it. I think I should buy new dresses for Jessie, who wants them about as much as anybody else in the village – that is to say, not at all." There's a parson for you, Sey, my boy. Only wish we had one of his sort at Seldon.'

'He certainly doesn't want to get anything out of you,' I answered.

That evening at dinner a queer little episode happened. The man with the eyebrows began talking to me across the table in his usual fashion, full of his wearisome concession on the Upper Amazon. I was trying to squash him as politely as possible, when I caught Amelia's eye. Her look amused me. She was engaged in making signals to Charles at her side to observe the little curate's curious cuff-links. I glanced at them, and saw at once they were a singular possession for so unobtrusive a person. They consisted each of a short gold bar for one arm of the link, fastened by a tiny chain of the same material to what seemed – to my tolerably experienced eye – a first-rate diamond. Pretty big diamonds, too, and of remarkable shape, brilliancy and cutting. In a moment I knew what Amelia meant. She owned a diamond *rivière*, said to be of Indian origin, but short by two stones for the circumference of her tolerably ample neck. Now, she had long been wanting two diamonds like these to match her set; but owing to the unusual shape and antiquated cutting of her own gems, she had never been able to complete the necklet, at least without removing an extravagant amount from a much larger stone of the first water.

The Scotch lassie's eyes caught Amelia's at the same time, and she broke into a pretty smile of good-humoured amusement. 'Taken in another person, Dick, dear!' she exclaimed, in her breezy way, turning to her husband. 'Lady Vandrift is observing your diamond cuff-links.'

'They're very fine gems,' Amelia observed incautiously. (A most unwise admission if she desired to buy them.)

But the pleasant little curate was too transparently simple a soul to take advantage of her slip of judgement. 'They *are* good stones,' he replied; 'very good stones – considering. They're not diamonds at all, to tell you the truth. They're best old-fashioned Oriental paste. My great-grandfather bought them, after the siege of Seringapatam, for a few rupees, from a sepoy who had looted them from Tippoo Sahib's palace. He thought, like you, he had got a good thing. But it turned out, when they came to be examined by experts, they were only paste – very wonderful paste; it is supposed they had even imposed upon Tippoo himself, so fine is the imitation. But they are worth – well, say, fifty shillings at the utmost.'

While he spoke Charles looked at Amelia, and Amelia looked at Charles. Their eyes spoke volumes. The *rivière* was also supposed to have come from Tippoo's collection. Both drew at once an identical conclusion. These were two of the same stones, very likely torn apart and disengaged from the rest in the *mêlée* at the capture of the Indian palace.

'Can you take them off?' Sir Charles asked blandly. He spoke in the tone that indicates business.

'Certainly,' the little curate answered, smiling. 'I'm accustomed to taking them off. They're always noticed. They've been kept in the family ever since the siege, as a sort of valueless heirloom, for the sake of the picturesqueness of the story, you know; and nobody ever sees them without asking, as you do, to examine them closely. They deceive even experts at first. But they're paste, all the same; unmitigated Oriental paste, for all that.'

He took them both off, and handed them to Charles. No man in England is a finer judge of gems than my brother-in-law. I watched him narrowly. He examined them close, first with the naked eye, then with the little pocket-lens which he always carries. 'Admirable imitation,' he muttered, passing them on to Amelia. 'I'm not surprised they should impose upon inexperienced observers.'

But from the tone in which he said it, I could see at once he had satisfied himself they were real gems of unusual value. I know Charles's way of doing business so well. His glance to Amelia meant, 'These are the very stones you have so long been in search of.'

The Scotch lassie laughed a merry laugh. 'He sees through them now, Dick,' she cried. 'I felt sure Sir Charles would be a judge of diamonds.'

Amelia turned them over. I know Amelia, too; and I knew from the way Amelia looked at them that she meant to have them. And when Amelia means to have anything, people who stand in the way may just as well spare themselves the trouble of opposing her.

They were beautiful diamonds. We found out afterwards the little curate's account was quite correct: these stones *had* come from the same necklet as Amelia's *rivière*, made for a favourite wife of Tippoo's who had presumably as expansive personal charms as our beloved sister-in-law's. More perfect diamonds have seldom been seen. They have excited the universal admiration of thieves and connoisseurs. Amelia told me afterwards that, according to legend, a sepoy stole the necklet at the sack of the palace, and then fought with another for it. It was believed that two stones got spilt in the scuffle, and were picked up and sold by a third person – a looker-on – who had no idea of the value of his booty. Amelia had been hunting for them for several years to complete her necklet.

'They are excellent paste,' Sir Charles observed, handing them back. 'It takes a first-rate judge to detect them from the reality. Lady Vandrift has a necklet much the same in character, but composed of genuine stones; and as these are so much like them, and would complete her set, to all outward appearances, I wouldn't mind giving you, say, ten pounds for the pair of them.'

Mrs Brabazon looked delighted. 'Oh, sell them to him, Dick,' she cried, 'and buy me a brooch with the money! A pair of common links would do for you just as well. Ten pounds for two paste stones! It's quite a lot of money.'

She said it so sweetly, with her pretty Scotch accent, that I couldn't imagine how Dick had the heart to refuse her. But he did, all the same.

'No, Jess, darling,' he answered. 'They're worthless, I know; but they have for me a certain sentimental value, as I've often told you. My dear mother wore them, while she lived, as earrings; and as soon as she died I had them set as links in order that I might always keep them about me. Besides, they have historical and family interest. Even a worthless heirloom, after all, *is* an heirloom.'

Dr Hector Macpherson looked across and intervened. 'There is a part of my concession,' he said, 'where we have reason to believe a perfect new Kimberley will soon be discovered. If at any time you would care, Sir Charles, to look at my diamonds – when I get them – it would afford me the greatest pleasure in life to submit them to your consideration.'

Sir Charles could stand it no longer. 'Sir,' he said, gazing across at him with his sternest air, 'if your concession were as full of diamonds as Sindbad the Sailor's valley, I would not care to turn my head to look at them. I am acquainted with the nature and practice of salting.' And he glared at the man with the overhanging eyebrows as if he would devour him raw. Poor Dr Hector Macpherson subsided instantly. We learnt a little later that he was a harmless lunatic, who went about the world with successive concessions for ruby mines and platinum reefs, because he had been ruined and driven mad by speculations in the two, and now recouped himself by imaginary grants in Burma and Brazil, or anywhere else that turned up handy. And his eyebrows, after all, were of nature's handicraft. We were sorry for the incident; but a man in Sir Charles's position is such a mark for rogues that, if he did not take means to protect himself promptly, he would be forever overrun by them.

When we went up to our *salon* that evening, Amelia flung herself on the sofa. 'Charles,' she broke out in the voice of a tragedy queen, 'those are real diamonds, and I shall never be happy again till I get them.'

'They are real diamonds,' Charles echoed. 'And you shall have them, Amelia. They're worth not less than three thousand pounds. But I shall bid them up gently.'

So, next day, Charles set to work to haggle with the curate. Brabazon, however, didn't care to part with them. He was no money-grubber, he said. He cared more for his mother's gift and a family tradition than for a hundred pounds, if Sir Charles were to offer it. Charles's eye gleamed. 'But if I give you two hundred!' he said insinuatingly. 'What opportunities for good! You could build a new wing to your village schoolhouse!'

'We have ample accommodation,' the curate answered. 'No, I don't think I'll sell them.'

Still, his voice faltered somewhat, and he looked down at them enquiringly.

Charles was too precipitate.

'A hundred pounds more or less matters little to me,' he said; 'and my wife has set her heart on them. It's every man's duty to please his wife – isn't it, Mrs Brabazon? – I offer you three hundred.'

The little Scotch girl clasped her hands.

'Three hundred pounds! Oh, Dick, just think what fun we could have, and what good we could do with it! Do let him have them.'

Her accent was irresistible. But the curate shook his head.

'Impossible,' he answered. 'My dear mother's ear-rings! Uncle Aubrey would be so angry if he knew I'd sold them. I daren't face Uncle Aubrey.'

'Has he expectations from Uncle Aubrey?' Sir Charles asked of White Heather.

Mrs Brabazon laughed. 'Uncle Aubrey! Oh, dear, no. Poor

dear old Uncle Aubrey! Why, the darling old soul hasn't a penny to bless himself with, except his pension. He's a retired post captain.' And she laughed melodiously. She was a charming woman.

'Then I should disregard Uncle Aubrey's feelings,' Sir Charles said decisively.

'No, no,' the curate answered. 'Poor dear old Uncle Aubrey! I wouldn't do anything for the world to annoy him. And he'd be sure to notice it.'

We went back to Amelia. 'Well, have you got them?' she asked.

'No,' Sir Charles answered. 'Not yet. But he's coming round, I think. He's hesitating now. Would rather like to sell them himself, but is afraid what "Uncle Aubrey" would say about the matter. His wife will talk him out of his needless considerations for Uncle Aubrey's feelings; and tomorrow we'll finally clinch the bargain.'

Next morning we stayed late in our *salon*, where we always breakfasted, and did not come down to the public rooms till just before *déjeuner*, Sir Charles being busy with me over arrears of correspondence. When we *did* come down, the *concierge* stepped forward with a twisted little feminine note for Amelia. She took it and read it. Her countenance fell. 'There, Charles,' she cried, handing it to him, 'you've let the chance slip. I shall *never* be happy now! They've gone off with the diamonds.'

Charles seized the note and read it. Then he passed it on to me. It was short, but final:

Thursday, 6 a.m.

Dear Lady Vandrift – *Will* you kindly excuse our having gone off hurriedly without bidding you goodbye? We have just had a horrid telegram to say that Dick's favourite sister is *dangerously* ill of fever in Paris. I wanted to shake hands with you before we left – you have all been so sweet to us – but we go by the morning train, absurdly early, and I wouldn't for worlds disturb you. Perhaps someday we may meet again – though, buried as we are in a north-country village, it isn't likely; but, in any case, you have secured the grateful recollection of

Yours very cordially,

JESSIE BRABAZON

PS – Kindest regards to Sir Charles and those *dear* Wentworths, and a kiss for yourself, if I may venture to send you one.

'She doesn't even mention where they've gone,' Amelia exclaimed, in a very bad humour.

'The *concierge* may know,' Isabel suggested, looking over my shoulder.

We asked at his office.

Yes, the gentleman's address was the Reverend Richard Peploe Brabazon, Holme Bush Cottage, Empingham, Northumberland.

Any address where letters might be sent at once, in Paris?

For the next ten days, or till further notice, Hôtel des Deux Mondes, Avenue de l'Opéra.

Amelia's mind was made up at once.

'Strike while the iron's hot,' she cried. 'This sudden illness, coming at the end of their honeymoon, and involving ten days' more stay at an expensive hotel, will probably upset the curate's budget. He'll be glad to sell now. You'll get them for three hundred. It was absurd of Charles to offer so much at first; but offered once, of course we must stick to it.'

'What do you propose to do?' Charles asked. 'Write, or telegraph?'

'Oh, how silly men are!' Amelia cried. 'Is this the sort of business to be arranged by letter, still less by telegram? No. Seymour must start off at once, taking the night train to Paris;

and the moment he gets there, he must interview the curate or Mrs Brabazon. Mrs Brabazon's the best. She has none of this stupid, sentimental nonsense about Uncle Aubrey.'

It is no part of a secretary's duties to act as a diamond broker. But when Amelia puts her foot down, she puts her foot down – a fact which she is unnecessarily fond of emphasising in that identical proposition. So the selfsame evening saw me safe in the train on my way to Paris; and next morning I turned out of my comfortable sleeping-car at the Gare de Strasbourg. My orders were to bring back those diamonds, alive or dead, so to speak, in my pocket to Lucerne; and to offer any needful sum, up to two thousand five hundred pounds, for their immediate purchase.

When I arrived at the Deux Mondes I found the poor little curate and his wife both greatly agitated. They had sat up all night, they said, with their invalid sister; and the sleeplessness and suspense had certainly told upon them after their long railway journey. They were pale and tired, Mrs Brabazon, in particular, looking ill and worried – too much like White Heather. I was more than half ashamed of bothering them about the diamonds at such a moment, but it occurred to me that Amelia was probably right – they would now have reached the end of the sum set apart for their Continental trip, and a little ready cash might be far from unwelcome.

I broached the subject delicately. It was a fad of Lady Vandrift's, I said. She had set her heart upon those useless trinkets. And she wouldn't go without them. She must and would have them. But the curate was obdurate. He threw Uncle Aubrey still in my teeth. Three hundred? – no, never! A mother's present; impossible, dear Jessie! Jessie begged and prayed; she had grown really attached to Lady Vandrift, she said; but the curate wouldn't hear of it. I went up tentatively to four hundred. He shook his head gloomily. It wasn't a question of money, he said. It was a question of affection. I saw it was no use trying that tack any longer. I struck out a new line. 'These stones,' I said, 'I think I ought to inform you, are really diamonds. Sir Charles is certain of it. Now, is it right for a man of your profession and position to be wearing a pair of big gems like those, worth several hundred pounds, as ordinary cuff-links? A woman? – yes, I grant you. But for a man, is it manly? And you a cricketer!'

He looked at me and laughed. 'Will nothing convince you?' he cried. 'They have been examined and tested by half a dozen jewellers, and we know them to be paste. It wouldn't be right of me to sell them to you under false pretences, however unwilling on my side. I *couldn't* do it.'

'Well, then,' I said, going up a bit in my bids to meet him, 'I'll put it like this. These gems are paste. But Lady Vandrift has an unconquerable and unaccountable desire to possess them. Money doesn't matter to her. She is a friend of your wife's. As a personal favour, won't you sell them to her for a thousand?'

He shook his head. 'It would be wrong,' he said – 'I might even add, criminal.'

'But we take all risk,' I cried.

He was absolutely adamant. 'As a clergyman,' he answered, 'I feel I cannot do it.'

'Will *you* try, Mrs Brabazon?' I asked.

The pretty little Scotchwoman leant over and whispered. She coaxed and cajoled him. Her ways were winsome. I couldn't hear what she said, but he seemed to give way at last. 'I should love Lady Vandrift to have them,' she murmured turning to me. 'She *is* such a dear!' And she took out the links from her husband's cuffs and handed them across to me.

'How much?' I asked.

'Two thousand?' she answered interrogatively. It was a big rise, all at once; but such are the ways of women.

'Done!' I replied. 'Do you consent?'

The curate looked up as if ashamed of himself.

'I consent,' he said slowly, 'since Jessie wishes it. But as a clergyman, and to prevent any future misunderstanding, I should like you to give me a statement in writing that you buy them on my distinct and positive declaration that they are made of paste – old Oriental paste – not genuine stones, and that I do not claim any other qualities for them.'

I popped the gems into my purse, well pleased.

'Certainly,' I said, pulling out a paper. Charles, with his unerring business instinct, had anticipated the request, and given me a signed agreement to that effect.

'You will take a cheque?' I enquired.

He hesitated.

'Notes of the Bank of France would suit me better,' he answered.

'Very well,' I replied. 'I will go out and get them.'

How very unsuspicious some are! He allowed me to go off – with the stones in my pocket!

Sir Charles had given me a blank cheque, not exceeding two thousand five hundred pounds. I took it to our agents and cashed it for notes of the Bank of France. The curate clasped them with pleasure. And right glad I was to go back to Lucerne that night, feeling that I had got those diamonds into my hands for about a thousand pounds under their real value!

At Lucerne railway station Amelia met me. She was positively agitated.

'Have you bought them, Seymour?' she asked.

'Yes,' I answered, producing my spoils in triumph.

'Oh, how dreadful!' she cried, drawing back. 'Do you think they're real? Are you sure he hasn't cheated you?'

'Certain of it,' I replied, examining them. 'No one can take me in, in the matter of diamonds. Why on earth should you doubt them?'

'Because I've been talking to Mrs O'Hagan, at the hotel, and she says there's a well-known trick just like that – she's read of it in a book. A swindler has two sets – one real, one false; and he makes you buy the false ones by showing you the real, and pretending he sells them as a special favour.'

'You needn't be alarmed,' I answered. 'I am a judge of diamonds.'

'I shan't be satisfied,' Amelia murmured, 'till Charles has seen them.'

We went up to the hotel. For the first time in my life I saw Amelia really nervous as I handed the stones to Charles to examine. Her doubt was contagious. I half feared, myself, he might break out into a deep monosyllabic interjection, losing his temper in haste, as he often does when things go wrong. But he looked at them with a smile, while I told him the price.

'Eight hundred pounds less than their value,' he answered, well satisfied.

'You have no doubt of their reality?' I asked.

'Not the slightest,' he replied, gazing at them. 'They are genuine stones, precisely the same in quality and type as Amelia's necklet.'

Amelia drew a sigh of relief. 'I'll go upstairs,' she said slowly, 'and bring down my own for you both to compare with them.'

One minute later she rushed down again, breathless. Amelia is far from slim, and I never before knew her exert herself so actively.

'Charles, Charles!' she cried, 'do you know what dreadful thing has happened? Two of my own stones are gone. He's stolen a couple of diamonds from my necklet, and sold them back to me.'

She held out the *rivière.* It was all too true. Two gems were missing – and these two just fitted the empty places!

A light broke in upon me. I clapped my hand to my head. 'By Jove,' I exclaimed, 'the little curate is – Colonel Clay!'

Charles clapped his own hand to his brow in turn. 'And Jessie,' he cried, 'White Heather – that innocent little Scotchwoman! I often detected a familiar ring in her voice, in spite of the charming Highland accent. Jessie is – Madame Picardet!'

We had absolutely no evidence; but, like the commissary at Nice, we felt instinctively sure of it.

Sir Charles was determined to catch the rogue. This second deception put him on his mettle. 'The worst of the man is,' he said, 'he has a method. He doesn't go out of his way to cheat us; he makes us go out of ours to be cheated. He lays a trap, and we tumble headlong into it. Tomorrow, Sey, we must follow him on to Paris.'

Amelia explained to him what Mrs O'Hagan had said. Charles took it all in at once, with his usual sagacity. 'That explains,' he said, 'why the rascal used this particular trick to draw us on by. If we had suspected him he could have shown the diamonds were real, and so escaped detection. It was a blind to draw us off from the fact of the robbery. He went to Paris to be out of the way when the discovery was made, and to get a clear day's start on us. What a consummate rogue! And to do me twice running!'

'How did they get at my jewel-case, though?' Amelia exclaimed.

'That's the question,' Charles answered. 'You *do* leave it about so!'

'And why didn't he steal the whole *rivière* at once, and sell the gems?' I enquired.

'Too cunning,' Charles replied. 'This was much better business. It isn't easy to dispose of a big thing like that. In the first place, the stones are large and valuable; in the second place, they're well known – every dealer has heard of the Vandrift *rivière*, and seen pictures of the shape of them. They're marked gems, so to speak. No, he played a better game – took a couple of them off, and offered them to the only person on earth who was likely to buy them without suspicion. He came here, meaning to work this very trick; he had the links made right to the shape beforehand, and then he stole the stones and slipped them into their places. It's a wonderfully clever trick. Upon my soul, I almost admire the fellow.'

For Charles is a businessman himself, and can appreciate business capacity in others.

How Colonel Clay came to know about that necklet, and to appropriate two of the stones, we only discovered much later. I will not here anticipate that disclosure. One thing at a time is a good rule in life. For the moment he succeeded in baffling us altogether.

However, we followed him on to Paris, telegraphing beforehand to the Bank of France to stop the notes. It was all in vain. They had been cashed within half an hour of my paying them. The curate and his wife, we found, quitted the Hôtel des Deux Mondes for parts unknown that same afternoon. And, as usual with Colonel Clay, they vanished into space, leaving no clue behind them. In other words, they changed their disguise, no doubt, and reappeared somewhere else that night in altered characters. At any rate, no such person as the Reverend Richard Peploe Brabazon was ever afterwards heard of – and, for the matter of that, no such village exists as Empingham, Northumberland.

We communicated the matter to the Parisian police. They were *most* unsympathetic. 'It is no doubt Colonel Clay,' said the official whom we saw; 'but you seem to have little just ground of complaint against him. As far as I can see messieurs, there is not much to choose between you. You, Monsieur le Chevalier, desired to buy diamonds at the price of paste. You, madame, feared you had bought paste at the price of diamonds. You, monsieur the secretary, tried to get the stones from an unsuspecting person for half their value. He took you all in, that brave Colonel Caoutchouc – it was diamond cut diamond.'

Which was true, no doubt, but by no means consoling.

We returned to the Grand Hôtel. Charles was fuming with indignation. 'This is really too much,' he exclaimed. 'What an audacious rascal! But he will never again take me in, my dear Sey. I only hope he'll try it on. I should love to catch him. I'd know him another time, I'm sure, in spite of his disguises. It's absurd my being tricked twice running like this. But never again while I live! Never again, I declare to you!'

'Jamais de la vie!' a courier in the hall close by murmured responsively. We stood under the verandah of the Grand Hotel, in the big glass courtyard. And I verily believe that courier was really Colonel Clay himself in one of his disguises.

But perhaps we were beginning to suspect him everywhere.

CLARENCE ROOK

Clarence Rook (1863–1915) was an American writer who lived in London from the latter years of the nineteenth century and became a witty chronicler of the Edwardian scene. He was most admired for his novel of working-class life *The Hooligan Nights* (1899). Rook's sleuth was a American female investigator, operating in the British capital. Female detectives were quite rare when the story 'The Stir outside the Café Royal' was published in the *Harmsworth Magazine* in 1898, but it was rarer for a male writer to use one as his central character.

The Stir Outside the Café Royal

Colonel Mathurin was one of the aristocrats of crime; at least Mathurin was the name under which he had accomplished a daring bank robbery in Detroit, which had involved the violent death of the manager, though it was generally believed by the police that the Rossiter who was at the bottom of some long firm frauds in Melbourne was none other than Mathurin under another name, and that the designer and chief gainer in a sensational murder case in the Midlands was the same mysterious and ubiquitous personage.

But Mathurin had for some years successfully eluded pursuit: indeed it was generally known that he was the most desperate among criminals, and was determined never to be taken alive. Moreover, as he invariably worked through subordinates who knew nothing of his whereabouts and were scarcely acquainted with his appearance, the police had but a slender clue to his identity.

As a matter of fact, only two people beyond his immediate

associates in crime could have sworn to Mathurin if a they had met him face to face. One of them was the Detroit bank manager whom he had shot with his own hand before the eyes of his fiancée. It was through the other that Mathurin was arrested, extradited to the States, and finally made to atone for his life of crime. It all happened in a distressingly commonplace way, so far as the average spectator was concerned. But the story, which I have pieced together from the details supplied – first, by a certain detective sergeant whom I met in a tavern hard by Westminster; and second, by a certain young woman named Miss van Snoop – has an element of romance, if you look below the surface.

It was about half-past one o'clock, on a bright and pleasant day, that a young lady was driving down Regent Street in a hansom which she had picked up outside her boarding-house near Portland Place Station. She had told the cabman to drive slowly, as she was nervous behind a horse, and so she had leisure to scan, with the curiosity of a stranger, the strolling crowd that at nearly all hours of the day throngs Regent Street. It was sunny and everybody looked cheerful. Ladies were shopping or looking in at the shop windows; men about town were collecting an appetite for lunch; flower girls were selling 'nice vi'lets, sweet vi'lets, penny a bunch'; and the girl in the cab leaned one arm on the apron and regarded the scene with alert attention. She was not exactly pretty, for the symmetry of her features was discounted by a certain hardness in the set of the mouth, but her hair, so dark as to be almost black, and her eyes, of greyish blue, set her beyond comparison with the commonplace.

Just outside the Café Royal there was a slight stir, and a temporary block in the foot traffic. A brougham was setting down, behind it was a victoria, and behind that a hansom; and as the girl glanced round the heads of the pair in the brougham, she saw several men standing on the steps. Leaning back suddenly, she opened the trap-door in the roof.

'Stop here,' she called up, 'I've changed my mind.'

The driver drew up by the kerb, and the girl skipped out.

'You shan't lose by the change,' she said, handing him half a crown.

There was a tinge of American accent in the voice; and the cabman, pocketing the half-crown with thanks, smiled.

'They may talk about that McKinley tariff,' he soliloquised as he crawled along the kerb towards Piccadilly Circus, 'but it's better 'n free trade!'

Meanwhile the girl walked slowly back towards the Café Royal, and, with a quick glance at the men who were standing there, entered. One or two of the men raised their eyebrows; but the girl was quite unconscious, and went on her way to the luncheon-room.

'American, you bet,' said one of the loungers. 'They'll go anywhere and do anything.'

Just in front of her as she entered was a tall, clean-shaven man, faultlessly dressed in glossy silk hat and frock-coat, with a flower in his buttonhole. He looked around for a moment in search of a convenient table. As he hesitated, the girl hesitated, but when the waiter waved him to a small table laid for two, the girl immediately sat down behind him at the next table.

'Excuse me, madam,' said the waiter, 'this table is set for four; would you mind – '

'I guess,' said the girl, 'I'll stay where I am.' And the look in her eyes, as well as a certain sensation in the waiter's palm, ensured her against further disturbance.

The restaurant was full of people lunching, singly or in twos, in threes and even in larger parties; and many curious glances were directed at the girl who sat at a table alone and pursued her way calmly through the menu. But the girl appeared to notice no one. When her eyes were off her plate they were fixed straight ahead – on the back of the man who had entered in front of her. The man, who had drunk a half-bottle of champagne with his lunch, ordered a liqueur to accompany his coffee. The girl, who had drunk an aerated water, leaned back in her chair and wrinkled her brows. They were very straight brows that seemed to meet over her nose when she wrinkled them in perplexity. Then she called a waiter.

'Bring me a sheet of notepaper, please,' she said, 'and my bill.'

The waiter laid the sheet of paper before her, and the girl proceeded, after a few moments' thought, to write a few lines in pencil upon it. When this was done, she folded the sheet carefully, and laid it in her purse. Then, having paid her bill, she returned her purse to her dress pocket, and waited patiently.

In a few minutes the clean-shaven man at the next table settled his bill and made preparations for departure. The girl at the same time drew on her gloves, keeping her eyes immovably upon her neighbour's back. As the man rose to depart, and passed the table at which the girl had been sitting, the girl was looking into the mirror upon the wall, and patting her hair. Then she turned and followed the man out of the restaurant, while a pair at an adjacent table remarked to one another that it was a rather curious coincidence for a man and woman to enter and leave at the same moment when they had no apparent connection.

But what happened outside was even more curious.

The man halted for a moment upon the steps at the entrance. The porter, who was in conversation with a policeman, turned, whistle in hand.

'Hansom, sir?' he asked.

'Yes,' said the clean-shaven man.

The porter was raising his whistle to his lips when he noticed the girl behind.

'Do you wish for a cab, madam?' he asked, and blew upon his whistle.

As he turned again for an answer, he plainly saw the girl, who was standing close behind the clean-shaven man, slip her hand under his coat, and snatch from his hip pocket something which she quickly transferred to her own.

'Well, I'm – ' began the clean-shaven man, swinging round and feeling in his pocket.

'Have you missed anything, sir?' said the porter, standing full in front of the girl to bar her exit.

'My cigarette case is gone,' said the man, making from one side to another.

'What's this?' said the policeman, stepping forward.

'I saw the woman's hand in the gentleman's pocket, plain as a pikestaff,' said the porter.

'Oh, that's it, is it?' said the policeman, coming close to the girl. 'I thought as much.'

'Come now,' said the clean-shaven man, 'I don't want to make a fuss. Just hand back that cigarette-case, and we'll say no more about it.'

'I haven't got it,' said the girl. 'How dare you? I never touched your pocket.'

The man's face darkened.

'Oh, come now!' said the porter.

'Look here, that won't do,' said the policeman, 'you'll have to come along of me. Better take a four-wheeler, eh, sir?'

A knot of loafers, seeing something interesting in the wind, had collected round the entrance.

A four-wheeler was called, and the girl entered, closely followed by the policeman and the clean-shaven man.

'I was never so insulted in my life,' said the girl.

Nevertheless, she sat back quite calmly in the cab, as though she was perfectly ready to face this or any other situation, while the policeman watched her closely to make sure that she did not dispose in any surreptitious way of the stolen article.

At the police-station hard by, the usual formalities were gone through, and the clean-shaven man was constituted prosecutor. But the girl stoutly denied having been guilty of any offence.

The inspector in charge looked doubtful.

'Better search her,' he said, and the girl was led off to a room for an interview with the female searcher.

The moment the door closed, the girl put her hand into her pocket, pulled out the cigarette-case and laid it upon the table.

'There you are,' she said. 'That will fix matters so far.'

The woman looked rather surprised.

'Now,' said the girl, holding out her arms, 'feel in this other pocket, and find my purse.'

The woman picked out the purse.

'Open it and read the note on the bit of paper inside.'

On the sheet of paper which the waiter had given her, the girl had written these words, which the searcher read in a muttered undertone.

> I am going to pick this man's pocket as the best way of getting him into a police-station without violence. He is Colonel Mathurin, alias Rossiter, alias Connell, and he is wanted in Detroit, New York, Melbourne, Colombo and London. Get four men to pin him unawares, for he is armed and desperate. I am a member of the New York Detective Force – Nora van Snoop.

'It's all right,' said Miss van Snoop, quickly, as the searcher looked up at her after reading the note. 'Show that to the boss – right away.'

The searcher opened the door. After whispered consultation the inspector appeared, holding the note in his hand.

'Now then, be spry,' said Miss van Snoop. 'Oh, you needn't worry! I've got my credentials right here,' and she dived into another pocket.

'But do you know – can you be sure,' said the inspector, 'that this is the man who shot the Detroit bank manager?'

'Great heavens! Didn't I see him shoot Will Stevens with my own eyes! And didn't I take service with the police to hunt him out?'

The girl stamped her foot, and the inspector left. For two, three, four minutes, she stood listening intently. Then a muffled shout reached her ears. Two minutes later the inspector returned.

'I think you're right,' he said. 'We have found enough evidence on him to identify him. But why didn't you give him in charge before to the police?'

'I wanted to arrest him myself,' said Miss van Snoop, 'and I have. Oh, Will! Will!'

Miss van Snoop sank into a cane-bottomed chair, laid her head upon the table, and cried. She had earned the luxury of hysterics. In half an hour she left the station, and, proceeding to a post-office, cabled her resignation to the head of the detective force in New York.

O. HENRY

William Sydney Porter (1862–1910), a short-story writer who used the pen name O. Henry, was born at Greensboro, North Carolina, son of a doctor. After leaving school he worked for five years in his father's dispensary, then went to Texas and was successively a ranch hand, a bank teller and editor and publisher of the humorous magazine *The Rolling Stone*. Some time later he was charged with having embezzled bank funds, and though he seems to have been only technically guilty he cleared off to South America, where he associated with law breakers and refugees. In 1897 he returned to Texas because of the illness of his wife and was arrested and sentenced to five years in the penitentiary, where he is thought to have taken the pseudonym of O. Henry from the name of a French pharmacist, Etienne-Ossian Henry, he found in the *U.S. Dispensatory*. Set at liberty in 1901, he roamed New York, living from hand to mouth and consuming an average of a quart of whiskey a day. He supported himself by his short stories, of which he wrote some six hundred, and eventually died in hospital of cirrhosis of the liver. With their use of ironical coincidence and unexpected endings they set a fashion in American literature. In 1918 the American Society of Arts and Sciences founded the O. Henry Memorial Award for the best American short story of each year.

Holding Up a Train

NOTE. The man who told me these things was for several years an outlaw in the South-West and a follower of the pursuit he so frankly describes. His description of the *modus operandi* should prove interesting, his counsel of value to the potential passenger in some future 'hold-up', while his estimate of the pleasures of train robbing will hardly induce anyone to adopt it as a profession. I give the story in almost exactly his own words. O. H.

Most people would say, if their opinion was asked for, that holding up a train would be a hard job. Well, it isn't; it's easy. I have contributed some to the uneasiness of railroads and the insomnia of express companies, and the most trouble I ever had about a hold-up was in being swindled by unscrupulous people while spending the money I got. The danger wasn't anything to speak of, and we didn't mind the trouble.

One man has come pretty near robbing a train by himself; two have succeeded a few times; three can do it if they are hustlers, but five is about the right number. The time to do it and the place depend upon several things.

The first 'stick-up' I was ever in happened in 1890. Maybe the way I got into it will explain how most train robbers start in the business. Five out of six Western outlaws are just cowboys out of a job and gone wrong. The sixth is a tough from the East who dresses up like a bad man and plays some low-down trick that gives the boys a bad name. Wire fences and 'nesters' made five of them; a bad heart made the sixth.

Jim S— and I were working on the 101 Ranch in Colorado. The nesters had the cowman on the go. They had taken up the land and elected officers who were hard to get along with. Jim and I rode into La Junta one day, going south from a round-up. We were having a little fun without malice towards anybody when a farmer administration cut in and tried to harvest us. Jim shot a deputy-marshal, and I kind of corroborated his side of the argument. We skirmished up and down the main street, the boomers having bad luck all the time. After awhile we leaned forward and shoved for the ranch down on the Ceriso. We were riding a couple of horses that couldn't fly, but they could catch birds.

A few days after that, a gang of the La Junta boomers came to the ranch and wanted us to go back with them. Naturally, we declined. We had the house on them, and before we were done refusing, the old 'dobe was plumb full of lead. When dark came we fagged 'em a batch of bullets and shoved out the back door for the rocks. They sure smoked us as we went. We had to drift, which we did, and rounded up down in Oklahoma.

Well, there wasn't anything we could get there, and, being mighty hard up, we decided to transact a little business with the railroads. Jim and I joined forces with Tom and Ike Moore – two brothers who had plenty of sand they were willing to convert into dust. I can call their names, for both of them are dead. Tom was shot while robbing a bank in Arkansas; Ike was killed during the more dangerous pastime of attending a dance laid on by the Creek Nation.

We selected a place on the Santa Fé where there was a bridge across a deep creek surrounded by heavy timber. All passenger trains took water at the tank close to one end of the bridge. It was a quiet place, the nearest house being five miles away. The day before it happened, we rested our horses and 'made medicine' as to how we should get about it. Our plans were not at all elaborate, as none of us had ever engaged in a hold-up before.

The Santa Fé Flyer was due at the tank at 11.15 p.m. At eleven, Tom and I lay down on one side of the track, and Jim and Ike took the other. As the train rolled up, the headlight flashing far down the track and the steam hissing from the engine, I turned weak all over. I would have worked a whole year on the ranch for nothing to have been out of that affair right then. Some of the nerviest men in the business have told me that they felt the same way the first time.

The engine had hardly stopped when I jumped on the running-board on one side, while Jim mounted the other. As soon as the engineer and fireman saw our guns they threw up their hands without being told and begged us not to shoot, saying they would do anything we wanted them to.

'Hit the ground,' I ordered, and they both jumped off. We drove them before us down the side of the train. While this was happening, Tom and Ike had been blazing away, one on each side of the train, yelling like Apaches so as to keep the passengers herded in the cars. Some fellow stuck a little 22-calibre out one of the coach windows and fired it straight up in the air. I let drive and smashed the glass just over his head. That settled everything like resistance from that direction.

By this time all my nervousness was gone. I felt a kind of pleasant excitement as if I were at a dance or a frolic of some sort. The lights were all out in the coaches, and, as Tom and Ike gradually quit firing and yelling, it got to be almost as still as a graveyard. I remember hearing a little bird chirping in a bush at the side of the track, as if it were complaining at being waked up.

I made the fireman get a lantern, and then I went to the express car and yelled to the messenger to open up or get perforated. He slid the door back and stood in it with his hands up. 'Jump overboard, son,' I said, and he hit the dirt like a lump of lead. There were two safes in the car – a big one and a little one. By the way, I first located the messenger's arsenal – a double-barrelled shotgun with buckshot cartridges and a thirty-eight in a drawer. I drew the cartridges from the shot-gun, pocketed the pistol, and called the messenger inside. I shoved my gun against his nose, and put him to work. He couldn't open the big safe, but he did the little one. There was only nine hundred dollars in it. That was mighty small winnings for our trouble, so we decided to go through the passengers. We took our prisoners to the smoking-car, and from there sent the engineer through the train to light up the coaches. Beginning with the first one, we placed a man at each door and ordered the passengers to stand between the seats with their hands up.

If you want to find out what cowards the majority of men are, all you have to do is rob a passenger train. I don't mean because they don't resist – I'll tell you later on why they can't do that – but it makes a man feel sorry for them the way they lose their heads. Big, burly drummers and farmers and ex-soldiers and high-collared dudes and sports that, a few moments before, were filling the car with noise and bragging, get so scared that their ears flop.

There were very few people in the day coaches at that time of night, so we made a slim haul until we got to the sleeper. The Pullman conductor met me at one door while Jim was going round to the other one. He very politely informed me that I could not go into that car as it did not belong to the railroad company, and besides, the passengers had already been greatly disturbed by the shouting and firing. Never in all my life have I met with a finer instance of official dignity and reliance upon the power of Mr Pullman's great name. I jabbed my six-shooter so hard against Mr Conductor's front that I afterwards found one of his vest-buttons so firmly wedged in the end of the barrel that I had to shoot it out. He just shut up like a weak-springed knife and rolled down the car steps.

I opened the door of the sleeper and stepped inside. A big, fat old man came wobbling up to me, puffing and blowing. He had one coat-sleeve on and was trying to put his vest on over that. I don't know who he thought I was.

'Young man, young man,' says he, 'you must keep cool and not get excited. Above everything keep cool.'

'I can't,' says I. 'Excitement's just eating me up.' And then I let out a yell and turned loose my forty-five through the skylight.

That old man tried to dive into one of the lower berths, but a screech came out of it and a bare foot that took him in the breadbasket and landed him on the floor. I saw Jim coming in the other door, and I hollered for everybody to climb out and line up.

They commenced to scramble down, and for awhile we had a three-ringed circus. The men looked as frightened and tame as a lot of rabbits in a deep snow. They had on, on an average, about a quarter of a suit of clothes and one shoe apiece. One chap was sitting on the floor of the aisle, looking as if he were working a hard sum in arithmetic. He was trying, very solemn, to pull a lady's number-two shoe on his number-nine foot.

The ladies didn't stop to dress. They were so curious to see a real, live train robber, bless 'em, that they just wrapped blankets and sheets around themselves and came out, squeaky and fidgety looking. They always show more curiosity and sand than the men do.

We got them all lined up and pretty quiet, and I went through the bunch. I found very little on them – I mean in the way of valuables. One man in the line was a sight. He was one of those big, overgrown, solemn snoozers that sit on the platform at lectures and look wise. Before crawling out he had managed to put on his long, frock-tailed coat and his high silk hat. The rest of him was nothing but pyjamas and bunions. When I dug into that Prince Albert, I expected to drag out at least a block of gold-mine stock or an armful of Government bonds, but all I found was a little boy's French harp about four inches long. What it was there for, I don't know. I felt a little mad because he had fooled me so. I stuck the harp up against his mouth.

'If you can't pay – play,' I says.

'I can't play,' says he.

'Then learn right off quick,' says I, letting him smell the end of my gun-barrel.

He caught hold of the harp, turned red as a beet, and commenced to blow. He blew a dinky little tune I remembered hearing when I was a kid:

> Prettiest little gal in the country – oh!
> Mammy and Daddy told me so.

I made him keep on playing it all the time we were in the car. Now and then he'd get weak and off the key, and I'd turn my gun on him and ask what was the matter with that little gal, and whether he had any intention of going back on her, which would make him start up again like sixty. I think that old boy standing there in his silk hat and bare feet playing his little French harp was the funniest sight I ever saw. One little red-headed woman in the line broke out laughing at him. You could have heard her in the next car.

Then Jim held them steady while I searched the berths. I grappled around in those beds and filled a pillowcase with the strangest assortment of stuff you ever saw. Now and then I'd come across a little pop-gun pistol, just about right for plugging teeth with, which I'd throw out the window. When I finished with the collection, I dumped the pillowcase load in the middle of the aisle. There were a good many watches, bracelets, rings and pocketbooks, with a sprinkling of false teeth, whiskey flasks, face-powder boxes, chocolate caramels and heads of hair of various colours and lengths. There were also about a dozen ladies' stockings into which jewellery, watches and rolls of bills had been stuffed and then wadded up tight and stuck under the mattresses. I offered to return what I called the 'scalps', saying that we were not Indians on the warpath, but none of the ladies seemed to know to whom the hair belonged.

One of the women – and a good-looker she was – wrapped in a striped blanket, saw me pick up one of the stockings that was pretty chunky and heavy about the toe, and she snapped out: 'That's mine, sir. You're not in the business of robbing women, are you?'

Now, as this was our first hold-up, we hadn't agreed upon any code of ethics, so I hardly knew what to answer. But, any-way, I replied: 'Well, not as a speciality. If this contains your personal property you can have it back.'

'It just does,' she declared eagerly, and reached out her hand for it.

'You'll excuse my taking a look at the contents,' I said, holding the stocking up by the toe. Out dumped a big gent's gold watch, worth two hundred; a gent's leather pocketbook that we afterwards found to contain six hundred dollars; a 32-calibre revolver; and the only thing of the lot that could have been a lady's personal property was a silver bracelet worth about fifty cents.

I said, 'Madame, here's your property,' and handed her the bracelet. 'Now,' I went on, 'how can you expect us to act square with you when you try to deceive us in this manner? I'm surprised at such conduct.'

The young woman flushed up as if she had been caught doing something dishonest. Some other woman down the line called out: 'The mean thing!' I never knew whether she meant the other lady or me.

When we finished our job we ordered everybody back to bed, told 'em good-night very politely at the door and left. We rode forty miles before daylight and then divided the stuff. Each one of us got $1,752.85 in money. We lumped the jewellery around. Then we scattered, each man for himself.

That was my first train robbery, and it was about as easily done as any of the ones that followed. But that was the last and only time I ever went through the passengers. I don't like that part of the business. Afterwards I stuck strictly to the express car. During the next eight years I handled a good deal of money.

The best haul I made was just seven years after the first one. We found out about a train that was going to bring out a lot of money to pay off the soldiers at a Government post. We stuck that train up in broad daylight. Five of us lay in the sandhills near a little station. Ten soldiers were guarding the money on the train, but they might just as well have been at home on a furlough. We didn't even allow them to stick their heads out the windows to see the fun. We had no trouble at all in getting the money, which was all in gold. Of course, a big howl was raised at the time about the robbery. It was Government stuff, and the Government got sarcastic and wanted to know what the convoy of soldiers went along for. The only excuse given was that nobody was expecting an attack among those bare sandhills in daytime. I don't know what the Government thought about the excuse, but I know that it was a good one. The surprise – that is the keynote of the train-robbing business. The papers published all kinds of stories about the loss, finally agreeing that it was between nine thousand and ten thousand dollars. The Government sawed wood. Here are the correct figures, printed for the first time – forty-eight thousand dollars. If anybody will take the trouble to look over Uncle Sam's private accounts for that little debit to profit and loss, he will find that I am right to a cent.

By that time we were expert enough to know what to do. We rode due west twenty miles, making a trail that a Broadway policeman could have followed, and then we doubled back, hiding our tracks. On the second night after the hold-up, while posses were scouring the country in every direction, Jim and I were eating supper in the second storey of a friend's house in the town where the alarm started from. Our friend pointed out to us, in an office across the street, a printing-press at work striking off handbills offering a reward for our capture.

I have been asked what we do with the money we get. Well, I never could account for a tenth part of it after it was spent. It goes fast and freely. An outlaw has to have a good many friends. A highly respected citizen may, and often does, get along with very few, but a man on the dodge has got to have 'side-kickers'. With angry posses and reward-hungry officers cutting out a hot trail for him, he must have a few places scattered about the country where he can stop and feed himself and his horse and get a few hours' sleep without having to keep both eyes open.

When he makes a haul he feels like dropping some of the coin with these friends, and he does it liberally. Sometimes I have, at the end of a hasty visit at one of these havens of refuge, flung a handful of gold and bills into the laps of the kids playing on the floor, without knowing whether my contribution was a hundred dollars or a thousand.

When old-timers make a big haul they generally go far away to one of the big cities to spend their money. Green hands, however successful a hold-up they make, nearly always give themselves away by showing too much money near the place where they got it.

I was in a job in '94 where we got twenty thousand dollars. We followed our favourite plan for a getaway – that is, doubled on our trail – and laid low for a time near the scene of the train's bad luck. One morning I picked up a newspaper and read an article with big headlines stating that the marshal, with eight deputies and a posse of thirty armed citizens, had the train robbers surrounded in a mesquite thicket on the Cimarron and that it was a question of only a few hours before they would be dead men or prisoners. While I was reading that article I was sitting at breakfast in one of the most elegant private residences in Washington City, with a flunky in knee pants standing behind my chair. Jim was sitting across the table talking to his half-uncle, a retired naval officer, whose name you have often seen in the accounts of doings in the capital. We had gone there and bought rattling outfits of good clothes, and were resting from our labours among the nabobs. We must have been killed in that mesquite thicket, for I can make an affidavit that we didn't surrender.

Now I propose to tell why it is easy to hold up a train, and, then, why no one should ever do it.

In the first place, the attacking party has all the advantage. That is, of course, supposing that they are old-timers with the necessary experience and courage. They have the outside and are protected by the darkness, while the others are in the light, hemmed into a small space, and exposed the moment they show a head at a window or door to the aim of a man who is a dead shot and who won't hesitate to shoot.

But, in my opinion, the main condition that makes train robbing easy is the element of surprise in connection with the imagination of the passengers. If you have ever seen a horse that has eaten loco weed you will understand what I mean when I say that the passengers get locoed. That horse gets the awfullest imagination on him in the world. You can't coax him to cross a little branch stream two feet wide. It looks as big to him as the Mississippi River. That's just the way with the passenger. He thinks there are a hundred men yelling and shooting outside, when maybe there are only two or three. And the muzzle of a forty-five looks like the entrance to a tunnel. The passenger is all right, although he may do mean little tricks, like hiding a wad of money in his shoe and forgetting to dig up until you jostle his ribs some with the end of your six-shooter; but there's no harm in him.

As to the train crew, we never had any more trouble with them than if they had been so many sheep. I don't mean that they are cowards; I mean that they have got sense. They know they're not up against a bluff. It's the same way with the officers. I've seen secret-service men, marshals and railroad detectives fork over their change as meek as Moses. I saw one of the bravest marshals I ever knew hide his gun under his seat and dig up along with the rest while I was taking toll. He wasn't afraid; he simply knew that we had the drop on the whole outfit. Besides, many of those officers have families and they feel that they oughtn't to take chances; whereas death has no terrors for the man who holds up a train. He expects to get killed some day, and he generally does. My advice to you, if you should ever be in a hold-up, is to line up with the cowards and save your bravery for an occasion when it may be of some benefit to you.

Another reason why officers are backward about mixing things with a train robber is a financial one. Every time there is a scrimmage and somebody gets killed, the officers lose money. If the train robber gets away they swear out a warrant against John Doe *et al.* and travel hundreds of miles and sign vouchers for thousands on the trail of the fugitives, and the Government foots the bills. So, with them, it is a question of mileage rather than courage.

I will give one instance to support my statement that the surprise is the best card in playing for a hold-up.

Along in '92 the Daltons were cutting out a hot trail for the officers down in the Cherokee Nation. Those were their lucky days, and they got so reckless and sandy that they used to announce beforehand what job they were going to undertake. Once they gave it out that they were going to hold up the M. K. & T. Flyer on a certain night at the station of Pryor Creek, in Indian Territory.

That night the railroad company got fifteen deputy marshals in Muscogee and put them on the train. Beside them they had fifty armed men hid in the depot at Pryor Creek.

When the Katy Flyer pulled in not a Dalton showed up. The next station was Adair, six miles away. When the train reached there and the deputies were having a good time explaining what they would have done to the Dalton Gang if they had turned up, all at once it sounded like an army firing outside. The conductor and brake-man came running into the car yelling, 'Train robbers!'

Some of those deputies lit out of the door, hit the ground, and kept on running. Some of them hid their Winchesters under the seats. Two of them made a fight and were both killed.

It took the Daltons just ten minutes to capture the train and whip the escort. In twenty minutes more they robbed the express car of twenty-seven thousand dollars and made a clean get-away.

My opinion is that those deputies would have put up a stiff fight at Pryor Creek, where they were expecting trouble, but they were taken by surprise and 'locoed' at Adair, just as the Daltons, who knew their business, expected they would be.

I don't think I ought to close without giving some deductions from my experience of eight years 'on the dodge'. It doesn't pay to rob trains. Leaving out the question of right and morals, which I don't think I ought to tackle, there is very little to envy in the life of an outlaw. After awhile money ceases to have any value in his eyes. He gets to looking upon the railroads and express companies as his bankers, and his six-shooter as a chequebook good for any amount. He throws away money right and left. Most of the time he is on the jump, riding day and night, and he lives so hard between times that he doesn't enjoy the taste of high life when he gets it. He knows that his time is bound to come to lose his life or liberty, and that the accuracy of his aim, the speed of his horse, and the fidelity of his 'sider', are all that postpone the inevitable.

It isn't that he loses any sleep over danger from the officers of the law. In all my experience I never knew officers to attack a band of outlaws unless they outnumbered them at least three to one.

But the outlaw carries one thought constantly in his mind – and that is what makes him so sore against life, more than anything else – he knows where the marshals get their recruits of deputies. He knows that the majority of these upholders of the law were once lawbreakers, horse thieves, rustlers, highwaymen and outlaws like himself, and that they gained their positions and immunity by turning state's evidence, by turning traitor and delivering up their comrades to imprisonment and death. He knows that some day – unless he is shot first – his Judas will set to work, the trap will be laid, and he will be the surprised instead of a surpriser at a stick-up.

That is why the man who holds up trains picks his company

with a thousand times the care with which a careful girl chooses a sweetheart. That is why he raises himself from his blanket of nights and listens to the tread of every horse's hoofs on the distant road. That is why he broods suspiciously for days upon a jesting remark or an unusual movement of a tried comrade, or the broken mutterings of his closest friend, sleeping by his side.

And it is one of the reasons why the train-robbing profession is not so pleasant a one as either of its collateral branches – politics or cornering the market.

G. K. CHESTERTON

Gilbert Keith Chesterton was born in Kensington in 1874. He was a late developer, only reaching adolescence in his late teens, leaving him with a somewhat skewed perspective on life. His childlike qualities of clarity and belief inspired his most famous creation, Father Brown. During his life Chesterton produced a considerable number of works in various styles including novels, plays, poems and non-fiction but he remains best known for his ingenious short stories about crime. He converted to Roman Catholicism in 1922 and wrote a number of books about his faith, most famously *Orthodoxy*. His 'friendly enemy', George Bernard Shaw, described him as 'a man of colossal genius'. He died in 1936.

The Point of a Pin

Father Brown always declared that he solved this problem in his sleep. And this was true, though in rather an odd fashion; because it occurred at a time when his sleep was rather disturbed. It was disturbed very early in the morning by the hammering that began in the huge building, or half-building, that was in process of erection opposite to his rooms; a colossal pile of flats still mostly covered with scaffolding and with boards announcing Messrs Swindon & Sand as the builders and owners. The hammering was renewed at regular intervals and was easily recognisable because Messrs Swindon & Sand specialised in some new American system of cement flooring which, in spite of its subsequent smoothness, solidity, impenetrability and permanent comfort (as described in the advertisements), had to be clamped down at certain points with heavy tools. Father Brown endeavoured, however, to extract exiguous comfort from it, saying that it always woke him up in time for the very earliest mass, and was therefore something almost in the nature of a carillon. After all, he said, it was almost as poetic that Christians should be awakened by hammers as by bells. As a fact, however, the building operations were a little on his nerves for another reason. For there was hanging like a cloud over the half-built skyscraper the possibility of a labour crisis, which the newspapers doggedly insisted on describing as a strike. As a matter of fact, if it ever happened, it would be a lock-out. But he worried a good deal about whether it would happen. And it might be questioned whether hammering is more of a strain on the attention because it may go on for ever, or because it may stop at any minute.

'As a mere matter of taste and fancy,' said Father Brown, staring up at the edifice with his owlish spectacles, 'I rather wish it would stop. I wish all houses would stop while they still have the scaffolding up. It seems almost a pity that houses are ever finished. They look so fresh and hopeful with all that fairy filigree of white wood, all light and bright in the sun; and a man so often only finishes a house by turning it into a tomb.'

As he turned away from the object of his scrutiny, he nearly ran into a man who had just darted across the road towards him. It was a man whom he knew slightly, but sufficiently to regard him (in the circumstances) as something of a bird of ill-omen. Mr Mastyk was a squat man with a square head that looked hardly European, dressed with a heavy dandyism that seemed rather too consciously Europeanised. But Brown had seen him lately talking to young Sand of the building firm; and he did not like it. This man Mastyk was the head of an organisation rather new in English industrial politics; produced by extremes at both ends; a definite army of non-Union and largely alien labour hired out in gangs to various firms; and he was obviously hovering about in the hope of hiring it out to this one. In short, he might negotiate some way of outmanoeuvring the trade union and flooding the works with blacklegs. Father Brown had been drawn into some of the debates, being in some sense called in on both sides. And as the capitalists all reported that, to their positive knowledge, he was a Bolshevist; and as the Bolshevists all testified that he was a reactionary rigidly attached to bourgeois ideologies, it may be inferred that he talked a certain amount of sense without any appreciable effect on anybody. The news brought by Mr Mastyk, however, was calculated to jerk everybody out of the ordinary rut of the dispute.

'They want you to go over there at once,' said Mr Mastyk, in awkwardly accented English. 'There is a threat to murder.'

Father Brown followed his guide in silence up several stairways and ladders to a platform of the unfinished building on which were grouped the more or less familiar figures of the heads of the building business. They included even what had once been the head of it; though the head had been for some time rather a head in the clouds. It was at least a head in a coronet, that hid it from human sight like a cloud. Lord Stanes, in other words, had not only retired from the business but been caught up into the House of Lords and disappeared. His rare reappearances were languid and somewhat dreary; but this one, in conjunction with that of Mastyk, seemed none the less menacing. Lord Stanes was a lean, long-headed, hollow-eyed man with very faint fair hair fading into baldness; and he was the most evasive person the priest had ever met. He was unrivalled in the true Oxford talent of saying, 'No doubt you're right,' so as to sound like, 'No doubt you think you're right,' or of merely remarking, 'You think so?' so as to imply the acid addition, 'You would.' But Father Brown fancied that the man was not merely bored but faintly embittered, though whether at being called down from Olympus to control such trade squabbles, or merely at not being really any longer in control of them, it was difficult to guess.

On the whole, Father Brown rather preferred the more bourgeois group of partners, Sir Hubert Sand and his nephew Henry; though he doubted privately whether they really had very many ideologies. True, Sir Hubert Sand had obtained considerable celebrity in the newspapers, both as a patron of sport and as a patriot in many crises during and after the Great War. He had won notable distinction in France, for a man of his years, and had afterwards been featured as a triumphant captain of industry overcoming difficulties among the munition-workers. He had been called a Strong Man; but that was not his fault. He was in fact a heavy, hearty Englishman; a great swimmer; a good squire; an admirable amateur colonel. Indeed, something that can only be called a military make-up pervaded his appearance. He was growing stout, but he kept his shoulders set back; his curly hair and moustache were still brown while the colours of his face were already somewhat withered and faded. His nephew was a burly youth of the pushing, or rather shouldering, sort with a relatively small head thrust out on a thick neck, as if he went at things with his head down; a gesture somehow rendered rather quaint and boyish by the pince-nez that were balanced on his pugnacious pug-nose.

Father Brown had looked at all these things before; and at that moment everybody was looking at something entirely new. In the centre of the woodwork there was nailed up a large loose flapping piece of paper on which something was scrawled in crude and almost crazy capital letters, as if the writer were either almost illiterate or were affecting or parodying illiteracy. The words actually ran: 'The Council of the Workers warns Hubert Sand that he will lower wages and lock out workmen at his peril. If the notices go out tomorrow, he will be dead by the justice of the people.'

Lord Stanes was just stepping back from his examination of the paper, and, looking across at his partner, he said with rather a curious intonation: 'Well, it's you they want to murder. Evidently I'm not considered worth murdering.'

One of those still electric shocks of fancy that sometimes thrilled Father Brown's mind in an almost meaningless way shot through him at that particular instant. He had a queer notion that the man who was speaking could not now be murdered, because he was already dead. It was, he cheerfully admitted, a perfectly senseless idea. But there was something that always gave him the creeps about the cold disenchanted detachment of the noble senior partner; about his cadaverous colour and inhospitable eyes. 'The fellow,' he thought in the same perverse mood, 'has green eyes and looks as if he had green blood.'

Anyhow, it was certain that Sir Hubert Sand had not got green blood. His blood, which was red enough in every sense, was creeping up into his withered or weather-beaten cheeks with all the warm fullness of life that belongs to the natural and innocent indignation of the good-natured.

'In all my life,' he said, in a strong voice and yet shakily, 'I have never had such a thing said or done about me. I may have differed – '

'We can none of us differ about this,' struck in his nephew impetuously. 'I've tried to get on with them, but this is a bit too thick.'

'You don't really think,' began Father Brown, 'that your workmen – '

'I say we may have differed,' said old Sand, still a little tremulously, 'God knows I never like the idea of threatening English workmen with cheaper labour – '

'We none of us liked it,' said the young man, 'but if I know you, uncle, this has about settled it.'

Then after a pause he added, 'I suppose, as you say, we did disagree about details; but as to real policy – '

'My dear fellow,' said his uncle, comfortably, 'I hoped there would never be any real disagreement.' From which anybody who understands the English nation may rightly infer that there had been very considerable disagreement. Indeed the uncle and nephew differed almost as much as an Englishman and an American. The uncle had the English ideal of getting outside the business, and setting up a sort of an alibi as a country gentleman. The nephew had the American ideal of getting inside the business; of getting inside the very mechanism like a mechanic. And, indeed, he had worked with most of the mechanics and was familiar with most of the processes and tricks of the trade. And he was American, again, in the fact that he did this partly as an employer to keep his men up to the mark, but in some vague way also as an equal, or at least with a pride in showing himself also as a worker. For this reason he had often appeared almost as a representative of the workers, on technical points which were a hundred miles away from his uncle's popular eminence in politics or sport. The memory of those many occasions when young Henry had practically come out of the workshop in his shirt sleeves, to demand some concession about the conditions of the work, lent a peculiar force and even violence to his present reaction the other way.

'Well, they've damned-well locked themselves out this time,' he cried. 'After a threat like that there's simply nothing left but to defy them. There's nothing left but to sack them all now; instanter; on the spot. Otherwise we'll be the laughing-stock of the world.'

Old Sand frowned with equal indignation, but began slowly: 'I shall be very much criticised – '

'Criticised!' cried the young man shrilly. 'Criticised if you defy a threat of murder! Have you any notion how you'll be criticised if you don't defy it? Won't you enjoy the headlines? "Great Capitalist Terrorised" – "Employer Yields to Murder Threat".

'Particularly,' said Lord Stanes, with something faintly

unpleasant in his tone. 'Particularly when he has been in so many headlines already as "The Strong Man of Steel-Building".'

Sand had gone very red again and his voice came thickly from under his thick moustache. 'Of course you're right there. If these brutes think I'm afraid – '

At this point there was an interruption in the conversation of the group and a slim young man came towards them swiftly. The first notable thing about him was that he was one of those whom men, and women too, think are just a little too nice-looking to look nice. He had beautiful dark curly hair and a silken moustache and he spoke like a gentleman, but with almost too refined and exactly modulated an accent. Father Brown knew him at once as Rupert Rae, the secretary of Sir Hubert, whom he had often seen pottering about in Sir Hubert's house; but never with such impatience in his movements or such a wrinkle on his brow.

'I'm sorry, sir,' he said to his employer, 'but there's a man been hanging about over there. I've done my best to get rid of him. He's only got a letter, but he swears he must give it to you personally.'

'You mean he went first to my house?' said Sand, glancing swiftly at his secretary. 'I suppose you've been there all the morning.'

'Yes, sir,' said Mr Rupert Rae.

There was a short silence; and then Sir Hubert Sand curtly intimated that the man had better be brought along; and the man duly appeared.

Nobody, not even the least fastidious lady, would have said that the newcomer was too nice-looking. He had very large ears and a face like a frog, and he stared before him with an almost ghastly fixity, which Father Brown attributed to his having a glass eye. In fact, his fancy was tempted to equip the man with two glass eyes, with so glassy a stare did he contemplate the company. But the priest's experience, as distinct from his fancy, was able to suggest several natural causes for that unnatural waxwork glare, one of them being an abuse of the divine gift of fermented liquor. The man was short and shabby and carried a large bowler hat in one hand and a large sealed letter in the other.

Sir Hubert Sand looked at him; and then said quietly enough, but in a voice that somehow seemed curiously small, coming out of the fullness of his bodily presence: 'Oh – it's you.'

He held out his hand for the letter; and then looked around apologetically, with poised finger, before ripping it open and reading it. When he had read it, he stuffed it into his inside pocket and said hastily and a little harshly: 'Well, I suppose all this business is over, as you say. No more negotiations possible now; we couldn't pay the wages they want anyhow. But I shall want to see you again, Henry, about – about winding things up generally.'

'All right,' said Henry, a little sulkily perhaps, as if he would have preferred to wind them up by himself. 'I shall be up in number 188 after lunch; got to know how far they've got up there.'

The man with the glass eye, if it was a glass eye, stumped stiffly away; and the eye of Father Brown (which was by no means a glass eye) followed him thoughtfully as he threaded his way down the ladders and disappeared into the street.

It was on the following morning that Father Brown had the unusual experience of oversleeping himself; or at least of starting from sleep with a subjective conviction that he must be late. This was partly due to his remembering, as a man may remember a dream, the fact of having been half-awakened at a more regular hour and fallen asleep again; a common enough occurrence with most of us, but a very uncommon occurrence with Father Brown. And he was afterwards oddly convinced, with that mystic side of him which was normally turned away from the world, that in that detached dark islet of dreamland, between the two wakings, there lay like buried treasure the truth of this tale.

As it was, he jumped up with great promptitude, plunged into his clothes, seized his big knobby umbrella and bustled out into the street, where the bleak white morning was breaking like splintered ice about the huge black building facing him. He was surprised to find that the streets shone almost empty in the cold crystalline light; the very look of it told him it could hardly be so late as he had feared. Then suddenly the stillness was cloven by the arrowlike swiftness of a long grey car which halted before the big deserted flats. Lord Stanes unfolded himself from within and approached the door, carrying (rather languidly) two large suitcases. At the same moment the door opened, and somebody seemed to step back instead of stepping out into the street. Stanes called twice to the man within, before that person seemed to complete his original gesture by coming out on to the doorstep; then the two held a brief colloquy, ending in the nobleman carrying his suitcases upstairs, and the other coming out into full daylight and revealing the heavy shoulders and peering head of young Henry Sand.

Father Brown made no more of this rather odd meeting until two days later the young man drove up in his own car, and implored the priest to enter it. 'Something awful has happened,' he said, 'and I'd rather talk to you than Stanes. You know Stanes arrived the other day with some mad idea of camping in one of the flats that's just finished. That's why I had to go there early and open the door to him. But all that will keep. I want you to come up to my uncle's place at once.'

'Is he ill?' enquired the priest quickly.

'I think he's dead,' answered the nephew.

'What do you mean by saying you think he's dead?' asked Father Brown a little briskly. 'Have you got a doctor?'

'No,' answered the other. 'I haven't got a doctor or a patient either . . . It's no good calling in doctors to examine the body; because the body has run away. But I'm afraid I know where it has run to . . . the truth is – we kept it dark for two days; but he's disappeared.'

'Wouldn't it be better,' said Father Brown mildly, 'if you told me what has really happened from the beginning?'

'I know,' answered Henry Sand; 'it's an infernal shame to talk flippantly like this about the poor old boy; but people get like that when they're rattled. I'm not much good at hiding things; the long and the short of it is – well, I won't tell you the long of it now. It's what some people would call rather a long shot; shooting suspicions at random and so on. But the short of it is that my unfortunate uncle has committed suicide.'

They were by this time skimming along in the car through the last fringes of the town and the first fringes of the forest and park beyond it; the lodge gates of Sir Hubert Sand's small estate were about half a mile farther on amid the thickening throng of the beeches. The estate consisted chiefly of a small park and a large ornamental garden, which descended in terraces of a certain classical pomp to the very edge of the chief river of the district. As soon as they arrived at the house, Henry took the priest somewhat hastily through the old Georgian rooms and out upon the other side; where they silently descended the slope, a rather steep slope embanked with flowers, from which they could see the pale river spread out before them almost as flat as in a bird's-eye view. They were just turning the corner of the path under an enormous classical urn crowned with a somewhat incongruous garland of geraniums, when Father Brown saw a movement in the bushes and thin trees just below him that seemed as swift as a movement of startled birds.

In the tangle of thin trees by the river two figures seemed to divide or scatter; one of them glided swiftly into the shadows and the other came forward to face them, bringing them to a halt and an abrupt and rather unaccountable silence. Then

Henry Sand said in his heavy way: 'I think you know Father Brown . . . Lady Sand.'

Father Brown did know her; but at that moment he might almost have said that he did not know her. The pallor and constriction of her face was like a mask of tragedy; she was much younger than her husband, but at that moment she looked somehow older than everything in that old house and garden. And the priest remembered, with a subconscious thrill, that she was indeed older in type and lineage and was the true possessor of the place. For her own family had owned it as impoverished aristocrats before she had restored its fortunes by marrying a successful businessman. As she stood there, she might have been a family picture, or even a family ghost. Her pale face was of that pointed yet oval type seen in some old pictures of Mary Queen of Scots; and its expression seemed almost to go beyond the natural unnaturalness of a situation in which her husband had vanished under suspicion of suicide. Father Brown, with the same subconscious movement of the mind, wondered who it was with whom she had been talking among the trees.

'I suppose you know all this dreadful news,' she said, with a comfortless composure. 'Poor Hubert must have broken down under all this revolutionary persecution, and been just maddened into taking his own life. I don't know whether you can do anything; or whether these horrible Bolsheviks can be made responsible for hounding him to death.'

'I am terribly distressed, Lady Sand,' said Father Brown. 'And still, I must own, a little bewildered. You speak of persecution; do you think that anybody could hound him to death merely by pinning up that paper on the wall?'

'I fancy,' answered the lady, with a darkening brow, 'that there were other persecutions besides the paper.'

'It shows what mistakes one may make,' said the priest sadly. 'I never should have thought he would be so illogical as to die in order to avoid death.'

'I know,' she answered, gazing at him gravely. 'I should never have believed it, if it hadn't been written with his own hand.'

'What?' cried Father Brown, with a little jump like a rabbit that has been shot at.

'Yes,' said Lady Sand calmly. 'He left a confession of suicide; so I fear there is no doubt about it.' And she passed on up the slope alone, with all the inviolable isolation of the family ghost.

The spectacles of Father Brown were turned in mute enquiry to the eyeglasses of Mr Henry Sand. And the latter gentleman, after an instant's hesitation, spoke again in his rather blind and plunging fashion: 'Yes, you see, it seems pretty clear now what he did. He was always a great swimmer and used to come down in his dressing-gown every morning for a dip in the river. Well, he came down as usual, and left his dressing-gown on the bank; it's lying there still. But he also left a message saying he was going for his last swim and then death, or something like that.'

'Where did he leave the message?' asked Father Brown.

'He scrawled it on that tree there, overhanging the water, I suppose the last thing he took hold of; just below where the dressing-gown's lying. Come and see for yourself.'

Father Brown ran down the last short slope to the shore and peered under the hanging tree, whose plumes were almost dipping in the stream. Sure enough, he saw on the smooth bark the words scratched conspicuously and unmistakably: 'One more swim and then drowning. Goodbye. Hubert Sand.' Father Brown's gaze travelled slowly up the bank till it rested on a gorgeous rag of raiment, all red and yellow with gilded tassels. It was the dressing-gown and the priest picked it up and began to turn it over. Almost as he did so he was conscious that a figure had flashed across his field of vision, a tall dark figure that slipped from one clump of trees to another, as if following the trail of the vanishing lady. He had little doubt that it was the companion from whom she had lately parted. He had still less doubt that it was the dead man's secretary, Mr Rupert Rae.

'Of course, it might be a final afterthought to leave the message,' said Father Brown, without looking up, his eye riveted on the red and gold garment. 'We've all heard of love-messages written on trees; and I suppose there might be death-messages written on trees too.'

'Well, he wouldn't have anything in the pockets of his dressing-gown, I suppose,' said young Sand. 'And a man might naturally scratch his message on a tree if he had no pens, ink or paper.'

'Sounds like French exercises,' said the priest dismally. 'But I wasn't thinking of that.' Then, after a silence, he said in a rather altered voice: 'To tell the truth, I was thinking whether a man might not naturally scratch his message on a tree, even if he had stacks of pens, and quarts of ink and reams of paper.'

Henry was looking at him with a rather startled air, his eye-glasses crooked on his pug-nose. 'And what do you mean by that?' he asked sharply.

'Well,' said Father Brown slowly, 'I don't exactly mean that postmen will carry letters in the form of logs, or that you will ever drop a line to a friend by putting a postage stamp on a pine tree. It would have to be a particular sort of position – in fact, it would have to be a particular sort of person, who really preferred this sort of arboreal correspondence. But, given the position and the person, I repeat what I said. He would still write on a tree, as the song says, if all the world were paper and all the sea were ink; if that river flowed with everlasting ink or all these woods were a forest of quills and fountain-pens.'

It was evident that Sand felt something creepy about the priest's fanciful imagery; whether because he found it incomprehensible or because he was beginning to comprehend.

'You see,' said Father Brown, turning the dressing-gown over slowly as he spoke, 'a man isn't expected to write his very best handwriting when he chips it on a tree. And if the man were not the man, if I make myself clear – Hello!'

He was looking down at the red dressing-gown, and it seemed for the moment as if some of the red had come off on his finger; but both the faces turned towards it were already a shade paler.

'Blood!' said Father Brown; and for the instant there was a deadly stillness save for the melodious noises of the river.

Henry Sand cleared his throat and nose with noises that were by no means melodious. Then he said rather hoarsely: 'Whose blood?'

'Oh, mine,' said Father Brown; but he did not smile.

A moment after he said: 'There was a pin in this thing and I pricked myself. But I don't think you quite appreciate the point . . . the point of the pin. I do' – and he sucked his finger like a child.

'You see,' he said, after another silence, 'the gown was folded up and pinned together; nobody could have unfolded it – at least without scratching himself. In plain words, Hubert Sand never *wore* this dressing-gown. Any more than Hubert Sand ever wrote on that tree. Or drowned himself in that river.'

The pince-nez tilted on Henry's enquiring nose fell off with a click; but he was otherwise motionless, as if rigid with surprise.

'Which brings us back,' went on Father Brown cheerfully, 'to somebody's taste for writing his private correspondence on trees, like Hiawatha and his picture-writing. Sand had all the time there was, before drowning himself. Why didn't he leave a note for his wife like a sane man? Or, shall we say . . . Why didn't the Other Man leave a note for the wife like a sane man? Because he would have had to forge the husband's handwriting; always a tricky thing now that experts are so nosey about it. But nobody can be expected to imitate even his own handwriting, let alone somebody else's, when he carves capital letters in the bark of a tree. This is not a suicide, Mr Sand. If it's anything at all, it's a murder.'

The bracken and bushes of the undergrowth snapped and

crackled as the big young man rose out of them like a leviathan, and stood lowering, with his thick neck thrust forward.

'I'm no good at hiding things,' he said, 'and I half-suspected something like this – expected it, you might say, for a long time. To tell the truth, I could hardly be civil to the fellow – to either of them, for that matter.'

'What exactly do you mean?' asked the priest, looking him gravely full in the face.

'I mean,' said Henry Sand, 'that you have shown me the murder and I think I could show you the murderers.'

Father Brown was silent and the other went on rather jerkily.

'You said people sometimes wrote love-messages on trees. Well, as a fact, there are some of them on that tree; there are two sort of monograms twisted together up there under the leaves – I suppose you know that Lady Sand was the heiress of this place long before she married; and she knew that damned dandy of a secretary even in those days. I guess they used to meet here and write their vows upon the trysting tree. They seem to have used the trysting tree for another purpose later on. Sentiment, no doubt, or economy.'

'They must be very horrible people,' said Father Brown.

'Haven't there been any horrible people in history or the *Police News*?' demanded Sand with some excitement. 'Haven't there been lovers who made love seem more horrible than hate? Don't you know about Bothwell and all the bloody legends of such lovers?'

'I know the legend of Bothwell,' answered the priest. 'I also know it to be quite legendary. But of course it's true that husbands have been sometimes put away like that. By the way, where was he put away? I mean, where did they hide the body?'

'I suppose they drowned him, or threw him in the water when he was dead,' snorted the young man impatiently.

Father Brown blinked thoughtfully and then said: 'A river is a good place to hide an imaginary body. It's a rotten bad place to hide a real one. I mean, it's easy to say you've thrown it in, because it might be washed away to sea. But if you really did throw it in, it's about a hundred to one it wouldn't; the chances of it going ashore somewhere are enormous. I think they must have had a better scheme for hiding the body than that – or the body would have been found by now. And if there were any marks of violence – '

'Oh, bother hiding the body,' said Henry, with some irritation; 'haven't we witness enough in the writing on their own devilish tree?'

'The body is the chief witness in every murder,' answered the other. 'The hiding of the body, nine times out of ten, is the practical problem to be solved.'

There was a silence; and Father Brown continued to turn over the red dressing-gown and spread it out on the shining grass of the sunny shore; he did not look up. But, for some time past he had been conscious that the whole landscape had been changed for him by the presence of a third party; standing as still as a statue in the garden.

'By the way,' he said, lowering his voice, 'how do you explain that little guy with the glass eye, who brought your poor uncle a letter yesterday? It seemed to me he was entirely altered by reading it; that's why I wasn't surprised at the suicide, when I thought it was a suicide. That chap was a rather low-down private detective, or I'm much mistaken.'

'Why,' said Henry in a hesitating manner, 'why, he might have been – husbands do sometimes put on detectives in domestic tragedies like this, don't they? I suppose he'd got the proofs of their intrigue; and so they – '

'I shouldn't talk too loud,' said Father Brown, 'because your detective is detecting us at this moment, from about a yard beyond those bushes.'

They looked up, and sure enough the goblin with the glass eye was fixing them with that disagreeable optic, looking all the more grotesque for standing among the white and waxen blooms of the classical garden.

Henry Sand scrambled to his feet again with a rapidity that seemed breathless for one of his bulk, and asked the man very angrily and abruptly what he was doing, at the same time telling him to clear out at once.

'Lord Stanes,' said the goblin of the garden, 'would be much obliged if Father Brown would come up to the house and speak to him.'

Henry Sand turned away furiously; but the priest put down his fury to the dislike that was known to exist between him and the nobleman in question. As they mounted the slope, Father Brown paused a moment as if tracing patterns on the smooth tree-trunk, glanced upwards once at the darker and more hidden hieroglyph said to be a record of romance; and then stared at the wider and more sprawling letters of the confession, or supposed confession of suicide.

'Do those letters remind you of anything?' he asked. And when his sulky companion shook his head, he went on: 'They remind me of the writing on that placard that threatened him with the vengeance of the strikers.'

'This is the hardest riddle and the queerest tale I have ever tackled,' said Father Brown, a month later, as he sat opposite Lord Stanes in the recently furnished apartment of No. 188, the end flat which was the last to be finished before the interregnum of the industrial dispute and the transfer of work from the trade union. It was comfortably furnished; and Lord Stanes was presiding over grog and cigars, when the priest made his confession with a grimace. Lord Stanes had become rather surprisingly friendly, in a cool and casual way.

'I know that is saying a good deal, with your record,' said Stanes, 'but certainly the detectives, including our seductive friend with the glass eye, don't seem at all able to see the solution.'

Father Brown laid down his cigar and said carefully: 'It isn't that they can't see the solution. It is that they can't see the problem.'

'Indeed,' said the other, 'perhaps I can't see the problem either.'

'The problem is unlike all other problems, for this reason,' said Father Brown. 'It seems as if the criminal deliberately did two different things, either of which might have been successful; but which, when done together, could only defeat each other. I am assuming, what I firmly believe, that the same murderer pinned up the proclamation threatening a sort of Bolshevik murder, and also wrote on the tree confessing to an ordinary suicide. Now you may say it is after all possible that the proclamation was a proletarian proclamation; that some extremist workmen wanted to kill their employer, and killed him. Even if that were true, it would still stick at the mystery of why they left, or why anybody left, a contrary trail of private self-destruction. But it certainly isn't true. None of these workmen, however bitter, would have done a thing like that. I know them pretty well; I know their leaders quite well. To suppose that people like Tom Bruce or Hogan would assassinate somebody they could go for in the newspapers, and damage in all sorts of different ways, is the sort of psychology that sensible people call lunacy. No; there was somebody, who was not an indignant workman, who first played the part of an indignant workman, and then played the part of a suicidal employer. But, in the name of wonder, why? If he thought he could pass it off smoothly as a suicide, why did he first spoil it all by publishing a threat of murder? You might say it was an afterthought to fix up the suicide story, as less provocative than the murder story. But it wasn't less provocative *after* the murder story. He must have known he had already turned our thoughts towards murder, when it should have been his whole object to keep our thoughts away from it. If it was an afterthought, it was the afterthought of a very thoughtless person. And I have a notion that this assassin is a very thoughtful person. Can you make anything of it?'

'No; but I see what you mean,' said Stanes, 'by saying that I didn't even see the problem. It isn't merely who killed Sand; it's why anybody should accuse somebody else of killing Sand and then accuse Sand of killing himself.'

Father Brown's face was knotted and the cigar was clenched in his teeth; the end of it glowed and darkened rhythmically like the signal of some burning pulse of the brain. Then he spoke as if to himself: 'We've got to follow very closely and very clearly. It's like separating threads of thought from each other; something like this. Because the murder charge really rather spoilt the suicide charge, he wouldn't normally have made the murder charge. But he did make it; so he had some other reason for making it. It was so strong a reason that perhaps it reconciled him even to weakening his other line of defence: that it was a suicide. In other words, the murder charge wasn't really a murder charge. I mean he wasn't using it as a murder charge; he wasn't doing it so as to shift to somebody else the guilt of murder; he was doing it for some other extraordinary reason of his own. His plan had to contain a proclamation that Sand would be murdered; whether it threw suspicion on other people or not. Somehow or other the mere proclamation itself was necessary. But why?'

He smoked and smouldered away with the same volcanic concentration for five minutes before he spoke again. 'What could a murderous proclamation do, besides suggesting that the strikers were the murderers? What *did* it do? One thing is obvious; it inevitably did the opposite of what it said. It told Sand not to lock out his men; and it was perhaps the only thing in the world that would really have made him do it. You've got to think of the sort of man and the sort of reputation. When a man has been called a Strong Man in our silly sensational newspapers, when he is fondly regarded as a Sportsman by all the most distinguished asses in England, he simply can't back down because he is threatened with a pistol. It would be like walking about at Ascot with a white feather stuck in his absurd white hat. It would break that inner idol or ideal of oneself, which every man not a downright dastard does really prefer to life. And Sand wasn't a dastard; he was courageous; he was also impulsive. It acted instantly like a charm: his nephew, who had been more or less mixed up with the workmen, cried out instantly that the threat must be absolutely and instantly defied.'

'Yes,' said Lord Stanes, 'I noticed that.' They looked at each other for an instant, and then Stanes added carelessly: 'So you think the thing the criminal wanted was – '

'The lock-out!' cried the priest energetically. 'The strike or whatever you call it; the cessation of work, anyhow. He wanted the work to stop at once; perhaps the blacklegs to come in at once; certainly the trade unionists to go out at once. That is what he really wanted; God knows why. And he brought that off, I think, really without bothering much about its other implication of the existence of Bolshevist assassins. But then . . . then I think something went wrong. I'm only guessing and groping very slowly here; but the only explanation I can think of is that something began to draw attention to the real seat of the trouble; to the reason, whatever it was, of his wanting to bring the building to a halt. And then belatedly, desperately and rather inconsistently, he tried to lay the other trail that led to the river, simply and solely because it led away from the flats.'

He looked up through his moonlike spectacles, absorbing all the quality of the background and furniture; the restrained luxury of a quiet man of the world; and contrasting it with the two suitcases with which its occupant had arrived so recently in a newly finished and unfurnished flat. Then he said rather abruptly: 'In short, the murderer was frightened of something or somebody in the flats. By the way, why did *you* come to live in the flats? . . . Also by the way, young Henry told me you made an early appointment with him when you moved in. Is that true?'

'Not in the least,' said Stanes. 'I got the key from his uncle the night before. I've no notion why Henry came here that morning.'

'Ah,' said Father Brown, 'then I think I have some notion of why he came . . . I *thought* you startled him by coming in just when he was coming out.'

'And yet,' said Stanes, looking across with a glitter in his grey-green eyes, 'you do rather think that I also am a mystery.'

'I think you are two mysteries,' said Father Brown. 'The first is why you originally retired from Sand's business. The second is why you have since come back to live in Sand's buildings.'

Stanes smoked reflectively, knocked out his ash, and rang a bell on the table before him. 'If you'll excuse me,' he said, 'I will summon two more to the council. Jackson, the little detective you know of, will answer the bell; and I've asked Henry Sand to come in a little later.'

Father Brown rose from his seat, walked across the room and looked down frowning into the fireplace.

'Meanwhile,' continued Stanes, 'I don't mind answering both your questions. I left the Sand business because I was sure there was some hanky-panky in it and somebody was pinching all the money. I came back to it, and took this flat, because I wanted to watch for the real truth about old Sand's death – on the spot.'

Father Brown faced round as the detective entered the room; he stood staring at the hearthrug and repeated: 'On the spot.'

'Mr Jackson will tell you,' said Stanes, 'that Sir Hubert commissioned him to find out who was the thief robbing the firm; and he brought a note of his discoveries the day before old Hubert disappeared.'

'Yes,' said Father Brown, 'and I know now where he disappeared to. I know where the body is.'

'Do you mean – ?' began his host hastily.

'It is here,' said Father Brown, and stamped on the hearthrug. 'Here, under the elegant Persian rug in this cosy and comfortable room.'

'Where in the world did you find that?'

'I've just remembered,' said Father Brown, 'that I found it in my sleep.'

He closed his eyes as if trying to picture a dream, and went on dreamily: 'This is a murder story turning on the problem of How to Hide the Body; and I found it in my sleep. I was always woken up every morning by hammering from this building. On that morning I half-woke up, went to sleep again and woke once more, expecting to find it late; but it wasn't. Why? Because there *had* been hammering that morning, though all the usual work had stopped; short, hurried hammering in the small hours before dawn. Automatically a man sleeping stirs at such a familiar sound. But he goes to sleep again, because the usual sound is not at the usual hour. Now why did a certain secret criminal want all the work to cease suddenly; and only new workers come in? Because, if the old workers had come in next day, they would have found a new piece of work done in the night. The old workers would have known where they left off; and they would have found the whole flooring of this room already nailed down. Nailed down by a man who knew how to do it; having mixed a good deal with the workmen and learned their ways.'

As he spoke, the door was pushed open and a head poked in with a thrusting motion; a small head at the end of a thick neck and a face that blinked at them through glasses.

'Henry Sand said,' observed Father Brown, staring at the ceiling, 'that he was no good at hiding things. But I think he did himself an injustice.'

Henry Sand turned and moved swiftly away down the corridor.

'He not only hid his thefts from the firm quite successfully for years,' went on the priest with an air of abstraction, 'but when his uncle discovered them, he hid his uncle's corpse in an entirely new and original manner.'

At the same instant Stanes again rang a bell, with a long strident steady ringing; and the little man with the glass eye was propelled or shot along the corridor after the fugitive, with something of the rotatory motion of a mechanical figure in a zoetrope. At the same moment, Father Brown looked out of the window, leaning over a small balcony, and saw five or six men start from behind bushes and railings in the street below and spread out equally mechanically like a fan or net, opening out after the fugitive who had shot like a bullet out of the front door. Father Brown saw only the pattern of the story, which had never strayed from that room; where Henry had strangled Hubert and hid his body under impenetrable flooring, stopping the whole work on the building to do it. A pin-prick had started his own suspicions; but only to tell him he had been led down the long loop of a lie. The point of the pin was that it was pointless.

He fancied he understood Stanes at last, and he liked to collect queer people who were difficult to understand. He realised that this tired gentleman, whom he had once accused of having green blood, had indeed a sort of cold green flame of conscientiousness or conventional honour that had made him first shift out of a shady business, and then feel ashamed of having shifted it on to others; and come back as a bored laborious detective; pitching his camp on the very spot where the corpse had been buried; so that the murderer, finding him sniffing so near the corpse, had wildly staged the alternative drama of the dressing-gown and the drowned man. All that was plain enough, but, before he withdrew his head from the night air and the stars, Father Brown threw one glance upwards at the vast black bulk of the cyclopean building heaved far up into the night, and remembered Egypt and Babylon, and all that is at once eternal and ephemeral in the work of man.

'I was right in what I said first of all,' he said. 'It reminds one of Coppée's poem about the Pharaoh and the Pyramid. This house is supposed to be a hundred houses; and yet the whole mountain of building is only one man's tomb.'

ARTHUR CONAN DOYLE

Sir Arthur Conan Doyle (1859–1930) was a Scottish physician and author, most noted for his stories about the detective Sherlock Holmes, generally considered without equal in the field of crime fiction. He was a prolific writer whose other works include science-fiction stories, plays, romances, historical novels, poetry and non-fiction. Conan Doyle was also a fervent advocate of justice and personally investigated two closed cases, which led to two men being exonerated from the crimes of which they were accused.

The Adventure of the Noble Bachelor

The Lord St Simon marriage, and its curious termination, have long ceased to be a subject of interest in those exalted circles in which the unfortunate bridegroom moves. Fresh scandals have eclipsed it, and their more piquant details have drawn the gossips away from this four-year-old drama. As I have reason to believe, however, that the full facts have never been revealed to the general public, and as my friend Sherlock Holmes had a considerable share in clearing the matter up, I feel that no memoir of him would be complete without some little sketch of this remarkable episode.

It was a few weeks before my own marriage, during the days when I was still sharing rooms with Holmes in Baker Street, that he came home from an afternoon stroll to find a letter on the table waiting for him. I had remained indoors all day, for the weather had taken a sudden turn to rain, with high autumnal winds, and the Jezail bullet which I had brought back in one of my limbs as a relic of my Afghan campaign throbbed with dull persistence. With my body in one easy-chair and my legs upon another, I had surrounded myself with a cloud of newspapers until at last, saturated with the news of the day, I tossed them all aside and lay listless, eyeing the huge crest and monogram gracing the envelope upon the table and wondering lazily who my friend's noble correspondent could be.

'Here is a very fashionable epistle,' I remarked as he entered. 'Your morning letters, if I remember right, were from a fish-monger and a tide-waiter.'

'Yes, my correspondence has certainly the charm of variety,' he answered, smiling, 'and the humbler are usually the more interesting. This looks like one of those unwelcome social summonses which call upon a man either to be bored or to lie.'

He broke the seal and glanced over the contents.

'Oh, come, it may prove to be something of interest, after all.'

'Not social, then?'

'No, distinctly professional.'

'And from a noble client?'

'One of the highest in England.'

'My dear fellow, I congratulate you.'

'I assure you, Watson, without affectation, that the status of my client is a matter of less moment to me than the interest of his case. It is just possible, however, that that also may not be wanting in this new investigation. You have been reading the papers diligently of late, have you not?'

'It looks like it,' said I ruefully, pointing to a huge bundle in the corner. 'I have had nothing else to do.'

'It is fortunate, for you will perhaps be able to post me up. I read nothing except the criminal news and the agony column. The latter is always instructive. But if you have followed recent events so closely you must have read about Lord St Simon and his wedding?'

'Oh, yes, with the deepest interest.'

'That is well. The letter which I hold in my hand is from Lord St Simon. I will read it to you, and in return you must turn over these papers and let me have whatever bears upon the matter. This is what he says:

'My dear Mr Sherlock Holmes – Lord Backwater tells me that I may place implicit reliance upon your judgement and discretion. I have determined, therefore, to call upon you and to consult you in reference to the very painful event which has occurred in connection with my wedding. Mr Lestrade, of Scotland Yard, is acting already in the matter, but he assures me that he sees no objection to your co-operation, and that he even thinks that it might be of some assistance. I will call at four o'clock in the afternoon, and should you have any other engagement at that time, I hope that you will postpone it, as this matter is of paramount importance. Yours faithfully,

St Simon.

'It is dated from Grosvenor Mansions, written with a quill pen, and the noble lord has had the misfortune to get a smear of ink upon the outer side of his right little finger,' remarked Holmes as he folded up the epistle.

'He says four o'clock. It is three now. He will be here in an hour.'

'Then I have just time, with your assistance, to get clear upon the subject. Turn over those papers and arrange the extracts in their order of time, while I take a glance as to who our client is.' He picked a red-covered volume from a line of books of reference beside the mantelpiece. 'Here he is,' said he, sitting down and flattening it out upon his knee. ' "Lord Robert Walsingham de Vere St Simon, second son of the Duke of Balmoral". Hum! "Arms: Azure, three caltrops in chief over a fess sable. Born in 1846." He's forty-one years of age, which is mature for marriage. Was Under-Secretary for the Colonies in a late administration. The Duke, his father, was at one time Secretary for Foreign Affairs. They inherit Plantagenet blood by direct descent, and Tudor on the distaff side. Ha! Well, there is nothing very instructive in all this. I think that I must turn to you, Watson, for something more solid.'

'I have very little difficulty in finding what I want,' said I, 'for the facts are quite recent, and the matter struck me as remarkable. I feared to refer them to you, however, as I knew that you had an enquiry on hand and that you disliked the intrusion of other matters.'

'Oh, you mean the little problem of the Grosvenor Square furniture van. That is quite cleared up now – though, indeed, it was obvious from the first. Pray give me the results of your newspaper selections.'

'Here is the first notice which I can find. It is in the personal column of the *Morning Post*, and dates, as you see, from some weeks back: "A marriage has been arranged," it says, "and will, if rumour is correct, very shortly take place, between Lord Robert St Simon, second son of the Duke of Balmoral, and Miss Hatty Doran, the only daughter of Aloysius Doran, Esq., of San Francisco, California, USA." That is all.'

'Terse and to the point,' remarked Holmes, stretching his long, thin legs towards the fire.

'There was a paragraph amplifying this in one of the society papers of the same week. Ah, here it is: "There will soon be a call for protection in the marriage market, for the present free-trade principle appears to tell heavily against our home product. One by one the management of the noble houses of Great Britain is passing into the hands of our fair cousins from across the Atlantic. An important addition has been made during the last week to the list of the prizes which have been borne away by these charming invaders. Lord St Simon, who has shown himself for over twenty years proof against the little god's arrows, has now definitely announced his approaching marriage with Miss Hatty Doran, the fascinating daughter of a California millionaire. Miss Doran, whose graceful figure and striking face attracted much attention at the Westbury House festivities, is an only child, and it is currently reported that her dowry will run to considerably over the six figures, with expectancies for the future. As it is an open secret that the Duke of Balmoral has been compelled to sell his pictures within the last few years, and as Lord St Simon has no property of his own save the small estate of Birchmoor, it is obvious that the Californian heiress is not the only gainer by an alliance which will enable her to make the easy and common transition from a Republican lady to a British peeress." '

'Anything else?' asked Holmes, yawning.

'Oh, yes; plenty. Then there is another note in the *Morning Post* to say that the marriage would be an absolutely quiet one, that it would be at St George's, Hanover Square, that only half a dozen intimate friends would be invited, and that the party would return to the furnished house at Lancaster Gate recently taken by Mr Aloysius Doran. Two days later – that is, on Wednesday last – there is a curt announcement that the wedding has taken place, and that the honeymoon will be passed at Lord Backwater's place, near Petersfield. Those are all the notices which appeared before the disappearance of the bride.'

'Before the what?' asked Holmes with a start.

'The vanishing of the lady.'

'When did she vanish, then?'

'At the wedding breakfast.'

'Indeed. This is more interesting than it promised to be; quite dramatic, in fact.'

'Yes; it struck me as being a little out of the common.'

'They often vanish before the ceremony, and occasionally during the honeymoon; but I cannot call to mind anything quite so prompt as this. Pray let me have the details.'

'I warn you that they are very incomplete.'

'Perhaps we may make them less so.'

'Such as they are, they are set forth in a single article of a morning paper of yesterday, which I will read to you. It is headed,

Singular Occurrence at a Fashionable Wedding

The family of Lord Robert St Simon has been thrown into the greatest consternation by the strange and painful episodes which have taken place in connection with his wedding. The ceremony, as shortly announced in the papers of yesterday, occurred on the previous morning; but it is only now that it has been possible to confirm the strange rumours which have been so persistently floating about. In spite of the attempts of friends to hush the matter up, so much public attention has now been drawn to it that no good purpose can be served by affecting to disregard what is a common subject for conversation.

The ceremony, which was performed at St George's, Hanover Square, was a very quiet one, no one being present save the father of the bride, Mr Aloysius Doran, the Duchess of Balmoral, Lord Backwater, Lord Eustace and Lady Clara St Simon (the younger brother and sister of the bridegroom) and Lady Alicia Whittington. The whole party proceeded afterwards to the house of Mr Aloysius Doran, at Lancaster Gate, where breakfast had been prepared. It appears that some little trouble was caused by a woman, whose name has not been ascertained, who endeavoured to force her way into the house after the bridal party, alleging that she had some claim upon Lord St Simon. It was only after a painful and prolonged scene that she was ejected by the butler and the footman. The bride, who had fortunately entered the house before this unpleasant interruption, had sat down to breakfast with the rest when she complained of a sudden indisposition and retired to her room. Her prolonged absence having caused some comment, her father followed her, but learned from her maid that she had only come up to her chamber for an instant, caught up an ulster and bonnet, and hurried down to the passage. One of the footmen declared that he had seen a lady leave the house thus apparelled, but had refused to credit that it was his mistress, believing her to be with the company. On ascertaining that his daughter had disappeared, Mr Aloysius Doran, in conjunction with the bridegroom, instantly put themselves in communication with the police, and very energetic enquiries are being made, which will probably result in a speedy clearing up of this very singular business. Up to a late hour last night, however, nothing had transpired as to the whereabouts of the missing lady. There are rumours of foul play in the matter, and it is said that the police have caused the arrest of the woman who had caused the original disturbance, in the belief that, from jealousy or some other motive, she may have been concerned in the strange disappearance of the bride.'

'And is that all?'

'Only one little item in another of the morning papers, but it is a suggestive one.'

'And it is – '

'That Miss Flora Millar, the lady who had caused the disturbance, has actually been arrested. It appears that she was formerly a *danseuse* at the Allegro, and that she has known the bridegroom for some years. There are no further particulars, and the whole case is in your hands now – so far as it has been set forth in the public press.'

'And an exceedingly interesting case it appears to be. I would not have missed it for worlds. But there is a ring at the bell, Watson, and as the clock makes it a few minutes after four, I have no doubt that this will prove to be our noble client. Do not dream of going, Watson, for I very much prefer having a witness, if only as a check to my own memory.'

'Lord Robert St Simon,' announced our pageboy, throwing open the door. A gentleman entered, with a pleasant, cultured face, high-nosed and pale, with something perhaps of petulance about the mouth, and with the steady, well-opened eye of a man whose lot it had ever been to command and to be obeyed. His manner was brisk, and yet his general appearance gave an undue impression of age, for he had a slight forward stoop and a little bend of the knees as he walked. His hair, too, as he swept off his very curly-brimmed hat, was grizzled round the edges and thin upon the top. As to his dress, it was careful to the verge of foppishness, with high collar, black frock-coat, white waistcoat, yellow gloves, patent-leather shoes and light-coloured gaiters. He advanced slowly into the room, turning his head from left to right and swinging in his right hand the cord which held his golden eyeglasses.

'Good-day, Lord St Simon,' said Holmes, rising and bowing. 'Pray take the basket-chair. This is my friend and colleague, Dr Watson. Draw up a little to the fire, and we will talk this matter over.'

'A most painful matter to me, as you can most readily imagine, Mr Holmes. I have been cut to the quick. I understand that you have already managed several delicate cases of this sort, sir, though I presume that they were hardly from the same class of society.'

'No, I am descending.'

'I beg pardon.'

'My last client of the sort was a king.'

'Oh, really! I had no idea. And which king?'

'The King of Scandinavia.'

'What! Had he lost his wife?'

'You can understand,' said Holmes suavely, 'that I extend to the affairs of my other clients the same secrecy which I promise to you in yours.'

'Of course! Very right! very right! I'm sure I beg pardon. As to my own case, I am ready to give you any information which may assist you in forming an opinion.'

'Thank you. I have already learned all that is in the public prints, nothing more. I presume that I may take it as correct – this article, for example, as to the disappearance of the bride.'

Lord St Simon glanced over it. 'Yes, it is correct, as far as it goes.'

'But it needs a great deal of supplementing before anyone can offer an opinion. I think that I may arrive at my facts most directly by questioning you.'

'Pray do so.'

'When did you first meet Miss Hatty Doran?'

'In San Francisco, a year ago.'

'You were travelling in the States?'

'Yes.'

'Did you become engaged then?'

'No.'

'But you were on a friendly footing?'

'I was amused by her society, and she could see that I was amused.'

'Her father is very rich?'

'He is said to be the richest man on the Pacific slope.'

'And how did he make his money?'

'In mining. He had nothing a few years ago. Then he struck gold, invested it, and came up by leaps and bounds.'

'Now, what is your own impression as to the young lady's – your wife's character?'

The nobleman swung his glasses a little faster and stared down into the fire. 'You see, Mr Holmes,' said he, 'my wife was twenty before her father became a rich man. During that time she ran free in a mining camp and wandered through woods or mountains, so that her education has come from nature rather than from the schoolmaster. She is what we call in England a tomboy, with a strong nature, wild and free, unfettered by any sort of traditions. She is impetuous – volcanic, I was about to say. She is swift in making up her mind and fearless in carrying out her resolutions. On the other hand, I would not have given her the name which I have the honour to bear' – he gave a little stately cough – 'had I not thought her to be at bottom a noble woman. I believe that she is capable of heroic self-sacrifice and that anything dishonourable would be repugnant to her.'

'Have you her photograph?'

'I brought this with me.' He opened a locket and showed us the full face of a very lovely woman. It was not a photograph but an ivory miniature, and the artist had brought out the full effect of the lustrous black hair, the large dark eyes, and the exquisite mouth. Holmes gazed long and earnestly at it. Then he closed the locket and handed it back to Lord St Simon.

'The young lady came to London, then, and you renewed your acquaintance?'

'Yes, her father brought her over for this last London season. I met her several times, became engaged to her, and have now married her.'

'She brought, I understand, a considerable dowry?'

'A fair dowry. Not more than is usual in my family.'

'And this, of course, remains to you, since the marriage is a *fait accompli*?'

'I really have made no enquiries on the subject.'

'Very naturally not. Did you see Miss Doran on the day before the wedding?'

'Yes.'

'Was she in good spirits?'

'Never better. She kept talking of what we should do in our future lives.'

'Indeed! That is very interesting. And on the morning of the wedding?'

'She was as bright as possible – at least until after the ceremony.'

'And did you observe any change in her then?'

'Well, to tell the truth, I saw then the first signs that I had ever seen that her temper was just a little sharp. The incident, however, was too trivial to relate and can have no possible bearing upon the case.'

'Pray let us have it, for all that.'

'Oh, it is childish. She dropped her bouquet as we went towards the vestry. She was passing the front pew at the time, and it fell over into the pew. There was a moment's delay, but the gentleman in the pew handed it up to her again, and it did not appear to be the worse for the fall. Yet when I spoke to her of the matter, she answered me abruptly; and in the carriage, on our way home, she seemed absurdly agitated over this trifling cause.'

'Indeed! You say that there was a gentleman in the pew. Some of the general public were present, then?'

'Oh, yes. It is impossible to exclude them when the church is open.'

'This gentleman was not one of your wife's friends?'

'No, no; I call him a gentleman by courtesy, but he was quite a common-looking person. I hardly noticed his appearance. But really I think that we are wandering rather far from the point.'

'Lady St Simon, then, returned from the wedding in a less cheerful frame of mind than she had gone to it. What did she do on re-entering her father's house?'

'I saw her in conversation with her maid.'

'And who is her maid?'

'Alice is her name. She is an American and came from California with her.'

'A confidential servant?'

'A little too much so. It seemed to me that her mistress allowed her to take great liberties. Still, of course, in America they look upon these things in a different way.'

'How long did she speak to this Alice?'

'Oh, a few minutes. I had something else to think of.'

'You did not overhear what they said?'

'Lady St Simon said something about "jumping a claim". She was accustomed to use slang of the kind. I have no idea what she meant.'

'American slang is very expressive sometimes. And what did your wife do when she finished speaking to her maid?'

'She walked into the breakfast-room.'

'On your arm?'

'No, alone. She was very independent in little matters like that. Then, after we had sat down for ten minutes or so, she rose hurriedly, muttered some words of apology, and left the room. She never came back.'

'But this maid, Alice, as I understand, deposes that she went to her room, covered her bride's dress with a long ulster, put on a bonnet, and went out.'

'Quite so. And she was afterwards seen walking into Hyde Park in company with Flora Millar, a woman who is now in custody, and who had already made a disturbance at Mr Doran's house that morning.'

'Ah, yes. I should like a few particulars as to this young lady, and your relations to her.'

Lord St Simon shrugged his shoulders and raised his eyebrows. 'We have been on a friendly footing for some years – I may say on a *very* friendly footing. She used to be at the Allegro. I have not treated her ungenerously, and she had no just cause of complaint against me, but you know what women are, Mr Holmes. Flora was a dear little thing, but exceedingly hot headed and devotedly attached to me. She wrote me dreadful letters when she heard that I was about to be married, and, to tell the truth, the reason why I had the marriage celebrated so quietly was that I feared lest there might be a scandal in the church. She came to Mr Doran's door just after we returned, and she endeavoured to push her way in, uttering very abusive expressions towards my wife, and even threatening her, but I had foreseen the possibility of something of the sort, and I had two police fellows there in private clothes, who soon pushed her out again. She was quiet when she saw that there was no good in making a row.'

'Did your wife hear all this?'

'No, thank goodness, she did not.'

'And she was seen walking with this very woman afterwards?'

'Yes. That is what Mr Lestrade, of Scotland Yard, looks upon as so serious. It is thought that Flora decoyed my wife out and laid some terrible trap for her.'

'Well, it is a possible supposition.'

'You think so, too?'

'I did not say a probable one. But you do not yourself look upon this as likely?'

'I do not think Flora would hurt a fly.'

'Still, jealousy is a strange transformer of characters. Pray what is your own theory as to what took place?'

'Well, really, I came to seek a theory, not to propound one. I have given you all the facts. Since you ask me, however, I may say that it has occurred to me as possible that the excitement of this affair, the consciousness that she had made so immense a social stride, had the effect of causing some little nervous disturbance in my wife.'

'In short, that she had become suddenly deranged?'

'Well, really, when I consider that she has turned her back – I will not say upon me, but upon so much that many have aspired to without success – I can hardly explain it in any other fashion.'

'Well, certainly that is also a conceivable hypothesis,' said Holmes, smiling. 'And now, Lord St Simon, I think that I have nearly all my data. May I ask whether you were seated at the breakfast-table so that you could see out of the window?'

'We could see the other side of the road and the park.'

'Quite so. Then I do not think that I need to detain you longer. I shall communicate with you.'

'Should you be fortunate enough to solve this problem – ' said our client, rising.

'I have solved it.'

'Eh? What was that?'

'I say that I have solved it.'

'Where, then, is my wife?'

'That is a detail which I shall speedily supply.'

Lord St Simon shook his head. 'I am afraid that it will take wiser heads than yours or mine,' he remarked, and bowing in a stately, old-fashioned manner he departed.

'It is very good of Lord St Simon to honour my head by putting it on a level with his own,' said Sherlock Holmes, laughing. 'I think that I shall have a whisky and soda and a cigar after all this cross-questioning. I had formed my conclusions as to the case before our client came into the room.'

'My dear Holmes!'

'I have notes of several similar cases, though none, as I remarked before, which were quite as prompt. My whole examination served to turn my conjecture into a certainty. Circumstantial evidence is occasionally very convincing, as when you find a trout in the milk, to quote Thoreau's example.'

'But I have heard all that you have heard.'

'Without, however, the knowledge of pre-existing cases which serves me so well. There was a parallel instance in Aberdeen some years back, and something on very much the same lines at Munich the year after the Franco-Prussian War. It is one of these cases – but, hello, here is Lestrade! Good-afternoon, Lestrade! You will find an extra tumbler upon the sideboard, and there are cigars in the box.'

The official detective was attired in a pea-jacket and cravat, which gave him a decidedly nautical appearance, and he carried a black canvas bag in his hand. With a short greeting he seated himself and lit the cigar which had been offered to him.

'What's up, then?' asked Holmes with a twinkle in his eye. 'You look dissatisfied.'

'And I feel dissatisfied. It is this infernal St Simon marriage case. I can make neither head nor tail of the business.'

'Really! You surprise me.'

'Who ever heard of such a mixed affair? Every clue seems to slip through my fingers. I have been at work upon it all day.'

'And very wet it seems to have made you,' said Holmes laying his hand upon the arm of the pea-jacket.

'Yes, I have been dragging the Serpentine.'

'In heaven's name, what for?'

'In search of the body of Lady St Simon.'

Sherlock Holmes leaned back in his chair and laughed heartily.

'Have you dragged the basin of Trafalgar Square fountain?' he asked.

'Why? What do you mean?'

'Because you have just as good a chance of finding this lady in the one as in the other.'

Lestrade shot an angry glance at my companion. 'I suppose you know all about it,' he snarled.

'Well, I have only just heard the facts, but my mind is made up.'

'Oh, indeed! Then you think that the Serpentine plays no part in the matter?'

'I think it very unlikely.'

'Then perhaps you will kindly explain how it is that we found this in it?' He opened his bag as he spoke, and tumbled on to the floor a wedding-dress of watered silk, a pair of white satin shoes and a bride's wreath and veil, all discoloured and soaked in water. 'There,' said he, putting a new wedding-ring upon the top of the pile. 'There is a little nut for you to crack, Master Holmes.'

'Oh, indeed!' said my friend, blowing blue rings into the air. 'You dragged them from the Serpentine?'

'No. They were found floating near the margin by a park-keeper. They have been identified as her clothes, and it seemed to me that if the clothes were there the body would not be far off.'

'By the same brilliant reasoning, every man's body is to be found in the neighbourhood of his wardrobe. And pray what did you hope to arrive at through this?'

'At some evidence implicating Flora Millar in the disappearance.'

'I am afraid that you will find it difficult.'

'Are you, indeed, now?' cried Lestrade with some bitterness. 'I am afraid, Holmes, that you are not very practical with your deductions and your inferences. You have made two blunders in as many minutes. This dress does implicate Miss Flora Millar.'

'And how?'

'In the dress is a pocket. In the pocket is a card-case. In the card-case is a note. And here is the very note.' He slapped it down upon the table in front of him. 'Listen to this: "You will see me when all is ready. Come at once. F.H.M." Now my theory all along has been that Lady St Simon was decoyed away by Flora Millar, and that she, with confederates, no doubt, was responsible for her disappearance. Here, signed with her initials, is the very note which was no doubt quietly slipped into her hand at the door and which lured her within their reach.'

'Very good, Lestrade,' said Holmes, laughing. 'You really are very fine indeed. Let me see it.' He took up the paper in a listless way, but his attention instantly became riveted, and he gave a little cry of satisfaction. 'This is indeed important,' said he.

'Ha! you find it so?'

'Extremely so. I congratulate you warmly.'

Lestrade rose in his triumph and bent his head to look. 'Why,' he shrieked, 'you're looking at the wrong side!'

'On the contrary, this is the right side.'

'The right side? You're mad! Here is the note written in pencil over here.'

'And over here is what appears to be the fragment of a hotel bill, which interests me deeply.'

'There's nothing in it. I looked at it before,' said Lestrade. ' "Oct. 4th, room 8*s*., breakfast 2*s*. 6*d*., cocktail 1*s*., lunch 2*s*. 6*d*., glass sherry, 8*d*." I see nothing in that.'

'Very likely not. It is most important, all the same. As to the note, it is important also, or at least the initials are, so I congratulate you again.'

'I've wasted time enough,' said Lestrade, rising. 'I believe in hard work and not in sitting by the fire spinning fine theories. Good-day, Mr Holmes, and we shall see which of us gets to the bottom of the matter first.' He gathered up the garments, thrust them into the bag, and made for the door.

'Just one hint to you, Lestrade,' drawled Holmes before his rival vanished; 'I will tell you the true solution of the matter. Lady St Simon is a myth. There is not, and there never has been, any such person.'

Lestrade looked sadly at my companion. Then he turned to me, tapped his forehead three times, shook his head solemnly and hurried away.

He had hardly shut the door behind him when Holmes rose to put on his overcoat. 'There is something in what the fellow says about outdoor work,' he remarked, 'so I think, Watson, that I must leave you to your papers for a little.'

It was after five o'clock when Sherlock Holmes left me, but I had no time to be lonely, for within an hour there arrived a confectioner's man with a very large flat box. This he unpacked, with the help of a youth whom he had brought with him, and presently, to my very great astonishment, a quite epicurean little cold supper began to be laid out upon our humble lodging-house mahogany. There were a couple of brace of cold woodcock, a pheasant, a *pâté de foie gras* pie with a group of ancient and cobwebby bottles. Having laid out all these luxuries, my two visitors vanished away, like the genii of the *Arabian Nights*, with no explanation save that the things had been paid for and were ordered to this address.

Just before nine o'clock Sherlock Holmes stepped briskly into the room. His features were gravely set, but there was a light in his eye which made me think that he had not been disappointed in his conclusions.

'They have laid the supper, then,' he said, rubbing his hands.

'You seem to expect company. They have laid for five.'

'Yes, I fancy we may have some company dropping in,' said he. 'I am surprised that Lord St Simon has not already arrived. Ha! I fancy that I hear his step now upon the stairs.'

It was indeed our visitor of the afternoon who came bustling in, dangling his glasses more vigorously than ever, and with a very perturbed expression upon his aristocratic features.

'My messenger reached you, then?' asked Holmes.

'Yes, and I confess that the contents startled me beyond measure. Have you good authority for what you say?'

'The best possible.'

Lord St Simon sank into a chair and passed his hand over his forehead.

'What will the duke say,' he murmured, 'when he hears that one of the family has been subjected to such humiliation?'

'It is the purest accident. I cannot allow that there is any humiliation.'

'Ah, you look on these things from another standpoint.'

'I fail to see that anyone is to blame. I can hardly see how the lady could have acted otherwise, though her abrupt method of doing it was undoubtedly to be regretted. Having no mother, she had no one to advise her at such a crisis.'

'It was a slight, sir, a public slight,' said Lord St Simon, tapping his fingers upon the table.

'You must make allowance for this poor girl, placed in so unprecedented a position.'

'I will make no allowance. I am very angry indeed, and I have been shamefully used.'

'I think that I heard a ring,' said Holmes. 'Yes, there are steps on the landing. If I cannot persuade you to take a lenient view of the matter, Lord St Simon, I have brought an advocate here who may be more successful.' He opened the door and ushered in a lady and gentleman. 'Lord St Simon,' said he, 'allow me to introduce you to Mr and Mrs Francis Hay Moulton. The lady, I think, you have already met.'

At the sight of these newcomers our client had sprung from his seat and stood very erect, with his eyes cast down and his hand thrust into the breast of his frock-coat, a picture of offended dignity. The lady had taken a quick step forward and had held out her hand to him, but he still refused to raise his eyes. It was as well for his resolution, perhaps, for her pleading face was one which it was hard to resist.

'You're angry, Robert,' said she. 'Well, I guess you have every cause to be.'

'Pray make no apology to me,' said Lord St Simon bitterly.

'Oh, yes, I know that I have treated you real bad and that I should have spoken to you before I went; but I was kind of rattled, and from the time when I saw Frank here again I just didn't know what I was doing or saying. I only wonder I didn't fall down and do a faint right there before the altar.'

'Perhaps, Mrs Moulton, you would like my friend and me to leave the room while you explain this matter?'

'If I may give an opinion,' remarked the strange gentleman, 'we've had just a little too much secrecy over this business already. For my part, I should like all Europe and America to hear the rights of it.' He was a small, wiry, sunburnt man, clean-shaven, with a sharp face and alert manner.

'Then I'll tell our story right away,' said the lady. 'Frank here and I met in 1884, in McQuire's camp, near the Rockies, where pa was working a claim. We were engaged to each other, Frank and I; but then one day father struck a rich pocket and made a pile, while poor Frank here had a claim that petered out and came to nothing. The richer pa grew the poorer was Frank; so at last pa wouldn't hear of our engagement lasting any longer, and he took me away to 'Frisco. Frank wouldn't throw up his hand, though; so he followed me there, and he saw me without pa knowing anything about it. It would only have made him mad to know, so we just fixed it all up for ourselves. Frank said that he would go and make his pile, too, and never come back to claim me until he had as much as pa. So then I promised to wait for him to the end of time and pledged myself not to marry anyone else while he lived. "Why shouldn't we be married right away, then," said he, "and then I will feel sure of you; and I won't claim to be your husband until I come back?" Well, we talked it over, and he had fixed it all up so nicely, with a clergyman all ready in waiting, that we just did it right there; and then Frank went off to seek his fortune, and I went back to pa.

'The next I heard of Frank was that he was in Montana, and then he went prospecting in Arizona, and then I heard of him from New Mexico. After that came a long newspaper story about how a miners' camp had been attacked by Apache Indians, and there was my Frank's name among the killed. I fainted dead away, and I was very sick for months after. Pa thought I had a decline and took me to half the doctors in 'Frisco. Not a word of news came for a year and more, so that I never doubted that Frank was really dead. Then Lord St Simon came to 'Frisco, and we came to London, and a marriage was arranged, and pa was very pleased, but I felt all the time that no man on this earth would ever take the place in my heart that had been given to my poor Frank.

'Still, if I had married Lord St Simon, of course I'd have done my duty by him. We can't command our love, but we can our actions. I went to the altar with him with the intention to make him just as good a wife as it was in me to be. But you may imagine what I felt when, just as I came to the altar rails, I glanced back and saw Frank standing and looking at me out of the first pew. I thought it was his ghost at first; but when I looked again there he was still, with a kind of question in his eyes, as if to ask me whether I were glad or sorry to see him. I wonder I didn't drop. I know that everything was turning round, and the words of the clergyman were just like the buzz of a bee in my ear. I didn't know what to do. Should I stop the service and make a scene in the church? I glanced at him again, and he seemed to know what I was thinking, for he raised his finger to his lips to tell me to be still. Then I saw him scribble on a piece of paper, and I knew that he was writing me a note. As I passed his pew on the way out I dropped my bouquet over to him, and he slipped the note into my hand when he returned me the flowers. It was only a line asking me to join him when he made the sign to me to do so. Of course I never doubted for a moment that my first duty was now to him, and I determined to do just whatever he might direct.

'When I got back I told my maid, who had known him in California, and had always been his friend. I ordered her to say nothing, but to get a few things packed and my ulster ready. I know I ought to have spoken to Lord St Simon, but it was dreadful hard before his mother and all those great people. I just made up my mind to run away and explain afterwards. I hadn't been at the table ten minutes before I saw Frank out of the window at the other side of the road. He beckoned to me and then began walking into the park. I slipped out, put on my things, and followed him. Some woman came talking something or other about Lord St Simon to me – seemed to me from the little I heard as if he had a little secret of his own before marriage also – but I managed to get away from her and soon overtook Frank. We got into a cab together, and away we drove to some lodgings he had taken in Gordon Square, and that was my true wedding after all those years of waiting. Frank had been a prisoner among the Apaches, had escaped, came on to 'Frisco, found that I had given him up for dead and had came to England, followed me here, and had come upon me at last on the very morning of my second wedding.'

'I saw it in a paper,' explained the American. 'It gave the name and the church but not where the lady lived.'

'Then we had a talk as to what we should do, and Frank was all for openness, but I was so ashamed of it all that I felt as if I should like to vanish away and never see any of them again – just sending a line to pa, perhaps, to show him that I was alive. It was awful to me to think of all those lords and ladies sitting round that breakfast-table and waiting for me to come back. So Frank took my wedding-clothes and things and made a bundle of them, so that I should not be traced, and dropped them away somewhere where no one could find them. It is likely that we should have gone on to Paris tomorrow, only that this good gentleman, Mr Holmes, came round to us this evening, though how he found us is more than I can think, and he showed us very clearly and kindly that I was wrong and that Frank was right, and that we should be putting ourselves in the wrong if we were so secret. Then he offered to give us a chance of talking to Lord St Simon alone, and so we came right away round to his rooms at once. Now, Robert, you have heard it all, and I am very sorry if I have given you pain, and I hope that you do not think very meanly of me.'

Lord St Simon had by no means relaxed his rigid attitude, but had listened with a frowning brow and a compressed lip to this long narrative.

'Excuse me,' he said, 'but it is not my custom to discuss my most intimate personal affairs in this public manner.'

'Then you won't forgive me? You won't shake hands before I go?'

'Oh, certainly, if it would give you any pleasure.' He put out his hand and coldly grasped that which she extended to him.

'I had hoped,' suggested Holmes, 'that you would have joined us in a friendly supper.'

'I think that there you ask a little too much,' responded his lordship. 'I may be forced to acquiesce in these recent developments, but I can hardly be expected to make merry over them. I think that with your permission I will now wish you all a very good-night.' He included us all in a sweeping bow and stalked out of the room.

'Then I trust that you at least will honour me with your company,' said Sherlock Holmes. 'It is always a joy to meet an American, Mr Moulton, for I am one of those who believe that the folly of a monarch and the blundering of a minister in far-gone years will not prevent our children from being someday citizens of the same worldwide country under a flag which shall be a quartering of the Union Jack with the Stars and Stripes.'

'The case has been an interesting one,' remarked Holmes, when our visitors had left us, 'because it serves to show very clearly how simple the explanation may be of an affair which at first sight seems to be almost inexplicable. Nothing could be more natural than the sequence of events as narrated by this lady, and nothing stranger than the result when viewed, for instance, by Mr Lestrade of Scotland Yard.'

'You were not yourself at fault at all, then?'

'From the first, two facts were very obvious to me, the one that the lady had been quite willing to undergo the wedding ceremony, the other that she had repented of it within a few minutes of returning home. Obviously something had occurred during the morning, then, to cause her to change her mind. What could that something be? She could not have spoken to anyone when she was out, for she had been in the company of the bridegroom. Had she seen someone, then? If she had, it must be someone from America because she had spent so short a time in this country that she could hardly have allowed anyone to acquire so deep an influence over her that the mere sight of him would induce her to change her plans so completely. You see we have already arrived, by a process of exclusion, at the idea that she might have seen an American. Then who could this American be, and why should he possess so much influence over her? It might be a lover; it might be a husband. Her young womanhood had, I knew, been spent in rough scenes and under strange conditions. So far I had got before I ever heard Lord St Simon's narrative. When he told us of a man in a pew, of the change in the bride's manner, of so transparent a device for obtaining a note as the dropping of a bouquet, of her resort to her confidential maid, and of her very significant allusion to claim-jumping – which in miners' parlance means taking possession of that which another person has a prior claim to – the whole situation became absolutely clear. She had gone off with a man, and the man was either a lover or was a previous husband – the chances being in favour of the latter.'

'And how in the world did you find them?'

'It might have been difficult, but friend Lestrade held information in his hands the value of which he did not himself know. The initials were, of course, of the highest importance, but more valuable still was it to know that within a week he had settled his bill at one of the most select London hotels.'

'How did you deduce the select?'

'By the select prices. Eight shillings for a bed and eightpence for a glass of sherry pointed to one of the most expensive hotels. There are not many in London which charge at that rate. In the second one which I visited, in Northumberland Avenue, I learned by an inspection of the book that Francis H. Moulton, an American gentleman, had left only the day before, and on looking over the entries against him, I came upon the very items which I had seen in the duplicate bill. His letters were to be forwarded to 226 Gordon Square, so thither I travelled, and being fortunate enough to find the loving couple at home, I ventured to give them some paternal advice and to point out to them that it would be better in every way that they should make their position a little clearer both to the general public and to Lord St Simon in particular. I invited them to meet him here, and, as you see, I made him keep the appointment.'

'But with no very good result,' I remarked. 'His conduct was certainly not very gracious.'

'Ah, Watson,' said Holmes, smiling, 'perhaps you would not be very gracious either, if, after all the trouble of wooing and wedding, you found yourself deprived in an instant of wife and of fortune. I think that we may judge Lord St Simon very mercifully and thank our stars that we are never likely to find ourselves in the same position. Draw your chair up and hand me my violin, for the only problem we have still to solve is how to while away these bleak autumnal evenings.'

BRETT HARTE

Francis Brett Harte (1836–1902) was an American author who was born in Albany, New York. He went to California in 1854, and became a compositor in San Francisco. Sketches of his experiences among the miners attracted much attention. He was secretary of the US Mint in San Francisco (1864–70) and during this period wrote some of his most famous poems, among them 'John Burns of Gettysburg' and 'The Society upon the Stanislau'. In 1868 he founded and edited the *Overland Monthly,* to which he contributed, among other short stories, *The Luck of Roaring Camp* and *The Outcasts of Poker Flat*. He was American consul in Krefeld (1878–80) and in Glasgow (1880–5) and then lived in London until his death.

The Stolen Cigar-Case

I found Hemlock Jones in the old Brook Street lodgings, musing before the fire. With the freedom of an old friend I at once threw myself in my old familiar attitude at his feet, and gently caressed his boot. I was induced to do this for two reasons: one that it enabled me to get a good look at his bent, concentrated face, and the other that it seemed to indicate my reverence for his superhuman insight. So absorbed was he, even then, in tracking some mysterious clue, that he did not seem to notice me. But therein I was wrong – as I always was in my attempt to understand that powerful intellect.

'It is raining,' he said, without lifting his head.

'You have been out then?' I said quickly.

'No. But I see that your umbrella is wet, and that your overcoat, which you threw off on entering, has drops of water on it.'

I sat aghast at his penetration. After a pause he said carelessly, as if dismissing the subject, 'Besides, I hear the rain on the window. Listen.'

I listened. I could scarcely credit my ears, but there was the soft pattering of drops on the pane. It was evident, there was no deceiving this man!

'Have you been busy lately?' I asked, changing the subject. 'What new problem – given up by Scotland Yard as inscrutable – has occupied that gigantic intellect?'

He drew back his foot slightly, and seemed to hesitate ere he returned it to its original position. Then he answered wearily: 'Mere trifles – nothing to speak of. The Prince Kopoli has been here to get my advice regarding the disappearance of certain rubies from the Kremlin; the Rajah of Pootibad, after vainly beheading his entire bodyguard, has been obliged to seek my assistance to recover a jewelled sword. The Grand Duchess of Pretzel-Brauntswig is desirous of discovering where her husband was on the night of the 14th of February, and last night' – he lowered his voice slightly – 'a lodger in this very house, meeting me on the stairs, wanted to know why they don't answer his bell.'

I could not help smiling – until I saw a frown gathering on his inscrutable forehead.

'Pray to remember,' he said coldly, 'that it was through such an apparently trivial question that I found out why Paul Ferroll killed his wife!'

I became dumb at once. He paused for a moment, and then suddenly changing back to his usual pitiless, analytical style, he said: 'When I say these are trifles – they are so in comparison to an affair that is now before me. A crime has been committed, and, singularly enough, against myself. You start,' he said; 'you wonder who would have dared to attempt it! So did I; nevertheless, it has been done. *I* have been *robbed*!'

'*You* robbed – you, Hemlock Jones, the Terror of Peculators!'

I gasped in amazement, rising and gripping the table as I faced him.

'Yes; listen. I would confess it to no other. But you who have followed my career; who know my methods; you, for whom I have partly lifted the veil that conceals my plans from ordinary humanity; you, who have for years rapturously accepted my confidences, passionately admired my inductions and inferences, placed yourself at my beck and call, become my slave, grovelled at my feet, given up your practice except those few unremunerative and rapidly decreasing patients to whom, in moments of abstraction over my problems, you have administered strychnine for quinine and arsenic for Epsom salts; you, who have sacrificed everything and everybody to me – *you* I make my confidant!'

I rose and embraced him warmly, yet he was already so engrossed in thought that at the same moment he mechanically placed his hand upon his watch chain as if to consult the time. 'Sit down,' he said; 'have a cigar?'

'I have given up cigar smoking,' I said.

'Why?' he asked.

I hesitated, and perhaps coloured. I had really given it up because, with my diminished practice, it was too expensive. I could only afford a pipe. 'I prefer a pipe,' I said laughingly. 'But tell me of this robbery. What have you lost?'

He rose, and, planting himself before the fire with his hands under his coat tails, looked down upon me reflectively for a moment. 'Do you remember the cigar-case presented to me by the Turkish ambassador for discovering the missing favourite of the Grand Vizier in the fifth chorus girl at the Hilarity Theatre? It was that one. It was encrusted with diamonds. I mean the cigar-case.'

'And the largest one had been supplanted by paste,' I said.

'Ah,' he said with a reflective smile, 'you know that.'

'You told me yourself. I remember considering it a proof of

your extraordinary perception. But, by Jove, you don't mean to say you have lost it.'

He was silent for a moment. 'No; it has been stolen, it is true, but I shall still find it. And by myself alone! In your profession, my dear fellow, when a member is severely ill he does not prescribe for himself, but calls in a brother doctor. Therein we differ. I shall take this matter into my own hands.'

'And where could you find better?' I said enthusiastically. 'I should say the cigar-case is as good as recovered already.'

'I shall remind you of that again,' he said lightly. 'And now, to show you my confidence in your judgement, in spite of my determination to pursue this alone, I am willing to listen to any suggestions from you.'

He drew a memorandum book from his pocket, and, with a grave smile, took up his pencil.

I could scarcely believe my reason. He, the great Hemlock Jones! accepting suggestions from a humble individual like myself! I kissed his hand reverently and began in a joyous tone: 'First I should advertise offering a reward; I should give the same intimation in handbills, distributed at the pubs and the pastry-cooks. I should next visit the different pawnbrokers; I should give notice at the police station. I should examine the servants. I should thoroughly search the house and my own pockets. I speak relatively,' I added with a laugh, 'of course, I mean *your* own.'

He gravely made an entry of these details.

'Perhaps,' I added, 'you have already done this?'

'Perhaps,' he returned enigmatically. 'Now, my dear friend,' he continued, putting the notebook in his pocket, and rising – 'would you excuse me for a few moments? Make yourself perfectly at home until I return; there may be some things,' he added with a sweep of his hand towards his heterogeneously filled shelves, 'that may interest you and while away the time. There are pipes and tobacco in that corner and whisky on the table.' And nodding to me with the same inscrutable face, he left the room. I was too well accustomed to his methods to think much of his unceremonious withdrawal, and made no doubt he was off to investigate some clue which had suddenly occurred to his active intelligence.

Left to myself, I cast a cursory glance over his shelves. There were a number of small glass jars, containing earthy substances, labelled 'Pavement and road sweepings', from the principal thoroughfares and suburbs of London, with the sub-directions 'for identifying foot tracks'. There were several other jars, labelled 'Fluff from omnibus and road-car seats', 'Coconut fibre and rope strands from mattings in public places', 'Cigarette stumps and match ends from floor of Palace Theatre. Row A, 1 to 50'. Everywhere were evidences of this wonderful man's system and perspicacity.

I was thus engaged when I heard the slight creaking of a door, and I looked up as a stranger entered. He was a rough-looking man, with a shabby overcoat, a still more disreputable muffler round his throat, and a cap on his head. Considerably annoyed at his intrusion I turned upon him rather sharply, when, with a mumbled, growling apology for mistaking the room, he shuffled out again and closed the door. I followed him quickly to the landing and saw that he disappeared down the stairs.

With my mind full of the robbery, the incident made a singular impression on me. I knew my friend's habits of hasty absences from his room in his moments of deep inspiration; it was only too probable that with his powerful intellect and magnificent perceptive genius concentrated on one subject, he should be careless of his own belongings, and, no doubt, even forget to take the ordinary precaution of locking up his drawers. I tried one or two and found that I was right – although for some reason I was unable to open one to its fullest extent. The handles were sticky, as if someone had opened them with dirty fingers. Knowing Hemlock's fastidious cleanliness, I resolved to inform him of this circumstance, but I forgot it, alas! until – but I am anticipating my story.

His absence was strangely prolonged. I at last seated myself by the fire, and lulled by warmth and the patter of the rain on the window, I fell asleep. I may have dreamt, for during my sleep I had a vague semi-consciousness of hands being softly pressed on my pockets – no doubt induced by the story of the robbery. When I came fully to my senses, I found Hemlock Jones sitting on the other side of the hearth, his deeply concentrated gaze fixed on the fire.

'I found you so comfortably asleep that I could not bear to waken you,' he said with a smile.

I rubbed my eyes. 'And what news.' I asked. 'How have you succeeded?'

'Better than I expected,' he said, 'and I think,' he added, tapping his notebook – 'I owe much to *you*.'

Deeply gratified, I awaited more. But in vain. I ought to have remembered that in his moods Hemlock Jones was reticence itself. I told him simply of the strange intrusion, but he only laughed.

Later, when I rose to go, he looked at me playfully. 'If you were a married man,' he said, 'I would advise you not to go home until you had brushed your sleeve. There are a few short, brown sealskin hairs on the inner side of the forearm – just where they would have adhered if your arm had encircled a sealskin *sacque* with some pressure!'

'For once you are at fault,' I said triumphantly; 'the hair is my own as you will perceive; I have just had it cut at the hairdressers, and no doubt this arm projected beyond the apron.'

He frowned slightly, yet nevertheless, on my turning to go, he embraced me warmly – a rare exhibition in that man of ice. He even helped me on with my overcoat and pulled out and smoothed down the flaps of my pockets. He was particular, too, in fitting my arm in my overcoat sleeve, shaking the sleeve down from the armhole to the cuff with his deft fingers. 'Come again soon!' he said, clapping me on the back.

'At any and all times,' I said enthusiastically. 'I only ask ten minutes twice a day to eat a crust at my office and four hours' sleep at night, and the rest of my time is devoted to you always – as you know.'

'It is, indeed,' he said, with his impenetrable smile.

Nevertheless I did not find him at home when I next called. One afternoon, when nearing my own home, I met him in one of his favourite disguises – a long, blue, swallow-tailed coat, striped cotton trousers, large turn-over collar, blacked face and white hat, carrying a tambourine. Of course to others the disguise was perfect, although it was known to myself, and I passed him – according to an old understanding between us – without the slightest recognition, trusting to a later explanation. At another time, as I was making a professional visit to the wife of a publican in the East End, I saw him in the disguise of a broken-down artisan looking into the window of an adjacent pawnshop. I was delighted to see that he was evidently following my suggestions, and in my joy I ventured to tip him a wink; it was abstractedly returned.

Two days later I received a note appointing a meeting at his lodgings that night. That meeting, alas! was the one memorable occurrence of my life, and the last meeting I ever had with Hemlock Jones! I will try to set it down calmly, though my pulses still throb with the recollection of it.

I found him standing before the fire with that look upon his face which I had seen only once or twice in our acquaintance – a look which I may call an absolute concatenation of inductive and deductive ratiocination – from which all that was human, tender or sympathetic was absolutely discharged. He was simply an icy, algebraic symbol! Indeed his whole being was concentrated to such an extent that his clothes fitted loosely, and his head was absolutely so much reduced in size by his mental compression that his hat tipped back from his forehead and literally hung on his massive ears.

After I had entered, he locked the doors, fastened the windows, and even placed a chair before the chimney. As I watched those significant precautions with absorbing interest, he suddenly drew a revolver and, presenting it to my temple, said in low icy tones: 'Hand over that cigar-case!'

Even in my bewilderment, my reply was truthful, spontaneous, and involuntary. 'I haven't got it,' I said.

He smiled bitterly, and threw down his revolver. 'I expected that reply! Then let me now confront you with something more awful, more deadly, more relentless and convincing than that mere lethal weapon – the damning inductive and deductive proofs of your guilt!' He drew from his pocket a roll of paper and a notebook.

'But surely,' I gasped, 'you are joking! You could not for a moment believe – '

'Silence!' he roared. 'Sit down!'

I obeyed.

'You have condemned yourself,' he went on pitilessly. 'Condemned yourself on my processes – processes familiar to you, applauded by you, accepted by you for years! We will go back to the time when you first saw the cigar-case. Your expressions,' he said in cold, deliberate tones, consulting his paper, 'were: "How beautiful! I wish it were mine." This was your first step in crime – and my first indication. From "I *wish* it were mine" to "I *will* have it mine", and the mere detail, "How *can* I make it mine?", the advance was obvious. Silence! But as in my methods, it was necessary that there should be an overwhelming inducement to the crime, that unholy admiration of yours for the mere trinket itself was not enough. You are a smoker of cigars.'

'But,' I burst out passionately, 'I told you I had given up smoking cigars.'

'Fool!' he said coldly, 'that is the *second* time you have committed yourself. Of course, you *told* me! What more natural than for you to blazon forth that prepared and unsolicited statement to *prevent* accusation. Yet, as I said before, even that wretched attempt to cover up your tracks was not enough. I still had to find that overwhelming, impelling motive necessary to affect a man like you. That motive I found in *passion*, the strongest of all impulses – love, I suppose you would call it,' he added bitterly; 'that night you called, you had brought the damning proof of it in your sleeve.'

'But – ' I almost screamed.

'Silence,' he thundered. 'I know what you would say. You would say that even if you had embraced some young person in a sealskin sacque what had that to do with the robbery. Let me tell you then that that sealskin sacque represented the quality and character of your fatal entanglement! If you are at all conversant with light sporting literature you would know that a sealskin sacque indicates a love induced by sordid mercenary interests. You bartered your honour for it – that stolen cigar-case was the purchaser of the sealskin sacque! Without money, with a decreasing practice, it was the only way you could ensure your passion being returned by that young person, whom, for your sake, I have not even pursued. Silence! Having thoroughly established your motive, I now proceed to the commission of the crime itself. Ordinary people would have begun with that – with an attempt to discover the whereabouts of the missing object. These are not my methods.'

So overpowering was his penetration, that although I knew myself innocent, I licked my lips with avidity to hear the further details of this lucid exposition of my crime.

'You committed that theft the night I showed you the cigar-case and after I had carelessly thrown it in that drawer. You were sitting in that chair, and I had risen to take something from that shelf. In that instant you secured your booty without rising. Silence! Do you remember when I helped you on with your overcoat the other night? I was particular about fitting your arm in. While doing so I measured your arm with a spring tape measure from the shoulder to the cuff. A later visit to your tailor confirmed that measurement. It proved to be *the exact distance between your chair and that drawer*!'

I sat stunned.

'The rest are mere corroborative details! You were again tampering with the drawer when I discovered you doing so. Do not start! The stranger that blundered into the room with the muffler on – was myself. More, I had placed a little soap on the drawer handles when I purposely left you alone. The soap was on your hand when I shook it at parting. I softly felt your pockets when you were asleep for further developments. I embraced you when you left – that I might feel if you had the cigar-case, or any other articles, hidden on your body. This confirmed me in the belief that you had already disposed of it in the manner and for the purpose I have shown you. As I still believed you capable of remorse and confession, I allowed you to see I was on your track twice, once in the garb of an itinerant negro minstrel, and the second time as a workman looking in the window of the pawnshop where you pledged your booty.'

'But,' I burst out, 'if you had asked the pawnbroker you would have seen how unjust –'

'Fool!' he hissed; 'that was one of *your* suggestions to search the pawnshops. Do you suppose I followed any of your suggestions – the suggestions of the thief? On the contrary, they told me what to avoid.'

'And I suppose,' I said bitterly, 'you have not even searched your drawer.'

'No,' he said calmly.

I was for the first time really vexed. I went to the nearest drawer and pulled it out sharply. It stuck as it had before, leaving a part of the drawer unopened. By working it, however,

I discovered that it was impeded by some obstacle that had slipped to the upper part of the drawer and held it firmly fast. Inserting my hand, I pulled out the impeding object. It was the missing cigar-case. I turned to him with a cry of joy.

But I was appalled at his expression. A look of contempt was now added to his acute, penetrating gaze. 'I have been mistaken,' he said slowly. 'I had not allowed for your weakness and cowardice. I thought too highly of you even in your guilt; but I see now why you tampered with that drawer the other night. By some incredible means – possibly another theft – you took the cigar-case out of pawn, and like a whipped hound restored it to me in this feeble, clumsy fashion. You thought to deceive me, Hemlock Jones; more, you thought to destroy my infallibility. Go! I give you your liberty. I shall not summon the three policemen who wait in the adjoining room – but, out of my sight for ever!'

As I stood once more dazed and petrified, he took me firmly by the ear and led me into the hall, closing the door behind him. This reopened presently wide enough to permit him to thrust out my hat, overcoat, umbrella and overshoes, and then closed against me for ever!

I never saw him again. I am bound to say, however, that thereafter my business increased – I recovered much of my old practice – and a few of my patients recovered also. I became rich. I had a brougham and a house in the West End. But I often wondered, pondering on that wonderful man's penetration and insight, if, in some lapse of consciousness, I had not really stolen his cigar-case!

CHARLES DICKENS

Charles Dickens (1812–70) was perhaps the greatest novelist of the nineteenth century. All his novels are still in print and they present a rich canvas of life and behaviour at all levels of contemporary society. Many of his works, such as *Oliver Twist*, *Great Expectations*, *David Copperfield*, *A Tale of Two Cities* and *A Christmas Carol*, have been filmed, televised and presented as both straight plays and musicals, revealing the power and the timelessness of his writing.

The Trial for Murder

I have always noticed a prevalent want of courage, even among persons of superior intelligence and culture, as to imparting their own psychological experiences when those have been of a strange sort. Almost all men are afraid that what they could relate in such wise would find no parallel or response in a listener's internal life, and might be suspected or laughed at. A truthful traveller, who should have seen some extraordinary creature in the likeness of a sea-serpent, would have no fear of mentioning it; but the same traveller, having had some singular presentiment, impulse, vagary of thought, vision (so-called), dream, or other remarkable mental impression, would hesitate considerably before he would own to it. To this reticence I attribute much of the obscurity in which such subjects are involved. We do not habitually communicate our experiences of these subjective things as we do our experiences of objective creation. The consequence is that the general stock of experience in this regard appears exceptional, and really is so, in respect of being miserably imperfect.

In what I am going to relate, I have no intention of setting up, opposing or supporting any theory whatever. I know the history of the Bookseller of Berlin, I have studied the case of the wife of a late Astronomer-Royal as related by Sir David Brewster, and I have followed the minutest details of a much more remarkable case of Spectral Illusion occurring within my private circle of friends. It may be necessary to state as to this last, that the sufferer (a lady) was in no degree, however distant, related to me. A mistaken assumption on that head might suggest an explanation of a part of my own case – but only a part – which would be wholly without foundation. It cannot be referred to my inheritance of any developed peculiarity, nor had I ever before any at all similar experience, nor have I ever had any at all similar experience since.

It does not signify how many years ago, or how few, a certain murder was committed in England, which attracted great attention. We hear more than enough of murderers as they rise in succession to their atrocious eminence, and I would bury the memory of this particular brute, if I could, as his body was buried in Newgate Jail. I purposely abstain from giving any direct clue to the criminal's individuality.

When the murder was first discovered, no suspicion fell – or I ought rather to say, for I cannot be too precise in my facts, it was nowhere publicly hinted that any suspicion fell – on the man who was afterwards brought to trial. As no reference was at that time made to him in the newspapers, it is obviously impossible that any description of him can at that time have been given in the newspapers. It is essential that this fact be remembered.

Unfolding at breakfast my morning paper, containing the account of that first discovery, I found it to be deeply interesting, and I read it with close attention. I read it twice, if not three times. The discovery had been made in a bedroom, and, when I laid down the paper, I was aware of a flash – rush – flow – I do not know what to call it – no word I can find is satisfactorily descriptive – in which I seemed to see that bedroom passing through my room, like a picture impossibly painted on a running river. Though almost instantaneous in its passing, it was perfectly clear; so clear that I distinctly, and with a sense of relief, observed the absence of the dead body from the bed.

It was in no romantic place that I had this curious sensation, but in chambers in Piccadilly, very near to the corner of St James's Street. It was entirely new to me. I was in my easy-chair at the moment, and the sensation was accompanied by a peculiar shiver which started the chair from its position. (But it is to be noted that the chair ran easily on casters.) I went to one of the windows (there are two in the room, and the room is on the second floor) to refresh my eyes with the moving objects down in Piccadilly. It was a bright autumn morning, and the street was sparkling and cheerful. The wind was high. As I looked out, it brought down from the Park a quantity of fallen leaves, which a gust took and whirled into a spiral pillar. As the pillar fell and the leaves dispersed, I saw two men on the opposite side of the way, going from west to east. They were one behind the other. The foremost man often looked back over his shoulder. The second man followed him, at a distance of some thirty paces, with his right hand menacingly raised. First, the singularity and steadiness of this threatening gesture in so public a thoroughfare attracted my attention; and next, the more remarkable circumstance that nobody heeded it. Both men threaded their way among the other passengers with a smoothness hardly consistent even with the action of walking on a pavement; and no single creature, that I could see, gave them place, touched them, or looked after them. In passing before my windows, they both stared up at me. I saw their two faces very distinctly, and I knew that I could recognise them anywhere. Not that I had consciously noticed anything very remarkable in either face, except that the man who went first had an unusually lowering appearance, and that the face of the man who followed him was of the colour of impure wax.

I am a bachelor, and my valet and his wife constitute my whole establishment. My occupation is in a certain Branch Bank, and I wish that my duties as head of a department were as light as they are popularly supposed to be. They kept me in town that autumn, when I stood in need of change. I was not ill, but I was not well. My reader is to make the most that can be reasonably made of my feeling jaded, having a depressing sense upon me of a monotonous life, and being 'slightly dyspeptic'. I am assured by my renowned doctor that my real state of health at that time justifies no stronger description, and I quote his own from his written answer to my request for it.

As the circumstances of the murder, gradually unravelling, took stronger and stronger possession of the public mind, I kept them away from mine by knowing as little about them as was possible in the midst of the universal excitement. But I knew that a verdict of Wilful Murder had been found against the suspected murderer, and that he had been committed to Newgate for trial. I also knew that his trial had been postponed over one Sessions of the Central Criminal Court, on the ground of general prejudice and want of time for the preparation of the defence. I may further have known, but I believe I did not, when, or about when, the Sessions to which his trial stood postponed would come on.

My sitting-room, bedroom and dressing-room are all on one floor. With the last there is no communication but through the bedroom. True, there is a door in it, once communicating with the staircase; but a part of the fitting of my bath has been – and had then been for some years – fixed across it. At the same period, and as a part of the same arrangement, the door had been nailed up and canvassed over.

I was standing in my bedroom late one night, giving some directions to my servant before he went to bed. My face was towards the only available door of communication with the dressing-room, and it was closed. My servant's back was towards that door. While I was speaking to him, I saw it open, and a man look in, who very earnestly and mysteriously beckoned to me. That man was the man who had gone second of the two along Piccadilly, and whose face was the colour of impure wax.

The figure, having beckoned, drew back, and closed the door. With no longer pause than was made by my crossing the bedroom, I opened the dressing-room door, and looked in. I had a lighted candle already in my hand. I felt no inward expectation of seeing the figure in the dressing-room, and I did not see it there.

Conscious that my servant stood amazed, I turned round to him, and said: 'Derrick, could you believe that in my cool senses I fancied I saw a – ' As I there laid my hand upon his breast, with a sudden start he trembled violently, and said, 'Oh, Lord, yes, sir! A dead man beckoning!'

Now I do not believe that this John Derrick, my trusty and attached servant for more than twenty years, had any impression whatever of having seen any such figure, until I touched him. The change in him was so startling, when I touched him, that I fully believe he derived his impression in some occult manner from me at that instant.

I bade John Derrick bring some brandy, and I gave him a dram, and was glad to take one myself. Of what had preceded that night's phenomenon, I told him not a single word. Reflecting on it, I was absolutely certain that I had never seen that face before, except on the one occasion in Piccadilly. Comparing its expression when beckoning at the door with its expression when it had stared up at me as I stood at my window, I came to the conclusion that on the first occasion it had sought to fasten itself upon my memory, and that on the second occasion it had made sure of being immediately remembered.

I was not very comfortable that night, though I felt a certainty, difficult to explain, that the figure would not return. At daylight I fell into a heavy sleep, from which I was awakened by John Derrick's coming to my bedside with a paper in his hand.

This paper, it appeared, had been the subject of an altercation at the door between its bearer and my servant. It was a summons to me to serve upon a jury at the forthcoming Sessions of the Central Criminal Court at the Old Bailey. I had never before been summoned on such a jury, as John Derrick well knew. He believed – I am not certain at this hour whether with reason or otherwise – that that class of jurors were customarily chosen on a lower qualification than mine, and he had at first refused to accept the summons. The man who served it had taken the matter very coolly. He had said that my attendance or non-attendance was nothing to him; there the summons was; and I should deal with it at my own peril, and not at his.

For a day or two I was undecided whether to respond to this call or take no notice of it. I was not conscious of the slightest mysterious bias, influence or attraction one way or another. Of that I am strictly sure as of every other statement that I make here. Ultimately I decided, as a break in the monotony of my life, that I would go.

The appointed morning was a raw morning in the month of November. There was a dense brown fog in Piccadilly, and it became positively black and in the last degree oppressive east of Temple Bar. I found the passages and staircases of the court-house flaringly lighted with gas, and the court itself similarly illuminated. I *think* that, until I was conducted by officers into the Old Court and saw its crowded state, I did not know that the murderer was to be tried that day. I *think* that, until I was so helped into the Old Court with considerable difficulty, I did not know into which of the two courts sitting my summons would take me. But this must not be received as a positive assertion, for I am not completely satisfied in my mind on either point.

I took my seat in the place appropriated to jurors in waiting, and I looked about the court as well as I could through the cloud of fog and breath that was heavy in it. I noticed the black vapour hanging like a murky curtain outside the great windows, and I noticed the stifled sound of wheels on the straw or tan that was littered in the street; also, the hum of the people gathered there, which a shrill whistle, or a louder song or hail than the rest, occasionally pierced. Soon afterwards the judges, two in number, entered, and took their seats. The buzz in the court was awfully hushed. The direction was given to put the murderer to the bar. He appeared there. And in that same instant I recognised in him the first of the two men who had gone down Piccadilly.

If my name had been called then, I doubt if I could have answered to it audibly. But it was called about sixth or eighth in the panel, and I was by the time able to say 'Here!' Now observe. As I stepped into the box, the prisoner, who had been looking on attentively, but with no sign of concern, became violently agitated, and beckoned to his attorney. The prisoner's wish to challenge me was so manifest that it occasioned a pause, during which the attorney with his hand upon the dock whispered with his client and shook his head. I afterwards had it from the gentleman that the prisoner's first affrighted words to him were, '*At all hazards, challenge that man!*' But that, as he would give no reason for it, and admitted that he had not even known my name until he heard it called and I appeared, it was not done.

Both on the ground already explained, that I wish to avoid reviving the unwholesome memory of that murderer, and also because a detailed account of his long trial is by no means indispensable to my narrative, I shall confine myself closely to such incidents in the ten days and nights during which we, the jury, were kept together, as directly bear on my own curious personal experience. It is in that, and not in the murderer, that I seek to interest my reader. It is to that, and not to a page of the Newgate Calendar, that I beg attention.

I was chosen foreman of the jury. On the second morning of the trial, after evidence had been taken for two hours (I heard the church clocks strike), happening to cast my eyes over my brother jurymen, I found an inexplicable difficulty in counting them. I counted them several times, yet always with the same difficulty. In short, I made them one too many.

I touched the brother juryman whose place was next to me, and I whispered to him, 'Oblige me by counting us.' He looked surprised by the request, but turned his head and counted. 'Why,' said he suddenly, 'we are thirt – but no, it's not possible. No. We are twelve.'

According to my counting that day, we were always right in detail, but in the gross we were always one too many. There was no appearance – no figure – to account for it; but I had now an inward foreshadowing of the figure that was surely coming.

The jury were housed at the London Tavern. We all slept in one large room on separate tables, and we were constantly in the charge and under the eye of the officer sworn to hold us in safe keeping. I see no reason for suppressing the real name of that officer. He was intelligent, highly polite and obliging, and (I was glad to hear) much respected in the City. He had an agreeable presence, good eyes, enviable black whiskers and a fine sonorous voice. His name was Mr Harker.

When we turned into our twelve beds at night, Mr Harker's bed was drawn across the door. On the night of the second day, not being disposed to lie down, and seeing Mr Harker sitting on his bed, I went and sat beside him, and offered him a pinch of snuff. As Mr Harker's hand touched mine in taking it from my box, a peculiar shiver crossed him, and he said, 'Who is this?'

Following Mr Harker's eyes, and looking along the room, I saw again the figure I expected – the second of the two men who had gone down Piccadilly. I rose, and advanced a few steps; stopped, and looked round at Mr Harker. He was quite unconcerned, laughed, and said in a pleasant way, 'I thought for a moment we had a thirteenth juryman, without a bed. I see it is the moonlight.'

Making no revelation to Mr Harker, but inviting him to take a walk with me to the end of the room, I watched what the figure did. It stood for a few moments by the bedside of each of my eleven brother jurymen, close to the pillow. It always went to the right-hand side of the bed, and always passed out crossing the foot of the next bed. It seemed, from the action of the head, merely to look down pensively at each recumbent figure. It took no notice of me, or of my bed, which was the nearest to Mr Harker's. It seemed to go out where the moonlight came in, through a high window, as by an aerial flight of stairs.

Next morning at breakfast, it appeared that everybody present had dreamed of the murdered man last night, except myself and Mr Harker. I now felt as convinced that the second man who had gone down Piccadilly was the murdered man (so to speak), as if it had been borne into my comprehension by his immediate testimony. But even this took place, and in a manner for which I was not at all prepared.

On the fifth day of the trial, when the case for the prosecution was drawing to a close, a miniature of the murdered man, missing from his bedroom upon the discovery of the deed, and afterwards found in a hiding-place where the murderer had been seen digging, was put in evidence. Having been identified by the witness under examination, it was handed up to the bench, and thence handed down to be inspected by the jury. As an officer in a black gown was making his way with it across to me, the figure of the second man who had gone down Piccadilly impetuously started from the crowd, caught the miniature from the officer, and gave it to me with his own hands, at the same time saying, in a low and hollow tone – before I saw the miniature, which was in a locket – 'I was younger then, and my face was not then drained of blood.' It also came between me and the brother juryman to whom I would have given the miniature, and the brother juryman to whom he would have given it, and so passed it on through the whole of our number, and back into my possession. Not one of them, however, detected this.

At table, and generally when we were shut up together in Mr Harker's custody, we had from the first naturally discussed the day's proceedings a good deal. On that fifth day, the case for the prosecution being closed, and we having that side of the question in a completed shape before us, our discussion was more animated and serious. Among our number was a vestryman – the densest idiot I have ever seen at large – who met the plainest evidence with the most preposterous objections, and who was sided with by two flabby parochial parasites; all the three empanelled from a district so delivered over to fever that they ought to have been upon their own trial for five hundred murders. When these mischievous blockheads were at their loudest, which was towards midnight, while some of us were already preparing for bed, I again saw the murdered man. He stood grimly behind them, beckoning to me. On my going towards them, and striking into the conversation, he immediately retired. This was the beginning of a separate series of appearances, confined to that long room in which we were confined. Whenever a knot of my brother jurymen laid their heads together, I saw the head of the murdered man among theirs. Whenever their comparison of notes was going against him, he would solemnly and irresistibly beckon to me.

It will be borne in mind that down to the production of the miniature, on the fifth day of the trial, I had never seen the Appearance in court. Three changes occurred now that we entered on the case for the defence. Two of them I will mention together, first. The figure was now in court continually, and it never there addressed itself to me, but always to the person who was speaking at the time. For instance: the throat of the murdered man had been cut straight across. In the opening speech for the defence, it was suggested that the deceased might have cut his own throat. At that very moment, the figure, with its throat in the dreadful condition referred to (this it had concealed before), stood at the speaker's elbow, motioning across and across its windpipe, now with the right hand, now with the left, vigorously suggesting to the speaker himself the impossibility of such a wound having been self-inflicted by either hand. For another instance: a witness to character, a woman, deposed to the prisoner's being the most amiable of mankind. The figure at that instant stood on the floor before her, looking her full in the face, and pointing out the prisoner's evil countenance with an extended arm and an outstretched finger.

The third change now to be added impressed me strongly as the most marked and striking of all. I do not theorise upon it; I accurately state it, and there leave it. Although the Appearance was not itself perceived by those whom it addressed, its coming close to such persons was invariably attended by some trepidation or disturbance on their part. It seemed to me as if it were prevented by laws to which I was not amenable from fully revealing itself to others, and yet as if it could invisibly, dumbly and darkly overshadow their minds. When the leading counsel for the defence suggested that hypothesis of suicide, and the figure stood at the learned gentleman's elbow, frightfully sawing at its severed throat, it is undeniable that the counsel faltered in his speech, lost for a few seconds the thread of his ingenious discourse, wiped his forehead with his handkerchief, and turned extremely pale. When the witness to character was confronted by the Appearance, her eyes most certainly did follow the direction of its pointed finger, and rest in great hesitation and trouble over the prisoner's face. Two additional illustrations will suffice. On the eighth day of the trial, after the pause which was every day made early in the afternoon for a few minutes rest and refreshment, I came back into court with the rest of the jury some little time before the return of the judges. Standing up in the box and looking about me, I thought the figure was not there, until, chancing to raise my eyes to the gallery, I saw it bending forward, and leaning over a very decent woman, as if to assure itself whether the judges had resumed their seats or not. Immediately afterwards the woman screamed, fainted and was carried out. So with the venerable, sagacious and patient judge who conducted the trial. When the case was over, and he settled himself and his papers to sum up, the murdered man, entering by the judges' door, advanced to his Lordship's desk, and looked eagerly over his shoulder at the pages of his notes which he was turning. A change came over his Lordship's face; his hand stopped; the peculiar shiver, that I knew so well, passed over him; he faltered, 'Excuse me, gentlemen, for a few moments I am somewhat oppressed by the vitiated air,' and did not recover until he had drunk a glass of water.

Through all the monotony of six of those interminable ten days – the same judge and others on the bench, the same murderer in the dock, the same lawyers at the table, the same tones of question and answer rising to the roof of the court, the same scratching of the judge's pen, the same ushers going in and out, the same lights kindled at the same hour when there had been any natural light of day, the same foggy curtain outside the great windows when it was foggy, the same rain pattering and dripping when it was rainy, the same footmarks of turnkeys and prisoner day after day on the same sawdust, the same keys locking and unlocking the same heavy doors – through all the wearisome monotony which made me feel as if I had been foreman of the jury for a vast period of time, and Piccadilly had flourished coevally with Babylon, the murdered man never lost one trace of his distinctness in my eyes, nor was he at any moment less distinct than anybody else. I must not omit, as a matter of fact, that I never once saw the Appearance which I call by the name of the murdered man look at the murderer. Again and again I wondered, 'Why does he not?' But he never did.

Nor did he look at me, after the production of the miniature, until the last closing minutes of the trial arrived. We retired to consider, at seven minutes before ten at night. The idiotic vestryman and his two parochial parasites gave us so much trouble that we twice returned into court to beg to have certain extracts from the judge's notes reread. Nine of us had not the slightest doubt about those passages, neither, I believe, had anyone in the court; the dunderhead triumvirate, however, having no idea but obstruction, disputed them for that very reason. At length we prevailed, and finally the jury returned into court at ten minutes past twelve.

The murdered man at that time stood directly opposite the jury box, on the other side of the court. As I took my place, his eyes rested on me with great attention; he seemed satisfied, and slowly shook a great grey veil, which he carried on his arm for the first time, over his head and whole form. As I gave in our verdict, 'Guilty', the veil collapsed, all was gone, and his place was empty.

The murderer, being asked by the judge, according to usage, whether he had anything to say before sentence of death should be passed upon him, indistinctly muttered something which was described in the leading newspapers of the following day as 'a few rambling, incoherent, and half-audible words, in which he was understood to complain that he had not had a fair trial, because the foreman of the jury was prepossessed against him'. The remarkable declaration that he really made was this: 'My Lord, I knew I was a doomed man when the foreman of my jury came into the box. My Lord, I knew he would never let me off, because, before I was taken, he somehow got to my bedside in the night, woke me, and put a rope round my neck.'

EDGAR ALLAN POE

Edgar Poe was born in Boston in 1809 to travelling actors David Poe and Elizabeth Arnold Hopkins. His mother died in December 1811 and his father died or disappeared soon afterwards, leading to Edgar's being brought up by John Allan, a prosperous Virginian merchant. Five of his formative years were spent with the Allans in England. On their return to the States, Edgar attended the University of Virginia before enlisting as a private soldier. He published his first poems in 1827 but it was not until he was discharged from the army and won a literary prize for his tale 'MS Found in a Bottle' that he started to achieve fame as a short-story writer. He gained the position of editor at the *Southern Literary Messenger* and distinguished himself writing journalism, literary criticism, stories and poems. He had his greatest successes in 1845 when 'The Raven' and a new collection of his *Tales* were published to national acclaim. His wife Virginia, a cousin whom he had married when she was only thirteen, died early and this led to the depression and reliance on drink that have scarred his reputation and dominated the interpretation of his work. He himself died in mysterious circumstances in 1849 and the details of his biography remain controversial and disputed.

The Murders in the Rue Morgue

> What song the Syrens sang, or what name Achilles assumed when he hid himself among women, although puzzling questions, are not beyond *all* conjecture.
>
> SIR THOMAS BROWNE

The mental features discoursed of as the analytical are, in themselves, but little susceptible of analysis. We appreciate them only in their effects. We know of them, among other things, that they are always to their possessor, when inordinately possessed, a source of the liveliest enjoyment. As the strong man exults in his physical ability, delighting in such exercises as call his muscles into action, so glories the analyst in that moral activity which *disentangles*. He derives pleasure from even the most trivial occupations bringing his talent into play. He is fond of enigmas, of conundrums, of hieroglyphics; exhibiting in his solutions of each a degree of acumen which appears to the ordinary apprehension preternatural. His results, brought about by the very soul and essence of method, have, in truth, the whole air of intuition.

The faculty of resolution is possibly much invigorated by mathematical study, and especially by that highest branch of it which, unjustly, and merely on account of its retrograde operations, has been called, as if *par excellence*, analysis. Yet to calculate is not in itself to analyse. A chess-player, for example, does the one, without effort at the other. It follows that the game of chess, in its effects upon mental character, is greatly misunderstood. I am not now writing a treatise, but simply prefacing a somewhat peculiar narrative by observations very much at random; I will, therefore, take occasion to assert that the higher powers of the reflective intellect are more decidedly and more usefully tasked by the unostentatious game of draughts than by all the elaborate frivolity of chess. In this latter, where the pieces have different and bizarre motions, with various and variable values, what is only complex is mistaken (a not unusual error) for what is profound. The *attention* is here called powerfully into play. If it flag for an instant, an oversight is committed, resulting in injury or defeat. The possible moves being not only manifold, but involute, the chances of such oversights are multiplied; and in nine cases out of ten, it is the more concentrative rather than the more acute player who conquers. In draughts, on the contrary, where the moves are *unique* and have but little variation, the probabilities of inadvertence are diminished, and the mere attention being left comparatively unemployed, what advantages are obtained by either party are obtained by superior acumen. To be less abstract – Let us suppose a game of draughts where the pieces are reduced to four kings, and where, of course, no oversight is to be expected. It is obvious that here the victory can be decided (the players being at all equal) only by some *recherché* movement, the result of some strong exertion of the intellect. Deprived of ordinary resources, the analyst throws himself into the spirit of his opponent, identifies himself therewith, and not unfrequently sees thus, at a glance, the sole methods (sometimes indeed absurdly simple ones) by which he may seduce into error or hurry into miscalculation.

Whist has long been noted for its influence upon what is termed the calculating power; and men of the highest order of intellect have been known to take an apparently unaccountable delight in it, while eschewing chess as frivolous. Beyond doubt there is nothing of a similar nature so greatly tasking the faculty of analysis. The best chess-player in Christendom *may* be little more than the best player of chess; but proficiency in whist implies capacity for success in all these more important undertakings where mind struggles with mind. When I say proficiency, I mean that perfection in the game which includes a comprehension of *all* the sources whence legitimate advantage may be derived. These are not only manifold, but multiform, and lie frequently among recesses of thought altogether inaccessible to the ordinary understanding. To observe attentively is to remember distinctly; and, so far, the concentrative chess-player will do very well at whist; while the rules of Hoyle (themselves based upon the mere mechanism of the game) are sufficiently and generally comprehensible. Thus to have a retentive memory, and to proceed by 'the book', are points commonly regarded as the sum total of good playing. But it is in matters beyond the limits of mere rule that the skill of the analyst is evinced. He makes, in silence, a host of observations and inferences. So, perhaps, do his companions; and the difference in the extent of the information obtained lies not so much in the validity of the inference as in the quality of the observation. The necessary knowledge is that of *what* to observe. Our player confines himself not at all; nor, because the game is the object, does he reject deductions from things external to the game. He examines the countenance of his partner, comparing it carefully with that of each of his opponents. He considers the mode of assorting the cards in each hand, often counting trump by trump, and honour by honour, through the glances bestowed by their holders upon each. He notes every variation of face as the play progresses, gathering a fund of thought from the differences in the expression of certainty, of surprise, of triumph or chagrin. From the manner of gathering up a trick he judges whether the person taking it can make another in the suit. He recognises what is played through feint by the air with which it is thrown upon the table. A casual or inadvertent word; the accidental dropping or turning of a card, with the accompanying anxiety or carelessness in regard to its concealment; the counting of the tricks, with the order of their arrangement; embarrassment, hesitation, eagerness or trepidation – all afford, to his apparently intuitive perception, indications of the true state of affairs. The first two or three rounds having been played, he is in full possession of the contents of each hand, and thenceforward puts down his cards with as absolute a precision of purpose as if the rest of the party had turned outward the faces of their own.

The analytical power should not be confounded with simple ingenuity; for while the analyst is necessarily ingenious, the ingenious man is often remarkably incapable of analysis. The constructive or combining power, by which ingenuity is usually manifested, and to which the phrenologists (I believe erroneously) have assigned a separate organ, supposing it a primitive faculty, has been so frequently seen in those whose intellect bordered otherwise upon idiocy as to have attracted general observation among writers on morals. Between ingenuity and the analytic ability there exists a difference far greater, indeed, than that between the fancy and the imagination, but of a character very strictly analogous. It will be found, in fact, that the ingenious are always fanciful, and the *truly* imaginative never otherwise than analytic.

The narrative which follows will appear to the reader somewhat in the light of a commentary upon the propositions just advanced.

Residing in Paris during the spring and part of the summer of 18—, I there became acquainted with a Monsieur C. Auguste Dupin. This young gentleman was of an excellent – indeed of an illustrious family, but, by a variety of untoward events, had been reduced to such poverty that the energy of his character succumbed beneath it, and he ceased to bestir himself in the world, or to care for the retrieval of his fortunes. By courtesy of his creditors there still remained in his possession a small remnant of his patrimony; and, upon the income arising from this, he managed, by means of a rigorous economy, to procure the necessaries of life, without troubling himself about its superfluities. Books, indeed, were his sole luxuries, and in Paris these are easily obtained.

Our first meeting was at an obscure library in the Rue Montmartre, where the accident of our both being in search of the same very rare and very remarkable volume brought us into closer communion. We saw each other again and again. I was deeply interested in the little family history which he detailed to me with all that candour which a Frenchman indulges whenever mere self is the theme. I was astonished, too, at the vast extent of his reading; and, above all, I felt my soul enkindled within me by the wild fervour and the vivid freshness of his imagination. Seeking in Paris the objects I then sought, I felt that the society of such a man would be to me a treasure beyond price; and this feeling I frankly confided to him. It was at length arranged that we should live together during my stay in the city; and as my worldly circumstances were somewhat less embarrassed than his own, I was permitted to be at the expense of renting, and furnishing in a style which suited the rather fantastic gloom of our common temper, a time-eaten and grotesque mansion, long deserted through superstitions into which we did not enquire, and tottering to its fall in a retired and desolate portion of the Faubourg St Germain.

Had the routine of our life at this place been known to the world, we should have been regarded as madmen – although, perhaps, as madmen of a harmless nature. Our seclusion was perfect. We admitted no visitors. Indeed the locality of our retirement had been carefully kept a secret from my own former associates; and it had been many years since Dupin had ceased to know or be known in Paris. We existed within ourselves alone.

It was a freak of fancy in my friend (for what else shall I call it?) to be enamoured of the night for her own sake; and into this *bizarrerie*, as into all his others, I quietly fell, giving myself up to his wild whims with a perfect abandon. The sable divinity would not herself dwell with us always; but we could counterfeit her presence. At the first dawn of the morning we closed all the massy shutters of our old building; lighted a couple of tapers which, strongly perfumed, threw out only the ghastliest and feeblest of rays. By the aid of these we then busied our souls in dreams – reading, writing or conversing, until warned by the clock of the advent of the true Darkness. Then we sallied forth into the streets, arm in arm, continuing the topics of the day, or roaming far and wide until a late hour, seeking, amid the wild lights and shadows of the populous city, that infinity of mental excitement which quiet observation can afford.

At such times I could not help remarking and admiring (although from his rich ideality I had been prepared to expect it) a peculiar analytic ability in Dupin. He seemed, too, to take an eager delight in its exercise – if not exactly in its display – and did not hesitate to confess the pleasure thus derived. He boasted to me, with a low chuckling laugh, that most men, in respect to himself, wore windows in their bosoms, and was wont to follow up such assertions by direct and very startling proofs of his intimate knowledge of my own. His manner at these moments was frigid and abstract; his eyes were vacant in expression; while his voice, usually a rich tenor, rose into a treble which would have sounded petulantly but for the deliberateness and entire distinctness of the enunciation. Observing him in these moods, I often dwelt meditatively upon the old philosophy of the bi-part soul, and amused myself with the fancy of a double Dupin – the creative and the resolvent.

Let it not be supposed, from what I have just said, that I am detailing any mystery, or penning any romance. What I have described in the Frenchman was merely the result of an excited or perhaps of a diseased intelligence. But of the character of his remarks at the periods in question an example will best convey the idea.

We were strolling one night down a long dirty street in the

vicinity of the Palais Royal. Being both, apparently, occupied with thought, neither of us had spoken a syllable for fifteen minutes at least. All at once Dupin broke forth with these words – 'He is a very little fellow, that's true, and would do better for the Théâtre des Variétés.'

'There can be no doubt of that,' I replied unwittingly, and not at first observing (so much had I been absorbed in reflection) the extraordinary manner in which the speaker had chimed in with my meditations. In an instant afterwards I recollected myself, and my astonishment was profound.

'Dupin,' said I, gravely, 'this is beyond my comprehension. I do not hesitate to say that I am amazed, and can scarcely credit my senses. How was it possible you should know I was thinking of – ?' Here I paused, to ascertain beyond a doubt whether he really knew of whom I thought.

'Of Chantilly,' said he; 'why do you pause? You were remarking to yourself that his diminutive figure unfitted him for tragedy.'

This was precisely what had formed the subject of my reflections. Chantilly was a quondam cobbler of the Rue St Denis, who, becoming stage-mad, had attempted the role of Xerxes, in Crébillon's tragedy so called, and been notoriously pasquinaded for his pains.

'Tell me, for heaven's sake,' I exclaimed, 'the method – if method there is – by which you have been enabled to fathom my soul in this matter.' In fact I was even more startled than I would have been willing to express.

'It was the fruiterer,' replied my friend, 'who brought you to the conclusion that the mender of soles was not of sufficient height for Xerxes *et id genus omne*.'

'The fruiterer! – you astonish me – I know no fruiterer.'

'The man who ran up against you as we entered the street – it may have been fifteen minutes ago.'

I now remembered that, in fact, a fruiterer, carrying upon his head a large basket of apples, had nearly thrown me down, by accident, as we passed from the Rue C— into the thoroughfare where we stood; but what this had to do with Chantilly I could not possibly understand.

There was not a particle of *charlatanerie* about Dupin.

'I will explain,' he said, 'and that you may comprehend all clearly, we will first retrace the course of your meditations, from the moment in which I spoke to you until that of the rencontre with the fruiterer in question. The larger links of the chain run thus – Chantilly, Orion, Dr Nichols, Epicurus, Stereotomy, the street stones, the fruiterer.'

There are few persons who have not, at some period of their lives, amused themselves in retracing the steps by which particular conclusions of their own minds have been attained. The occupation is often full of interest; and he who attempts it for the first time is astonished by the apparently illimitable distance and incoherence between the starting-point and the goal. What, then, must have been my amazement when I heard the Frenchman speak what he had just spoken, and when I could not help acknowledging that he had spoken the truth!

He continued: 'We had been talking of horses, if I remember aright, just before leaving the Rue C—. This was the last subject we discussed. As we crossed into the street, a fruiterer, with a large basket upon his head, brushing quickly past us, thrust you upon a pile of paving-stones collected at a spot where the causeway is undergoing repair. You stepped upon one of the loose fragments, slipped, slightly strained your ankle, appeared vexed or sulky, muttered a few words, turned to look at the pile, and then proceeded in silence. I was not particularly attentive to what you did; but observation has become with me, of late, a species of necessity.

'You kept your eyes upon the ground – glancing, with a petulant expression, at the holes and ruts in the pavement (so that I saw you were still thinking of the stones), until we reached the little alley called Lamartine, which has been paved, by way of experiment, with the overlapping and riveted blocks. Here your countenance brightened up, and, perceiving your lips move, I could not doubt that you murmured the word "stereotomy", a term very affectedly applied to this species of pavement. I knew that you could not say to yourself "stereotomy" without being brought to think of atomics, and thus of the theories of Epicurus; and since, when we discussed this subject not very long ago, I mentioned to you how singularly, yet with how little notice, the vague guesses of that noble Greek had met with confirmation in the late nebular cosmogony, I felt that you could not avoid casting your eyes upward to the great nebula in Orion, and I certainly expected that you would do so. You did look up; and I was now assured that I had correctly followed your steps. But in that bitter tirade upon Chantilly, which appeared in yesterday's *Musée*, the satirist, making some disgraceful allusions to the cobbler's change of name upon assuming the buskin, quoted a Latin line about which we have often conversed. I mean the line:

> Perdidit antiquum litera prima sonum.
> [The first letter has lost its original sound.]

I had told you that this was in reference to Orion, formerly written Urion; and, from certain pungencies connected with this explanation, I was aware that you could not have forgotten it. It was clear, therefore, that you would not fail to combine the two ideas of Orion and Chantilly. That you did combine them I saw by the character of the smile which passed over your lips. You thought of the poor cobbler's immolation. So far, you had been stooping in your gait; but now I saw you draw yourself up to your full height. I was then sure that you reflected upon the diminutive figure of Chantilly. At this point I interrupted your meditations to remark that as, in fact, he *was* a very little fellow, that Chantilly, he would do better at the Théâtre des Variétés.'

Not long after this, we were looking over an evening edition of the *Gazette des Tribunaux* when the following paragraphs arrested our attention:

EXTRAORDINARY MURDERS

This morning, about three o'clock, the inhabitants of the Quartier St Roch were aroused from sleep by a succession of terrific shrieks, issuing, apparently, from the fourth storey of a house in the Rue Morgue, known to be in the sole occupancy of one Mme L'Espanaye, and her daughter, Mlle Camille L'Espanaye. After some delay, occasioned by a fruitless attempt to procure admission in the usual manner, the gateway was broken in with a crowbar, and eight or ten of the neighbours entered, accompanied by two gendarmes. By this time the cries had ceased; but, as the party rushed up the first flight of stairs, two or more rough voices, in angry contention, were distinguished, and seemed to proceed from the upper part of the house. As the second landing was reached, these sounds, also, had ceased, and everything remained perfectly quiet. The party spread themselves, and hurried from room to room. Upon arriving at a large back chamber in the fourth storey (the door of which, being found locked, with the key inside, was forced open), a spectacle presented itself which struck everyone present not less with horror than with astonishment.

The apartment was in the wildest disorder – the furniture broken and thrown about in all directions. There was only one bedstead; and from this the bed had been removed, and thrown into the middle of the floor. On a chair lay a razor, besmeared with blood. On the hearth were two or three long and thick tresses of grey human hair, also dabbled in blood, and seeming to have been pulled out by the roots. Upon the floor were found four napoleons, an earring of topaz, three large silver spoons, three smaller of métal d'Alger, and two bags, containing nearly four thousand francs in gold. The drawers of a bureau, which stood in one corner, were open, and had been, apparently, rifled, although many articles still remained in them. A small iron safe was discovered under the *bed* (not under the bedstead). It was open, with a key still in the door. It had no contents beyond a few old letters, and other papers of little consequence.

Of Mme L'Espanaye no traces were here seen; but an unusual quantity of soot being observed in the fireplace, a search was made in the chimney, and (horrible to relate!) the corpse of the daughter, head downward, was dragged therefrom; it having been thus forced up the narrow aperture for a considerable distance. The body was quite warm. Upon examining it, many excoriations were perceived, no doubt occasioned by the violence with which it had been thrust up and disengaged. Upon the face were many severe scratches, and, upon the throat, dark bruises, and deep indentations of finger-nails, as if the deceased had been throttled to death.

After a thorough investigation of every portion of the house, without further discovery, the party made its way into a small paved yard in the rear of the building, where lay the corpse of the old lady, with her throat so entirely cut that, upon an attempt to raise her, the head fell off. The body, as well as the head, was fearfully mutilated – the former so much so as scarcely to retain any semblance of humanity.

To this horrible mystery there is not as yet, we believe, the slightest clue.

The next day's paper had these additional particulars:

THE TRAGEDY IN THE RUE MORGUE

Many individuals have been examined in relation to this most extraordinary and frightful affair [the word '*affaire*' has not yet in France that levity of import which it conveys with us], but nothing whatever has transpired to throw light upon it. We give below all the material testimony elicited.

Pauline Dubourg, laundress, deposes that she has known both the deceased for three years, having washed for them during that period. The old lady and her daughter seemed on good terms – very affectionate towards each other. They gave her excellent pay. Could not speak in regard to their mode or means of living. Believed that Mme L. told fortunes for a living. Was reputed to have money put by. Never met any persons in the house when she called for the clothes or took them home. Was sure that they had no servant in employ. There appeared to be no furniture in any part of the building, except in the fourth storey.

Pierre Moreau, tobacconist, deposes that he has been in the habit of selling small quantities of tobacco and snuff to Mme L'Espanaye for nearly four years. Was born in the neighbourhood, and has always resided there. The deceased and her daughter had occupied the house in which the corpses were found for more than six years. It was formerly occupied by a jeweller, who under-let the upper rooms to various persons. The house was the property of Mme L. She became dissatisfied with the abuse of the premises by her tenant, and moved into them herself, refusing to let any portion. The old lady was childish. Witness had seen the daughter some five or six times during the six years. The two lived an exceedingly retired life – were reputed to have money.

Had heard it said among the neighbours that Mme L. told fortunes – did not believe it. Had never seen any person enter the door except the old lady and her daughter, a porter once or twice, and a physician some eight or ten times.

Many other persons, neighbours, gave evidence to the same effect. No one was spoken of as frequenting the house. It was not known whether there were any living connections of Mme L. and her daughter. The shutters of the front windows were seldom opened. Those in the rear were always closed, with the exception of the large back room, fourth storey. The house was a good house – not very old.

Isidore Mustè, gendarme, deposes that he was called to the house about three o'clock in the morning, and found some twenty or thirty persons at the gateway, endeavouring to gain admittance. Forced it open, at length, with a bayonet – not with a crowbar. Had but little difficulty in getting it open, on account of its being a double or folding gate, and bolted neither at bottom nor top. The shrieks were continued until the gate was forced – and then suddenly ceased. They seemed to be screams of some person (or persons) in great agony – were loud and drawn out, not short and quick. Witness led the way upstairs. Upon reaching the first landing, heard two voices in loud and angry contention – the one a gruff voice, the other much shriller – a very strange voice. Could distinguish some words of the former, which was that of a Frenchman. Was positive that it was not a woman's voice. Could distinguish the words 'sacré' and 'diable'. The shrill voice was that of a foreigner. Could not be sure whether it was the voice of a man or of a woman. Could not make out what was said, but believed the language to be Spanish. The state of the room and of the bodies was described by this witness as we described them yesterday.

Henri Duval, a neighbour, and by trade a silversmith, deposes that he was one of the party who first entered the house. Corroborates the testimony of Mustè in general. As soon as they forced an entrance, they reclosed the door, to keep out the crowd, which collected very fast, notwithstanding the lateness of the hour. The shrill voice, this witness thinks, was that of an Italian. Was certain it was not French. Could not be sure that it was a man's voice. It might have been a woman's. Was not acquainted with the Italian language. Could not distinguish the words, but was convinced by the intonation that the speaker was an Italian. Knew Mme L. and her daughter. Had conversed with both frequently. Was sure that the shrill voice was not that of either of the deceased.

Herr Odenheimer, restaurateur. This witness volunteered his testimony. Not speaking French, was examined through an interpreter. Is a native of Amsterdam. Was passing the house at the time of the shrieks. They lasted for several minutes – probably ten. They were long and loud – very awful and distressing. Was one of those who entered the building. Corroborated the previous evidence in every respect but one. Was sure that the shrill voice was that of a man – of a Frenchman. Could not distinguish the words uttered. They were loud and quick – unequal – spoken apparently in fear as well as in anger. The voice was harsh – not so much shrill as harsh. Could not call it a shrill voice. The gruff voice said repeatedly 'sacré' and 'diable', and once 'mon Dieu'.

Jules Mignaud, banker, of the firm of Mignaud et Fils, Rue Deloraine. Is the elder Mignaud. Mme L'Espanaye had some property. Had opened an account with his banking house in the spring of the year, eight years previously. Made frequent deposits in small sums. Had withdrawn nothing until the third day before her death, when she took out in person the sum of four thousand francs. This sum was paid in gold, and a clerk sent home with the money.

Adolphe Le Bon, clerk to Mignaud et Fils, deposes that on the day in question, about noon, he accompanied Mme L'Espanaye to her residence with the 4000 francs put up in two bags. Upon the door being opened, Mlle L. appeared and took from his hands one of the bags, while the old lady relieved him of the other. He then bowed and departed. Did not see any person in the street at the time. It is a by-street – very lonely.

William Bird, tailor, deposes that he was one of the party who entered the house. Is an Englishman. Has lived in Paris two years. Was one of the first to ascend the stairs. Heard the voices in contention. The gruff voice was that of a Frenchman. Could make out several words, but cannot now remember all. Heard distinctly 'sacré' and 'mon Dieu'. There was a sound at the moment as if of several persons struggling – a scraping and scuffling sound. The shrill voice was very loud – louder than the gruff one. Is sure that it was not the voice of an Englishman. Appeared to be that of a German. Might have been a woman's voice. Does not understand German.

Four of the above-named witnesses, being recalled, deposed that the door of the chamber in which was found the body of Mlle L. was locked on the inside when the party reached it. Everything was perfectly silent – no groans or noises of any kind. Upon forcing the door no person was seen. The windows, both of the back and front room, were down and firmly fastened from within. A door between the two rooms was closed, but not locked. The door leading from the front room into the passage was locked, with the key on the inside. A small room in the front of the house, on the fourth storey, at the head of the passage, was open, the door being ajar. This room was crowded with old beds, boxes, and so forth. These were carefully removed and searched. There was not an inch of any portion of the house which was not carefully searched. Sweeps were sent up and down the chimneys. The house was a four-storey one, with garrets (*mansardes*). A trap-door on the roof was nailed down very securely – did not appear to have been opened for years. The time elapsing between the hearing of the voices in contention and the breaking open of the room door was variously stated by the witnesses. Some made it as short as three minutes – some as long as five. The door was opened with difficulty.

Alfonzo Garcio, undertaker, deposes that he resides in the Rue Morgue. Is a native of Spain. Was one of the party who entered the house. Did not proceed upstairs. Is nervous, and was apprehensive of the consequences of agitation. Heard the voices in contention. The gruff voice was that of a Frenchman. Could not distinguish what was said. The shrill voice was that of an Englishman – is sure of this. Does not understand the English language, but judges by the intonation.

Alberto Montani, confectioner, deposes that he was among the first to ascend the stairs. Heard the voices in question. The gruff voice was that of a Frenchman. Distinguished several words. The speaker appeared to be expostulating. Could not make out the words of the shrill voice. Spoke quick and unevenly. Thinks it the voice of a Russian. Corroborates the general testimony. Is an Italian. Never conversed with a native of Russia.

Several witnesses, recalled, here testified that the chimneys of all the rooms on the fourth storey were too narrow to admit the passage of a human being. By 'sweeps' were meant cylindrical sweeping-brushes, such as are employed by those who clean chimneys. These brushes were passed up and down every flue in the house. There is no back passage by which anyone could have descended while the party proceeded upstairs. The body of Mlle L'Espanaye was so firmly wedged in the chimney that it could not be got down until four or five of the party united their strength.

Paul Dumas, physician, deposes that he was called to view the bodies about daybreak. They were both then lying on the sacking of the bedstead in the chamber where Mlle L. was found. The corpse of the young lady was much bruised and excoriated. The fact that it had been thrust up the chimney would sufficiently account for these appearances. The throat was greatly chafed. There were several deep scratches just below the chin, together with a series of livid spots which were evidently the impression of fingers. The face was fearfully discoloured, and the eyeballs protruded. The tongue had been partially bitten through. A large bruise was discovered upon the pit of the stomach, produced apparently, by the pressure of a knee. In the opinion of M. Dumas, Mlle L'Espanaye had been throttled to death by some person or persons unknown. The corpse of the mother was horribly mutilated. All the bones of the right leg and arm were more or less shattered. The left tibia much splintered, as well as all the ribs of the left side. Whole body dreadfully bruised and discoloured. It was not possible to say how the injuries had been inflicted. A heavy club of wood, or a broad bar of iron, or a chair – any large, heavy and obtuse weapon would have produced such results, if wielded by the hands of a very powerful man. No woman could have inflicted the blows with any weapon. The head of the deceased, when seen by witness, was entirely separated from the body, and was also greatly shattered. The throat had evidently been cut with some very sharp instrument – probably with a razor.

Alexandre Etienne, surgeon, was called with M. Dumas, to view the bodies. Corroborated the testimony and the opinions of M. Dumas.

Nothing further of importance was elicited, although several other persons were examined. A murder so mysterious, and so perplexing in all its particulars, was never before committed in Paris – if indeed a murder has been committed at all. The police are entirely at a loss – an unusual occurrence in affairs of this nature. There is not, however, the shadow of a clue apparent.

The evening edition of the paper stated that the greatest excitement still continued in the Quartier St Roch – that the premises in question had been carefully re-searched, and fresh examinations of witnesses instituted, but all to no purpose. A postscript, however, mentioned that Adolphe Le Bon had been arrested and imprisoned – although nothing appeared to criminate him, beyond the facts already detailed.

Dupin seemed singularly interested in the progress of this affair – at least so I judged from his manner, for he made no comments. It was only after the announcement that Le Bon had been imprisoned that he asked me my opinion respecting the murders.

I could merely agree with all Paris in considering them an insoluble mystery. I saw no means by which it would be possible to trace the murderer.

'We must not judge of the means,' said Dupin, 'by this shell of an examination. The Parisian police, so much extolled for acumen, are cunning, but no more. There is no method in their proceedings, beyond the method of the moment. They make a vast parade of measures; but, not unfrequently, these are so ill adapted to the objects proposed as to put us in mind of M. Jourdain's calling for his *robe-de-chambre – pour mieux entendre la musique*. The results attained by them are not unfrequently surprising, but, for the most part, are brought about by simple diligence and activity. When these qualities are unavailing, their schemes fail. Vidocq, for example, was a good guesser, and a persevering man. But, without educated thought, he erred continually by the very intensity of his investigations. He impaired his vision by holding the object too close. He might see, perhaps, one or two points with unusual clearness, but in so doing, he, necessarily, lost sight of the matter as a whole. Thus there is such a thing as being too profound. Truth is not always in a well. In fact, as regards the more important knowledge, I do believe that she is invariably superficial. The depth lies in the valleys where we seek her, and not upon the mountain-top where she is found. The modes and sources of this kind of error are well typified in the contemplation of the heavenly bodies. To look at a star by glances – to view it in a sidelong way, by turning towards it the exterior portions of the retina (more susceptible of feeble impressions of light than the interior), is to behold the star distinctly – is to have the best appreciation of its lustre – a lustre which grows dim just in proportion as we turn our vision *fully* upon it. A greater number of rays actually fall upon the eye in the latter case, but, in the former, there is the more refined capacity for comprehension. By undue profundity we perplex and enfeeble thought; and it is possible to make even Venus herself vanish from the firmament by a scrutiny too sustained, too concentrated or too direct.

'As for these murders, let us enter into some examinations for ourselves before we make up an opinion respecting them. An enquiry will afford us amusement' (I thought this an odd term, so applied, but said nothing), 'and, besides, Le Bon once rendered me a service for which I am not ungrateful. We will go and see the premises with our own eyes. I know G—, the Prefect of Police, and shall have no difficulty in obtaining the necessary permission.'

The permission was obtained, and we proceeded at once to the Rue Morgue. This is one of those miserable thoroughfares which intervene between the Rue Richelieu and the Rue St Roch. It was late in the afternoon when we reached it, as this quarter is at a great distance from that in which we resided. The house was readily found; for there were still many persons gazing up at the closed shutters, with an objectless curiosity, from the opposite side of the way. It was an ordinary Parisian house, with a gateway, on one side of which was a glazed watch-box, with a sliding panel in the window, indicating a *loge de concierge*. Before going in we walked up the street, turned down an alley, and then, again turning, passed in the rear of the building – Dupin, meanwhile, examining the whole neighbourhood, as well as the house, with a minuteness of attention for which I could see no possible object.

Retracing our steps, we came again to the front of the dwelling, rang, and having shown our credentials, were admitted by the agents in charge. We went upstairs – into the chamber where the body of Mlle L'Espanaye had been found, and where both the deceased still lay. The disorders of the room had, as usual, been suffered to exist. I saw nothing beyond what had been stated in the *Gazette des Tribunaux*. Dupin scrutinised everything – not excepting the bodies of the victims. We then went into the other rooms, and into the yard, a gendarme accompanying us throughout. The examination occupied us until dark, when we took our departure. On our way home my companion stepped in for a moment at the office of one of the daily papers.

I have said that the whims of my friend were manifold, and that *je les ménageais* – for this phrase there is no English equivalent [perhaps, 'I humoured them with cautious respect].

It was his humour, now, to decline all conversation on the subject of the murders, until about noon the next day. He then asked me, suddenly, if I had observed anything *peculiar* at the scene of the atrocity.

There was something in his manner of emphasising the word 'peculiar', which caused me to shudder, without knowing why.

'No, nothing *peculiar*,' I said; 'nothing more, at least, than we both saw stated in the paper.'

'The *Gazette*,' he replied, 'has not entered, I fear, into the unusual horror of the thing. But dismiss the idle opinions of this print. It appears to me that this mystery is considered insoluble for the very reason which should cause it to be regarded as easy of solution – I mean for the *outré* character of its features. The police are confounded by the seeming absence of motive – not for the murder itself, but for the atrocity of the murder. They are puzzled, too, by the seeming impossibility of reconciling the voices heard in contention with the facts that no one was discovered upstairs but the assassinated Mlle L'Espanaye, and that there were no means of egress without the notice of the party ascending. The wild disorder of the room; the corpse thrust, with the head downward, up the chimney; the frightful mutilation of the body of the old lady; these considerations, with those just mentioned, and others which I need not mention, have sufficed to paralyse the powers, by putting completely at fault the boasted acumen, of the government agents. They have fallen into the gross but common error of confounding the unusual with the abstruse. But it is by these deviations from the plane of the ordinary that reason feels its way, if at all, in its search for the true. In investigations such as we are now pursuing, it should not be so much asked "what has occurred?" as "what has occurred that has never occurred before?" In fact, the facility with which I shall arrive, or have arrived, at the solution of this mystery, is in the direct ratio of its apparent insolubility in the eyes of the police.'

I stared at the speaker in mute astonishment.

'I am now awaiting,' continued he, looking towards the door of our apartment – 'I am now awaiting a person who, although perhaps not the perpetrator of these butcheries, must have been in some measure implicated in their perpetration. Of the worst portion of the crimes committed, it is probable that he is innocent. I hope that I am right in this supposition; for upon it I build my expectation of reading the entire riddle. I look for the man here – in this room – every moment. It is true that he may not arrive; but the probability is that he will. Should he come, it will be necessary to detain him. Here are pistols; and we both know how to use them when occasion demands their use.'

I took the pistols, scarcely knowing what I did, or believing what I heard, while Dupin went on, very much as if in a soliloquy. I have already spoken of his abstract manner at such times. His discourse was addressed to myself; but his voice, although by no means loud, had that intonation which is commonly employed in speaking to someone at a great distance. His eyes, vacant in expression, regarded only the wall.

'That the voices heard in contention,' he said, 'by the party upon the stairs were not the voices of the women themselves was fully proved by the evidence. This relieves us of all doubt upon the question whether the old lady could have first destroyed the daughter, and afterwards have committed suicide. I speak of this point chiefly for the sake of method; for the strength of Mme L'Espanaye would have been utterly unequal to the task of thrusting her daughter's corpse up the chimney as it was found; and the nature of the wounds upon her own person entirely precludes the idea of self-destruction. Murder, then, has been committed by some third party; and the voices of this third party were those heard in contention. Let me now advert, not to the whole testimony respecting these voices, but to what was peculiar in that testimony. Did you observe anything peculiar about it?'

I remarked that, while all the witnesses agreed in supposing the gruff voice to be that of a Frenchman, there was much disagreement in regard to the shrill, or, as one individual termed it, the harsh voice.

'That was the evidence itself,' said Dupin, 'but it was not the peculiarity of the evidence. You have observed nothing distinctive. Yet there *was* something to be observed. The witnesses, as you remark, agreed about the gruff voice; they were here unanimous. But in regard to the shrill voice, the peculiarity is – not that they disagreed – but that, while an Italian, an Englishman, a Spaniard, a Hollander and a Frenchman attempted to describe it, each one spoke of it as that *of a foreigner*. Each is sure that it was not the voice of one of his own countrymen. Each likens it not to the voice of an individual of any nation with whose language he is conversant – but the converse. The Frenchman supposes it the voice of a Spaniard, and "might have distinguished some words *had he been acquainted with the Spanish*". The Dutchman maintains it to have been that of a Frenchman; but we find it stated that, "*not understanding French, this witness was examined through an interpreter*". The Englishman thinks it the voice of a German, and "*does not understand German*". The Spaniard "is sure" that it was that of an Englishman, but "judges by the intonation" altogether, "*as he has no knowledge of the English*". The Italian believes it the voice of a Russian, but "*has never conversed with a native of Russia*". A second Frenchman differs, moreover, with the first, and is positive that the voice was that of an Italian; but, *not being cognisant of that tongue*, is, like the Spaniard, "convinced by the intonation". Now, how strangely unusual must that voice have really been, about which such testimony as this *could* have been elicited! – in whose *tones*, even, denizens of the five great divisions of Europe could recognise nothing familiar! You will say that it might have been the voice of an Asiatic – of an African. Neither Asiatics nor Africans abound in Paris; but, without denying the inference, I will now merely call your attention to three points. The voice is termed by one witness "harsh rather than shrill". It is represented by two others to have been "quick and *unequal*". No words – no sounds resembling words – were by any witness mentioned as distinguishable.

'I know not,' continued Dupin, 'what impression I may have made, so far, upon your own understanding; but I do not hesitate to say that legitimate deductions even from this portion of the testimony – the portion respecting the gruff and shrill voices – are in themselves sufficient to engender a suspicion which should give direction to all further progress in the investigation of the mystery. I said "legitimate deductions"; but my meaning is not thus fully expressed. I designed to imply that the deductions are the *sole* proper ones, and that the suspicion arises *inevitably* from them as the single result. What the suspicion is, however, I will not say just yet. I merely wish you to bear in mind that, with myself, it was sufficiently forcible to give a definite form – a certain tendency – to my enquiries in the chamber.

'Let us now transport ourselves, in fancy, to this chamber. What shall we first seek here? The means of egress employed by the murderers. It is not too much to say that neither of us believes in preternatural events. Mme and Mlle L'Espanaye were not destroyed by spirits. The doers of the deed were material, and escaped materially. Then how? Fortunately, there is but one mode of reasoning upon the point, and that mode *must* lead us to a definite decision. Let us examine, each by each, the possible means of egress. It is clear that the assassins were in the room where Mlle L'Espanaye was found, or at least in the room adjoining, when the party ascended the stairs. It is, then, only from these two apartments that we have to seek issues. The police have laid bare the floors, the ceilings, and the masonry of the walls, in every direction. No *secret* issues could have escaped their vigilance. But, not trusting to *their* eyes, I examined with my own. There were, then, *no* secret issues. Both doors leading from the rooms into the passage were securely locked, with the keys inside. Let us turn to the chimneys. These, although of ordinary width for some eight or ten feet above the hearths, will not admit, throughout their extent, the body of a large cat. The impossibility of egress, by means already stated, being thus absolute, we are reduced to the windows. Through those of the front room no one could have escaped without notice from the crowd in the street. The murderers *must* have passed, then, through those of the back room. Now, brought to this conclusion in so unequivocal a manner as we are, it is not our part, as reasoners, to reject it on account of apparent impossibilities. It is only left for us to prove that these apparent "impossibilities" are, in reality, not such.

'There are two windows in the chamber. One of them is unobstructed by furniture, and is wholly visible. The lower portion of the other is hidden from view by the head of the unwieldy bedstead which is thrust close up against it. The former was found securely fastened from within. It resisted the utmost force of those who endeavoured to raise it. A large gimlet hole had been pierced in its frame to the left, and a very stout nail was found fitted therein, nearly to the head. Upon examining the other window, a similar nail was seen similarly fitted in it; and a vigorous attempt to raise this sash, failed also. The police were now entirely satisfied that egress had not been in these directions. And, *therefore*, it was thought a matter of supererogation to withdraw the nails and open the windows.

'My own examination was somewhat more particular, and was so for the reason I have just given – because here it was, I knew, that all apparent impossibilities *must* be proved to be not such in reality.

'I proceeded to think thus – *a posteriori*. The murderers *did* escape from one of these windows. This being so, they could not have re-fastened the sashes from the inside, as they were found fastened – the consideration which put a stop, through its obviousness, to the scrutiny of the police in this quarter. Yet the sashes *were* fastened. They *must*, then, have the power of fastening themselves. There was no escape from this conclusion. I stepped to the unobstructed casement, withdrew the nail with some difficulty, and attempted to raise the sash. It resisted all my efforts, as I had anticipated. A concealed spring must, I now knew, exist; and this corroboration of my idea convinced me that my premises, at least, were correct, however mysterious still appeared the circumstances attending the nails. A careful search soon brought to light the hidden spring. I pressed it, and, satisfied with the discovery, forbore to upraise the sash.

'I now replaced the nail and regarded it attentively. A person passing out through this window might have reclosed it, and the spring would have caught – but the nail could not have been replaced. The conclusion was plain, and again narrowed in the field of my investigations. The assassins *must* have escaped through the other window. Supposing, then, the springs upon each sash to be the same, as was probable, there *must* be found a difference between the nails, or at least between the modes of their fixture. Getting upon the sacking of the bedstead, I looked over the headboard minutely at the second casement. Passing my hand down behind the board, I readily discovered and pressed the spring, which was, as I had supposed, identical in character with its neighbour. I now looked at the nail. It was as stout as the other, and apparently fitted in the same manner – driven in nearly up to the head.

'You will say that I was puzzled; but, if you think so, you must have misunderstood the nature of the inductions. To use a sporting phrase, I had not been once "at fault". The scent had never for an instant been lost. There was no flaw in any link of the chain. I had traced the secret to its ultimate result – and that result was *the nail*. It had, I say, in every respect, the appearance of its fellow in the other window; but this fact was an absolute nullity (conclusive as it might seem to be) when compared with the consideration that here, at this point, terminated the clue. "There *must* be something wrong," I said, "about the nail." I touched it; and the head, with about a quarter of an inch of the shank, came off in my fingers. The rest of the shank was in the gimlet hole, where it had been broken off. The fracture was an old one (for its edges were encrusted with rust), and had apparently been accomplished by the blow of a hammer, which had partially embedded, in the top of the bottom sash, the head portion of the nail. I now carefully replaced this head portion in the indentation whence I had taken it, and the resemblance to a perfect nail was complete – the fissure was invisible. Pressing the spring, I gently raised the sash for a few inches; the head went up with it, remaining firm in its bed. I closed the window, and the semblance of the whole nail was again perfect.

'The riddle, so far, was now unriddled. The assassin had escaped through the window which looked upon the bed. Dropping of its own accord upon his exit (or perhaps purposely closed), it had become fastened by the spring; and it was the retention of this spring which had been mistaken by the police for that of the nail – further enquiry being thus considered unnecessary.

'The next question is that of the mode of descent. Upon this point I had been satisfied in my walk with you around the building. About five feet and a half from the casement in question there runs a lightning-rod. From this rod it would have been impossible for anyone to reach the window itself, to say nothing of entering it. I observed, however, that the shutters of the fourth storey were of the peculiar kind called by Parisian carpenters *ferrades* – a kind rarely employed at the present day, but frequently seen upon very old mansions at Lyons and Bordeaux. They are in the form of an ordinary door (a single, not a folding door), except that the lower half is latticed or worked in open trellis – thus affording an excellent hold for the hands. In the present instance these shutters are fully three feet and a half broad. When we saw them from the rear of the house, they were both about half open – that is to say, they stood off at right angles from the wall. It is probable that the police, as well as myself, examined the back of the tenement; but, if so, in looking at these *ferrades* in the line of their breadth (as they must have done), they did not perceive this great breadth itself, or, at all events, failed to take it into due consideration. In fact, having once satisfied themselves that no egress could have been made in this quarter, they would naturally bestow here a very cursory examination. It was clear to me, however, that the shutter belonging to the window at the head of the bed, would, if swung fully back to the wall, reach to within two feet of the lightning-rod. It was also evident that, by exertion of a very unusual degree of activity and courage, an entrance into the window, from the rod, might have been thus effected. By reaching to the distance of two feet and a half (we now suppose the shutter open to its whole extent) a robber might have taken a firm grasp upon the trellis-work. Letting go, then, his hold upon the rod, placing his feet securely against the wall, and springing boldly from it, he might have swung the shutter so as to close it, and, if we imagine the window open at the time, might even have swung himself into the room.

'I wish you to bear especially in mind that I have spoken of a *very* unusual degree of activity as requisite to success in so hazardous and so difficult a feat. It is my design to show you, first, that the thing might possibly have been accomplished; but, secondly and *chiefly*, I wish to impress upon your understanding the *very extraordinary* – the almost preternatural character of that agility which could have accomplished it.

'You will say, no doubt, using the language of the law, that "to make out my case" I should rather undervalue than insist upon a full estimation of the activity required in this matter. This may be the practice in law, but it is not the usage of reason.

My ultimate object is only the truth. My immediate purpose is to lead you to place in juxtaposition that *very unusual* activity of which I have just spoken, with that *very peculiar* shrill (or harsh) and *unequal* voice, about whose nationality no two persons could be found to agree, and in whose utterance no syllabification could be detected.'

At these words a vague and half-formed conception of the meaning of Dupin flitted over my mind. I seemed to be upon the verge of comprehension, without power to comprehend – as men, at times, find themselves upon the brink of remembrance, without being able in the end, to remember. My friend went on with his discourse.

'You will see,' he said, 'that I have shifted the question from the mode of egress to that of ingress. It was my design to convey the idea that both were effected in the same manner, at the same point. Let us now revert to the interior of the room. Let us survey the appearances here. The drawers of the bureau, it is said, had been rifled, although many articles of apparel still remained within them. The conclusion here is absurd. It is a mere guess – a very silly one – and no more. How are we to know that the articles found in the drawers were not all these drawers had originally contained? Mme L'Espanaye and her daughter lived an exceedingly retired life – saw no company – seldom went out – had little use for numerous changes of habiliment. Those found were at least of as good quality as any likely to be possessed by these ladies. If a thief had taken any, why did he not take the best – why did he not take all? In a word, why did he abandon four thousand francs in gold to encumber himself with a bundle of linen? The gold *was* abandoned. Nearly the whole sum mentioned by M. Mignaud, the banker, was discovered, in bags, upon the floor. I wish you, therefore, to discard from your thoughts the blundering idea of *motive* engendered in the brains of the police by that portion of the evidence which speaks of money delivered at the door of the house. Coincidences ten times as remarkable as this (the delivery of the money, and murder committed within three days upon the party receiving it), happen to all of us every hour of our lives, without attracting even momentary notice. Coincidences, in general, are great stumbling-blocks in the way of that class of thinkers who have been educated to know nothing of the theory of probabilities – that theory to which the most glorious objects of human research are indebted for the most glorious of illustration. In the present instance, had the gold been gone, the fact of its delivery three days before would have formed something more than a coincidence. It would have been corroborative of this idea of motive. But, under the real circumstances of the case, if we are to suppose gold the motive of this outrage, we must also imagine the perpetrator so vacillating an idiot as to have abandoned his gold and his motive together.

'Keeping now steadily in mind the points to which I have drawn your attention – that peculiar voice, that unusual agility and that startling absence of motive in a murder so singularly atrocious as this – let us glance at the butchery itself. Here is a woman strangled to death by manual strength, and thrust up a chimney, head downward. Ordinary assassins employ no such modes of murder as this. Least of all, do they thus dispose of the murdered. In the manner of thrusting the corpse up the chimney, you will admit that there was something *excessively outré* – something altogether irreconcilable with our common notions of human action, even when we suppose the actors the most depraved of men. Think, too, how great must have been that strength which could have thrust the body *up* such an aperture so forcibly that the united vigour of several persons was found barely sufficient to drag it *down*!

'Turn, now, to other indications of the employment of a vigour most marvellous. On the hearth were thick tresses – very thick tresses – of grey human hair. These had been torn out by the roots. You are aware of the great force necessary in tearing thus from the head even twenty or thirty hairs together. You saw the locks in question as well as myself. Their roots (a hideous sight!) were clotted with fragments of the flesh of the scalp – sure token of the prodigious power which had been exerted in uprooting perhaps half a million of hairs at a time. The throat of the old lady was not merely cut, but the head absolutely severed from the body: the instrument was a mere razor. I wish you also to look at the *brutal* ferocity of these deeds. Of the bruises upon the body of Mme L'Espanaye I do not speak. M. Dumas, and his worthy coadjutor M. Etienne, have pronounced that they were inflicted by some obtuse instrument; and so far these gentlemen are very correct. The obtuse instrument was clearly the stone pavement of the yard, upon which the victim had fallen from the window which looked in upon the bed. This idea, however simple it may now seem, escaped the police for the same reason that the breadth of the shutters escaped them – because, by the affair of the nails, their perceptions had been hermetically sealed against the possibility of the windows having ever been opened at all.

'If now, in addition to all these things, you have properly reflected upon the odd disorder of the chamber, we have gone so far as to combine the ideas of an agility astounding, a strength superhuman, a ferocity brutal, a butchery without motive, a *grotesquerie* in horror absolutely alien from humanity, and a voice foreign in tone to the ears of men of many nations, and devoid of all distinct or intelligible syllabification. What result, then, has ensued? What impression have I made upon your fancy?'

I felt a creeping of the flesh as Dupin asked me the question. 'A madman,' I said, 'has done this deed – some raving maniac escaped from a neighbouring Maison de Santé.'

'In some respects,' he replied, 'your idea is not irrelevant. But the voices of madmen, even in their wildest paroxysms, are never found to tally with that peculiar voice heard upon the stairs. Madmen are of some nation, and their language, however incoherent in its words, has always the coherence of syllabification. Besides, the hair of a madman is not such as I now hold in my hand. I disentangled this little tuft from the rigidly clutched fingers of Mme L'Espanaye. Tell me what you can make of it.'

'Dupin,' I said, completely unnerved; 'this hair is most unusual – this is no *human* hair.'

'I have not asserted that it is,' said he; 'but, before we decide this point, I wish you to glance at the little sketch I have here traced upon this paper. It is a facsimile drawing of what has been described in one portion of the testimony as "dark bruises, and deep indentations of fingernails", upon the throat of Mlle L'Espanaye, and in another (by Messrs Dumas and Etienne), as a "series of livid spots, evidently the impression of fingers".

'You will perceive,' continued my friend, spreading out the paper upon the table before us, 'that this drawing gives the idea of a firm and fixed hold. There is no *slipping* apparent. Each finger has retained – possibly until the death of the victim – the fearful grasp by which it originally embedded itself. Attempt, now, to place all your fingers, at the same time, in the respective impressions as you see them.'

I made the attempt in vain.

'We are possibly not giving this matter a fair trial,' he said. 'The paper is spread out upon a plane surface; but the human throat is cylindrical. Here is a *billot* of wood, the circumference of which is about that of the throat. Wrap the drawing round it, and try the experiment again.'

I did so; but the difficulty was even more obvious than before. 'This,' I said, 'is the mark of no human hand.'

'Read now,' replied Dupin, 'this passage from Cuvier.'

It was a minute anatomical and generally descriptive account of the large fulvous orang-utan of the East Indian Islands. The gigantic stature, the prodigious strength and activity, the wild ferocity and the imitative propensities of these mammalia are sufficiently well known to all. I understood the full horrors of the murder at once.

'The description of the digits,' said I, as I made an end of reading, 'is in exact accordance with this drawing. I see that no animal but an orang-utan, of the species here mentioned, could have impressed the indentations, as you have traced them. This tuft of tawny hair, too, is identical in character with that of the beast of Cuvier. But I cannot possibly comprehend the particulars of this frightful mystery. Besides, there were *two* voices heard in contention, and one of them was unquestionably the voice of a Frenchman.'

'True; and you will remember an expression attributed almost unanimously, by the evidence, to this voice – the expression "Mon Dieu!" This, under the circumstances, has been justly characterised by one of the witnesses (Montani, the confectioner) as an expression of remonstrance or expostulation. Upon these two words, therefore, I have mainly built my hopes of a full solution of the riddle. A Frenchman was cognisant of the murder. It is possible – indeed it is far more than probable – that he was innocent of all participation in the bloody transactions which took place. The orang-utan may have escaped from him. He may have traced it to the chamber; but, under the agitating circumstances which ensued, he could never have recaptured it. It is still at large. I will not pursue these guesses – for I have no right to call them more – since the shades of reflection upon which they are based are scarcely of sufficient depth to be appreciable to my own intellect and since I could not pretend to make them intelligible to the understanding of another. We will call them guesses, then, and speak of them as such. If the Frenchman in question is indeed, as I suppose, innocent of this atrocity, this advertisement, which I left last night, upon our return home, at the office of *Le Monde* (a paper devoted to the shipping interest, and much sought by sailors), will bring him to our residence.'

He handed me a paper, and I read thus:

CAUGHT

> In the Bois de Boulogne, early in the morning of the — inst. [the morning of the murder], a very large, tawny orang-utan of the Bornese species. The owner (who is ascertained to be a sailor, belonging to a Maltese vessel), may have the animal again, upon identifying it satisfactorily, and paying a few charges arising from its capture and keeping. Call at No. —, Rue —, Faubourg St Germain, au troisième.

'How was it possible,' I asked, 'that you should know the man to be a sailor, and belonging to a Maltese vessel?'

'I do *not* know it,' said Dupin. 'I am not *sure* of it. Here, however, is a small piece of ribbon, which from its form, and from its greasy appearance, has evidently been used in tying the hair in one of those long queues of which sailors are so fond. Moreover, this knot is one which few besides sailors can tie, and is peculiar to the Maltese. I picked the ribbon up at the foot of the lightning-rod. It could not have belonged to either of the deceased. Now if, after all, I am wrong in my induction from this ribbon that the Frenchman was a sailor belonging to a Maltese vessel, still I can have done no harm in saying what I did in the advertisement. If I am in error, he will merely suppose that I have been misled by some circumstance into which he will not take the trouble to enquire. But if I am right, a great point is gained. Cognisant although innocent of the murder, the Frenchman will naturally hesitate about replying to the advertisement – about demanding the orang-utan. He will reason thus: "I am innocent; I am poor; my orang-utan is of great value – to one in my circumstances a fortune of itself – why should I lose it through idle apprehensions of danger? Here it is within my grasp. It was found in the Bois de Boulogne – at a vast distance from the scene of that butchery. How can it ever be suspected that a brute beast should have done the deed? The police are at fault – they have failed to procure the slightest clue. Should they even trace the animal, it would be impossible to prove me cognisant of the murder, or to implicate me in guilt on account of that cognisance. Above all, *I am known*. The advertiser designates me as the possessor of the beast. I am not sure to what limit his knowledge may extend. Should I avoid claiming a property of so great value, which it is known that I possess, I will render the animal at least liable to suspicion. It is not my policy to attract attention either to myself or to the beast. I will answer the advertisement, get the orang-utan, and keep it close until this matter has blown over." '

At this moment we heard a step upon the stairs.

'Be ready,' said Dupin, 'with your pistols, but neither use them nor show them until at a signal from myself.'

The front door of the house had been left open, and the visitor had entered, without ringing, and advanced several steps upon the staircase. Now, however, he seemed to hesitate. Presently we heard him descending. Dupin was moving quickly to the door, when we again heard him coming up. He did not turn back a second time, but stepped up with decision, and rapped at the door of our chamber.

'Come in,' said Dupin, in a cheerful and hearty tone.

A man entered. He was a sailor, evidently – a tall, stout and muscular-looking person, with a certain daredevil expression of countenance, not altogether unprepossessing. His face, greatly sunburnt, was more than half hidden by whisker and mustachio. He had with him a huge oaken cudgel, but appeared to be otherwise unarmed. He bowed awkwardly, and bade us 'good-evening', in French accents, which although somewhat Neufchâtelish were still sufficiently indicative of a Parisian origin.

'Sit down, my friend,' said Dupin. 'I suppose you have called about the orang-utan. Upon my word, I almost envy you the possession of him; a remarkably fine, and no doubt a very valuable animal. How old do you suppose him to be?'

The sailor drew a long breath, with the air of a man relieved of some intolerable burden, and then replied, in an assured tone, 'I have no way of telling – but he can't be more than four or five years old. Have you got him here?'

'Oh no; we had no conveniences for keeping him here. He is at a livery stable in the Rue Dubourg, just by. You can get him in the morning. Of course you are prepared to identify the property?'

'To be sure I am, sir.'

'I shall be sorry to part with him,' said Dupin.

'I don't mean that you should be at all this trouble for nothing, sir,' said the man. 'Couldn't expect it. I'm very willing to pay a reward for the finding of the animal – that is to say, anything in reason.'

'Well,' replied my friend, 'that is all very fair, to be sure. Let me think! – what should I have? Oh! I will tell you. My reward shall be this. You shall give me all the information in your power about these murders in the Rue Morgue.'

Dupin said the last words in a very low tone, and very quietly. Just as quietly, too, he walked towards the door, locked it and put the key in his pocket. He then drew a pistol from his bosom, and placed it, without the least flurry, upon the table.

The sailor's face flushed up as if he were struggling with suffocation. He started to his feet and grasped his cudgel; but the next moment he fell back into his seat, trembling violently, and with the countenance of death itself. He spoke not a word. I pitied him from the bottom of my heart.

'My friend,' said Dupin, in a kind tone, 'you are alarming yourself unnecessarily – you are indeed. We mean you no harm whatever. I pledge you the honour of a gentleman, and of a Frenchman, that we intend you no injury. I perfectly well know that you are innocent of the atrocities in the Rue Morgue. It will not do, however, to deny that you are in some measure implicated in them. From what I have already said, you must know that I have had means of information about this matter – means of which you could never have dreamed. Now the thing stands thus. You have done nothing which you could have avoided – nothing, certainly, which renders you culpable. You were not even guilty of robbery, when you might have robbed with impunity. You have nothing to conceal. You have no reason for concealment. On the other hand, you are bound by every principle of honour to confess all you know. An innocent man is now imprisoned, charged with that crime of which you can point out the perpetrator.'

The sailor had recovered his presence of mind, in a great measure, while Dupin uttered these words; but his original boldness of bearing was all gone.

'So help me God,' said he, after a brief pause, 'I *will* tell you all I know about this affair; but I do not expect you to believe one half I say – I would be a fool indeed if I did. Still, I *am* innocent, and I will make a clean breast if I die for it.'

What he stated was, in substance, this. He had lately made a voyage to the Indian Archipelago. A party, of which he formed one, landed at Borneo, and passed into the interior on an excursion of pleasure. Himself and a companion had captured the orang-utan. This companion dying, the animal fell into his own exclusive possession. After great trouble, occasioned by the intractable ferocity of his captive during the home voyage, he at length succeeded in lodging it safely at his own residence in Paris, where, not to attract towards himself the unpleasant curiosity of his neighbours, he kept it carefully secluded, until such time as it should recover from a wound in the foot, received from a splinter on board ship. His ultimate design was to sell it.

Returning home from some sailors' frolic on the night, or rather in the morning of the murder, he found the beast occupying his own bedroom, into which it had broken from a closet adjoining, where it had been, as was thought, securely confined. Razor in hand, and fully lathered, it was sitting before a looking-glass, attempting the operation of shaving, in which it had no doubt previously watched its master through the keyhole of the closet. Terrified at the sight of so dangerous a weapon in the possession of an animal so ferocious, and so well able to use it, the man, for some moments, was at a loss what to do. He had been accustomed, however, to quiet the creature, even in its fiercest moods, by the use of a whip, and to this he now resorted. Upon sight of it, the orang-utan sprang at once through the door of the chamber, down the stairs, and thence, through a window, unfortunately open, into the street.

The Frenchman followed in despair; the ape, razor still in hand, occasionally stopping to look back and gesticulate at its pursuer, until the latter had nearly come up with it. It then again made off. In this manner the chase continued for a long time. The streets were profoundly quiet, as it was nearly three o'clock in the morning. In passing down an alley in the rear of the Rue Morgue, the fugitive's attention was arrested by a light gleaming from the open window of Mme L'Espanaye's chamber, in the fourth storey of her house. Rushing to the building, it perceived the lightning-rod, clambered up with inconceivable agility, grasped the shutter, which was thrown fully back against the wall, and, by its means, swung itself directly upon the headboard of the bed. The whole feat did not occupy a minute. The shutter was kicked open again by the orang-utan as it entered the room.

The sailor, in the meantime, was both rejoiced and perplexed. He had strong hopes of now recapturing the brute, as it could scarcely escape from the trap into which it had ventured, except by the rod, where it might be intercepted as it came down. On the other hand, there was much cause for anxiety as to what it might do in the house. This latter reflection urged the man still to follow the fugitive. A lightning-rod is ascended without difficulty, especially by a sailor; but, when he had arrived as high as the window, which lay far to his left, his career was stopped; the most that he could accomplish was to reach over so as to obtain a glimpse of the interior of the room. At this glimpse he nearly fell from his hold through excess of horror. Now it was that those hideous shrieks arose upon the night, which had startled from slumber the inmates of the Rue Morgue. Mme L'Espanaye and her daughter, habited in their nightclothes, had apparently been occupied in arranging some papers in the iron chest already mentioned, which had been wheeled into the middle of the room. It was open, and its contents lay beside it on the floor. The victims must have been sitting with their backs towards the window; and, from the time elapsing between the ingress of the beast and the screams, it seems probable that it was not immediately perceived. The flapping-to of the shutter would naturally have been attributed to the wind.

As the sailor looked in, the gigantic animal had seized Mme L'Espanaye by the hair (which was loose, as she had been combing it), and was flourishing the razor about her face, in imitation of the motions of a barber. The daughter lay prostrate and motionless; she had swooned. The screams and struggles of the old lady (during which the hair was torn from her head) had the effect of changing the probably pacific purposes of the orang-utan into those of wrath. With one determined sweep of its muscular arm it nearly severed her head from her body. The sight of blood inflamed its anger into frenzy. Gnashing its teeth, and flashing fire from its eyes, it flew upon the body of the girl, and embedded its fearful talons in her throat, retaining its grasp until she expired. Its wandering and wild glances fell at this moment upon the head of the bed, over which the face of its master, rigid with horror, was just discernible. The fury of the beast, who no doubt bore still in mind the dreaded whip, was instantly converted into fear. Conscious of having deserved punishment, it seemed desirous of concealing its bloody deeds, and skipped about the chamber in an agony of nervous agitation, throwing down and breaking the furniture as it moved, and dragging the bed from the bedstead. In conclusion, it seized first the corpse of the daughter, and thrust it up the chimney, as it was found; then that of the old lady, which it immediately hurled through the window headlong.

As the ape approached the casement with its mutilated burden, the sailor shrank aghast to the rod, and rather gliding than clambering down it, hurried at once home – dreading the consequences of the butchery, and gladly abandoning, in his terror, all solicitude about the fate of the orang-utan. The words heard by the party upon the staircase were the Frenchman's exclamations of horror and affright, commingled with the fiendish jabberings of the brute.

I have scarcely anything to add. The orang-utan must have escaped from the chamber, by the rod, just before the breaking of the door. It must have closed the window as it passed through it. It was subsequently caught by the owner himself, who obtained for it a very large sum at the Jardin des Plantes. Le Bon was instantly released upon our narration of the circumstances (with some comments from Dupin) at the bureau of the Prefect of Police. This functionary, however well disposed to my friend, could not altogether conceal his chagrin at the turn which affairs had taken, and was fain to indulge in a sarcasm or two about the propriety of every person minding his own business.

'Let him talk,' said Dupin, who had not thought it necessary to reply. 'Let him discourse; it will ease his conscience. I am satisfied with having defeated him in his own castle. Nevertheless, that he failed in the solution of this mystery is by no means that matter for wonder which he supposes it; for, in truth, our friend the prefect is somewhat too cunning to be profound. In his wisdom is no *staying power*. It is all head and no body, like the pictures of the goddess Laverna – or, at best, all head and shoulders, like a codfish. But he is a good creature after all. I like him especially for one masterstroke of cant, by which he has attained his reputation for ingenuity. I mean the tendency he has "*de nier ce qui est, et d'expliquer ce qui n'est pas*" [to deny what is, and explain what is not].'*

* Rousseau, *Nouvelle Héloïse*.

AMELIA B. EDWARDS

Amelia Ann Blandford Edwards, the daughter of one of the Duke of Wellington's officers, was born in London in 1831. At a very early age she displayed considerable literary and artistic talent. She became a contributor to various magazines and newspapers, and besides many miscellaneous works she wrote eight novels, the most successful of which were *Debenham's Vow* (1870) and *Lord Brackenbury* (1880). In the winter of 1873–4 she visited Egypt and was profoundly impressed by the new openings for archaeological research. She learnt the hieroglyphic characters and made a considerable collection of Egyptian antiquities. In 1877 she published *A Thousand Miles Up the Nile*, with illustrations by herself, and in 1882 was largely instrumental in founding the Egypt Exploration Fund. It was at this point that she abandoned her other literary work, writing only on Egyptology. She died in Weston-super-Mare, Somerset, in 1892, bequeathing her valuable collection of Egyptian antiquities to University College, London, together with a sum to found a chair of Egyptology.

The Four-Fifteen Express

The events which I am about to relate took place between nine and ten years ago. Sebastopol had fallen in the early spring, the Peace of Paris had been concluded since March, our commercial relations with the Russian empire were but recently renewed; and I, returning home after my first northward journey since the war, was well pleased with the prospect of spending the month of December under the hospitable and thoroughly English roof of my excellent friend, Jonathan Jelf,

Esquire, of Dumbleton Manor, Clayborough, East Anglia. Travelling in the interests of the well-known firm in which it is my lot to be a junior partner, I had been called upon to visit not only the capitals of Russia and Poland, but had found it also necessary to pass some weeks among the trading ports of the Baltic; whence it came that the year was already far spent before I again set foot on English soil, and that, instead of shooting pheasants with him, as I had hoped, in October, I came to be my friend's guest during the more genial Christmastide.

My voyage over, and a few days given up to business in Liverpool and London, I hastened down to Clayborough with all the delight of a schoolboy whose holidays are at hand. My way lay by the Great East Anglian Line as far as Clayborough station, where I was to be met by one of the Dumbleton carriages and conveyed across the remaining nine miles of country. It was a foggy afternoon, singularly warm for the 4th of December, and I had arranged to leave London by the 4:15 express. The early darkness of winter had already closed in; the lamps were lighted in the carriages; a clinging damp dimmed the windows, adhered to the door-handles, and pervaded all the atmosphere; while the gas-jets at the neighbouring bookstand diffused a luminous haze that only served to make the gloom of the terminus more visible. Having arrived some seven minutes before the starting of the train, and, by the connivance of the guard, taken sole possession of an empty compartment, I lighted my travelling-lamp, made myself particularly snug, and settled down to the undisturbed enjoyment of a book and a cigar. Great, therefore, was my disappointment when, at the last moment, a gentleman came hurrying along the platform, glanced into my carriage, opened the locked door with a private key, and stepped in.

It struck me at the first glance that I had seen him before – a tall, spare man, thin-lipped, light-eyed, with an ungraceful stoop in the shoulders and scant grey hair worn somewhat long upon the collar. He carried a light waterproof coat, an umbrella and a large brown japanned deed-box, which last he placed under the seat. This done, he felt carefully in his breast-pocket, as if to make certain of the safety of his purse or pocketbook, laid his umbrella in the netting overhead, spread the waterproof across his knees, and exchanged his hat for a travelling-cap of some Scotch material. By this time the train was moving out of the station and into the faint grey of the wintry twilight beyond.

I now recognised my companion. I recognised him from the moment when he removed his hat and uncovered the lofty, furrowed and somewhat narrow brow beneath. I had met him, as I distinctly remembered, some three years before, at the very house for which, in all probability, he was now bound, like myself. His name was Dwerrihouse, he was a lawyer by profession, and, if I was not greatly mistaken, was first cousin to the wife of my host. I knew also that he was a man eminently 'well-to-do', both as regarded his professional and private means. The Jelfs entertained him with that sort of observant courtesy which falls to the lot of the rich relation, the children made much of him, and the old butler, albeit somewhat surly 'to the general', treated him with deference. I thought, observing him by the vague mixture of lamplight and twilight, that Mrs Jelf's cousin looked all the worse for the three years' wear and tear which had gone over his head since our last meeting. He was very pale, and had a restless light in his eye that I did not remember to have observed before. The anxious lines, too, about his mouth were deepened, and there was a cavernous, hollow look about his cheeks and temples which seemed to speak of sickness or sorrow. He had glanced at me as he came in, but without any gleam of recognition in his face. Now he glanced again, as I fancied, somewhat doubtfully. When he did so for the third or fourth time I ventured to address him.

'Mr John Dwerrihouse, I think?'

'That is my name,' he replied.

'I had the pleasure of meeting you at Dumbleton about three years ago.'

Mr Dwerrihouse bowed. 'I thought I knew your face,' he said; 'but your name, I regret to say – '

'Langford – William Langford. I have known Jonathan Jelf since we were boys together at Merchant Taylors', and I generally spend a few weeks at Dumbleton in the shooting season. I suppose we are bound for the same destination?'

'Not if you are on your way to the manor,' he replied. 'I am travelling upon business – rather troublesome business too – while you, doubtless, have only pleasure in view.'

'Just so. I am in the habit of looking forward to this visit as to the brightest three weeks in all the year.'

'It is a pleasant house,' said Mr Dwerrihouse.

'The pleasantest I know.'

'And Jelf is thoroughly hospitable.'

'The best and kindest fellow in the world!'

'They have invited me to spend Christmas week with them,' pursued Mr Dwerrihouse, after a moment's pause.

'And you are coming?'

'I cannot tell. It must depend on the issue of this business which I have in hand. You have heard perhaps that we are about to construct a branch line from Blackwater to Stockbridge.'

I explained that I had been for some months away from England, and had therefore heard nothing of the contemplated improvement. Mr Dwerrihouse smiled complacently.

'It *will* be an improvement,' he said, 'a great improvement. Stockbridge is a flourishing town, and needs but a more direct railway communication with the metropolis to become an important centre of commerce. This branch was my own idea. I brought the project before the board, and have myself superintended the execution of it up to the present time.'

'You are an East Anglian director, I presume?'

'My interest in the company,' replied Mr Dwerrihouse, 'is

threefold. I am a director, I am a considerable shareholder, and, as head of the firm of Dwerrihouse, Dwerrihouse & Craik, I am the company's principal solicitor.'

Loquacious, self-important, full of his pet project, and apparently unable to talk on any other subject, Mr Dwerrihouse then went on to tell of the opposition he had encountered and the obstacles he had overcome in the cause of the Stockbridge branch. I was entertained with a multitude of local details and local grievances. The rapacity of one squire, the impracticability of another, the indignation of the rector whose glebe was threatened, the culpable indifference of the Stockbridge townspeople, who could *not* be brought to see that their most vital interests hinged upon a junction with the Great East Anglian Line, the spite of the local newspaper, and the unheard-of difficulties attending the Common question, were each and all laid before me with a circumstantiality that possessed the deepest interest for my excellent fellow-traveller, but none whatever for myself. From these, to my despair, he went on to more intricate matters: to the approximate expenses of construction per mile; to the estimates sent in by different contractors; to the probable traffic returns of the new line; to the provisional clauses of the new act as enumerated in Schedule D of the company's last half-yearly report; and so on and on and on, till my head ached and my attention flagged and my eyes kept closing in spite of every effort that I made to keep them open. At length I was roused by these words: 'Seventy-five thousand pounds, cash down.'

'Seventy-five thousand pounds, cash down,' I repeated, in the liveliest tone I could assume. 'That is a heavy sum.'

'A heavy sum to carry here,' replied Mr Dwerrihouse, pointing significantly to his breast pocket, 'but a mere fraction of what we shall ultimately have to pay.'

'You do not mean to say that you have seventy-five thousand pounds at this moment upon your person?' I exclaimed.

'My good sir, have I not been telling you so for the last half-hour?' said Mr Dwerrihouse, testily. 'That money has to be paid over at half-past eight o'clock this evening, at the office of Sir Thomas's solicitors, on completion of the deed of sale.'

'But how will you get across by night from Blackwater to Stockbridge with seventy-five thousand pounds in your pocket?'

'To Stockbridge!' echoed the lawyer. 'I find I have made myself very imperfectly understood. I thought I had explained how this sum only carries us as far as Mallingford – the first stage, as it were, of our journey – and how our route from Blackwater to Mallingford lies entirely through Sir Thomas Liddell's property.'

'I beg your pardon,' I stammered. 'I fear my thoughts were wandering. So you only go as far as Mallingford tonight?'

'Precisely. I shall get a conveyance from the Blackwater Arms. And you?'

'Oh, Jelf sends a trap to meet me at Clayborough! Can I be the bearer of any message from you?'

'You may say, if you please, Mr Langford, that I wished I could have been your companion all the way, and that I will come over, if possible, before Christmas.'

'Nothing more?'

Mr Dwerrihouse smiled grimly. 'Well,' he said, 'you may tell my cousin that she need not burn the hall down in my honour this time, and that I shall be obliged if she will order the blue-room chimney to be swept before I arrive.'

'That sounds tragic. Had you a conflagration on the occasion of your last visit to Dumbleton?'

'Something like it. There had been no fire lighted in my bedroom since the spring, the flue was foul and the jackdaws had built in it; so when I went up to dress for dinner I found the room full of smoke and the chimney on fire. Are we already at Blackwater?'

The train had gradually come to a pause while Mr Dwerrihouse was speaking, and, on putting my head out of the window, I could see the station some few hundred yards ahead. There was another train before us blocking the way, and the guard was making use of the delay to collect the Blackwater tickets. I had scarcely ascertained our position when the ruddy-faced official appeared at our carriage door.

'Tickets, sir!' said he.

'I am for Clayborough,' I replied, holding out the pink card.

He took it, glanced at it by the light of his little lantern, gave it back, looked, as I fancied, somewhat sharply at my fellow-traveller, and disappeared.

'He did not ask for yours,' I said, with some surprise.

'They never do,' replied Mr Dwerrihouse; 'they all know me, and of course I travel free.'

'Blackwater! Blackwater!' cried the porter, running along the platform beside us as we glided into the station.

Mr Dwerrihouse pulled out his deed-box, put his travelling-cap in his pocket, resumed his hat, took down his umbrella, and prepared to be gone.

'Many thanks, Mr Langford, for your society,' he said, with old-fashioned courtesy. 'I wish you a good-evening.'

'Good-evening,' I replied, putting out my hand.

But he either did not see it or did not choose to see it, and, slightly lifting his hat, stepped out upon the platform. Having done this, he moved slowly away and mingled with the departing crowd.

Leaning forward to watch him out of sight, I trod upon something which proved to be a cigar-case. It had fallen, no doubt, from the pocket of his waterproof coat, and was made of dark morocco leather, with a silver monogram upon the side. I sprang out of the carriage just as the guard came up to lock me in.

'Is there a minute to spare?' I asked, eagerly. 'The gentleman who travelled down with me from town has dropped his cigar-case; he is not yet out of the station.'

'Just a minute and a half, sir,' replied the guard. 'You must be quick.'

I dashed along the platform as fast as my feet could carry me. It was a large station, and Mr Dwerrihouse had by this time got more than halfway to the farther end.

I, however, saw him distinctly, moving slowly with the stream. Then, as I drew nearer, I saw that he had met some friend, that they were talking as they walked, that they presently fell back somewhat from the crowd and stood aside in earnest conversation. I made straight for the spot where they were waiting. There was a vivid gas-jet just above their heads, and the light fell full upon their faces. I saw both distinctly – the face of Mr Dwerrihouse and the face of his companion. Running, breathless, eager as I was, getting in the way of porters and passengers, and fearful every instant lest I should see the train going on without me, I yet observed that the newcomer was considerably younger and shorter than the director, that he was sandy-haired, mustachioed, small-featured, and dressed in a close-cut suit of Scotch tweed. I was now within a few yards of them. I ran against a stout gentleman, I was nearly knocked down by a luggage-truck, I stumbled over a carpetbag; I gained the spot just as the driver's whistle warned me to return.

To my utter stupefaction, they were no longer there. I had seen them but two seconds before – and they were gone! I stood still; I looked to right and left; I saw no sign of them in any direction. It was as if the platform had gaped and swallowed them.

'There were two gentlemen standing here a moment ago,' I said to a porter at my elbow; 'which way can they have gone?'

'I saw no gentlemen, sir,' replied the man. The whistle shrilled out again. The guard, far up the platform, held up his arm, and shouted to me to 'come on!'

'If you're going on by this train, sir,' said the porter, 'you must run for it.'

I did run for it, just gained the carriage as the train began to move, was shoved in by the guard, and left, breathless and bewildered, with Mr Dwerrihouse's cigar-case still in my hand.

It was the strangest disappearance in the world; it was like a transformation trick in a pantomime. They were there one moment – palpably there, with the gaslight full upon their faces – and the next moment they were gone. There was no door near, no window, no staircase; it was a mere slip of barren platform, tapestried with big advertisements. Could anything be more mysterious?

It was not worth thinking about, and yet, for my life, I could not help pondering upon it – pondering, wondering, conjecturing, turning it over and over in my mind, and beating my brains for a solution of the enigma. I thought of it all the way from Blackwater to Clayborough. I thought of it all the way from Clayborough to Dumbleton, as I rattled along the smooth highway in a trim dog-cart, drawn by a splendid black mare and driven by the silentest and dapperest of East Anglian grooms.

We did the nine miles in something less than an hour, and pulled up before the lodge-gates just as the church clock was striking half-past seven. A couple of minutes more, and the warm glow of the lighted hall was flooding out upon the gravel, a hearty grasp was on my hand, and a clear jovial voice was bidding me 'welcome to Dumbleton'.

'And now, my dear fellow,' said my host, when the first greeting was over, 'you have no time to spare. We dine at eight, and there are people coming to meet you, so you must just get the dressing business over as quickly as may be. By the way, you will meet some acquaintances: the Biddulphs are coming, and Prendergast (Prendergast of the Skirmishers) is staying in the house. Adieu! Mrs Jelf will be expecting you in the drawing-room.'

I was ushered to my room – not the blue room, of which Mr Dwerrihouse had made disagreeable experience, but a pretty little bachelor's chamber, hung with a delicate chintz and made cheerful by a blazing fire. I unlocked my portmanteau. I tried to be expeditious, but the memory of my railway adventure haunted me. I could not get free of it; I could not shake it off. It impeded me, worried me, it tripped me up, it caused me to mislay my studs, to mis-tie my cravat, to wrench the buttons off my gloves. Worst of all, it made me so late that the party had all assembled before I reached the drawing-room. I had scarcely paid my respects to Mrs Jelf when dinner was announced, and we paired off, some eight or ten couples strong, into the dining-room.

I am not going to describe either the guests or the dinner. All provincial parties bear the strictest family resemblance, and I am not aware that an East Anglian banquet offers any exception to the rule. There was the usual country baronet and his wife; there were the usual country parsons and their wives; there was the sempiternal turkey and haunch of venison. *Vanitas vanitatum*. There is nothing new under the sun.

I was placed about midway down the table. I had taken one rector's wife down to dinner, and I had another at my left hand. They talked across me, and their talk was about babies; it was dreadfully dull. At length there came a pause. The entrées had just been removed, and the turkey had come upon the scene. The conversation had all along been of the languidest, but at this moment it happened to have stagnated altogether. Jelf was carving the turkey; Mrs Jelf looked as if she was trying to think of something to say; everybody else was silent. Moved by an unlucky impulse, I thought I would relate my adventure.

'By the way, Jelf,' I began, 'I came down part of the way today with a friend of yours.'

'Indeed!' said the master of the feast, slicing scientifically into the breast of the turkey. 'With whom, pray?'

'With one who bade me tell you that he should, if possible, pay you a visit before Christmas.'

'I cannot think who that could be,' said my friend, smiling.

'It must be Major Thorp,' suggested Mrs Jelf.

I shook my head. 'It was not Major Thorp,' I replied; 'it was a near relation of your own, Mrs Jelf.'

'Then I am more puzzled than ever,' replied my hostess. 'Pray tell me who it was.'

'It was no less a person than your cousin, Mr John Dwerrihouse.'

Jonathan Jelf laid down his knife and fork. Mrs Jelf looked at me in a strange, startled way, and said never a word.

'And he desired me to tell you, my dear madam, that you need not take the trouble to burn the hall down in his honour this time, but only to have the chimney of the blue room swept before his arrival.'

Before I had reached the end of my sentence I became aware of something ominous in the faces of the guests. I felt I had said something which I had better have left unsaid, and that for some unexplained reason my words had evoked a general consternation. I sat confounded, not daring to utter another syllable, and for at least two whole minutes there was dead silence round the table. Then Captain Prendergast came to the rescue.

'You have been abroad for some months, have you not, Mr Langford?' he said, with the desperation of one who flings himself into the breach. 'I heard you had been to Russia. Surely you have something to tell us of the state and temper of the country after the war?'

I was heartily grateful to the gallant Skirmisher for this diversion in my favour. I answered him, I fear, somewhat lamely; but he kept the conversation up, and presently one or two others joined in and so the difficulty, whatever it might have been, was bridged over – bridged over, but not repaired.

A something, an awkwardness, a visible constraint remained. The guests hitherto had been simply dull, but now they were evidently uncomfortable and embarrassed.

The dessert had scarcely been placed upon the table when the ladies left the room. I seized the opportunity to select a vacant chair next Captain Prendergast.

'In heaven's name,' I whispered, 'what was the matter just now? What had I said?'

'You mentioned the name of John Dwerrihouse.'

'What of that? I had seen him not two hours before.'

'It is a most astounding circumstance that you should have seen him,' said Captain Prendergast. 'Are you sure it was he?'

'As sure as of my own identity. We were talking all the way between London and Blackwater. But why does that surprise you?'

'*Because*,' replied Captain Prendergast, dropping his voice to the lowest whisper – '*because John Dwerrihouse absconded three months ago with seventy-five thousand pounds of the company's money, and has never been heard of since.*'

John Dwerrihouse had absconded three months ago – and I had seen him only a few hours back! John Dwerrihouse had embezzled seventy-five thousand pounds of the company's money, yet told me that he carried that sum upon his person! Were ever facts so strangely incongruous, so difficult to reconcile? How should he have ventured again into the light of day? How dared he show himself along the line? Above all, what had he been doing throughout those mysterious three months of disappearance?

Perplexing questions these – questions which at once suggested themselves to the minds of all concerned, but which admitted of no easy solution. I could find no reply to them. Captain Prendergast had not even a suggestion to offer. Jonathan Jelf, who seized the first opportunity of drawing me aside and learning all that I had to tell, was more amazed and bewildered than either of us.

He came to my room that night, when all the guests were gone, and we talked the thing over from every point of view; without, it must be confessed, arriving at any kind of conclusion.

'I do not ask you,' he said, 'whether you can have mistaken your man. That is impossible.'

'As impossible as that I should mistake some stranger for yourself.'

'It is not a question of looks or voice, but of facts. That he should have alluded to the fire in the blue room is proof enough of John Dwerrihouse's identity. How did he look?'

'Older, I thought; considerably older, paler, and more anxious.'

'He has had enough to make him look anxious, anyhow,' said my friend, gloomily, 'be he innocent or guilty.'

'I am inclined to believe that he is innocent,' I replied. 'He showed no embarrassment when I addressed him, and no uneasiness when the guard came round. His conversation was open to a fault. I might almost say that he talked too freely of the business which he had in hand.'

'That is strange, for I know no one more reticent on such subjects. He actually told you that he had the seventy-five thousand pounds in his pocket?'

'He did.'

'Humph! My wife has an idea about it, and she may be right –'

'What idea?'

'Well, she fancies – women are so clever, you know, at putting themselves inside people's motives – she fancies that he was tempted, that he did actually take the money, and that he has been concealing himself these three months in some wild part of the country, struggling possibly with his conscience all the time, and daring neither to abscond with his booty nor to come back and restore it.'

'But now that he has come back?'

'That is the point. She conceives that he has probably thrown himself upon the company's mercy, made restitution of the money, and, being forgiven, is permitted to carry the business through as if nothing whatever had happened.'

'The last,' I replied, 'is an impossible case. Mrs Jelf thinks like a generous and delicate-minded woman, but not in the least like a board of railway directors. They would never carry forgiveness so far.'

'I fear not; and yet it is the only conjecture that bears a semblance of likelihood. However we can run over to Clayborough tomorrow and see if anything is to be learned. By the way Prendergast tells me you picked up his cigar-case.'

'I did so, and here it is.'

Jelf took the cigar-case, examined it by the light of the lamp, and said at once that it was beyond doubt Mr Dwerrihouse's property, and that he remembered to have seen him use it.

'Here, too, is his monogram on the side,' he added – 'a big J transfixing a capital D. He used to carry the same on his note-paper.'

'It offers, at all events, a proof that I was not dreaming.'

'Ay, but it is time you were asleep and dreaming now. I am ashamed to have kept you up so long. Good-night.'

'Good-night, and remember that I am more than ready to go with you to Clayborough or Blackwater or London or anywhere, if I can be of the least service.'

'Thanks! I know you mean it, old friend, and it may be that I shall put you to the test. Once more, good-night.'

So we parted for that night, and met again in the breakfast-room at half-past eight next morning. It was a hurried, silent, uncomfortable meal; none of us had slept well, and all were thinking of the same subject. Mrs Jelf had evidently been crying. Jelf was impatient to be off, and both Captain Prendergast and myself felt ourselves to be in the painful position of outsiders who are involuntarily brought into a domestic trouble. Within twenty minutes after we had left the breakfast-table the dog-cart was brought round and my friend and I were on the road to Clayborough.

'Tell you what it is, Langford,' he said, as we sped along between the wintry hedges, 'I do not much fancy to bring up Dwerrihouse's name at Clayborough. All the officials know that he is my wife's relation, and the subject just now is hardly a pleasant one. If you don't much mind, we will make the 11:10 to Blackwater. It's an important station, and we shall stand a far better chance of picking up information there than at Clayborough.'

So we took the 11:10, which happened to be an express, and, arriving at Blackwater about a quarter before twelve, proceeded at once to prosecute our enquiry.

We began by asking for the station-master, a big, blunt, businesslike person, who at once averred that he knew Mr John Dwerrihouse perfectly well, and that there was no director on the line whom he had seen and spoken to so frequently.

'He used to be down here two or three times a week about three months ago,' said he, 'when the new line was first set afoot; but since then, you know, gentlemen – '

He paused significantly.

Jelf flushed scarlet.

'Yes, yes,' he said, hurriedly; 'we know all about that. The point now to be ascertained is whether anything has been seen or heard of him lately.'

'Not to my knowledge,' replied the station-master.

'He is not known to have been down the line any time yesterday, for instance?'

The station-master shook his head. 'The East Anglian, sir,' said he, 'is about the last place where he would dare to show himself. Why, there isn't a station-master, there isn't a guard, there isn't a porter, who doesn't know Mr Dwerrihouse by sight as well as he knows his own face in the looking-glass, or who wouldn't telegraph for the police as soon as he had set eyes on him at any point along the line. Bless you, sir! there's been a standing order out against him ever since the 25th of September last.'

'And yet,' pursued my friend, 'a gentleman who travelled down yesterday from London to Clayborough by the afternoon express testifies that he saw Mr Dwerrihouse in the train, and that Mr Dwerrihouse alighted at Blackwater station.'

'Quite impossible, sir,' replied the station-master promptly.

'Why impossible?'

'Because there is no station along the line where he is so well known or where he would run so great a risk. It would be just running his head into the lion's mouth; he would have been mad to come nigh Blackwater station; and if he had come he would have been arrested before he left the platform.'

'Can you tell me who took the Blackwater tickets of that train?'

'I can, sir. It was the guard, Benjamin Somers.'

'And where can I find him?'

'You can find him, sir, by staying here, if you please, till one o'clock. He will be coming through with the up express from Crampton, which stays in Blackwater for ten minutes.'

We waited for the up express, beguiling the time as best we could by strolling along the Blackwater road till we came almost to the outskirts of the town, from which the station was distant nearly a couple of miles. By one o'clock we were back again upon the platform and waiting for the train. It came punctually, and I at once recognised the ruddy-faced guard who had gone down with my train the evening before.

'The gentlemen want to ask you something about Mr Dwerrihouse, Somers,' said the station-master, by way of introduction.

The guard flashed a keen glance from my face to Jelf's and back again to mine. 'Mr John Dwerrihouse, the late director?' said he, interrogatively.

'The same,' replied my friend. 'Should you know him if you saw him?'

'Anywhere, sir.'

'Do you know if he was in the 4:15 express yesterday afternoon?'

'He was not, sir.'

'How can you answer so positively?'

'Because I looked into every carriage and saw every face in that train, and I could take my oath that Mr Dwerrihouse was not in it. This gentleman was,' he added, turning sharply upon me. 'I don't know that I ever saw him before in my life, but I remember *his* face perfectly. You nearly missed taking your seat in time at this station, sir, and you got out at Clayborough.'

'Quite true, guard,' I replied; 'but do you not remember the face of the gentleman who travelled down in the same carriage with me as far as here?'

'It was my impression, sir, that you travelled down alone,' said Somers, with a look of some surprise.

'By no means. I had a fellow-traveller as far as Blackwater, and it was in trying to restore him the cigar-case which he had dropped in the carriage that I nearly let you go on without me.'

'I remember your saying something about a cigar-case, certainly,' replied the guard; 'but – '

'You asked for my ticket just before we entered the station.'

'I did, sir.'

'Then you must have seen him. He sat in the corner next the very door to which you came.'

'No, indeed; I saw no one.'

I looked at Jelf. I began to think the guard was in the ex-director's confidence, and paid for his silence.

'If I had seen another traveller I should have asked for his ticket,' added Somers. 'Did you see me ask for his ticket, sir?'

'I observed that you did not ask for it, but he explained that by saying – ' I hesitated. I feared I might be telling too much, and so broke off abruptly.

The guard and the station-master exchanged glances. The former looked impatiently at his watch.

'I am obliged to go on in four minutes more, sir,' he said.

'One last question, then,' interposed Jelf, with a sort of desperation. 'If this gentleman's fellow traveller had been Mr John Dwerrihouse, and he had been sitting in the corner next the door in which you took the tickets, could you have failed to see and recognise him?'

'No, sir; it would have been quite impossible!'

'And you are certain you did *not* see him?'

'As I said before, sir, I could take my oath, I did not see him. And if it wasn't that I don't like to contradict a gentleman, I would say I could also take my oath that this gentlemen was quite alone in the carriage the whole way from London to Clayborough. Why, sir,' he added dropping his voice so as to be inaudible to the station-master, who had been called away to speak to some person close by, 'you expressly asked me to give you a compartment to yourself, and I did so. I locked you in, and you were so good as to give me something for myself.'

'Yes; but Mr Dwerrihouse had a key of his own.'

'I never saw him, sir; I saw no one in that compartment but yourself. Beg pardon, sir; my time's up.'

And with this the ruddy guard touched his cap and was gone. In another minute the heavy panting of the engine began afresh, and the train glided slowly out of the station.

We looked at each other for some moments in silence. I was the first to speak. 'Mr Benjamin Somers knows more than he chooses to tell,' I said.

'Humph! do you think so?'

'It must be. He could not have come to the door without seeing him; it's impossible.'

'There is one thing not impossible, my dear fellow.'

'What is that?'

'That you may have fallen asleep and dreamed the whole thing.'

'Could I dream of a branch line that I had never heard of? Could I dream of a hundred and one business details that had no kind of interest for me? Could I dream of the seventy-five thousand pounds?'

'Perhaps you might have seen or heard some vague account of the affair while you were abroad. It might have made no impression upon you at the time, and might have come back to you in your dreams, recalled perhaps by the mere names of the stations on the line.'

'What about the fire in the chimney of the blue room – should I have heard of that during my journey?'

'Well, no; I admit there is a difficulty about that point.'

'And what about the cigar-case?'

'Ay, by Jove! there is the cigar-case. That *is* a stubborn fact. Well, it's a mysterious affair, and it will need a better detective than myself, I fancy, to clear it up. I suppose we may as well go home.'

* * *

A week had not gone by when I received a letter from the secretary of the East Anglian Railway Company, requesting the favour of my attendance at a special board meeting not then many days distant. No reasons were alleged and no apologies offered for this demand upon my time, but they had heard, it was clear, of my enquiries about the missing director, and had a mind to put me through some sort of official examination upon the subject. Being still a guest at Dumbleton Hall, I had to go up to London for the purpose and Jonathan Jelf accompanied me. I found the direction of the Great East Anglian Line represented by a party of some twelve or fourteen gentlemen seated in solemn conclave round a huge green-baize table, in a gloomy boardroom adjoining the London terminus.

Being courteously received by the chairman (who at once began by saying that certain statements of mine respecting Mr John Dwerrihouse had come to the knowledge of the direction, and that they in consequence desired to confer with me on those points), I was placed at the table and the inquiry proceeded in due form.

I was first asked if I knew Mr John Dwerrihouse, how long I had been acquainted with him and whether I could identify him at sight. I was then asked when I had seen him last. To which I replied, 'On the 4th of this present month, December, 1856.' Then came the enquiry of where I had seen him on that fourth day of December; to which I replied that I met him in a first-class compartment of the 4:15 down express, that he got in just as the train was leaving the London terminus and that he alighted at Blackwater station. The chairman then enquired whether I had held any communication with my fellow-traveller; whereupon I related, as nearly as I could remember it, the whole bulk and substance of Mr John Dwerrihouse's diffuse information respecting the new branch line.

To all this the board listened with profound attention, while the chairman presided and the secretary took notes. I then produced the cigar-case. It was passed from hand to hand, and recognised by all. There was not a man present who did not remember that plain cigar-case with its silver monogram, or to whom it seemed anything less than entirely corroborative of my evidence. When at length I had told all that I had to tell, the chairman whispered something to the secretary; the secretary touched a silver handbell, and the guard, Benjamin Somers, was ushered into the room. He was then examined as carefully as myself. He declared that he knew Mr John Dwerrihouse perfectly well, that he could not be mistaken in him, that he remembered going down with the 4:15 express on the afternoon in question, that he remembered me, and that, there being one or two empty first-class compartments on that especial afternoon, he had, in compliance with my request, placed me in a carriage by myself. He was positive that I remained alone in that compartment all the way from London to Clayborough. He was ready to take his oath that Dwerrihouse was neither in that carriage with me nor in any other compartment of that train. He remembered distinctly to have examined my ticket to Blackwater; was certain that there was no one else at that time in the carriage; could not have failed to observe a second person, if there had been one; had that second person been Mr John Dwerrihouse, should have quietly double-locked the door of the carriage and have at once given information to the Blackwater station-master. So clear, so decisive, so ready, was Somers with this testimony that the board looked fairly puzzled.

'You hear this person's statement, Mr Langford,' said the chairman. 'It contradicts yours in every particular. What have you to say in reply?'

'I can only repeat what I said before. I am quite as positive of the truth of my own assertions as Mr Somers can be of the truth of his.'

'You say that Mr Dwerrihouse alighted in Blackwater, and that he was in possession of a private key. Are you sure that he had not alighted by means of that key before the guard came round for the tickets?'

'I am quite positive that he did not leave the carriage till the train had fairly entered the station, and the other Blackwater passengers alighted. I even saw that he was met there by a friend.'

'Indeed! Did you see that person distinctly?'

'Quite distinctly.'

'Can you describe his appearance?'

'I think so. He was short and very slight, sandy-haired, with a bushy moustache and beard, and he wore a closely fitting suit of grey tweed. His age I should take to be about thirty-eight or forty.'

'Did Mr Dwerrihouse leave the station in this person's company?'

'I cannot tell. I saw them walking together down the platform, and then I saw them standing inside under a gas-jet, talking earnestly. After that I lost sight of them quite suddenly, and just then my train went on, and I with it.'

The chairman and secretary conferred together in an undertone. The directors whispered to one another. One or two looked suspiciously at the guard. I could see that my evidence remained unshaken, and that, like myself, they suspected some complicity between the guard and the defaulter.

'How far did you conduct that 4:15 express on the day in question, Somers?' asked the chairman.

'All through, sir,' replied the guard, 'from London to Crampton.'

'How was it that you were not relieved at Clayborough? I thought there was always a change of guards at Clayborough.'

'There used to be, sir, till the new regulations came in force last midsummer, since when the guards in charge of express trains go the whole way through.'

The chairman turned to the secretary.

'I think it would be as well,' he said, 'if we had the daybook to refer to upon this point.'

Again the secretary touched the silver handbell, and desired the porter in attendance to summon Mr Raikes. From a word or two dropped by another of the directors I gathered that Mr Raikes was one of the under-secretaries.

He came, a small, slight, sandy-haired, keen-eyed man, with an eager, nervous manner, and a forest of light beard and moustache. He just showed himself at the door of the board-room, and, being requested to bring a certain daybook from a certain shelf in a certain room, bowed and vanished.

He was there such a moment, and the surprise of seeing him was so great and sudden, that it was not till the door had closed upon him that I found voice to speak. He was no sooner gone, however, than I sprang to my feet.

'That person,' I said, 'is the same who met Mr Dwerrihouse upon the platform at Blackwater!'

There was a general movement of surprise. The chairman looked grave and somewhat agitated.

'Take care, Mr Langford,' he said; 'take care what you say.'

'I am as positive of his identity as of my own.'

'Do you consider the consequences of your words? Do you consider that you are bringing a charge of the gravest character against one of the company's servants?'

'I am willing to be put upon my oath, if necessary. The man who came to that door a minute since is the same whom I saw talking with Mr Dwerrihouse on the Blackwater platform. Were he twenty times the company's servant, I could say neither more nor less.'

The chairman turned again to the guard.

'Did you see Mr Raikes in the train or on the platform?' he asked.

Somers shook his head. 'I am confident Mr Raikes was not in the train,' he said, 'and I certainly did not see him on the platform.'

The chairman turned next to the secretary.

'Mr Raikes is in your office, Mr Hunter,' he said. 'Can you remember if he was absent on the 4th instant?'

'I do not think he was,' replied the secretary, 'but I am not prepared to speak positively. I have been away most afternoons myself lately, and Mr Raikes might easily have absented himself if he had been disposed.'

At this moment the under-secretary returned with the day-book under his arm.

'Be pleased to refer, Mr Raikes,' said the chairman, 'to the entries of the 4th instant, and see what Benjamin Somers's duties were on that day.'

Mr Raikes threw open the cumbrous volume, and ran a practised eye and finger down some three or four successive columns of entries. Stopping suddenly at the foot of a page, he then read aloud that Benjamin Somers had on that day conducted the 4:15 express from London to Crampton.

The chairman leaned forward in his seat, looked the under-secretary full in the face, and said, quite sharply and suddenly: 'Where were you, Mr Raikes, on the same afternoon?'

'*I*, sir?'

'You, Mr Raikes. Where were you on the afternoon and evening of the 4th of the present month?'

'Here, sir, in Mr Hunter's office. Where else should I be?'

There was a dash of trepidation in the under-secretary's voice as he said this, but his look of surprise was natural enough.

'We have some reason for believing, Mr Raikes, that you were absent that afternoon without leave. Was this the case?'

'Certainly not, sir. I have not had a day's holiday since September. Mr Hunter will bear me out in this.'

Mr Hunter repeated what he had previously said on the subject, but added that the clerks in the adjoining office would be certain to know. Whereupon the senior clerk, a grave, middle-aged person in green glasses, was summoned and interrogated.

His testimony cleared the under-secretary at once. He declared that Mr Raikes had in no instance, to his knowledge, been absent during office hours since his return from his annual holiday in September.

I was confounded. The chairman turned to me with a smile, in which a shade of covert annoyance was scarcely apparent.

'You hear, Mr Langford?' he said.

'I hear, sir; but my conviction remains unshaken.'

'I fear, Mr Langford, that your convictions are very

insufficiently based,' replied the chairman, with a doubtful cough. 'I fear that you "dream dreams", and mistake them for actual occurrences. It is a dangerous habit of mind, and might lead to dangerous results. Mr Raikes here would have found himself in an unpleasant position had he not proved so satisfactory an alibi.'

I was about to reply, but he gave me no time.

'I think, gentlemen,' he went on to say, addressing the board, 'that we should be wasting time to push this inquiry further. Mr Langford's evidence would seem to be of an equal value throughout. The testimony of Benjamin Somers disproves his first statement, and the testimony of the last witness disproves his second. I think we may conclude that Mr Langford fell asleep in the train on the occasion of his journey to Clayborough, and dreamed an unusually vivid and circumstantial dream, of which, however, we have now heard quite enough.'

There are few things more annoying than to find one's positive convictions met with incredulity. I could not help feeling impatience at the turn that affairs had taken. I was not proof against the civil sarcasm of the chairman's manner. Most intolerable of all, however, was the quiet smile lurking about the corners of Benjamin Somers's mouth, and the half-triumphant, half-malicious gleam in the eyes of the under-secretary. The man was evidently puzzled and somewhat alarmed. His looks seemed furtively to interrogate me. Who was I? What did I want? Why had I come there to do him an ill turn with his employers? What was it to me whether or no he was absent without leave?

Seeing all this, and perhaps more irritated by it than the thing deserved, I begged leave to detain the attention of the board for a moment longer. Jelf plucked me impatiently by the sleeve.

'Better let the thing drop,' he whispered. 'The chairman's right enough; you dreamed it, and the less said now the better.'

I was not to be silenced, however, in this fashion. I had yet something to say, and I would say it. It was to this effect: that dreams were not usually productive of tangible results, and that I requested to know in what way the chairman conceived I had evolved from my dream so substantial and well-made a delusion as the cigar-case which I had had the honour to place before him at the commencement of our interview.

'The cigar-case, I admit, Mr Langford,' the chairman replied, 'is a very strong point in your evidence. It is your *only* strong point, however, and there is just a possibility that we may all be misled by a mere accidental resemblance. Will you permit me to see the case again?'

'It is unlikely,' I said, as I handed it to him, 'that any other should bear precisely this monogram, and also be in all other particulars exactly similar.'

The chairman examined it for a moment in silence, and then passed it to Mr Hunter. Mr Hunter turned it over and over, and shook his head.

'This is no mere resemblance,' he said. 'It is John Dwerrihouse's cigar-case to a certainty. I remember it perfectly; I have seen it a hundred times.'

'I believe I may say the same,' added the chairman; 'yet how account for the way in which Mr Langford asserts that it came into his possession?'

'I can only repeat,' I replied, 'that I found it on the floor of the carriage after Mr Dwerrihouse had alighted. It was in leaning out to look after him that I trod upon it, and it was in running after him for the purpose of restoring it that I saw, or believed I saw, Mr Raikes standing aside with him in earnest conversation.'

Again I felt Jonathan Jelf plucking at my sleeve.

'Look at Raikes,' he whispered; 'look at Raikes!'

I turned to where the under-secretary had been standing a moment before, and saw him, white as death, with lips trembling and livid, stealing towards the door.

To conceive a sudden, strange and indefinite suspicion, to fling myself in his way, to take him by the shoulders as if he were a child, and turn his craven face, perforce, towards the board, were with me the work of an instant.

'Look at him!' I exclaimed. 'Look at his face! I ask no better witness to the truth of my words.'

The chairman's brow darkened.

'Mr Raikes,' he said, sternly, 'if you know anything you had better speak.'

Vainly trying to wrench himself from my grasp, the under-secretary stammered out an incoherent denial.

'Let me go,' he said. 'I know nothing – you have no right to detain me – let me go!'

'Did you, or did you not, meet Mr John Dwerrihouse at Blackwater station? The charge brought against you is either true or false. If true, you will do well to throw yourself upon the mercy of the board and make full confession of all that you know.'

The under-secretary wrung his hands in an agony of helpless terror. 'I was away!' he cried. 'I was two hundred miles away at the time! I know nothing about it – I have nothing to confess – I am innocent – I call God to witness I am innocent!'

'Two hundred miles away!' echoed the chairman. 'What do you mean?'

'I was in Devonshire. I had three weeks' leave of absence – I appeal to Mr Hunter – Mr Hunter knows I had three weeks' leave of absence! I was in Devonshire all the time; I can prove I was in Devonshire!'

Seeing him so abject, so incoherent, so wild with apprehension, the directors began to whisper gravely among themselves, while one got quietly up and called the porter to guard the door.

'What has your being in Devonshire to do with the matter?' said the chairman. 'When were you in Devonshire?'

'Mr Raikes took his leave in September,' said the secretary, 'about the time when Mr Dwerrihouse disappeared.'

'I never even heard that he had disappeared till I came back!'

'That must remain to be proved,' said the chairman. 'I shall at once put this matter in the hands of the police. In the meanwhile, Mr Raikes, being myself a magistrate and used to dealing with these cases, I advise you to offer no resistance but to confess while confession may yet do you service. As for your accomplice –'

The frightened wretch fell upon his knees.

'I had no accomplice!' he cried. 'Only have mercy upon me – only spare my life, and I will confess all! I didn't mean to harm him! I didn't mean to hurt a hair of his head! Only have mercy upon me, and let me go!'

The chairman rose in his place, pale and agitated.

'Good heavens!' he exclaimed, 'what horrible mystery is this? What does it mean?'

'As sure as there is a God in heaven,' said Jonathan Jelf, 'it means that murder has been done.'

'No! no! no!' shrieked Raikes, still upon his knees, and cowering like a beaten hound, 'not murder! No jury that ever sat could bring it in murder. I thought I had only stunned him – I never meant to do more than stun him! Manslaughter – manslaughter – not murder!'

Overcome by the horror of this unexpected revelation, the chairman covered his face with his hand and for a moment or two remained silent.

'Miserable man,' he said at length, 'you have betrayed yourself.'

'You bade me confess! You urged me to throw myself upon the mercy of the board!'

'You have confessed to a crime which no one suspected you of having committed,' replied the chairman, 'and which this board has no power either to punish or forgive. All that I can do for you is to advise you to submit to the law, to plead guilty, and to conceal nothing. When did you do this deed?'

The guilty man rose to his feet, and leaned heavily against the table. His answer came reluctantly, like the speech of one dreaming.

'On the 22nd of September!'

On the 22nd of September! I looked in Jonathan Jelf's face, and he in mine. I felt my own smiling with a strange sense of wonder and dread. I saw his blanch suddenly, even to the lips.

'Merciful Heaven!' he whispered. '*What was it, then, that you saw in the train?*'

What was it that I saw in the train? That question remains unanswered to this day. I have never been able to reply to it. I only know that it bore the living likeness of the murdered man, whose body had then been lying some ten weeks under a rough pile of branches and brambles and rotting leaves at the bottom of a deserted chalk-pit about halfway between Blackwater and Mallingford. I know that it spoke and moved and looked as that man spoke and moved and looked in life; that I heard, or seemed to hear, things revealed which I could never otherwise have learned; that I was guided, as it were, by that vision on the platform to the identification of the murderer; and that, a passive instrument myself, I was destined, by means of these mysterious teachings to bring about the ends of justice. For these things I have never been able to account.

As for that matter of the cigar-case, it proved, on enquiry, that the carriage in which I travelled down that afternoon to Clayborough had not been in use for several weeks, and was, in point of fact, the same in which poor John Dwerrihouse had performed his last journey. The case had doubtless been dropped by him, and had lain unnoticed till I found it.

Upon the details of the murder I have no need to dwell. Those who desire more ample particulars may find them, and the written confession of Augustus Raikes, in the files of *The*

Times for 1856. Enough that the under-secretary, knowing the history of the new line, and following the negotiation step by step through all its stages, determined to waylay Mr Dwerrihouse, rob him of the seventy-five thousand pounds and escape to America with his booty.

In order to effect these ends he obtained leave of absence a few days before the time appointed for the payment of the money, secured his passage across the Atlantic in a steamer advertised to start on the 23rd, provided himself with a heavily loaded 'life-preserver', and went down to Blackwater to await the arrival of his victim. How he met him on the platform with a pretended message from the board, how he offered to conduct him by a short cut across the fields to Mallingford, how, having brought him to a lonely place, he struck him down with the life-preserver, and so killed him, and how, finding what he had done, he dragged the body to the verge of an out-of-the-way chalk-pit, and there flung it in and piled it over with branches and brambles, are facts still fresh in the memories of those who, like the connoisseurs in De Quincey's famous essay, regard murder as a fine art. Strangely enough, the murderer having done his work, was afraid to leave the country. He declared that he had not intended to take the director's life, but only to stun and rob him and that, finding the blow had killed, he dared not fly for fear of drawing down suspicion upon his head. As a mere robber he would have been safe in the States, but as a murderer he would inevitably have been pursued and given up to justice. So he forfeited his passage, returned to the office as usual at the end of his leave, and locked up his ill-gotten thousands till a more convenient opportunity. In the meanwhile he had the satisfaction of finding that Mr Dwerrihouse was universally believed to have absconded with the money, no one knew how or whither.

Whether he meant murder or not, however, Mr Augustus Raikes paid the full penalty of his crime, and was hanged at the

Old Bailey in the second week of January 1857. Those who desire to make his further acquaintance may see him any day (admirably done in wax) in the Chamber of Horrors at Madame Tussaud's exhibition in Baker Street. He is there to be found in the midst of a select society of ladies and gentlemen of atrocious memory, dressed in the close-cut tweed suit which he wore on the evening of the murder and holding in his hand the identical life-preserver with which he committed it.

ARNOLD BENNETT

Arnold Bennett was born on 27 May 1867. He grew up in the environs of Hanley, Staffordshire, one of the Midlands pottery towns that later served as a backdrop for his celebrated *Five Towns* novels. The son of a solicitor, Bennett received a secondary education but was forced to leave school at the age of sixteen to be a clerk in his father's firm. Having twice failed his legal examinations, Bennett escaped to London in 1889 to work in law offices. Gradually drawn into literary and artistic circles, he abandoned the law in 1894 and embarked on a writing career, securing an editorial position with the weekly magazine *Woman.* The following year his story 'A Letter Home' appeared in the fashionable *Yellow Book*, and he soon brought out an autobiographical first novel, *A Man from the North* (1898). In 1902 Bennett completed two highly popular works: *The Grand Babylon Hotel* and *Anna of the Five Towns.* In 1903 Bennett settled in Paris, where he lived for much of the next decade. He scored a triumphant success in 1908 with the publication of *The Old Wives' Tale,* a masterful portrayal of English provincial life that rivals the novels of Flaubert and other French realists. Bennett enhanced his renown with the *Clayhanger* trilogy (1910–16) and enjoyed theatrical success in London with the plays *Milestones* (1912) and *The Great Adventure* (1913). Bennett's prominence declined temporarily following World War I but experienced a resurgence of popularity with *Riceyman Steps* (1923) and *Lord Raingo* (1926). In 1926 he began contributing a weekly book review to the London *Evening Standard*. His final novel, *Imperial Palace,* came out in 1930. Arnold Bennett died in London of typhoid fever on 27 March 1931.

Murder!

1

Many great ones of the earth have justified murder as a social act, defensible and even laudable in certain instances. There is something to be said for murder, though perhaps not much. All of us, or nearly all of us, have at one time or another had the desire and the impulse to commit murder. At any rate, murder is not an uncommon affair. On an average, two people are murdered every week in England, and probably about two hundred every week in the United States. And forty per cent of the murderers are not brought to justice. These figures take no account of the undoubtedly numerous cases where murder has been done but never suspected. Murders and murderesses walk safely abroad among us, and it may happen to us to shake hands with them. A disturbing thought! But such is life, and such is homicide.

2

Two men, named respectively Lomax Harder and John Franting, were walking side by side one autumn afternoon on the Marine Parade of the seaside resort and port of Quangate on the Channel coast. Both were well dressed and had the air of moderate wealth, and both were about thirty-five years of age. At this point the resemblances between them ceased. Lomax Harder had refined features, an enormous forehead, fair hair and a delicate, almost apologetic manner. John Franting was low-browed, heavy chinned, scowling, defiant, indeed what is called a tough customer. Lomax Harder corresponded in appearance with the popular notion of a poet – save that he was carefully barbered. He was in fact a poet, and not unknown in the tiny, trifling, mad world where poetry is a matter of first-rate interest. John Franting corresponded in appearance with the popular notion of a gambler, an amateur boxer and, in spare time, a deluder of women. Popular notions sometimes fit the truth.

Lomax Harder, somewhat nervously buttoning his overcoat, said in a quiet but firm and insistent tone: 'Haven't you got anything to say?'

John Franting stopped suddenly in front of a shop whose façade bore the sign: 'Gontle – Gunsmith'.

'Not in words,' answered Franting. 'I'm going in here.' And he brusquely entered the small, shabby shop.

Lomax Harder hesitated half a second, and then followed his companion.

The shopman was a middle-aged gentleman wearing a black velvet coat.

'Good-afternoon,' he greeted Franting, with an expression and in a tone of urbane condescension which seemed to indicate that Franting was a wise as well as a fortunate man in that he knew of the excellence of Gontle's and had the wit to come into Gontle's.

For the name of Gontle was favourably and respectfully known wherever triggers are pressed. Not only along the whole length of the Channel coast but throughout England was Gontle's renowned. Sportsmen would travel to Quangate from the far north, and even from London, to buy guns. To say: 'I bought it at Gontle's,' or, 'Old Gontle recommended it,' was sufficient to silence any dispute concerning the merits of a firearm. Experts bowed the head before the unique reputation of Gontle. As for old Gontle, he was extremely and pardonably conceited. His conviction that no other gunsmith in the wide world could compare with him was absolute. He sold guns and rifles with the gesture of a monarch conferring an honour. He never argued; he stated; and the customer who contradicted him was as likely as not to be courteously and icily informed by

Gontle of the geographical situation of the shop-door. Such shops exist in the English provinces, and nobody knows how they have achieved their renown. They could exist nowhere else.

' 'd-afternoon,' said Franting gruffly, and paused.

'What can I do for you?' asked Mr Gontle, as if saying: 'Now don't be afraid. This shop is tremendous, and I am tremendous; but I shall not eat you.'

'I want a revolver,' Franting snapped.

'Ah! A revolver!' commented Mr Gontle, as if saying: 'A gun or a rifle, yes! But a revolver – an arm without individuality, manufactured wholesale! . . . However, I suppose I must deign to accommodate you.'

'I presume you know something about revolvers?' asked Mr Gontle, as he began to produce the weapons.

'A little.'

'Do you know the Webley Mark III?'

'Can't say that I do.'

'Ah! It is the best for all common purposes.' And Mr Gontle's glance said: 'Have the goodness not to tell me it isn't.'

Franting examined the Webley Mark III.

'You see,' said Mr Gontle, 'the point about it is that until the breach is properly closed it cannot be fired. So that it can't blow open and maim or kill the would-be murderer.' Mr Gontle smiled archly at one of his oldest jokes.

'What about suicides?' Franting grimly demanded.

'Ah!'

'You might show me just how to load it,' said Franting.

Mr Gontle, having found ammunition, complied with this reasonable request.

'The barrel's a bit scratched,' said Franting.

Mr Gontle inspected the scratch with pain. He would have denied the scratch, but could not.

'Here's another one,' said he, 'since you're so particular.' He simply had to put customers in their place.

'You might load it,' said Franting.

Mr Gontle loaded the second revolver.

'I'd like to try it,' said Franting.

'Certainly,' said Mr Gontle, and led Franting out of the shop by the back exit and down to a cellar where revolvers could be experimented with.

Lomax Harder was now alone in the shop. He hesitated a long time and then picked up the revolver rejected by Franting, fingered it, put it down, and picked it up again. The back-door of the shop opened suddenly, and startled, Harder dropped the revolver into his overcoat pocket: a thoughtless, quite unpremeditated act. He dared not remove the revolver. The revolver was as fast in his pocket as though the pocket had been sewn up.

'And cartridges?' asked Mr Gontle of Franting.

'Oh,' said Franting, 'I've only had one shot. Five'll be more than enough for the present. What does it weigh?'

'Let me see. Four-inch barrel? Yes. One pound four ounces.'

Franting paid for the revolver, receiving thirteen shillings in change from a five-pound note, and strode out of the shop, weapon in hand. He was gone before Lomax Harder decided upon a course of action.

'And for you, sir?' said Mr Gontle, addressing the poet.

Harder suddenly comprehended that Mr Gontle had mistaken him for a separate customer, who had happened to enter the shop a moment after the first one. Harder and Franting had said not a word to one another during the purchase, and Harder well knew that in the most exclusive shops it is the custom utterly to ignore a second customer until the first one has been dealt with.

'I want to see some foils.' Harder spoke stammeringly the only words that came into his head.

'Foils!' exclaimed Mr Gontle, shocked, as if to say: 'Is it conceivable that you should imagine that I, Gontle, gunsmith, sell such things as foils?'

After a little talk Harder apologised and departed – a thief.

'I'll call later and pay the fellow,' said Harder to his restive conscience. 'No. I can't do that. I'll send him some anonymous postal orders.'

He crossed the Parade and saw Franting, a small left-handed figure all alone far below on the deserted sands, pointing the revolver. He thought that his ear caught the sound of a discharge, but the distance was too great for him to be sure. He continued to watch, and at length Franting walked westward diagonally across the beach.

'He's going back to the Bellevue,' thought Harder, the Bellevue being the hotel from which he had met Franting coming out half an hour earlier. He strolled slowly towards the white hotel. But Franting, who had evidently come up the face of the cliff in the penny lift, was before him. Harder, standing outside, saw Franting seated in the lounge. Then Franting rose and vanished down a long passage at the rear of the lounge. Harder entered the hotel rather guiltily. There was no hall-porter at the door, and not a soul in the lounge or in sight of the lounge. Harder went down the long passage.

3

At the end of the passage Lomax Harder found himself in a billiard-room – an extension built partly of brick and partly of wood on a sort of courtyard behind the main structure of the hotel. The roof, of iron and grimy glass, rose to a point in the middle. On two sides the high walls of the hotel obscured the light. Dusk was already closing in. A small fire burned feebly in the grate. A large radiator under the window was steel-cold, for though summer was finished, winter had not officially begun in the small economically-run hotel: so that the room was chilly; nevertheless, in deference to the English passion for fresh air and discomfort, the window was wide open.

Franting, in his overcoat and with an unlit cigarette between his lips, stood lowering with his back to the bit of fire. At sight of Harder he lifted his chin in a dangerous challenge.

'So you're still following me about,' he said resentfully to Harder.

'Yes,' said the latter, with his curious gentle primness of manner. 'I came down here specially to talk to you. I should have said all I had to say earlier, only you happened to be going out of the hotel just as I was coming in. You didn't seem to want to talk in the street; but there's some talking has to be done. I've a few things I must tell you.' Harder appeared to be perfectly calm, and he felt perfectly calm. He advanced from the door towards the billiard-table.

Franting raised his hand, displaying his square-ended, brutal fingers in the twilight.

'Now listen to me,' he said with cold, measured ferocity. 'You can't tell me anything I don't know. If there's some talking to be done I'll do it myself, and when I've finished you can get out. I know that my wife has taken a ticket for Copenhagen by the steamer from Harwich, and that she's been seeing to her passport, and packing. And of course I know that you have interests in Copenhagen and spend about half your precious time there. I'm not worrying to connect the two things. All that's got nothing to do with me. Emily has always seen a great deal of you, and I know that the last week or two she's been seeing you more than ever. Not that I mind that. I know that she objects to my treatment of her and my conduct generally. That's all right, but it's a matter that only concerns her and me. I mean that it's no concern of yours, for instance, or anybody else's. If she objects enough she can try and divorce me. I doubt if she'd succeed, but you can never be sure – with these new laws. Anyhow she's my wife till she does divorce me, and so she has the usual duties and responsibilities towards me – even though I was the worst husband in the world. That's how I look at it, in my old-fashioned way. I've just had a letter from her –

she knew I was here, and I expect that explains how you knew I was here.'

'It does,' said Lomax Harder quietly.

Franting pulled a letter from his inner pocket and unfolded it. 'Yes,' he said, glancing at it, and read some sentences aloud:

> 'I have absolutely decided to leave you, and I won't hide from you that I know you know who is doing what he can to help me. I can't live with you any longer. You may be very fond of me, as you say, but I find your way of showing your fondness too humiliating and painful. I've said this to you before, and now I'm saying it for the last time.

And so on and so on.'

Franting tore the letter in two, dropped one half on the floor, twisted the other half into a spill, turned to the fire, and lit his cigarette.

'That's what I think of her letter,' he proceeded, the cigarette between his teeth. 'You're helping her, are you? Very well. I don't say you're in love with her, or she with you. I'll make no wild statements. But if you aren't in love with her I wonder why you're taking all this trouble over her. Do you go about the world helping ladies who say they're unhappy just for the pure sake of helping? Never mind. Emily isn't going to leave me. Get that into your head. I shan't let her leave me. She has money, and I haven't. I've been living on her, and it would be infernally awkward for me if she left me for good. That's a reason for keeping her, isn't it? But you may believe me or not – it isn't my reason. She's right enough when she says I'm very fond of her. That's a reason for keeping her too. But it isn't my reason. My reason is that a wife's a wife, and she can't break her word just because everything isn't lovely in the garden. I've heard it said I'm unmoral. I'm not all unmoral. And I feel particularly strongly about what's called the marriage tie.' He drew the revolver from his overcoat pocket, and held it up to view. 'You see this thing. You saw me buy it. Now you needn't be afraid. I'm not threatening you; and it's no part of my game to shoot you. I've nothing to do with your goings-on. What I have to do with is the goings-on of my wife. If she deserts me – for you or for anybody or for nobody – I shall follow her, whether it's to Copenhagen or Bangkok or the North Pole, and I shall kill her – with just this very revolver that you saw me buy. And now you can get out.'

Franting replaced the revolver, and began to consume the cigarette with fierce and larger puffs.

Lomax Harder looked at the grim, set, brutal, scowling, bitter face, and knew that Franting meant what he had said. Nothing would stop him from carrying out his threat. The fellow was not an argufier; he could not reason; but he had unmistakable grit and would never recoil from the fear of consequences. If Emily left him, Emily was a dead woman; nothing in the end could protect her from the execution of her husband's menace. On the other hand, nothing would persuade her to remain with her husband. She had decided to go, and she would go. And indeed the mere thought of this lady to whom he, Harder, was utterly devoted, staying with her husband and continuing to suffer the tortures and humiliations which she had been suffering for years – this thought revolted him. He could not think it.

He stepped forward along the side of the billiard-table, and simultaneously Franting stepped forward to meet him. Lomax Harder snatched the revolver which was in his pocket, aimed and pulled the trigger.

Franting collapsed, with the upper half of his body somehow balanced on the edge of the billiard-table. He was dead. The sound of the report echoed in Harder's ear like the sound of a violin string loudly twanged by a finger. He saw a little reddish hole in Franting's bronzed right temple.

'Well,' he thought, 'somebody had to die. And it's better him than Emily.' He felt that he had performed a righteous act. Also he felt a little sorry for Franting.

Then he was afraid. He was afraid for himself, because he wanted not to die, especially on the scaffold; but also for Emily Franting, who would be friendless and helpless without him; he could not bear to think of her alone in the world – the central point of a terrific scandal. He must get away instantly . . .

Not down the corridor back into the hotel-lounge! No! That would be fatal! The window. He glanced at the corpse. It was more odd, curious, than affrighting. He had made the corpse. Strange! He could not unmake it. He had accomplished the irrevocable. Impressive! He saw Franting's cigarette glowing on the linoleum in the deepening dusk, and picked it up and threw it into the fender.

Lace curtains hung across the whole width of the window. He drew one aside, and looked forth. The light was much stronger in the courtyard than within the room. He put his gloves on. He gave a last look at the corpse, straddled the window-sill, and was on the brick pavement of the courtyard. He saw that the curtain had fallen back into the perpendicular.

He gazed around. Nobody! Not a light in any window! He saw a green wooden gate, pushed it; it yielded; then a sort of entry-passage . . . In a moment, after two half-turns, he was on the Marine Parade again. He was a fugitive. Should he fly to the right, to the left? Then he had an inspiration. An idea of genius for baffling pursuers. He would go into the hotel by the main-entrance. He went slowly and deliberately into the portico, where a middle-aged hall-porter was standing in the gloom.

'Good-evening, sir.'

'Good-evening. Have you got any rooms?'

'I think so, sir. The housekeeper is out, but she'll be back in a moment – if you'd like a seat. The manager's away in London.'

The hall-porter suddenly illuminated the lounge, and Lomax Harder, blinking, entered and sat down.

'I might have a cocktail while I'm waiting,' the murderer suggested with a bright and friendly smile. 'A Bronx.'

'Certainly, sir. The page is off duty. He sees to orders in the lounge, but I'll attend to you myself.'

'What a hotel!' thought the murderer, solitary in the chilly lounge, and gave a glance down the long passage. 'Is the whole place run by the hall-porter? But of course it's the dead season.'

Was it conceivable that nobody had heard the sound of the shot?

Harder had a strong impulse to run away. But no! To do so would be highly dangerous. He restrained himself.

'How much?' he asked of the hall-porter, who had arrived with surprising quickness, tray in hand and glass on tray.

'A shilling, sir.'

The murderer gave him eighteenpence, and drank off the cocktail.

'Thank you very much, sir.' The hall-porter took the glass.

'See here!' said the murderer. 'I'll look in again. I've got one or two little errands to do.'

And he went, slowly, into the obscurity of the Marine Parade.

4

Lomax Harder leant over the left arm of the sea-wall of the man-made port of Quangate. Not another soul was there. Night had fallen. The lighthouse at the extremity of the right arm was occulting. The lights – some red, some green, many white – of ships at sea passed in both directions in endless processions. Waves plashed gently against the vast masonry of the wall. The wind, blowing steadily from the north-west, was not cold. Harder, looking about – though he knew he was absolutely alone, took his revolver from his overcoat pocket and stealthily dropped it into the sea. Then he turned round and gazed across the small harbour at the mysterious amphitheatre of the lighted town, and heard public clocks and religious clocks striking the hour.

He was a murderer, but why should he not successfully escape detection? Other murderers had done so. He had all his wits. He was not excited. He was not morbid. His perspective of things was not askew. The hall-porter had not seen his first entrance into the hotel, nor his exit after the crime. Nobody had seen them. He had left nothing behind in the billiard-room. No fingermarks on the window-sill. (The putting-on of his gloves was in itself a clear demonstration that he had fully kept his presence of mind.) No footmarks on the hard, dry pavement of the courtyard.

Of course there was the possibility that some person unseen had seen him getting out of the window. Slight: but still a possibility! And there was also the possibility that someone who knew Franting by sight had noted him walking by Franting's side in the streets. If such a person informed the police and gave a description of him, enquiries might be made . . . No! Nothing in it. His appearance offered nothing remarkable to the eye of a casual observer – except his forehead, of which he was rather proud, but which was hidden by his hat.

It was generally believed that criminals always did something silly. But so far he had done nothing silly, and he was convinced that, in regard to the crime, he never would do anything silly. He had none of the desire, supposed to be common among murderers, to revisit the scene of the crime or to look upon the corpse once more. Although he regretted the necessity for his act, he felt no slightest twinge of conscience. Somebody had to die, and surely it was better that a brute should die than the heavenly, enchanting, martyrised creature whom his act had rescued for ever from the brute! He was aware within himself of an ecstasy of devotion to Emily Franting – now a widow and free. She was a unique woman. Strange that a woman of such gifts should have come under the sway of so obvious a scoundrel as Franting. But she was very young at the time, and such freaks of sex had happened before and would happen again; they were a widespread phenomenon in the history of the relations of men and women. He would have killed a hundred men if a hundred men had threatened her felicity. His heart was pure; he wanted nothing from Emily in exchange for what he had done in her defence. He was passionate in her defence. When he reflected upon the coarseness and cruelty of the gesture by which Franting had used Emily's letter to light his cigarette, Harder's cheeks grew hot with burning resentment.

A clock struck the quarter. Harder walked quickly to the harbour front, where there was a taxi-rank, and drove to the station . . . A sudden apprehension! The crime might have been discovered! Police might already be watching for suspicious-looking travellers! Absurd! Still, the apprehension remained despite its absurdity. The taxi-driver looked at him queerly. No! Imagination! He hesitated on the threshold of the station, then walked boldly in, and showed his return ticket to the ticket-inspector. No sign of a policeman. He got into the Pullman car, where five other passengers were sitting. The train started.

5

He nearly missed the boat-train at Liverpool Street because according to its custom the Quangate Flyer arrived twenty minutes late at Victoria. And at Victoria the foolish part of him, as distinguished from the common-sense part, suffered another spasm of fear. Would detectives, instructed by telegraph, be waiting for the train? No! An absurd idea! The boat-train from Liverpool Street was crowded with travellers, and the platform crowded with senders-off. He gathered from scraps of talk overheard that an international conference was about to take place in Copenhagen. And he had known nothing of it – not seen a word of it in the papers! Excusable perhaps; graver matters had held his attention.

Useless to look for Emily in the vast bustle of the compartments! She had her through ticket (which she had taken herself, in order to avoid possible complications), and she happened to be the only woman in the world who was never late and never in a hurry. She was certain to be on the train. But was she on the train? Something sinister might have come to pass. For instance, a telephone message to the flat that her husband had been found dead with a bullet in his brain.

The swift two-hour journey to Harwich was terrible for Lomax Harder. He remembered that he had left the unburnt part of the letter lying under the billiard-table. Forgetful! Silly! One of the silly things that criminals did! And on Parkeston Quay the confusion was enormous. He did not walk he was swept on to the great shaking steamer whose dark funnels rose amid wisps of steam into the starry sky. One advantage: detectives would have no chance in that multitudinous scene, unless indeed they held up the ship.

The ship roared a warning, and slid away from the quay, groped down the tortuous channel to the harbour mouth, and was in the North Sea; and England dwindled to naught but a string of lights. He searched every deck from stem to stern, and could not find Emily. She had not caught the train, or, if she had caught the train, she had not boarded the steamer because he had failed to appear. His misery was intense. Everything was going wrong. And on the arrival at Esbjerg would not detectives be lying in wait for the Copenhagen train? . . .

Then he descried her, and she him. She too had been searching. Only chance had kept them apart. Her joy at finding him was ecstatic; tears came into his eyes at sight of it. He was everything to her, absolutely everything. He clasped her right hand in both his hands and gazed at her in the dim, diffused light blended of stars, moon and electricity. No woman was ever like her: mature, innocent, wise, trustful, honest. And the touching beauty of her appealing, sad, happy face, and the pride of her carriage! A unique jewel – snatched from the brutal grasp of that fellow – who had ripped her solemn letter in two and used it as a spill for his cigarette! She related her movements; and he his. Then she said: 'Well?'

'I didn't go,' he answered. 'Thought it best not to. I'm convinced it wouldn't have been any use.'

He had not intended to tell her this lie. Yet when it came to the point, what else could he say? He had told one lie instead of twenty. He was deceiving her, but for her sake. Even if the worst occurred, she was for ever safe from that brutal grasp. And he had saved her. As for the conceivable complications of the future, he refused to confront them; he could live in the marvellous present. He felt suddenly the amazing beauty of the night at sea, but beneath all his other sensations was the obscure sensation of a weight at his heart.

'I expect you were right,' she angelically acquiesced.

6

The superintendent of police (Quangate was the county town of the western half of the county) and a detective-sergeant were in the billiard-room of the Bellevue. Both wore mufti. The powerful green-shaded lamps usual in billiard-rooms shone down ruthlessly on the green table, and on the reclining body of John Franting, which had not moved and had not been moved.

A charwoman was just leaving these officers when a stout gentleman, who had successfully beguiled a policeman guarding the other end of the long corridor, squeezed past her, greeted the two officers and shut the door.

The superintendent, a thin man, with lips to match, and a moustache, stared hard at the arrival.

'I am staying with my friend Dr Furnival,' said the arrival cheerfully. 'You telephoned for him, and as he had to go out to one of those cases in which nature will not wait, I offered to come in his place. I've met you before, superintendent, at Scotland Yard.'

'Dr Austin Bond!' exclaimed the superintendent.

'He,' said the other.

They shook hands, Dr Bond genially, the superintendent half-consequential, half-deferential, as one who had his dignity to think about; also as one who resented an intrusion, but dared not show resentment.

The detective-sergeant reeled at the dazzling name of the great amateur detective, a genius who had solved the famous mysteries of 'The Yellow Hat', 'The Three Towns', 'The Three Feathers', 'The Gold Spoon', etc., etc., etc., whose devilish perspicacity had again and again made professional detectives both look and feel foolish, and whose notorious friendship with the loftiest heads of Scotland Yard compelled all police forces to treat him very politely indeed.

'Yes,' said Dr Austin Bond, after detailed examination. 'Been shot about ninety minutes, poor fellow! Who found him?'

'That woman who's just gone out. Some servant here. Came in to look after the fire.'

'How long since?'

'Oh! About an hour ago.'

'Found the bullet? I see it hit the brass on that cue-rack there.'

The detective-sergeant glanced at the superintendent, who, however, resolutely remained unastonished.

'Here's the bullet,' said the superintendent.

'Ah!' commented Dr Austin Bond, glinting through his spectacles at the bullet as it lay in the superintendent's hand. 'Decimal 38, I see. Flattened. It would be.'

'Sergeant,' said the superintendent, 'you can get help and have the body moved now Dr Bond has made his examination. Eh, doctor?'

'Certainly,' answered Dr Bond, at the fireplace. 'He was smoking a cigarette, I see.'

'Either he or his murderer.'

'You've got a clue?'

'Oh yes,' the superintendent answered, not without pride. 'Look here. Your torch, sergeant.'

The detective-sergeant produced a pocket electric-lamp, and the superintendent turned to the window-sill.

'I've got a stronger one than that,' said Dr Austin Bond, producing another torch.

The superintendent displayed fingerprints on the window-frame, footmarks on the sill, and a few strands of inferior blue cloth. Dr Austin Bond next produced a magnifying glass, and inspected the evidence at very short range.

'The murderer must have been a tall man – you can judge that from the angle of fire; he wore a blue suit, which he tore slightly on this splintered wood of the window-frame; one of his boots had a hole in the middle of the sole, and he'd only three fingers on his left hand. He must have come in by the window and gone out by the window, because the hall-porter is sure that nobody except the dead man entered the lounge by any door within an hour of the time when the murder must have been committed.'

The superintendent proudly gave many more details, and ended by saying that he had already given instructions to circulate a description.

'Curious,' said Dr Austin Bond, 'that a man like John Franting should let anyone enter the room by the window! Especially a shabby-looking man!'

'You knew the deceased personally then?'

'No! But I know he was John Franting.'

'How, doctor?'

'Luck.'

'Sergeant,' said the superintendent, piqued. 'Tell the constable to fetch the hall-porter.'

Dr Austin Bond walked to and fro, peering everywhere, and picked up a piece of paper that had lodged against the step of the platform which ran round two sides of the room for the raising of the spectators' benches. He glanced at the paper casually, and dropped it again.

'My man,' the superintendent addressed the hall-porter. 'How can you be sure that nobody came in here this afternoon?'

'Because I was in my cubicle all the time, sir.'

The hall-porter was lying. But he had to think of his own welfare. On the previous day he had been reprimanded for quitting his post against the rule. Taking advantage of the absence of the manager, he had sinned once again, and he lived in fear of dismissal if found out.

'With a full view of the lounge?'

'Yes, sir.'

'Might have been in there beforehand,' Dr Austin Bond suggested.

'No,' said the superintendent. 'The charwoman came in twice. Once just before Franting came in. She saw the fire wanted making up and she went for some coal and then returned later with the scuttle. But the look of Franting frightened her, and she turned back with her coal.'

'Yes,' said the hall-porter. 'I saw that.'

Another lie.

At a sign from the superintendent he withdrew.

'I should like to have a word with that charwoman,' said Dr Austin Bond.

The superintendent hesitated. Why should the great amateur meddle with what did not concern him? Nobody had asked his help. But the superintendent thought of the amateur's relations with Scotland Yard, and sent for the charwoman.

'Did you clean the window here today?' Dr Austin Bond interrogated her.

'Yes, please, sir.'

'Show me your left hand.' The slattern obeyed. 'How did you lose your little finger?'

'In a mangle accident, sir.'

'Just come to the window, will you, and put your hands on it. But take off your left boot first.'

The slattern began to weep.

'It's quite all right, my good creature,' Dr Austin Bond reassured her. 'Your skirt is torn at the hem, isn't it?'

When the slattern was released from her ordeal and had gone, carrying one boot in her grimy hand, Dr Austin Bond said genially to the superintendent: 'Just a fluke. I happened to notice she'd only three fingers on her left hand when she passed me in the corridor. Sorry I've destroyed your evidence. But I felt sure almost from the first that the murderer hadn't either entered or decamped by the window.'

'How?'

'Because I think he's still here in the room.'

The two police officers gazed about them as if exploring the room for the murderer.

'I think he's there.'

Dr Austin Bond pointed to the corpse.

'And where did he hide the revolver after he'd killed himself?' demanded the thin-lipped superintendent icily, when he had somewhat recovered his aplomb.

'I'd thought of that, too,' said Dr Austin Bond, beaming. 'It is always a very wise course to leave a dead body absolutely untouched until a professional man has seen it. But *looking* at the body can do no harm. You see the left-hand pocket of the overcoat. Notice how it bulges. Something unusual in it. Something that has the shape of a – Just feel inside it, will you?'

The superintendent, obeying, drew a revolver from the overcoat pocket of the dead man.

'Ah! Yes!' said Dr Austin Bond. 'A Webley Mark III. Quite new. You might take out the ammunition.' The superintendent dismantled the weapon. 'Yes, yes! Three chambers empty. Wonder how he used the other two! Now, where's that bullet?

You see? He fired. His arm dropped, and the revolver happened to fall into the pocket.'

'Fired with his left hand, did he?' asked the superintendent, foolishly ironic.

'Certainly. A dozen years ago Franting was perhaps the finest amateur lightweight boxer in England. And one reason for it was that he bewildered his opponents by being left-handed. His lefts were much more fatal than his rights. I saw him box several times.'

Whereupon Dr Austin Bond strolled to the step of the platform near the door and picked up the fragment of very thin paper that was lying there.

'This,' said he, 'must have been blown from the hearth to here by the draught from the window when the door was opened. It's part of a letter. You can see the burnt remains of the other part in the corner of the fender. He probably lighted the cigarette with it. Out of bravado! His last bravado! Read this.'

The superintendent read:

> '. . . repeat that I realise how fond you are of me, but you have killed my affection for you, and I shall leave our home tomorrow. This is absolutely final. E.'

Dr Austin Bond, having for the nth time satisfactorily demonstrated in his own unique, rapid way that police officers were a set of numskulls, bade the superintendent a most courteous good-evening, nodded amicably to the detective-sergeant, and left in triumph.

7

'I must get some mourning and go back to the flat,' said Emily Franting.

She was sitting one morning in the lobby of the Palads Hotel, Copenhagen. Lomax Harder had just called on her with an English newspaper containing an account of the inquest at which the jury had returned a verdict of suicide upon the body of her late husband. Her eyes filled with tears.

'Time will put her right,' thought Lomax Harder, tenderly watching her. 'I was bound to do what I did. And I can keep a secret for ever.'

W. W. JACOBS

William Wymark Jacobs was born in Wapping in 1863, the son of an East London dock worker. He left school when he was sixteen to join the civil service as a clerk in the Post Office Savings Bank. Never really happy in his work, he began writing short stories, mostly concerned with the sea and nautical culture. In 1896, he published his first collection of short stories, *Many Cargoes*, which was well received. An excellent humourist, Jacobs became one of the most popular English writers of that genre in the early twentieth century. Today he is best remembered for his macabre story *The Monkey's Paw* (1902), which appeared first in *Harper's Monthly* and which was reprinted in his third collection of short stories, *The Lady of the Barge*, that same year. His other works include *More Cargoes* (1898), *Little Freights* (1901), *At Sunwich Port* (1902), *A Master of Craft* (1903), *Dialstone Lane* (1904), *Short Cruises* (1907), *Sailor's Knots* (1909), *Ship's Company* (1911), *Night Watches* (1914), *Castaways* (1916), *Deep Waters* (1919), *Sea Whispers* (1926) and *Snug Harbour* (1931). He died in 1943.

In the Library

The fire had burnt low in the library, for the night was wet and warm. It was now little more than a grey shell, and looked desolate. Trayton Burleigh, still hot, rose from his armchair, and turning out one of the gas-jets, took a cigar from a box on a side-table and resumed his seat again.

The apartment, which was on the third floor at the back of the house, was a combination of library, study and smoke-room, and was the daily despair of the old housekeeper who, with the assistance of one servant, managed the house. It was a bachelor establishment, and had been left to Trayton Burleigh and James Fletcher by a distant connection of both men some ten years before.

Trayton Burleigh sat back in his chair watching the smoke of his cigar through half-closed eyes. Occasionally he opened them a little wider and glanced round the comfortable, well-furnished room, or stared with a cold gleam of hatred at Fletcher as he sat sucking stolidly at his brier pipe. It was a comfortable room and a valuable house, half of which belonged to Trayton Burleigh; and yet he was to leave it in the morning and become a rogue and a wanderer over the face of the earth. James Fletcher had said so. James Fletcher, with the pipe still between his teeth and speaking from one corner of his mouth only, had pronounced his sentence.

'It hasn't occurred to you, I suppose,' said Burleigh, speaking suddenly, 'that I might refuse your terms.'

'No,' said Fletcher, simply.

Burleigh took a great mouthful of smoke and let it roll slowly out.

'I am to go out and leave you in possession?' he continued. 'You will stay here sole proprietor of the house; you will stay at the office sole owner and representative of the firm? You are a good hand at a deal, James Fletcher.'

'I am an honest man,' said Fletcher, 'and to raise sufficient money to make your defalcations good will not by any means leave me the gainer, as you very well know.'

'There is no necessity to borrow,' began Burleigh, eagerly. 'We can pay the interest easily, and in course of time make the principal good without a soul being the wiser.'

'That you suggested before,' said Fletcher, 'and my answer is the same. I will be no man's confederate in dishonesty; I will raise every penny at all costs, and save the name of the firm – and yours with it – but I will never have you darken the office again, or sit in this house after tonight.'

'You won't,' cried Burleigh, starting up in a frenzy of rage.

'I won't,' said Fletcher. 'You can choose the alternative: disgrace and penal servitude. Don't stand over me; you won't frighten me, I can assure you. Sit down.'

'You have arranged so many things in your kindness,' said Burleigh, slowly, resuming his seat again, 'have you arranged how I am to live?'

'You have two strong hands, and health,' replied Fletcher. 'I will give you the two hundred pounds I mentioned, and after that you must look out for yourself. You can take it now.'

He took a leather case from his breast pocket, and drew out a roll of notes. Burleigh, watching him calmly, stretched out his hand and took them from the table. Then he gave way to a sudden access of rage, and crumpling them in his hand, threw them into a corner of the room. Fletcher smoked on.

'Mrs Marl is out?' said Burleigh, suddenly.

Fletcher nodded. 'She will be away the night,' he said, slowly; 'and Jane too; they have gone together somewhere, but they will be back at half-past eight in the morning.'

'You are going to let me have one more breakfast in the old place, then,' said Burleigh. 'Half-past eight, half-past –'

He rose from his chair again. This time Fletcher took his pipe from his mouth and watched him closely. Burleigh stooped, and picking up the notes, placed them in his pocket.

'If I am to be turned adrift, it shall not be to leave you here,' he said, in a thick voice.

He crossed over and shut the door; as he turned back Fletcher rose from his chair and stood confronting him. Burleigh put his hand to the wall, and drawing a small Japanese sword from its sheath of carved ivory, stepped slowly towards him.

'I give you one chance, Fletcher,' he said, grimly. 'You are a man of your word. Hush this up and let things be as they were before, and you are safe.'

'Put that down,' said Fletcher, sharply.

'I warn you, I mean what I say!' cried the other.

'I mean what I said!' answered Fletcher.

He looked round at the last moment for a weapon, then he turned back at a sharp sudden pain, and saw Burleigh's clenched fist nearly touching his breast-bone. The hand came away from his breast again, and something with it. It went a long way off. Trayton Burleigh suddenly went to a great distance and the room darkened. It got quite dark, and Fletcher, with an attempt to raise his hands, let them fall to his sides instead, and fell in a heap to the floor.

He was so still that Burleigh could hardly realise that it was all over, and stood stupidly waiting for him to rise again. Then he took out his handkerchief as though to wipe the sword, but thinking better of it, put it back into his pocket again, and threw the weapon on to the floor.

The body of Fletcher lay where it had fallen, the white face turned up to the gas. In life he had been a commonplace-looking man, not to say vulgar; now Burleigh, with a feeling of nausea, drew back towards the door, until the body was hidden by the table, and relieved from the sight, he could think more clearly. He looked down carefully and examined his clothes and his boots. Then he crossed the room again, and with his face averted, turned out the gas. Something seemed to stir in the darkness, and with a faint cry he blundered towards the door before he had realised that it was the clock. It struck twelve.

He stood at the head of the stairs trying to recover himself; trying to think. The gas on the landing below, the stairs and the furniture, all looked so prosaic and familiar that he could not realise what had occurred. He walked slowly down and turned the light out. The darkness of the upper part of the house was now almost appalling, and in a sudden panic he ran downstairs into the lighted hall, and snatching a hat from the stand, went to the door and walked down to the gate.

Except for one window the neighbouring houses were in

darkness, and the lamps shone on a silent street. There was a little rain in the air, and the muddy road was full of pebbles. He stood at the gate trying to screw up his courage to enter the house again. Then he noticed a figure coming slowly up the road and keeping close to the palings.

The full realisation of what he had done broke in upon him when he found himself turning to fly from the approach of the constable. The wet cape glistening in the lamplight, the slow, heavy step, made him tremble. Suppose the thing upstairs was not quite dead and should cry out? Suppose the constable should think it strange for him to be standing there and follow him in? He assumed a careless attitude, which did not feel careless, and as the man passed bade him good-night, and made a remark as to the weather.

Ere the sound of the other's footsteps had gone quite out of hearing, he turned and entered the house again before the sense of companionship should have quite departed. The first flight of stairs was lighted by the gas in the hall, and he went up slowly. Then he struck a match and went up steadily, past the library door, and with firm fingers turned on the gas in his bedroom and lit it. He opened the window a little way, and sitting down on his bed, tried to think.

He had got eight hours. Eight hours and two hundred pounds in small notes. He opened his safe and took out all the loose cash it contained, and walking about the room, gathered up and placed in his pockets such articles of jewellery as he possessed.

The first horror had now to some extent passed, and was succeeded by the fear of death.

With this fear on him he sat down again and tried to think out the first moves in that game of skill of which his life was the stake. He had often read of people of hasty temper, evading the police for a time, and eventually falling into their hands for lack of the most elementary common sense. He had heard it said that they always made some stupid blunder, left behind them some damning clue. He took his revolver from a drawer and saw that it was loaded. If the worst came to the worst, he would die quickly.

Eight hours' start; two hundred odd pounds. He would take lodgings at first in some populous district, and let the hair on his face grow. When the hue-and-cry had ceased, he would go abroad and start life again. He would go out of a night and post letters to himself, or better still, postcards, which his landlady would read. Postcards from cheery friends, from a sister, from a brother. During the day he would stay in and write, as became a man who described himself as a journalist.

Or suppose he went to the sea? Who would look for him in flannels, bathing and boating with ordinary happy mortals? He sat and pondered. One might mean life, and the other death. Which?

His face burned as he thought of the responsibility of the choice. So many people went to the sea at that time of year that he would surely pass unnoticed. But at the sea one might meet acquaintances. He got up and nervously paced the room again. It was not so simple, now that it meant so much, as he had thought.

The sharp little clock on the mantelpiece rang out 'one', followed immediately by the deeper note of that in the library. He thought of the clock, which seemed the only live thing in that room, and shuddered. He wondered whether the thing lying by the far side of the table heard it. He wondered –

He started and held his breath with fear. Somewhere downstairs a board creaked loudly, then another. He went to the door, and opening it a little way, but without looking out, listened. The house was so still that he could hear the ticking of the old clock in the kitchen below. He opened the door a little wider and peeped out. As he did so there was a sudden sharp outcry on the stairs, and he drew back into the room and stood trembling before he had quite realised that the noise had been made by the cat. The cry was unmistakable; but what had disturbed it?

There was silence again, and he drew near the door once more. He became certain that something was moving stealthily on the stairs. He heard the boards creak again, and once the rails of the balustrade rattled. The silence and suspense were frightful. Suppose that the something which had been Fletcher waited for him in the darkness outside?

He fought his fears down, and opening the door, determined to see what was beyond. The light from his room streamed out on to the landing, and he peered about fearfully. Was it fancy, or did the door of Fletcher's room opposite close as he looked? Was it fancy, or did the handle of the door really turn?

In perfect silence, and watching the door as he moved, to see that nothing came out and followed him, he proceeded slowly down the dark stairs. Then his jaw fell, and he turned sick and faint again. The library door, which he distinctly remembered closing, and which, moreover, he had seen was closed when he went upstairs to his room, now stood open some four or five inches. He fancied that there was a rustling inside, but his brain refused to be certain. Then plainly and unmistakably he heard a chair pushed against the wall.

He crept to the door, hoping to pass it before the thing inside became aware of his presence. Something crept stealthily about the room. With a sudden impulse he caught the handle of the door and, closing it violently, turned the key in the lock, then he ran madly down the stairs.

A fearful cry sounded from the room, and a heavy hand beat upon the panels of the door. The house rang with the blows, but above them sounded the loud hoarse cries of human fear. Burleigh, halfway down to the hall, stopped with his hand on the balustrade and listened. The beating ceased, and a man's voice cried out loudly for God's sake to let him out.

At once Burleigh saw what had happened and what it might

mean for him. He had left the hall door open after his visit to the front, and some wandering bird of the night had entered the house. No need for him to go now. No need to hide either from the hangman's rope or the felon's cell. The fool above had saved him. He turned and ran upstairs again just as the prisoner in his furious efforts to escape wrenched the handle from the door.

'Who's there?' he cried, loudly.

'Let me out!' cried a frantic voice. 'For God's sake, open the door! There's something here.'

'Stay where you are!' shouted Burleigh, sternly. 'Stay where you are! If you come out, I'll shoot you like a dog!'

The only response was a smashing blow on the lock of the door. Burleigh raised his pistol, and aiming at the height of a man's chest, fired through the panel.

The report and the crashing of the wood made one noise, succeeded by an unearthly stillness, then the noise of a window hastily opened. Burleigh fled down the stairs, and flinging wide the hall door, shouted loudly for assistance.

It happened that a sergeant and the constable on the beat had just met in the road. They came towards the house at a run. Burleigh, with incoherent explanations, ran upstairs before them, and halted outside the library door. The prisoner was still inside, still trying to demolish the lock of the sturdy oaken door. Burleigh tried to turn the key, but the lock was too damaged to admit of its moving. The sergeant drew back and, shoulder foremost, hurled himself at the door and burst it open.

He stumbled into the room, followed by the constable, and two shafts of light from the lanterns at their belts danced round the room. A man lurking behind the door made a dash for it, and the next instant the three men were locked together.

Burleigh, standing in the doorway, looked on coldly, reserving himself for the scene which was to follow. Except for the stumbling of the men and the sharp catch of the prisoner's breath, there was no noise. A helmet fell off and bounced and rolled along the floor. The men fell; there was a sobbing snarl and a sharp click. A tall figure rose from the floor; the other, on his knees, still held the man down. The standing figure felt in his pocket, and, striking a match, lit the gas.

The light fell on the flushed face and fair beard of the sergeant. He was bare-headed and his hair dishevelled. Burleigh entered the room and gazed eagerly at the half-insensible man on the floor – a short, thick-set fellow with a white, dirty face and a black moustache. His lip was cut and bled down his neck. Burleigh glanced furtively at the table. The cloth had come off in the struggle and was now in the place where he had left Fletcher.

'Hot work, sir,' said the sergeant, with a smile. 'It's fortunate we were handy.'

The prisoner raised a heavy head and looked up with unmistakable terror in his eyes. 'All right, sir,' he said, trembling, as the constable increased the pressure of his knee. 'I 'ain't been in the house ten minutes altogether. I swear, I've not.'

The sergeant regarded him curiously.

'It don't signify,' he said, slowly; 'ten minutes or ten seconds won't make any difference.'

The man shook and began to whimper.

'It was 'ere when I come,' he said, eagerly; 'take that down, sir. I've only just come, and it was 'ere when I come. I tried to get away then, but I was locked in.'

'What was?' demanded the sergeant.

'That,' he said, desperately.

The sergeant, following the direction of the terror-stricken black eyes, stooped by the table. Then, with a sharp exclamation, he dragged away the cloth. Burleigh, with a convincing cry of horror, reeled back against the wall.

'All right, sir,' said the sergeant, catching him; 'all right. Turn your head away.'

He pushed him into a chair, and crossing the room, poured out a glass of whisky and brought it to him. The glass rattled against his teeth, but he drank it greedily, and then groaned faintly. The sergeant waited patiently. There was no hurry.

'Who is it, sir?' he asked at length.

'My friend – Fletcher,' said Burleigh, with an effort. 'We lived together.' He turned to the prisoner. 'You damned villain!'

'He was dead when I come in the room, gentlemen,' said the prisoner, strenuously. 'He was on the floor dead, and when I see 'im, I tried to get out. S' 'elp me he was. You heard me call out, sir. I shouldn't ha' called out if I'd killed him.'

'All right,' said the sergeant, gruffly; 'you'd better hold your tongue, you know.'

'You keep quiet,' urged the constable.

The sergeant knelt down and raised the dead man's head.

'I 'ad nothing to do with it,' repeated the man on the floor. 'I 'ad nothing to do with it. I never thought of such a thing. I've only been in the place ten minutes; put that down, sir.'

The sergeant groped with his left hand, and picking up the Japanese sword, held it at him.

'I've never seen it before,' said the prisoner, struggling.

'It used to hang on the wall,' said Burleigh. 'He must have snatched it down. It was on the wall when I left Fletcher a little while ago.'

'How long?' enquired the sergeant.

'Perhaps an hour, perhaps half an hour,' was the reply. 'I went to my bedroom.'

The man on the floor twisted his head and regarded him narrowly.

'You done it!' he cried, fiercely. 'You done it, and you want me to swing for it.'

'That'll do,' said the indignant constable.

The sergeant let his burden gently to the floor again.

'You hold your tongue, you devil!' he said, menacingly.

He crossed to the table and poured a little spirit into a glass and took it in his hand. Then he put it down again and crossed to Burleigh.

'Feeling better, sir?' he asked.

The other nodded faintly.

'You won't want this thing any more,' said the sergeant.

He pointed to the pistol which the other still held, and taking it from him gently, put it into his pocket.

'You've hurt your wrist, sir,' he said, anxiously.

Burleigh raised one hand sharply, and then the other.

'This one, I think,' said the sergeant. 'I saw it just now.'

He took the other's wrists in his hand, and suddenly holding them in the grip of a vice, whipped out something from his pocket – something hard and cold, which snapped suddenly on Burleigh's wrists, and held them fast.

'That's right,' said the sergeant; 'keep quiet.'

The constable turned round in amaze; Burleigh sprang towards him furiously.

'Take these things off!' he choked. 'Have you gone mad? Take them off!'

'All in good time,' said the sergeant.

'Take them off!' cried Burleigh again.

For answer the sergeant took him in a powerful grip, and staring steadily at his white face and gleaming eyes, forced him to the other end of the room and pushed him into a chair.

'Collins,' he said, sharply.

'Sir?' said the astonished subordinate.

'Run to the doctor at the corner hard as you can run!' said the other. 'This man is not dead!'

As the man left the room the sergeant took up the glass of spirits he had poured out, and kneeling down by Fletcher again, raised his head and tried to pour a little down his throat. Burleigh, sitting in his corner, watched like one in a trance. He saw the constable return with the breathless surgeon, saw the three men bending over Fletcher, and then saw the eyes of the dying man open and the lips of the dying man move. He was conscious that the sergeant made some notes in a pocket-book, and that all three men eyed him closely. The sergeant stepped towards him and placed his hand on his shoulder, and obedient to the touch, he arose and went with him out into the night.

EDGAR WALLACE

Edgar Wallace (1875–1932), journalist and novelist, born in Greenwich, the illegitimate son of an actor, was baptised Richard Horatio Edgar Wallace. Brought up by a Billingsgate fish-porter and his wife, he attended an elementary school at Peckham and left at twelve to become successively newsboy, errand boy, milk roundsman and labourer. At eighteen he enlisted in the Royal West Kent Regiment and served in South Africa. Discharged in 1899, he became a foreign correspondent for the *Daily Mail,* but was sacked for involving them in a libel suit. His first great success was *The Four Just Men* (1905), with its sequels *The Council of Justice* (1908) and *The Three Just Men* (1926). His early novels include a West African series – *Sanders of the River* (1911), *Bones* (1915) and others – but it was by his thrillers and detective stories that he became really famous. Well meriting his nickname of 'fiction factory', working with a dictaphone and a typist who held the record for speed-typing, he produced some one hundred and seventy books. Wallace also wrote a number of excellent plays in which excitement and horror are skilfully relieved by touches of humour. *People* (1926) is an autobiography. He died in Hollywood of pneumonia, and left an estate cumbered with £150,000 of debt, which his royalties paid off in two years. He was twice married.

Clues

I've got a smart Aleck of a detective-sergeant in my division who is strong for clues. The harder they are the better he likes 'em. He reckons fingerprints are too childishly easy for a full-grown officer of the CID.

'I believe there is a lot in that tobacco-ash theory, Sooper,' he said. 'It's fiction, I know – but there's a lot of truth in stories.'

So I put up to him the well-known case of the State against Uriah – or, better still, Uriah against David with Bathsheba intervening.

The chief was saying the other day that there has been nothing new in murder crime since the celebrated Cain and Abel affair.

'In fact, Sooper,' he said, 'you can dig down into the Old Book and find parallels for most every case that comes up at the Old Bailey.'

Which, in a way, is true. All the same, crime was a mighty simple affair round about 3000 BC. If a feller didn't like another feller he just dropped him down a well or snicked off his head, and what happened to the snicker depended on the kind of a pull he had with the chief priest or the king or whoever was the man on top.

There wasn't any comeback with Uriah, for instance, and no complications. They just handed him up to the front-line trenches and sent him out single-handed to see what the Amalekites were thinking up for tomorrow's battle.

But if Uriah had had a tough brother Bill or a sister named Lou, there would surely have been trouble for David, and worse still if Uriah, instead of getting himself carved up by the enemy, had sneaked back to headquarters by a roundabout way.

The David I'm thinking of was a mean man named Mr Penderbury Jonnes, who owned three stores on Oxford Street and had a country mansion near Hertford, to say nothing of a flat in Hanover Square. I happened to know Pen Jonnes. He was a Welshman on the soft-goods side of the race. A tall, red-faced fellow with eyes like a puppy dog's and a moustache like a cavalry officer's. We used to think that he was a bachelor in the sense that he hadn't any regular matrimonial arrangement. But this wasn't so.

He had a wife, though nobody seemed to have met her. She had been a shop-girl in one of his stores and he didn't find out until it was too late that her brother was Yorkshire Harry, the only cruiser-weight that ever went ten rounds with that Yankee fellow who held the title till some girl told him he looked grand in a dress suit.

Yorkshire Harry used to do a little blackmailing on the side, and he ran with the Stineys, who were cracksmen on the top scale. Anyway, Penderbury took the shortest way out of trouble and was married at the Henrietta Street Registry Office. I expect he was sorry, because Yorkshire Harry was caught the very next year and died in Gloucester Gaol from some fool thing.

I used to get a whole lot of anonymous letters about Penderbury – written in a woman's hand. Every second word was spelt wrong. Generally the letters had a Hertford postmark, and if half the things they accused Jonnes of doing were true, he'd have lived permanently in jail.

It was then I found out about Mrs Jonnes and got a specimen of her handwriting. After that we didn't take too much notice of the anonymous letters, whether they were signed 'A Frend' or 'A lover of Justise'. Interfering between man and wife is the very last instruction in the police code. I gathered that Mrs Jonnes did not like her husband and let it go at that.

One letter I remember very well – I'll spell it according to my ideas of how it ought to be spelt: 'If he wasn't afraid that the police would come after him, why does he keep all that money in his safe ready in case he has to jump out of the country?'

As a matter of fact, I did know that Penderbury kept a lot of money in his safe near Hertford, and so did somebody else. Two burglars tried to 'bust' the house once and it came out at the trial. As the judge says, 'This is not a court of morality,' and people can do pretty well anything they like so long as they don't obstruct the police in the execution of their duty or drive a car without a licence.

Jonnes had a cashier named Banford – Horace Angel Banford. I never quite got the hang of that 'Angel' and I never asked him, though I knew him pretty well. He was one of those Adam's apple tenors who sang so well that nothing could improve him. People used to say what a pity it was that he didn't go to a master for a few lessons. He was that kind of vocalist. But he went fine at our police orphanage concerts, and that is where I came to meet him. He was a tall, thin, sandy man with hollow cheeks, short sight and a schoolgirl complexion, and the last idea that he'd start was that he'd ever qualify for that 9 a.m. walk from cell to gallows.

Crime and music were his hobbies. I was surprised, when he invited me down to his little flat in Bloomsbury, to find the number of books he had about criminals. But he was sensible with it – never thought he could spot a homicide by the colour of his eyes and the curious way he wagged his ears. One thing he was certain about.

'Nine out of every ten murderers wouldn't be caught if they weren't boneheads,' he said to me one night. 'A crime is like any other job. You've got to be efficient to hold it down.'

We were all alone because his wife was out. She went out a lot – she was a great dancer.

'She goes with a lady friend,' said Mr Banford. 'Personally, dancing bores me, but she loves it,'

That made it all right. Anything Dora Banford loved – dresses, dancing, pretty little jewels – was all right. Banford's salary was ten pounds a week – that's about fifty dollars American, isn't it? And he did everything on that – Bloomsbury flat, a well-dressed wife, jewels and dances.

And it can't be done.

I went again, because he had a book on the Leamington murder which he'd lent and was getting back, and naturally, as I was the man who pinched Pike Gurney, I wanted to see if the feller that wrote the book had given me all the credit I deserved.

I met Mrs Banford in the hall: she was pulling on her gloves when I went in, and I can tell you she was a peach. One of those fluffy little things with wild golden hair that never stays put. She sort of gave me a look under her long lashes and said (not out loud, but my receptivity is pretty good), 'Who is the old bird with the big feet?' or something equally interesting.

Horace Angel fussed around her like a nanny before a baby's first party. He sort of leant over her and fanned her with his wings. Down to the street door he went with her, got her a cab and put her inside, and then he came back with his silly thin face all red and smirky.

'The best wife in the world!' he said.

I was with him for two hours and picked out all the bits in the book about me. I must say that the fellow who wrote it was an honest man and only made one mistake. He said I took Pike as he was going into the Branscombe House Hotel, when in fact I took him as he was coming out.

At one o'clock the next morning I had a pressing engagement with the reserves. We raided the Highlow Club in Fitzroy Square. We had information that Fogini, the manager, was selling booze out of hours and that everybody who went to the Highlow didn't go to dance. There was a baccarat game on the top floor, and there were all sorts of nice little private dining-rooms where people stayed who didn't play cards and weren't keen on dancing.

The raid went according to plan, and in Room 7 I found Mrs Banford and Mr Jonnes. They were sitting at a little table with a very large bottle of champagne, and as far as I could see when I opened the door, he was holding her two hands across the table. She snatched them away when I barged in, and I saw a puzzled sort of look walking alongside her fear – she was trying to place me.

Jonnes went redder than usual.

'What the devil is the idea of this?' he snapped.

'You're under arrest,' said I, 'for consuming spirituous liquor after the hours by law prescribed.'

Which is the classy way of saying that he was boozing out of hours.

That made his colour run.

'Can't this be squared?' he said. 'I'm Mr Jonnes, of Jonnes Mantle Corporation.'

He yanked out his pocket-book.

'Don't insult me with five,' I said, when he slipped me a note. 'My price is ten million. Who is the lady?'

Of course I knew, but I didn't let on. He seemed to have forgotten all about her.

'Oh – ' he said, like a man who had to bring his mind down to trifles, 'she's Mrs Smith – an Australian lady.'

I ordered him down to the dance room, where my boys were doing a little asking, and he went. This Mrs Banford's face was the colour of chalk and she was going after him when I called her back.

'I'm playing favourites for the first time in years,' I said. 'There's a pretty good fire-escape at the back – I'll show you the way.'

I did more than that, I took her down and tipped off the man on duty to let her pass out; said she was a highness and we didn't want any highnesses in this kind of scandal.

Jonnes came up next morning before the Marylebone magistrates and got his fine, and so far as I was concerned there was the end of the lady who went dancing with a girl friend.

Only things don't work out that way in life, which is a story that's continued an' continued. About six months after this I stepped into the charge room at Limber Street Station, and what did I see? Horace Angel in the steel pen. He had the colour of a man who wasn't expected to live. Poor old Horace, caught with the goods. Two thousand pounds' worth of embezzlement on his soul. And there, resting his arm on the sergeant's desk, was Jonnes.

Horace Angel had nothing to say, or if he had he was short on speech. The jailer put him below and I strolled up to Penderbury Jonnes.

'He has been swindling me for years. I hate doing this, because I know his wife, poor little woman . . . But I trusted him. Why, I've even sent him down to Hertford with the key of my safe, where there are thousands of pounds . . . '

That was his end of it. When I interviewed Horace Angel in his dugout he gave me another slant to the story. It wasn't easy to get it, I can tell you, because when he wasn't weeping he was cursing Dora Banford and Penderbury Jonnes, and when he wasn't cursing Dora he was forgiving her, though I didn't notice that he forgave Penderbury much.

'We're going to start fresh when I come out,' he said. 'I never gave the little girl a chance, Sooper. All I wanted to do was read an' sing, and that's pretty dull for a woman. I've been a scoundrel and dragged her name in the mud. How that hound caught me I don't know – somebody on the inside must have seen the duplicate set of books – '

'Where did you make them up?' I asked.

'At home,' he gulped. 'God, what a fool I was! And they came straight to my flat and found them, Sooper. The hired girl must have been in their pay.'

I let him go on.

'What's all this about Jonnes and your wife?' I asked.

'Nothing!' he said, very loud, but by and by I got it out of him.

Horace Angel had a friend who took a part in a West End revue. This friend was a genuine tenor and had a couple of Come-my-love-the-moon-is-shining numbers. The queer thing about a stage tenor is that his throat is always going wonky. Just before the curtain goes up he strolls into the manager's office and says: 'Sorry, old boy, but you'll have to put on the understudy,' and naturally that leads to his having a lot of fuss made over him both before and after. But sometimes his throat does really go wrong, and Horace Angel, being a sort of floating understudy, was sometimes sent for to take his place.

One night a hurry-up call came to him – it was just after his wife had gone out to meet her girl friend – and Horace Angel went down to the theatre and made up. He was rather glad she was out because she knew nothing about his understudying – Horace Angel was a little sensitive on the point of his voice.

His entry was towards the end of the first act. He was halfway through that love and moon stuff when he happened to look into the stage box. And there was Dora and Mr Jonnes. They were right at the back of the box and he gathered that they weren't interested in the play.

He got through the numbers and went home. There was a row, I suppose – he didn't tell me anything about that. And a few weeks later Jonnes pinched him.

Now whether Jonnes knew all the time that poor old Horace Angel was robbing him, and kept quiet because of the pull it gave him, or whether the auditors made the discovery, I've never found out.

At the Old Bailey the judge took a serious view of the crime and sent Banford down for three years. Two days after he was sentenced, Mrs Banford paid the rent in advance, locked up the flat, and went to Paris. Mr Jonnes followed the next day.

I had a talk with Uriah at Wormwood Scrubbs.

'There is only one way to hurt Jonnes,' he said, 'and when I come out I'm going to do it.'

You don't take much notice of what newly convicted people say, and I passed it. I said nothing about Mrs Bathsheba except to lie up a message from her to say that she was bearing her affliction patiently. But he got to know when he was in

Dartmoor. Every man has a friend who thinks that bad news is the only news worth knowing, and Horace Angel had several friends like that.

He said nothing; gave no trouble; went out of his cell at eight in the morning and had the key turned on him at four in the afternoon; sewed mailbags, helped with the laundry and sang solos in the prison choir; and nobody guessed how Horace Angel's mind was slipping back to Lombroso and Mantazinni and his little crime library.

I never saw Jonnes and Dora together – not that I had many opportunities, but I never did. One of our inspectors who went over to bring back a bank clerk who had left London hurriedly with a block of the bank's assets, told me that she had a flat in the Avenue Bois de Boulogne (which is going some) but personally I knew nothing about that till later. But just about then I met Mrs Jonnes. The anonymous letters were piling up at the office and the chief was getting a little tired of reading 'em.

'Go down and see this Mrs Jonnes, Sooper, and tell her from me that until we get short on regular crime, we haven't time to investigate the chicken-chasing propensities of the modern husband.'

I went down to Hertford midweek, because Mr Jonnes would be in town, and after a lot of difficulty I saw his wife. She had been a good looker, but years of Penderbury had sort of put an A in her face; if you've seen the nose lines and the drooping mouth of dissatisfied ladies you'll know what I mean. She had a Cockney accent with a sort of whistle in it, and what she didn't say about Mr Jonnes was that he was a perfect gentleman and a model husband.

'I live the life of a dog,' she said. 'One of these days I'll poison him – I will! If my poor darling brother was alive . . . !'

I got in a word or two about anonymous letters and she gave me her views on the police and the way they allowed wives to be beaten and locked up in rooms without food and treated like dirt by the servants.

'One of these days . . . !'

Those were her last words to me, and somehow I didn't feel that they were quite idle, for in Mrs Jonnes's veins ran the blood of three tough generations on both sides of the family.

When Horace was released I made it my business to call on him. He was sitting in the dining-room of the flat going through a lot of letters that had come during his absence. I remember that one of them had a cheque for his performance the night he peeked into the stage box.

'I'm starting all over again, Sooper,' he said, and he was very cheerful. 'A friend of mine has offered me a job in Peckham – not a big salary but enough to carry on with.'

He did not mention his wife but he did speak of Jonnes.

'There is a man who ought to be out of the world,' he said, as calmly as though he was talking about rice pie. 'The more one thinks about Jonnes the more useless a creature he seems. He has never done a stroke of work for the money he has. His father left him the stores and he uses his wealth to corrupt the pure and the foolish.'

'Quite a lot of people ought to be out of the world, Horace Angel,' I said, 'and sooner or later they will be. Give nature a chance and she'll put everybody where they belong.' He smiled at this: a sour, crooked smile. This was a Thursday afternoon. On Saturday afternoon at four o'clock, Penderbury Jonnes went out of his big house at Hertford with a gun under his arm. He said that he was going to shoot rabbits. Field Towers – which was the name of his house – stands in about eighty acres of good rough shooting. The estate is surrounded by a wall except for about three hundred yards, where a bean-shaped covert of beech and pine trees separates his land from Lord Forlmby's estate. At about 5.35 one of Lord Forlmby's gamekeepers, stalking a stoat, came through the covert and saw a man lying huddled up on the ground. He ran across the rough and saw that it was Penderbury Jonnes and that he was dead. He had been shot at close range through the right shoulder, and his gun was lying by his side.

The gamekeeper sent for the police, and just about that time I had taken over the duties of chief detective inspector in the absence on leave of Joe Frawlett. There are four chief inspectors attached to Scotland Yard, and these men have the four districts of London, so that when the Hertford police asked for assistance it was my job to go down.

I got to the Towers about nine o'clock that night. It was dark and raining, but on the advice of the local police the body hadn't been moved, and a ring of space had been kept clear around the hurdles which had been put up over the body.

'The man must have been killed by a discharge of the gun,' the doctor told me, 'though the wound is a very slight one. Probably a stray pellet reached his heart. One barrel of the gun has been fired, and the servants at the Towers say that they heard only one explosion.'

The gun had been carefully wrapped in oiled silk and taken to the house to be photographed for fingerprints. I had a talk with the chief constable of Hertford, who was on the spot.

'The shot was fired at about 4.15,' he said; 'the only person seen near the spot was a motor-cyclist who was sheltering from the rain under a hedge on Lord Forlmby's side of the plantation. And the only discovery we have made is this glove.'

He took it out of his pocket – a cheap cotton glove, right hand, slightly stained with mud and very damp.

'We found this at the end of the plantation,' said the chief constable. 'It was too dark to look for footprints and there is no other clue.'

I told off three of the Hertford police to make a search of the copse by hand-lamp, and then went up to the house to see Mrs Jonnes, and here I had my first shock.

She had left the Towers at some time in the afternoon.

'They'd been quarrelling all morning,' said the butler; 'the worst shindy I've ever heard!'

'Where did you see her last?' I asked.

'Going into the gun-room,' he said.

I made a search of the gun-room. Jonnes was a methodical man, who had little ivory labels on every stand showing the maker and date of purchase of every piece. And there were two blank spaces. One was the home of the gun that had been found by Jonnes's side, the other a new gun bought a week before.

I went up into Mrs Jonnes's room. The wardrobe door was open, but there had been no attempt to pack anything. I made further enquiries. Jonnes's two-seater car was gone – had been taken out of the garage some time between four and six.

I inspected the other rooms, and in one on the ground floor, which Jonnes used as a study, I saw the safe. The butler, who was beginning to get more at home with the police, and had lost the feeling that any word he uttered might hang him, became a little more chatty.

'The row was about a woman named Banford. He was throwing her in Mrs Jonnes's face, saying how wonderful she was. Mrs Jonnes went almost mad . . . she was a very jealous woman.'

About now the policemen I had sent to search the wood came back. They had made two finds. A rain-sodden sheet of newspaper in which something had been wrapped, and a small wooden box that somebody had hidden under a holly bush. The newspaper was a week-old copy of the *Echo de Paris*. The box was locked, but there wasn't much trouble in opening it. As a burglar kit it wasn't of much account. A couple of chisels, a jemmy, an electric torch, a key wrapped in tissue paper, a glazier's diamond and a folded square of fly-paper to hold a window pane when it was cut.

'That explains the glove,' I said. 'He carried them in his

pocket to avoid fingerprinting – but who goes travelling around with the *Echo de Paris*?'

The key interested me. I tried it on the safe and it opened the door.

There was one man to see, and that was Horace Angel. By twelve o'clock I was ringing the bell of his flat. I was a little surprised when he opened the door to me. He was dressed in an old suit and a pair of slippers, but before the fire was a pair of wet boots, and over the back of a chair was hung a pair of trousers that were wet to the knees.

'Been out?' I asked.

He had been to Wembley Exhibition, he said.

Now Wembley ran a guessing competition. When you entered you received a card on which you wrote down your guess of the number of people who would pay for admission the next day. It was a green card, and was almost the first thing I saw lying on the table.

'There's a chance of a hundred pounds, Sooper,' he said, and smiled as he took up the ticket and handed it to me.

'What time were you there?' I asked.

'About four,' he said.

'You're a bit of a motor-cyclist, aren't you?'

He shook his head.

'I've never ridden one,' he answered. 'Why do you ask?'

Before I could say a word there was a knock on the hall door, and immediately afterwards another knock. I was nearest. I went into the hall and opened the door. A woman was standing there, so drenched, so miserably dressed, that I did not recognise her. There was a light on the landing, and she must have recognised me, for she cowered back as if I was going to strike her.

'Come in, Mrs Banford,' I said, and slowly she shrank past me into the dining-room where Horace Angel was standing by the table. He said nothing; his wide-opened eyes were staring at her as though she were a ghost.

'Hello . . . Dora!' he whispered. 'My God . . . how awful!'

She looked as if she had found her dress on a junk heap. It was old and ill-fitting . . . I remember that there had been a sort of pattern worked in little beads. Some of the pattern was missing. Two or three threads were hanging loose, losing beads with every movement she made. Her hat was like a man's, shapeless and big and dripping from the brim.

'Hello . . . Horry!'

The words seemed to strangle her, and though she spoke to him her eyes were on me – big, round, blue eyes, set far back in dark hollows.

'Where have you come from, Mrs Banford?' I asked.

She wore old boots that were soggy with rain and grey with mud; her skirt looked as if it had been soaked in water.

'From Dover . . . I walked,' she said breathlessly. 'I've been waiting outside to see you, Horry – I knew you were in London. I went to the Bloomsbury Garage and saw your old motor-bicycle: they said that you had been in two hours.'

I looked at Horace Angel – who couldn't ride a motor-bicycle – but he had no eyes for me. He was tugging his handkerchief from his pocket to wipe his streaming face; the handkerchief came out and something else – a white cotton glove that fell on the table. It was the left glove, an exact fellow to the other that had been found in the covert.

I said nothing, waiting . . . Dora went on: 'I've been in England four days . . . Jonnes had me put in prison . . . a French prison.'

'Why?'

She shook her head. 'I was mad . . . I don't know . . . the knife was on the table and I was mad.'

'You attacked him and you were put into a French prison: when?'

She put her hand before her eyes as if she was trying to think. 'A year ago. There was no trial, and when he did not appear to sign some papers they released me. They do that sort of thing in France. They paid my fare, third-class to Dover, and I walked.'

'I'm sorry.' Horace Angel was so hoarse that he barked the words.

And then she looked at him, I think for the first time. 'Are you? I'm past that, Horry . . . My God! if that man hadn't come into the wood – !'

'What's that?' I asked sharply. 'Which wood?'

She turned her head.

'There's somebody at the door . . . police . . . but you're a policeman, aren't you?'

Her numbed fingers snapped back the catch of the shabby bag she carried.

'I don't want this – '

She laid a tiny automatic on the table.

And then the door opened slowly and a woman came in. I must have forgotten to fasten the outer door. It was Mrs Jonnes and she wore an oilskin cloak. I noticed this because she kept her hands hidden under it. Her face was white and her eyes were like red lamps.

'You're Dora Banford,' she said.

Dora nodded.

And then the hands came into view and the shotgun. I snatched it from her before her fingers could curl round the trigger, and she dropped into a chair and burst into tears.

I don't exactly remember how I got them all three to the station, but when I got them there it looked as if my troubles were just beginning, for which of them to charge I did not know.

Jonnes's doctor saved me a lot of time next morning.

'The man died of heart failure, as I warned him he would,' he telephoned me. 'The wound was accidental – he probably pulled the trigger as he fell, and anyway it would not have killed a rat.'

And so nobody hanged. Not Horace Angel, who went to

burgle the safe with a key that he'd pinched or copied years before; not Mrs Jonnes, who came after Dora with murder in her heart; nor Dora, who tramped to Hertford to settle accounts with the man who had broken her.

But the clues – gosh! I'll never get clues like those again!

STEPHEN CRANE

Stephen Crane was born in Newark, New Jersey, in 1871, the youngest son of a Methodist minister. After failing to settle at university, Crane moved to New York where he worked as a journalist and wrote his first novel *Maggie: A Girl of the Streets* in 1893. His second novel, *The Red Badge of Courage*, was far more successful, critically and commercially, and after its publication in 1895 he travelled as a newspaper correspondent to Mexico, to Cuba and to Greece. In 1897 he settled in England, where he met Joseph Conrad and Henry James. He died in Germany in 1900, aged twenty-eight.

Manacled

In the First Act there had been a farm scene, wherein real horses had drunk real water out of real buckets, afterwards dragging a real waggon off stage left.

The audience was consumed with admiration of this play, and the great Theatre Nouveau rang to its roof with the crowd's plaudits.

The Second Act was now well advanced. The hero, cruelly victimised by his enemies, stood in prison garb, panting with rage, while two brutal warders fastened real handcuffs on his wrists and real anklets on his ankles. And the hovering villain sneered.

' 'Tis well, Aubrey Pettingill,' said the prisoner. 'You have so far succeeded; but, mark you, there will come a time – '

The villain retorted with a cutting allusion to the young lady whom the hero loved.

'Curse you,' cried the hero, and he made as if to spring upon this demon; but, as the pitying audience saw, he could only take steps four inches long.

Drowning the mocking laughter of the villain came cries from both the audience and the people back of the wings. 'Fire! Fire! Fire!' Throughout the great house resounded the roaring crashes of a throng of human beings moving in terror, and even above this noise could be heard the screams of women more shrill than whistles. The building hummed and shook; it was like a glade which holds some bellowing cataract of the mountains. Most of the people who were killed on the stairs still clutched their play-bills in their hands as if they had resolved to save them at all costs.

The Theatre Nouveau fronted upon a street which was not of the first importance, especially at night, when it only aroused when the people came to the theatre, and aroused again when they came out to go home. On the night of the fire, at the time of the scene between the enchained hero and his tormentor, the thoroughfare echoed with only the scraping shovels of some street-cleaners, who were loading carts with blackened snow and mud. The gleam of lights made the shadowed pavement deeply blue, save where lay some yellow plum-like reflection.

Suddenly a policeman came running frantically along the street. He charged upon the fire-box on a corner. Its red light touched with flame each of his brass buttons and the municipal shield. He pressed a lever. He had been standing in the entrance of the theatre chatting to the lonely man in the box-office. To send an alarm was a matter of seconds.

Out of the theatre poured the first hundreds of fortunate ones, and some were not altogether fortunate. Women, their bonnets flying, cried out tender names; men, white as death, scratched and bleeding, looked wildly from face to face. There were displays of horrible blind brutality by the strong. Weaker men clutched and clawed like cats. From the theatre itself came the howl of a gale.

The policeman's fingers had flashed into instant life and action the most perfect counter-attack to the fire. He listened for some seconds, and presently he heard the thunder of a charging engine. She swept around a corner, her three shining enthrilled horses leaping. Her consort, the hose-cart, roared behind her. There were the loud clicks of the steel-shod hoofs, hoarse shouts, men running, the flash of lights, while the crevice-like streets resounded with the charges of other engines.

At the first cry of fire, the two brutal warders had dropped the arms of the hero and run off the stage with the villain. The hero cried after them angrily, 'Where are you going? Here, Pete – Tom – you've left me chained up, damn you!'

The body of the theatre now resembled a mad surf amid rocks, but the hero did not look at it. He was filled with fury at the stupidity of the two brutal warders in forgetting that they were leaving him manacled. Calling loudly, he hobbled off stage left, taking steps four inches long.

Behind the scenes he heard the hum of flames. Smoke, filled with sparks sweeping on spiral courses, rolled thickly upon him. Suddenly his face turned chalk-colour beneath his skin of manly bronze for the stage. His voice shrieked, 'Pete – Tom – damn you – come back – you've left me chained up.'

He had played in this theatre for seven years, and he could find his way without light through the intricate passages which mazed out behind the stage. He knew that it was a long way to the street door.

The heat was intense. From time to time masses of flaming wood sung down from above him. He began to jump. Each jump advanced him about three feet, but the effort soon became heart-breaking. Once he fell, and it took time to get upon his feet again.

There were stairs to descend. From the top of this flight he tried to fall feet first. He precipitated himself in a way that would have broken his hip under common conditions. But every step seemed covered with glue, and on almost every one he stuck for a moment. He could not even succeed in falling downstairs. Ultimately he reached the bottom, windless from the struggle.

There were stairs to climb. At the foot of the flight he lay for an instant with his mouth close to the floor trying to breathe. Then he tried to scale this frightful precipice up the face of which many an actress had gone at a canter.

Each succeeding step arose eight inches from its fellow. The hero dropped to a seat on the third step, and pulled his feet to the second step. From this position he lifted himself to a seat on the fourth step. He had not gone far in this manner before his frenzy caused him to lose his balance, and he rolled to the foot of the flight. After all, he could fall downstairs.

He lay there whispering. 'They all got out but I. All but I.' Beautiful flames flashed above him, some were crimson, some were orange, and here and there were tongues of purple, blue, green.

A curiously calm thought came into his head. 'What a fool I was not to foresee this! I shall have Rogers furnish manacles of papier-mâché tomorrow.'

The thunder of the fire-lions made the theatre have a palsy.

Suddenly the hero beat his handcuffs against the wall, cursing them in a loud wail. Blood started from under his finger-nails. Soon he began to bite the hot steel, and blood fell from his blistered mouth. He raved like a wolf.

Peace came to him again. There were charming effects amid the flames . . . He felt very cool, delightfully cool . . . 'They've left me chained up.'